Destined for Love

•

Trenton picked up the flute and began to play. The music reminded Aeneva of wind blowing through the tops of pine trees. She looked away from him. The beautiful sad melody and his presence were almost too much to bear. She finally turned to him when he stopped playing and asked, "Why did you come here?"

He looked into her velvety brown eyes and said, "I wanted to say goodbye." Then putting his arms around Aeneva, he drew her closer.

"You should go now. I am leaving early tomorrow. I must sleep."

She pretended to be distant and almost unaware of his presence. But this only made Trenton more insistent. He brought his face close to hers, so that their lips were nearly touching. "I am coming back for you," he whispered softly. "Do you hear me, Aeneva? Our hearts are locked together and our fate is sealed."

SWEET MEDICINE'S PROPHECY
by Karen A. Bale

#3 SWEET MEDICINE'S PROPHECY
WINTER'S LOVE SONG

BY KAREN A. BALE

ZEBRA BOOKS
KENSINGTON PUBLISHING CORP.

ZEBRA BOOKS

are published by

KENSINGTON PUBLISHING CORP.
475 Park Avenue South
New York, N.Y. 10016

For Linda

ACKNOWLEDGMENTS

Unlike many of the Plains Indians, the Cheyenne had a very well-organized system of government. Because of their nomadic way of life, their tribe was made up of ten major bands. The need for adequate grazing grounds for their horses forced them to wander in these relatively small bands, each of which rarely exceeded more than a few hundred people. Band loyalty was extremely important and relationships within the band were close. A Cheyenne could be recognized by band as well as by tribal allegiance, although the bands seldom came together except for special ceremonial occasions during the summer.

Chiefs were dominant members of their own bands and their attitudes set an example for other members of the band, but they were not the only members of the tribe who were greatly respected. All elderly people in the Cheyenne tribe were revered for their wisdom. The Cheyennes treasured the knowledge and experience of the old and whenever possible, that knowledge was passed on to successive generations.

When a Cheyenne died, it was believed that no burden of guilt was borne. According to their beliefs, the spirit of the departed traveled up the Hanging Road, the Milky Way, to Seyan, the place where Heammawihio, the Wise One Above, resided. In Seyan the deceased could follow the Cheyenne way and live forever among long-lost loved ones, hunting and living without worry.

Aside from George Bird Grinnell's *The Cheyenne Indians, Their History and Ways of Life*, Volumes I & II (Lincoln: University of Nebraska Press, 1972) and John Stands In Timber's *Cheyenne Memories*, with Margot Liberty and Robert M. Utley (Lincoln: University of Nebraska Press, 1967), which have been invaluable sources of information for me, I would like to name other sources that I have used in the writing of this book, and thank the authors and editors:

Chris Emmett, *Fort Union and the Winning of the Southwest* (Norman: University of Oklahoma Press, 1965); John A. Hawgood, *America's Western Frontiers* (New York: Alfred A. Knopf, Inc., 1967); David Lavender, *Bent's Fort* (Garden City, N.Y.: Country Life Press, 1954); W.P. Clark, *Indian Sign Language* (Philadelphia: L.R. Hamersly and Co., 1885); *English–Cheyenne Student Dictionary*, (Lame Deer, Montana: The Language Research Dept. of the Northern Cheyenne, 1976); George Bird Grinnell, *By Cheyenne Campfires* (Lincoln: University of Nebraska Press, 1962); Frank B. Linderman, *Pretty Shield, Medicine Woman of the Crows* (Lincoln: University of Nebraska Press, 1960); *American Indian Life,* edited by Elsie Clews Parsons (Lincoln: University of Nebraska Press, 1967); Melvin R. Gilmore, *Uses of Plants by the Indians of the Missouri River Region* (Lincoln: University of Nebraska Press, 1977).

CHAPTER 1

Hidden in a small grove of lodgepole pines, the Crow war party watched the Cheyennes below. The Crow war chief smiled grimly, looking down on the Cheyenne hunting party. This would be easy; much easier than he had hoped. Already he could feel the blood coursing through his veins at the thought of the ambush.

He watched the hunting party intently for a few more seconds, then lifted his rifle high into the air, his war cry resounding through the hills and down to the prairie below.

Aeneva looked at her brother, the fear evident in her eyes. She started for her horse.

"No. You must stay, Aeneva." Coyote Boy swung up onto his horse. "Ride back to the village. Tell them what has happened."

Aeneva watched as her brother rode toward the others and suddenly she was terrified. Her grandfather and oldest brother were in the hunting party, and now Coyote Boy was going to help them. If they were killed, there would be no one left but her and her grandmother. The Crows had already killed her parents; she would not let them do the same thing to the rest of her family.

She sheathed her skinning knife and quickly mounted her pony, pulling her rifle from its place on her horse's side. She checked and loaded it; then tucked it under her arm, pulling at her horse's reins and kneeing him into a gallop.

As she rode she heard a continuous volley of shots and she saw the battle taking place in the distance. She lowered her head, keeping it next to the horse's neck, taking aim at the first Crow she saw. She squeezed the trigger slowly and with great confidence, saw the Crow as he fell from his horse. Then noting two warriors converge on her brother, Brave Wolf, she turned her horse. She took aim and fired; again a warrior fell from his horse. Brave Wolf looked up for a moment, as did the Crow, but Brave Wolf was quick and smashed his rifle butt into the Crow's head.

"Aeneva, get back!"

Aeneva turned when she heard her grandfather's voice. She saw his face, and her anger, in spite of the danger, was renewed. She yelled and rode toward the Crows who fought against her grandfather. She squeezed off a shot with her right hand, and with her left, sent her war club crashing into a Crow warrior's neck. She jumped from her horse when she reached her grandfather, and together they stood to face their enemies.

A few Crows regarded her skeptically until she fired off some shots at them from her reloaded rifle; then they turned their horses and rode into the hills.

"Are you all right, Grandfather?" Aeneva encircled her grandfather's large frame with her arms.

"I am well, thanks to you, Aeneva," Stalking Horse replied heavily. "Why did you do such a thing, child? The danger was too great."

Aeneva looked at Stalking Horse for a moment, her face genuinely puzzled by his words. "I did not care about the danger, Grandfather. I only wanted to help you

10

and my brothers." She turned, suddenly aware that she hadn't seen either Brave Wolf or Coyote Boy. She smiled as she saw them running toward her.

"What a warrior this one is, eh, Grandfather?" Coyote Boy put his arm around his sister.

Brave Wolf did not look so happy. "I should beat you until you cannot walk," he said angrily, his voice shaking. "Do you know what it did to me to see you here among the enemy? I am lucky I was able to keep my head and fight."

Aeneva stepped forward, touching her eldest brother's arm lightly. "I am truly sorry, Brave Wolf. I only wanted to help. I could think of nothing but losing you and grandfather and Coyote Boy. Do not be angry with me."

Brave Wolf looked at his sister, who at fifteen summers old, was already taller than some of the boys her age. She was strong and lean, and she knew the ways of war better than most of the young warriors. She had practiced since she was a little girl to become a warrior and today she had proven she could fight like one. Brave Wolf reached out and pulled her to him, holding her tightly against him. He didn't want this for her; it was not the kind of life a woman should lead. "I am not angry with you, little Sister. I just do not want to see you fighting against experienced warriors. You know how I feel about this."

Aeneva nodded slightly; she knew. Brave Wolf had told her too many times that he thought it ridiculous for a girl to want to become a warrior. But more than anything, she knew it was because he feared for her life. "I know how you feel, Brave Wolf. You do not have to tell me again." She turned away, but felt Brave Wolf tug at her arm.

"You fought well today, little Sister. I was proud of

you.''

Aeneva smiled. She could receive no greater words of praise from Brave Wolf.

It was a solemn group which rode back to the Cheyenne village. Two of the hunters had been killed and another three wounded. It was the third such attack in two months. The word was spread throughout various Cheyenne bands that many Crows had ridden deep into Cheyenne territory and were raiding hunting parties and small bands which traveled alone.

Stalking Horse looked over at his grandchildren riding next to him and thought miserably that the trouble with the Crows had only grown worse. All of his life he had feared trouble with the white men; but most of his life he had spent fighting Indians. He had hoped that by the time his grandchildren were grown, the intertribal fighting would be less severe, but the hatred on both sides had only grown more intense. Too many lives had been lost, too many memories burned brightly. Again he looked at his grandchildren and knew they were prime examples of the hatred the Cheyennes held for the Crows. As long as they lived, they would never forget that their parents had been killed by Crows, or that many of those around them had died at the hands of the hated enemy. Indeed, it was not easy for Stalking Horse to forget the memory of his daughter and adopted son lying dead by their lodge, the bodies of two Crow warriors lying near. It was not easy to forget that they had been so very young.

He decided then that he wanted his grandchildren away for a while, until the threat of the Crows was less. He wanted to band together with some of the other Cheyennes and to drive the enemy out of their land. But he would wait until his grandchildren were safely away. He would not see them dead at the hands of the Crows.

"I want you to take all of the children away for a while."

Jean looked over at Stalking Horse, his eyebrows raising only slightly as he puffed on the pipe. "And do they know they are going?"

"They will not argue with me."

"Do you actually think Brave Wolf and Coyote Boy will go away with me when the band has been attacked by Crows? They are not boys any longer, *mon ami,* and I do not think they will leave. They are both experienced fighters."

Stalking Horse nodded. "When I was their age, I was an experienced horse-stealer. I had not fought in any wars."

"Times have changed, my friend, and we are talking of a different kind of survival now. They must know how to fight and fight well in order to live."

"And my granddaughter fights as well as any of the boys her age; better than some. I cannot even feel secure in the knowledge that she will marry and be happy with just that."

"You knew that a long time ago. Aeneva has shown the signs since she was a small girl. We all knew she would be as she is; yet we all hoped she would change."

"But she has not. You should have seen her, Jean. She fought well, riding right into the middle of the Crows." He stopped for a moment and laughed. "You should have seen them look at her. There was no fear in her. She knew what she had to do."

"You sound proud in spite of yourself."

"I am proud, but I am also frightened. You know that a warrior does not lead a long life."

"There is still time, *hoovehe.* Perhaps someday there

will be a man—''

''There is only one man who can handle Aeneva, and he has not come back.''

''Ah, the white boy. He said he had something to do in the white world and then he would come back. I believe him.''

''He seeks revenge; that is not good.''

''It is not for us to say, *mon ami*. Perhaps he has a right to seek his revenge.'' He stuck his hand into his long, fuzzy mane, scratching for a moment. ''Where do you want me to take them? We no longer have the rendezvous of the mountain men, and the damned fur company has taken over the trade fairs.''

''What about the city? The city you talk of sometimes.''

''St. Louis? You are crazy, friend. It is a wild place and will scare the youngsters to death.''

''But they have seen Indians there?''

''*Oui,* always there are Indians walking around. I don't know. The men, they get so crazy; I would worry constantly about Aeneva.''

''You and her brothers will be there to look after her.''

''I do not know. What if she became separated from us, eh?'' Jean mulled it over for a minute, twirling the pipe around in his hands. ''I would like them to see a city. There are good things there for them.''

''Good; it is settled. For this, you will take ten of my horses.''

''I do not want your horses, *mon ami*. I want your wife.''

''It has always been so. We are now old men and she an old woman, but still you want her.''

''We may be old men, but Sun Dancer is not an old woman. Look into her eyes, *mon ami*. They still have the

14

twinkle of youth."

"Yes, you are right. Sun Dancer will never grow old."

"I am too old for this," Sun Dancer groaned, getting up from her knees, picking up the basket filled with roots and plants.

"Why do you not let me do it for you, Grandmother? It is not right for you to be on your knees so much. You have enough to do healing the people of this band."

"Oh, Aeneva, if I did not do it, it would not be the same. I cannot ask you to do my work for me."

"But you could let me help."

"I do let you help." Sun Dancer smiled and leaned against her granddaughter. "When did you get so tall?"

"Grandfather says I am much like my father," she said proudly.

"Yes, you are very much like him."

"And my mother?" Aeneva asked gently.

"You are like her, too. You have her goodness of heart."

"I do not remember her well. Brave Wolf says she was small and delicate, like a flower."

"Yes, that is why we named her Little Flower. She was so fragile." Sun Dancer's eyes filled with tears. She seemed to cry more often these days. "But she was strong. She fought against the Crows who killed her and your father."

"Grandmother, I do not want to go to the city with *naxane*. I want to stay here. There is so much trouble with the Crows. It is not right that I and my brothers leave when we are needed."

"The war will not be ended while you are gone, child. This is something that will give Jean great pleasure. He is getting older now; he has lived over seventy winters. He

15

is afraid that he will not be able to take you children to see the city. Do this for him, Aeneva.''

"I cannot imagine life without *naxane*. I did not realize he was that old. He does not seem it. He does not even act it. He moves as well as some of the younger men.''

Sun Dancer laughed. "Yes, Jean is healthy, but he does not know for certain how long he will be that way. Go with him and see the white man's world through his eyes. Perhaps you can learn some things. If I were younger I would go with you.''

"But you could come—''

Sun Dancer lifted her hand. "No, it is too long a journey for me. But you and your brothers go and remember everything you see. Remember it clearly so one day you can tell your children about it.''

"Why do you not go to the rendezvous anymore, *naxane?*'' Aeneva asked Jean as they rode at a leisurely pace.

"It is not like the ones of old, girl. Now the men fight and murder each other because the demand for furs is no longer so great.''

"But they used to be good, eh, *naxane?*'' Coyote Boy asked.

"*Oui,* boy, they were great fun. We men of the mountains, who had not seen each other in a long time, would get together and drink, gamble, dance, and love the women.'' He looked over at Aeneva who caught his glance and smiled.

"It is all right, *naxane*. I have heard some of the stories about you and the men of the mountains. You would gamble half of your furs, sometimes all of them, just to spend the night with a beautiful Indian girl.''

"That is not true. I gambled, but I did not lose.''

16

"When was it that you were attacked by the Gros Ventres, *naxane?*"

"It was the rendezvous of 1832 at Pierre's Hole in the Tetons. The rendezvous broke up after a month and Sublette was leading a party of trappers to the Snake River. A few miles from the river they were attacked by a band of Gros Ventres. Sublette knew he couldn't fight the band, so he asked for a parley. He sent out Antoine Godin, the imbecile, and a Flathead Indian. Godin's father had been killed by a Blackfoot so he wanted revenge. When the Gros Ventre started to parley, Godin ordered the Flathead to shoot the Gros Ventre. The band of Gros Ventres withdrew to a nearby grove and began to dig rifle pits. The mountain men were reinforced by some two hundred more mountain men and about five hundred Flatheads and Nez Percés from the rendezvous camp. Even though the Gros Ventres were outnumbered, they held off the mountain men and Indians.

"That night the Gros Ventres sang their death songs and then yelled out to the mountain men that about six hundred more of their tribe were coming to reinforce them. It scared the hell out of most of the men and they slipped back to the rendezvous camp. In the morning they went back to the scene of the battle and found that the Gros Ventres had lied, using the trick to help them escape during the night."

"I must remember that if I am ever caught in such a situation," said Brave Wolf laughingly.

"It is better to fight," Coyote Boy said harshly.

"It is better to be alive, boy," Jean disagreed angrily, "especially if you can outwit the enemy without having to fight."

"I like that, *naxane*. The Gros Ventres were very smart." Aeneva smiled. "Grandfather says that when he

17

was growing up it was better not to take a man's life. There were not so many wars then and horse stealing was the most important thing.''

"*Oui,* and your grandfather was one of the best. Do you know that he stole two hundred horses to pay for your grandmother's bride price? That was no easy thing. He was gone for a long time. Your grandmother almost decided to give up on him.''

"It is a good thing she did not," Brave Wolf said seriously; "it would have been terrible to waste all those good horses!''

St. Louis was located on the western bank of the Mississippi River just below the mouth of the Missouri. It was in a perfect position to dominate western trade. Steamboats transported men and supplies from its port out to the beaver country and carried back pelts by the ton. The beaver pelts were known as "brown gold" and from 1815 to 1830 they brought almost four million dollars into the city.

The waterfront was lined with taverns and saloons where trappers, mountain men, river men, wagoners, soldiers, and drifters met to drink, gamble, boast, and fight. Although the waterfront was reserved for the more raucous brawling crowd, there was another part of St. Louis that retained the sophisticated ways of its original French settlers.

There was rivalry among the wealthy fur merchants to see who could build the most lavish mansion. The rooms of these mansions were usually imposing in size, their floors were made of black walnut, and huge chandeliers hung overhead. They were furnished in mahogany, crystal, velvet, and lace.

There was never a lack of entertainment. The city

boasted theaters where many plays were put on; and there were dances and parties to keep people busy. By the year 1820, there were three newspapers and a bookstore, as well as four hairdressers and many professional musicians.

While the brawlers and ruffians of the waterfront were quick to settle an argument with their fists, the more refined gentlemen of St. Louis sought redress through dueling. There was a place on the Mississippi called Bloody Island. There the duelists and their seconds would seek their honor. After pacing off, the duelists would raise their pistols and fire. This procedure left seven prominent citizens dead between the years 1810 and 1831.

All this Jean told his three young charges. He also informed them that thieves, thugs, and kidnappers prowled the streets at night. "But you stay with me and do as I say, and you will be fine. I have many friends here. You will be all right."

Aeneva and her brothers had reservations about going into a white man's city, but they were young and curious enough to want to see what it was like. The boys were anxious for their sister, for they had heard of the way whites treated Indians, but Jean didn't seem overly concerned. He said that St. Louis had seen all types and Indians were nothing new.

Aeneva's first impression of the city was that it was a monstrously busy and crowded place. She was frightened, but at the urging of Jean and her brothers, she rode with them through the town and down to the waterfront. Jean showed them the steamboats that ran up the Mississippi to places like Franklin, Council Bluffs, Fort Tecumseh, and Fort Union. He took them to the old part of the city, and the youngsters looked in awe at the huge limestone mansions of the wealthy.

"What do they do in such big places?" Aeneva asked in wonder.

"It's mostly for show. It's impossible to use all the rooms they have in those houses. But the bigger they build them, the more impressive it is to the other people in the city." At the young people's puzzled expressions, Jean explained further. "It is like one of your people owning five hundred horses. Not many people own that many. It makes him very important." The young people now understood and again looked at these huge places in wonder.

Jean searched the street and finally found what he was looking for: a hitching post in the shade, away from the busy street traffic. They dismounted and tied up their horses, the three Cheyennes obviously quite nervous about leaving their animals.

"It will be all right; no one will steal the horses. Come." They walked out into the dusty street and a carriage almost knocked Coyote Boy down. "Watch it, boy; you must look in the streets here. People will run you down without even looking backward." They walked past many stores until Jean found one he knew would interest Aeneva.

"Here is one where women can buy dresses, hats, gloves, and shoes—and all that other stuff they wear underneath."

Aeneva stared in wonder at the fine velvets and silks, awed by the beautiful colors and textures. She pointed to the shoes. "How do they wear such things on their feet? They must be very painful."

"They probably are. If you think those are painful, look at that." Jean pointed to a corseted mannequin. "They wear those things around their waists and pull them as tightly as they can. A woman can hardly breathe when she wears one.''

''Why do they do such things to themselves?'' Aeneva asked in astonishment.

''Because they all want to look the same, have small waists. Most of these women don't do anything but sit on their behinds and play cards and have tea, so they grow fat and have to wear those things.'' He put his arm around Aeneva. ''They are not like you and your women. You are always riding or walking or swimming to give you exercise. The most exercise these women have is to step from their carriages onto the sidewalks.''

The problem of eating was foremost in Jean's head. He knew he couldn't take them into a restaurant and expect them to eat with a fork when they had never in their lives used one. He knew of a few places on the waterfront that wouldn't care how they ate, but the kind of crowd that hung out there was not the kind he wanted Aeneva to be around. He solved the problem by going into a general store and purchasing cheese, meat, bread, apple cider, and some fruit. All of them were overjoyed by the vast quantities of fresh fruit. Jean bought plums, pears, peaches, apples, and some fruit in tin cans for them to have on the way home. They went to a place along the waterfront. It was peaceful and they could watch steamboats move up the river.

''Everything is so big here,'' Brave Wolf marveled. ''The lodges are like none I have ever seen; and these boats, they could hold many horses.''

''It is too noisy for me here,'' Coyote Boy complained. ''You cannot hear the birds or even the wolves at night. I miss the sounds of our land.''

''Yes, and the beauty. Here they cover up the land with their lodges. There is no room for anything.''

''It is the way with the whites, Aeneva; but not all are

21

like that. There are many who do not like the cities. They live on land much like yours, away from other white people, wanting only to grow their own food and raise their own animals. Just as not all Indians are alike, not all whites are alike.''

They slept at a spot outside the city where Jean thought they would be relatively safe. Jean made sure that the two boys stood watch, with Coyote Boy standing the first watch and Brave Wolf standing the second. Jean knew there were many men who might have ambushed them.

They had been in and around St. Louis for over a week when Aeneva saw Trenton. She recognized him immediately, although it had been over four years since she had seen him. She started to call out to him, but saw he was with a woman, a white woman, and so she said nothing. She watched him as he walked with the woman, aware of how tall he had grown, how much more manly he now was, and she watched as the woman possessively held onto his arm, and laughed up at him as he talked. He had said he would come back to her; merely a childhood promise, one he had never meant to keep. After all, he was half white, and that part of him was stronger than the Indian half. He belonged here, while she belonged back with her own people.

"What is it, *chérie?*" Jean came up to stand next to her.

Aeneva quickly turned her head, smiling up at Jean. "It is nothing, *naxane*. I was just watching some people."

But Jean saw Trenton and almost called out to him, until he saw the girl on his arm and the look on Aeneva's face. It was obvious that what Trenton had felt for Aeneva had just been childish love, but it was equally as obvious that what Aeneva felt for Trenton was something

22

more, something stronger and more lasting. Jean took her arm and led her in the opposite direction, trying to distract her. "I know something we can do. Come." Jean led them to the riverside.

The one thing Aeneva and her brothers were eager to do was ride on one of the riverboats. Jean decided it would be a good trip if they rode the boat to Fort Union, which was situated one thousand seven hundred sixty miles upriver above the mouth of the Yellowstone. From Fort Union, they could purchase supplies and strike overland to Cheyenne country and home.

Jean secured a room aboard the steamer for the journey, but the boys wanted to sleep with Jean outside on the deck. Aeneva was forced to take the room for herself. While she hated to be all alone in the room at night, she enjoyed the quiet and she even slept on the bed, although she didn't tell her brothers.

There was a large assortment of people on board: gamblers, businessmen, trappers, river men, gentlemen and their ladies, prostitutes who hoped to ply their trade on board, and soldiers going to Fort Union. The majority of the people were not unfriendly to Aeneva and her brothers; most merely looked curiously at them and left them alone. The wealthier people were somewhat shocked by the sight of Indians on the boat, but a nasty look from Jean kept them at a distance.

While on board, Jean bought food from the kitchen to supplement the food they had brought along, and they ate out in the fresh air on the deck. Aeneva and her brothers delighted in the steam whistles that blew when ships passed each other or when their ship signaled to someone on shore. There was almost always someone on shore, standing and waving excitedly at the sight of the large boat passing upriver. There were also flatboats which moved along up and down the river. They were literally flat, with a keel for stability, and decks fore and aft with walkways along each side. Midships was a cabin, and sometimes the boat was rigged with a square sail. The crew walked the length of the boat thrusting long poles into the bottom of the river to help propel the craft. They also used long ropes in places where men or animals could be used to pull the craft from the bank. Sometimes the wind came up and the square sail became useful. It was a slow, dangerous way to move along the river, but for people who were unable to pay the price of the steamboat trip, the flatboat was still their best way to travel.

Aeneva leaned over the top railing of the steamboat and looked down. She was on the second level, the bottom being the freight deck, and the top housing a pilothouse and hurricane deck, as well as the towering smokestacks. The boat had a paddle wheel in the rear—a stern-wheeler Jean had called it—and it enabled them to maneuver more easily in shallow water.

"I never realized you liked the water so much, girl."

Aeneva looked at Jean and smiled. "It is wonderful, *naxane*. I could grow very used to this."

Jean looked at the lush banks of the river and realized with a sudden pang that this was one thing he would miss when he was gone. "Life on the river is very different from anywhere else I've been. It can be dangerous, but it is always exciting. I shall miss it."

"You will be back again. Why do you talk like that?"

"Look at me, girl. Do your eyes not see how old I have grown, how gray my hair is, how wrinkled my skin has become? I do not think I will be back here again."

"Please, do not talk like that, *naxane*. You will outlive us all."

"I do not think so, Aeneva; but thank you. Besides, I

have seen enough in this life; I have done many, many things. I have traveled many places and met many people. I have a family that I can always come back to, and a home where I will always feel comfortable. I am not sorry for anything.''

Aeneva reached over and tucked her arm in his, leaning her head against his shoulder. She had never thought that Jean or her grandparents would die; she had just assumed that they would live forever.

"Where are Brave Wolf and Coyote Boy?" she asked suddenly, craning her neck around to see.

"They got into a little gambling game with some trappers." He laughed. "If those men aren't careful, Brave Wolf and Coyote Boy will steal their pants off them."

"Would you like to come inside with me, girl, and get something to drink?"

"No, *naxane*. I would not feel comfortable in there. You go. I like it here."

She watched him as he walked away, noticing for the first time how he limped slightly and how his left arm hung more stiffly. Why had she not seen it before? He had taken them here because he knew it was his last trip, too. She moved back to the railing, closing her eyes to the cool breeze sweeping over her face. Aeneva had never thought she would feel comfortable in any place outside of her land, but she liked this river and the way the boat moved over it. She liked the movement and the sound the paddle wheel made as it churned its way through the water.

She looked down at the rippling water and she was lost in thought until she sensed that someone was behind her. She turned abruptly, startled to see Trenton behind her. He moved toward her but stopped, seeing the hostility in her eyes. She turned back to the railing, steeling herself for the moment she had dreaded.

"Aeneva," he said softly, joining her at the rail; and she couldn't help but look up at his eyes. She hadn't remembered them as being quite so blue or quite so reflective of the emotions he felt. It was not only that he was bigger and older; it was also that he was dressed in a white man's shirt and pants that made him look so different. But there were still the same telltale signs of wildness: his light hair hung long, almost below his collar; and he wore the Indian necklace that her grandmother had given his father, as well as moccasins. Inadvertently, she reached up to the necklace he had given her. He saw the motion and smiled slightly. She shifted away from him, back toward the railing.

"I hardly recognized Brave Wolf and Coyote Boy," he said aimlessly, as if they were carrying on an amicable conversation, "but I would have recognized you anywhere."

Aeneva still did not answer. She found her strength in silence.

"You're going up to Fort Union. That's where I'm headed. Looks like we'll be seeing a lot of each other."

Aeneva looked at him once, implacably, then walked away, heading to her cabin. Trenton stopped her a few steps away from the railing, yanking roughly at her arm.

"Don't walk away; I want to talk to you."

Aeneva stared up at him, trying to pry herself from his rough hold, but Trenton held fast.

"Would you at least say something to me?"

"All right," she said flatly, reaching up to yank the necklace from her neck. "You can take this back. I no longer want it."

Perplexed but smiling, Trenton watched as she walked away. At least he could still arouse feelings of anger in

26

her. If she was angry, there was still some feeling left, and anger was not far from passion.

Aeneva looked at herself in the small, round mirror. It was strange for her to see herself. She smoothed back the short strands of hair that stubbornly escaped from the long braid down her back, and she stared in fascination at the reflection of the young girl she saw there. She had never before thought about what she looked like. She had seen rippled reflections in the water of the streams, but she supposed she looked like any other Cheyenne girl. Now she was startled to see that her face was one of some beauty, although not the kind that her mother or grandmother had possessed. Her eyes seemed too oval and more yellow than brown, and her nose seemed too small for her face; it should have been longer, more forceful. Her mouth was full and pouty, giving her the impression of impertinence. It was not at all the face she had thought it would be; it was not the face of a warrior.

She washed with the pitcher of water which was in her cabin and changed into the good dress and moccasins her grandmother had made for her. Her grandmother had made the dress and moccasins from the skins of young does, and they were of a much lighter color than her other dress. Sun Dancer had quilled various designs on the dress and from the long fringes on the arms hung various colors of beads and feathers. Aeneva tried standing high on her tiptoes to get a look at herself in the mirror, but decided that was a silly thing to do and walked away. What did it matter what she looked like? Her appearance had never bothered her before; indeed, she had never even been concerned with it.

She walked out of the room, eager to meet Jean and her brothers. But as she neared the deck she slowed her pace;

27

she wanted to make sure Trenton would be there. It was for him that she had put on her best dress and suddenly become so critical of her appearance. She had a momentary desire to flee back to her cabin to change into her ordinary dress, to change back into the person she really was, but she did not. She was this person, too.

Trenton was with her family. They were sitting on the deck, laughing and eating, and Trenton stood when he saw her approach.

"You look very fine in that dress, *chérie*," Jean said playfully. "I have not seen you wear it before."

Aeneva fired Jean a hostile glance before she reached down and grabbed some of the bread from his hand. "Grandmother made it for this trip. If I had not worn it sometime, she would have been disappointed."

"But of course," Jean said with a wave of his hand, cutting off a piece of meat and handing it to Aeneva.

She stood, eying Trenton warily, and moved away from him.

"Aeneva, come with me into the dining room. I would like you to eat dinner with me."

She turned, looking at him coldly. "I do not belong in the places of the white man or woman, Trenton. I belong here, with my family." She turned back to look out at the water.

"You have a right to eat in there, just as any of the other passengers do."

"I do not want to eat in there. I like it here." She sat down and dangled her legs over the side of the deck, swinging them back and forth as she chewed on her bread and meat. She tried to ignore Trenton's presence as he sat next to her, but it was a difficult thing to do.

"Well, if you won't eat in there with me, I will have to eat out here with you." Using his knife, he cut off a piece of cheese for Aeneva, who, tasting it for the first time in the city, had taken an instant liking to it. She took the proffered piece and stuck it on her bread. "Aeneva, why are you so angry with me?" Trenton's voice was so much deeper now, like that of a grown man.

Aeneva looked over at him. "I am not angry with you. Why should I be?"

"Maybe because I told you I would come back and I did not." His eyes met hers and held them. She looked away first.

"It was only a childish promise. I did not really believe it." She looked back out at the water, absently chewing on the bread and watching the banks of the river as they moved slowly by.

"But I meant it."

Aeneva threw the rest of her food into the water and turned to face Trenton, her eyes yellow with fury. "You did not mean what you said. It was a lie. You would have me believe that you would give up all you have learned and acquired in the white world to come back and live with me and my people?" She laughed bitterly. "I am old for my years, Trenton, and not as stupid as you think. You are white now; you are one of them. You even have a white woman. Will you give her up, too?" She pulled her legs in and stood up. "And you are wrong if you think I have been waiting for you. There are many who have asked for me in marriage. I have refused only because I am now too young. But when the time is right and a warrior comes along . . ." She turned abruptly, her thick braid swinging across her shoulder, and walked with long strides down the deck. Trenton stared after her.

"She does not suffer defeat easily, *mon ami.*"

Trenton looked at Jean. "What do you mean 'defeat'? She has not lost anything."

"She feels she has lost you to a white woman and the white world. It does not sit well with her."

"What white woman? What is she talking about?"

"We saw you in the city walking with a white woman. You looked to be more than friends."

"I'm just escorting her to Fort Union to be with her parents. It's nothing more than that."

"You do not have to explain to me," Jean replied innocently. "Are you still looking for the man who killed your father?"

"Yes. That's the main reason I haven't come back for Aeneva. I want to do this thing first."

"And if it takes you five years, ten years, twenty years? Did you expect Aeneva to wait for you?" Jean shook his head. "Ah, you are foolish, boy. Perhaps you *have* been in the white world too long."

Trenton felt the anger rise in him and he squatted next to Jean. "Every day that I have been in the white world has been too long, Jean. But when my mother died I knew it was the time to search out this man and make him pay for what he did to my father. I have kept track of the years. Aeneva is not yet sixteen years old. I know her better than you think. She will not marry just any man, if she even marries. The man she marries will have to be very strong and able to put up with her temper. And I know that what drives her is much the same thing that drives me: we want to avenge the murder of our parents. I know her well because she is like me. She will not marry until I come for her." Trenton stood up.

"You are very sure of yourself, eh, boy?" Jean looked up at the tall young man, a slight smile wrinkling his mouth.

"I am sure of myself and of Aeneva. We will be together one day."

CHAPTER II

The trip by riverboat to Fort Union usually lasted about three weeks, depending on the weather and the condition of the river. To Trenton, it was the longest three weeks he had ever lived through. It was not an easy task keeping Lydia away from Aeneva and Aeneva away from Lydia. Aeneva was outside almost all the time and Lydia occasionally wanted to take a stroll around the deck of the boat. It was inevitable that the three of them would meet. It happened in the passageway while Aeneva was walking to her cabin and Trenton was escorting Lydia out of hers. Aeneva's hostility was evident as she eyed both Trenton and Lydia disdainfully, then walked on by as if she owned the riverboat. Trenton smiled after her.

"Did you see that girl? Did you see the way she looked at us, Trenton?" Lydia hung on to Trenton's arm.

"How did she look at us, Lydia?"

"Well, so savagely. I'll bet she even carries a knife on her. They shouldn't allow those savages in the company of decent folk."

"Those savages have paid their way just like everybody else, Lydia, and if the captain sees fit for them to travel with us, then I guess you and everybody else had just better get used to it."

Lydia stared at Trenton in surprise, started to say something, then stopped. She had heard him speak about

Indians before and was shocked that he felt such compassion for them. Didn't he know what they had done to settlers in the East? And she had heard the stories of what they were now doing to the farmers and settlers who moved west, and of what they did to white women. She felt her cheeks flush a deep red.

"What's the matter, Lydia?"

"Nothing. I just don't understand you, that's all, Trenton Hawkins. If you're ever going to be promoted, you'd better keep your notions about Indians to yourself. If my father ever heard—"

"Your father has heard. It's no secret that I have a great sympathy for the Indians. Now, let's go outside before it gets too cold for you."

Several days passed and Trenton didn't see Aeneva. One night when he had had a little too much to drink with Jean and some soldiers, he went to Aeneva's cabin. Waiting outside, he tried to figure out what he was going to say. Finally, he knocked on the door. When she didn't open it, he kept knocking. She asked who it was in English, but he didn't answer. Trenton kept knocking until she opened the door slightly; then he pushed it open, knocking her backward. He shut the door behind him. Her hair was unbraided and hung loose around her shoulders and back. She stared at him, her eyes large, filled with anger and fear. The anger he could understand, the fear he could not.

"Why are you afraid of me?" he asked suddenly, moving closer to her.

She moved back involuntarily. "I fear no man," she replied in a not-quite-believable tone. She glanced around her and saw her sheathed knife lying on the table near the bed. Why had she been so stupid as to give in to the comforts of the white man? If she had not, her knife would be on her, where it belonged. She moved back slowly, never taking her eyes from Trenton. She lunged for the knife, unsheathing it and holding it in front of her. But Trenton was quick, too. As Aeneva unsheathed the knife, his hand was on her wrist. She was strong, very strong for a woman, and she fought hard, kicking and hitting him with her free hand, but he forced her to drop the knife and pinned both arms behind her, slamming her up against the wall.

"Would you have really used that knife on me, Aeneva?" His blue eyes drilled into hers and she turned her face away, unable to take this closeness.

"Yes," she seethed, "and I would have enjoyed it."

His hand moved to her hair, tugging at it until her head jerked back and he was able to stare down into her face. "I don't think you would have used it. You are hurt and angry and you are fighting back the only way you know how. There's no need to fight me, Aeneva." His face moved closer to hers and his mouth closed over hers, touching it, tasting the fullness of her lips. His hands loosened their hold on her and he leaned against her, his body pressing hers against the cold, wooden wall. She moved her arms up slowly until her hands rested on his chest, all the time delighting in the feel of his lips on hers and the touch of his body against hers. But the anger in her won out and with a hard push, she shoved him backward across the room, then stooped to pick up her knife. She faced him then, a wild tangled mass of hair around her shoulders, her lips red and her cheeks full of color.

Trenton smiled, but did not move. "Go ahead, use the knife."

She faced him, her chest heaving. She lifted the knife and sent it sailing across the small room, where it landed in the wall next to Trenton's head.

He still had not moved, and his smile had grown even broader. "It seems you have lost your skill with the knife, Aeneva. I know a time when you could not miss a target at much farther away."

"If I had wanted to kill you, you would be dead."

"I know," he said softly, pulling the knife out of the wall and walking over to hand it to her. "So it seems you are not so tough after all." He bent quickly and touched her lips once more with his, very softly, then he left the room.

She remained motionless until he was gone, thinking of what had happened between them. Her stomach felt strange and her heart pounded frantically; she wondered just exactly what it would be like to be Trenton's woman. She felt the cold metal of the knife in her hand and she gazed at it a moment, before throwing it onto the table. She would never be caught in such a situation again, not by any man; and not by Trenton—especially not by Trenton.

The sand bars along the river shifted periodically and their progress was slowed considerably. Once the boat hit a large rock which was completely covered by water. They stopped, so the engineer could make repairs, and the passengers were allowed to go ashore for a few hours. Jean, Aeneva, Brave Wolf, and Coyote Boy, all eager to be on land again, went ashore in a small rowboat. The land around the river was muddy and moist, almost swamplike, and the trees and undergrowth were dense and dark green. Low-hanging moss was everywhere, and it was easy for a person to get lost in a place where there was so little land to mark or track.

"It is strange in here, *naxane*." Aeneva peered around at the dark green shadows. "I would not be surprised if demons and spirits inhabited this place.''

"Demons and spirits, bah! I did not think you believed in such things, child.''

"I do not, but it would be easy to believe in them in a place such as this.''

"I do not like it either.'' Brave Wolf drew close to his sister.

"Where is your spirit of adventure? Come.''

"Do not worry, *naxane*. I will follow you. My brave brother and sister can stay behind.'' Coyote Boy laughed as he ran after Jean.

"There is something about this place, Brave Wolf. The sounds, they are so different. I do not recognize any of the animals.''

"Yes, there are many birds—and something else which I do not understand.'' He turned to Aeneva. "Do you want to wait here?''

"No, let us explore with *naxane*. I am sure nothing can hurt us.''

They moved into the dense undergrowth together, both unsure of why they felt so strange. They had both been in unfamiliar land before, but there was something about this place that bothered them both. They easily followed Jean's tracks in the moist dirt and soon realized that he was playing a game with them, leading them in circles but never taking them anywhere.

"Our uncle is trying to make us look like children, I think.'' Brave Wolf looked around him. "Have we not passed this place before?''

"Yes. I think we are getting a real lesson in tracking.''

"I think it would be best if we went back to the boat. I do not like it here, Aeneva.''

Aeneva looked at her brother. He was one of the bravest young men she knew, but there was something here which frightened him. And unaccountably, she felt the same. "Yes, let us go back. Uncle and Coyote Boy can play their games by themselves."

They started back slowly, Brave Wolf leading Aeneva by the hand, just as he had done when they were children. They looked for signs of things they had passed earlier—a tree, a muddy track, some stripped leaves or moss—but they soon found it was not such an easy thing to get out of this dark place. It was only after they both stepped into the quicksand and it started to pull them in that they realized they couldn't get out of it.

"Brave Wolf, I cannot move my legs. This mud is pulling at me."

"I also cannot move. We must try to walk out of it, back the way we came. Pull yourself, Aeneva."

They both reached for the hard ground outside the small circle of quicksand, but the harder they moved toward it, the harder they were sucked under by the deadly sand.

"I cannot move, Brave Wolf. It is pulling me harder."

Brave Wolf saw the fear in his sister's eyes and he knew the fear in his own heart. He had never before faced anything like this; this was not like something you could see, something you could fight with any weapon. He did not know how to deal with it, but seeing the look in his sister's eyes, he knew he had to do something. There was only one thing he knew of that might help them, something that had been taught to him early on as a young boy. He cupped his hands to his mouth and made the howl of the wolf, a wolf in trouble signaling to one of its own for help. There was nothing they could do but hope that Jean and Coyote Boy would hear his calls and come to help them.

* * *

Trenton looked up, his ear instantly attuned to the sound coming from the swamp.

"What is that awful sound?" Lydia moved closer to him, grabbing at his arm for protection. Trenton shook it free.

"I'm not sure." He listened for the sound again and it came, clear and familiar, as he had heard it many times as an Arapaho youth when he had played at war with Brave Wolf and Coyote Boy. One of them was in trouble. "Go back to the boat, Lydia."

"Where are you going, Trenton? Come back here."

"Lydia, go back to the boat. There are swamps in there with quicksand."

"But why are you going in there?"

"Someone's in trouble." He ran into the undergrowth, swinging at it with his arms, listening intently for the sound that would lead him to his friends. He stopped, cupping his hands to his mouth, making the sound, hoping that they would return his call. He heard it instantly and advanced cautiously through the swampy area, searching for the little pits of quicksand that were so easy to miss. He heard the call again and switched directions; he waited. It was different; someone was answering the first call. He followed the sound and when he felt he was within hearing distance, he yelled their names. "Aeneva, Brave Wolf, Coyote Boy." He shouted their names and the sound echoed throughout the swamp.

"Here, Trenton. Here." It was Brave Wolf. "Get Aeneva first."

Trenton wasted little time. "Don't move. Be still!" He searched the trees for a strong limb and broke it off. He took off his belt and tied it around the middle of the stick, tossing the end of the belt to Aeneva. She grabbed it and held on tightly as Trenton, his hands on either side of the belt, pulled at the stick. He felt the sand pulling at Aeneva and the harder he pulled, the harder the sand pulled at her.

"Aeneva, Brave Wolf." Jean's voice rang out.

"Here, Jean. Here," Trenton yelled furiously. Again he pulled at the stick and he felt Aeneva begin to move very slowly out of the sand. He heard Jean run up behind him and knew that he would get Brave Wolf out. As Aeneva drew nearer, Trenton dropped the stick and reached for her arms, pulling until he had the top half of her body on the hard ground. Her eyes were large and frightened, but she made no sound; she was only concerned about Brave Wolf. Trenton immediately ran to help Jean and Coyote Boy, but they had already pulled Brave Wolf out of the sand. He turned back to Aeneva, helping her to her feet and supporting her as she leaned against him. She regarded him for a moment, her eyes slightly moist. He put his arm around her.

"Here we go, my boy. *Sacré bleu!* This is enough to give an old man a heart attack."

"You should not play games with us then, Uncle," Brave Wolf said breathlessly, trying to brush some of the wet sand from his body.

"I was not playing games. I warned you of the dangers of the swamps. You young ones wanted to come in here. Is that not true?"

"It is true, *naxane,* but you did not have to leave us."

"I did not think you would be so stupid as to try to go back by yourselves. I left an easy enough trail for you to follow."

"Too easy. You were leading us around in circles."

"But you would have been safe if you had followed me or come with me, no? Instead you two chose to go off alone, as you have always done. What am I going to do with you two? I am too old for this. *Merde!*"

"It seems again we owe you a debt, my friend." Brave Wolf walked to Trenton, taking his shoulders in his hands. "Once before you saved Aeneva, and now you have saved us both. You must tell me how I can repay you."

"There is no need to repay me, Brave Wolf. You and Aeneva are my friends. You would have done as much for me."

"But we cannot leave it like this. You must come to our camp so I can repay you."

Trenton looked over at Aeneva. "I cannot come for a while, but when I do, I want no payment. All I want is your friendship and that of your family. That is payment enough."

"That you shall always have, my friend," Brave Wolf replied solemnly, placing his right hand on Trenton's forearm, while Trenton did the same.

"Are you all right, little Sister?" Brave Wolf moved to Aeneva.

"I am fine, Brother. It was strange, was it not? We could do nothing to fight it."

"It's deadly stuff and I shouldn't have let you two go off alone. If anything had happened to you, your grandfather would have tortured me in the worst way. *Merde,* I do not even like to think about it!"

The horn on the boat blasted and they all looked toward the river.

"It's time to go. The boat's fixed," Trenton said. "Everyone stay right behind each other this time. You lead, Jean."

"*Oui,*" Jean replied, setting off ahead of the others. Coyote Boy followed, then Brave Wolf, then Aeneva and Trenton.

39

They hadn't gone far when Aeneva stopped abruptly and turned to face Trenton. "Thank you for what you did for me. You make me feel so foolish."

"Why? You didn't know about the quicksand. I had never heard of it before I took this trip and the captain warned us all about it. I'm just glad I was near."

"Were you walking in the swamp also?"

"No, I was on the bank."

"With the white woman?"

Trenton met her eyes and nodded. "We were walking along the bank when I heard Brave Wolf's call."

Aeneva nodded half-heartedly and turned, starting to walk toward the river. She felt Trenton's arm on hers and she stopped, unable to fight with him.

"Aeneva, I do not love the white woman. I am taking her to her father. When I get to Fort Union I hope to find the man who murdered my father. Then I will come for you."

Aeneva stared into his light eyes, seeing his sincerity, knowing that he believed what he said. She reached up and touched his face. "You will not come back for me, Trenton, for you are one of them now. You do not yet realize it, but when the time comes for you to leave the white man's world, you will be unable to do so. There are some men like *naxane* who are more Indian than white, and others who will be white no matter how much Indian blood is in them. It is not bad. They are your people, too."

"No, you're wrong. I'll prove you wrong some day, Aeneva."

"I hope that you do, Swiftly Running Deer." She smiled then, taking his hand in hers, and they walked in companionable silence back to the river.

* * *

40

Fort Union had been built in 1828-29, three miles above the mouth of the Yellowstone River on the upper Missouri. The trip by steamboat from St. Louis to Fort Union was one thousand seven hundred sixty miles, and this made the steamboat practical for upriver travel.

Although Fort Union had started out as a trading post, it now had soldiers posted to it. Aeneva, Brave Wolf, and Coyote Boy were surprised at the number of soldiers. All three felt acutely uncomfortable in the confines of the structure, but Jean assured them that they wouldn't be bothered.

Jean planned to buy supplies; then they would follow the Yellowstone River to the Missouri, and from there ride into Cheyenne territory. There was a possibility that they might meet some Crows in the northern country, but Jean was fairly sure that the route they would take would be a comparatively safe one.

They were to stay at the fort for a night and then move on. Brave Wolf and Coyote Boy were anxious to return home; Aeneva had mixed feelings. She was eager to be with her people again, to be in her own land, but she was afraid she would never again see Trenton.

The travelers slept in a part of the fort where many Indians stayed to trade. While Jean was off drinking and swapping supplies with some trappers, Brave Wolf and Coyote Boy got involved in a gambling game with some of the Indians. Aeneva wandered around the fort alone. There was a trading post which carried everything. Jean had taken them inside earlier and had shown them many things: tins of food, candy, flour, sugar, coffee, tea, bolts of cloth, dresses, shirts, pants, guns, rifles, knives, and just about anything a person wanted. If the trading post didn't have it, the owner could order it and the next boat coming upriver would bring it. Surrounding the trading

41

post were small buildings for the officers and the men who were stationed at the fort.

Aeneva had seen nothing of Trenton until they left the boat. He had come over to her, offering to help carry her things. She had seen the white woman in the background. She was staring after Trenton in expectation, and seeing how lovely and delicate the fair-haired woman was, Aeneva realized how futile all her hopes were. Trenton was too much a part of this world now. She had thanked him, but had picked up her own things and walked past him, down the gangplank of the boat.

She sauntered back to their small camp, sat down on the ground, and rummaged through her parfleche for one of the sticks of candy Jean had bought for her. She stuck the sweet peppermint stick into her mouth, wondering if her mother had ever tasted a piece of candy. She often thought of her mother; she wished she had known her, wished she had been much older when she had died. But the word murdered also came to her mind—her mother and father had been murdered by Crows. She could never forget that. She never wanted to.

"What are you thinking about so intently?"

Aeneva stared at Trenton as he walked over to her, his face bright and smiling, his wild, wayward hair slightly tamed and combed. He had changed his shirt and he now wore one made of dark blue cloth which made his eyes seem a darker shade of blue. "I was not thinking about anything," she lied.

"I thought you might like to hear some music." He pulled a flute out of his back pocket and sat down next to her. "I've been practicing a lot since you gave this to me. I'll bet I'm even better than Brave Wolf now."

Aeneva smiled; he still had the flute she had made for him. "I am surprised you still have it. Jean tells me the whites make a flute out of metal and it makes a much better sound.''

"The sound this one makes is good enough for me. I want no other.'' He put the wooden instrument up to his mouth and blew into it; the sound that came out of it was similar to that made by the wind blowing through pine trees. He moved his fingers on the holes and the sounds turned into music, lovely music, the likes of which Aeneva had never before heard. She looked away from him, afraid that her eyes would betray her. The sad music and his presence were too much.

"Did you like it?'' Trenton moved forward, trying to see her face.

"It was beautiful. I have never heard anything like it.''

"I made it up myself.''

"Why did you come here?'' She turned to him, her eyes finally meeting his.

"Because I wanted to say good-by.''

"We said good-by on the boat.''

"*You* said good-by on the boat.''

"It does not matter.'' She turned away again, looking at the people around her, trying to act interested in everything that was going on.

"It matters to me.''

"*E-toneto*. It is cold.'' Aeneva automatically reverted to Cheyenne.

"*Ne-pevo-mohta-he?* Are you feeling well?'' Trenton asked with concern.

Aeneva did not seem to hear. She looked up at the sky, absently rubbing her arms. "Fall is almost here and then will come the winter. Aeneva. Why do you suppose my parents named me after something as cold and cruel as the winter?''

"Perhaps because they were so grateful that you survived it. It is a beautiful name, Aeneva.''

"You should go now. We are leaving early in the morning. I must sleep." She seemed to be preoccupied with something, unaware of his presence.

"If I don't find the man who killed my father soon, I will come for you. Do you hear me, Aeneva?''

She turned to him, her eyes distant and blank-looking. "I hear you, but I do not want to speak of the future. It is not good to plan things, for life is never as it should be. May the Great Father always look down on you with favor, Trenton." She looked away from him and began to lay out her robe.

Trenton stood up, completely puzzled by Aeneva's mood, but he realized it would do no good to push her. He took the necklace from his pocket and dropped it onto the robe beside her, then turned and walked away. He did not see her when she moved her head to watch him or when she picked up the necklace and clutched it in her hand as if it were the only thing that had ever mattered to her.

CHAPTER III

Aeneva rinsed the cloth in the bowl of water, handed it back to Sun Dancer, and watched as her grandmother cleansed the wound and applied one of her herbal poultices. It always amazed her that her grandmother worked so quickly and efficiently, never seeming to tire of all the people she helped or of the long, hard days she sometimes had. There were times when she had old ones to look after, warriors who had been wounded in battles, children who were sick, or women who were giving birth, but she never complained of any of it. They were all important to her. She was a healer and they needed her. It never occurred to her that she was doing too much.

When they left the lodge of Red Bull, Aeneva took the basket from her grandmother's arm. "You still do too much, Grandmother. Perhaps you should have a helper."

"I do have a helper. You."

"I?" Aeneva replied indignantly. "I am no healer; I am a warrior."

"You can be both. Healing comes easily to you, Aeneva. I have watched you many times. Your hands are quick and skillful, and your knowledge of the plants and roots is vast. You have learned much without even knowing it."

"I could not help it, Grandmother; your love of healing overflows. It was easy for me to learn much from you. I still remember when you told me that healing is as important as fighting.''

"It is true.'' Sun Dancer looked out at the prairie. "I am surprised you are not out with the hunters today. There are many buffalo to be killed and skinned before we move up into the mountains.''

"There are also many sick people to look after. I will not let you do it all yourself. There are many hunters, but only one healer.''

Sun Dancer stopped, looking up at the young girl who was now already taller than she. "You are a good girl, Aeneva. Have I told you that much?''

"No, you have not.'' Aeneva laughed.

Sun Dancer smiled. "I will truly miss you when I die. You have brought much happiness to my life.''

"Thank you, Grandmother; that is a generous thing to say. I know how much my mother meant to you. For you to say such a thing about me . . .''

Sun Dancer took Aeneva's hand, turning it over in hers. "Your hands are so rough and they have so many calluses on them. It should not be for one so young.''

"Oh, Grandmother, every girl has calluses on her hands. The work of a Cheyenne woman is difficult.''

"But you try to do the work of both a woman and a man. You must decide one of these days what you will do, child.''

"I know what I want to do, Grandmother. I want to fight. It has always been so.''

Sighing deeply, Sun Dancer nodded her head. "Yes, it has always been so. Your father knew it when you were only a few summers old. It frightened him, Aeneva. He did not want that kind of life for you.''

"But how could he know when I was so young?''

"You showed the signs even then.'' Sun Dancer was

silent for a moment, looking off into the distance. "Have you really thought about what this will mean for you, child? Do you understand that if you are good enough to ride with the warriors, no man will want to marry you. You will be alone, Aeneva."

Aeneva turned quickly away. "It does not matter. I do not wish to marry anyway. I want only to fight and to die as a true warrior."

"But you cannot mean that!" Sun Dancer grabbed Aeneva's arm and yanked her around. "That is foolish talk. When one has lived a long time, then he can choose the way he wishes to die. But when one is young . . ." Sun Dancer threw up her hands in exasperation. "There is no honor in dying young, Aeneva. I have never believed it, nor will I ever."

Aeneva stared at her grandmother, hardly believing that this was the same gentle woman she had known all her life. "You cannot really believe that, Grandmother. There is great honor in dying while fighting for your people no matter—"

"Do not speak to me of such things, child!" Sun Dancer screamed, her fists clenched, her voice shaking. "My brother died as a young man with honor, but I have longed to see him again since I was a young girl. And your parents—"

"My parents were murdered!" Aeneva protested angrily.

"We do not know that for sure."

"But my mother was shot in the back."

"Perhaps it was easier for her to die that way than to run away again. And your father, he was a good fighter. Your grandfather and Jean felt that he could have killed the two Crows. He wanted to die."

Aeneva turned away. "I do not want to hear any

47

more.''

''He wanted to die, Aeneva. Think about that when next you ride out to fight. Think how honorable it was for your parents to die at such a young age and leave three young children. You think about it, Aeneva; then you tell me how much honor there is in that!'' Sun Dancer pulled the basket from Aeneva's arm and walked away.

Aeneva started after her grandmother, unable or unwilling to comprehend all that she had said. She had not expected this from her; she had not expected to hear her grandmother speak against everything that she believed in. A sound came from deep within her and unable to understand it all, she cried out. Her mind was a mass of confusion, and her grandmother had instilled doubts in her that had never before existed.

Aeneva did not mind the winter as the others did, and often when it was not snowing and the snow on the ground was not too deep, she would walk and explore. She was careful never to wander far away from camp and she always laid a trail so she could follow it back. She had heard too many times the story of her grandmother having been lost in the snow and having to climb a tree to keep the wolves away from her.

At times like this when she was very solitary and very alone, she thought of Trenton. She wondered how she could feel so deeply for someone she had not known for very long. There had only been the spring and summer of her eleventh year, but it had seemed like a long enough time to know him. Those had been wonderful days, days full of laughter and fun, days when the only important thing was to be young. She thought of the riverboat ride and seeing Trenton again, and the feeling she had had that there was still a closeness between them, something untouched by their years apart. He had felt it too, she knew, but it was different for him now. His life would go in a different direction from hers.

She had often thought of what her grandmother had said to her and she wondered if, when the time came, she could die honorably. She was still so young and there was still so much yet to do; she wasn't sure she was ready to die.

"Why is it you can never sit still for very long, little Sister?"

Aeneva turned and smiled as she saw Brave Wolf coming behind her in the snow. "We sit still too much in the winter, Brother. •We must move around when we are able."

"Would you like to go on a hunt?"

Aeneva's face lit up. "Grandfather will let me go?"

"Yes, he says you can come. You, I, Coyote Boy, and some•of the other ones. We must return in a day if we do not find anything."

"Then the older ones will go out," Aeneva replied dryly.

"They are more experienced. If we cannot find something in a day, they do not want us wasting time. It is fair."

"Yes, I want to go. When do we leave?"

"Now. Come, you must pack your horse."

"Is grandmother angry that I am going?" Aeneva asked suddenly.

"As usual, she said nothing. She knows you will go anyway."

The elders thought the break in the bad weather would hold, but Aeneva was not so sure. The farther away from camp they got, the more dense the low-hanging clouds were. She looked up at the sky, hoping to see a path of blue, but there was none. Not many things frightened her, but one that did was snow and all the dangers it entailed. She had heard enough tales of people getting lost in the snow, freezing to death, losing arms or legs to frostbite, or becoming easy prey to some mountain lion or wolf. She did not relish dying like that. It was a distasteful way to die.

Brave Wolf held up his hand and the small hunting party stopped. He was the eldest of the group, and at nineteen summers the most experienced. He turned his horse so they could all hear him. "I am afraid the weather is growing worse. I think we should go back."

"But we cannot go back without some food, Brave Wolf," one of the young braves objected.

"It is true, Brother. If we do not get something now and it starts to snow again, we could be without meat for a long while," Coyote Boy added.

"We have enough dried meat and currants to last."

"But we need fresh meat."

"And we must show the elders that we are capable. We cannot go back without a kill."

Brave Wolf was silent for a time, looking over the small group; then his eyes met Aeneva's. Many times he had sought out her opinion. She always thought clearly and precisely; she was not a rash thinker like Coyote Boy. Many times she had seen the truth in things when he did not. "What do you think, little Sister?"

Aeneva looked at her brother, and up at the swirling clouds. She knew Brave Wolf was concerned for the lives of the young men he had brought with him; more than that, he was responsible for them. She had felt long ago that the weather was not good. "I think we should go back, Brave Wolf. The weather quickly grows worse."

She pointed to the mist that fell around them. "See the moisture. As it grows colder, that will turn into snow. I do not want to be caught out here without shelter in a blizzard."

Brave Wolf nodded in satisfaction. He had known she would feel the same as he.

"You seek out the opinion of a girl over us, Brave Wolf?" Spotted Feather asked. "Of course she would want to go back; she is a girl. But I say we go on. I do not want to return to my father without a fresh kill. I want to show him and the elders that we are strong and able to hunt, even in weather like this. I am going, even if you do not, Brave Wolf."

"I, too," chimed several others.

Brave Wolf looked at Coyote Boy, expecting him to feel the same. "And what of you, Brother? Do you feel the same as the others?"

"You are our leader and I will do as you say." Coyote Boy faced the others so they could better hear him. "I do not need to prove to the elders that I can go out into the snow and get myself killed. I would rather prove to them that I am smart and have chosen the right path. They all know I can hunt, better than most of them even." He smiled broadly at Brave Wolf. "I will follow my brother. He is right. You would be foolish to stay out in this weather."

"You three would stay together, or course," Spotted Feather said angrily. "But it still does not matter to me. You are not my chief, Brave Wolf, and I do not have to follow you. You can all go back to the camp like scared children while I go and hunt some fresh meat. We will see then whom the elders choose to honor."

The hunting party wound up divided equally. Two other hunters went with Brave Wolf, Aeneva, and Coyote Boy, while the other four chose to follow Spotted Feather. They had not ridden more than a mile when Brave Wolf stopped, his head hung low, his eyes staring at the whiteness on the ground.

"I cannot leave them," he said quietly.

"It was their decision, Brother," Coyote Boy said.

"I am responsible for them. Grandfather picked me to lead the hunting party. If something happens to them it will be my fault. He will blame me."

"Brave Wolf, you are being foolish. You did what you could. Now we must go back." Aeneva pleaded with her brother.

"I have made my decision. Coyote Boy, you lead this group back to camp; I will go after the others. It is the only way."

"You take this much too seriously, Brother. You are not a chief. Why are you acting like one? You are not responsible for them. It is their own fault if they die out there."

"It is my fault if I let them die out there, Coyote Boy. I must stay with them and make sure they get out. Do as I say and take Aeneva and the others back to camp."

"I am going with you, Brave Wolf." Aeneva locked eyes with her brother. "Do not try to talk me out of it. If you go, I go."

"And I," Coyote Boy added.

"We also," Hokiyo and Wounded Eye agreed.

Brave Wolf nodded in resignation. "All right then, let us hurry. It will be snowing soon."

As Brave Wolf and Aeneva had feared, the snow was raging full force within the hour. They barely had time to locate a hollowed-out tree and to find what little shelter there was beneath. Brave Wolf and his brother and sister

52

stayed together, and Hokiyo and Wounded Eye sought shelter in a nearby tree. They hastily gathered what branches were lying about, not buried in the snow, and piled them on top of their small shelter, in an attempt to keep the heavy snow from coming in. Aeneva took their dried food from the pack and secured their horses to the trees, removing their blankets to use as extra cover for themselves. She took the smoldering piece of buffalo chip from the parfleche her grandmother had given her and started a fire under the shelter. It did not give off much heat, as they could find very little dried wood, but they peeled off pieces of bark and it gave off enough heat for them to warm their hands.

"Those idiots!" Brave Wolf cried. "Why could they not open their eyes and see for themselves?"

"They wanted only to prove themselves, Brave Wolf. They did not think about the storm."

"Well, they will think about it now. And they will feel it to their very bones."

"*Haahe,* Hokiyo and Wounded Eye," Brave Wolf yelled out into the whiteness, "are you faring well?"

"There are other ways I would rather be keeping warm," Wounded Eye yelled back, "but I will not say them in front of Aeneva. We are doing well enough, Brave Wolf."

They all laughed and were glad for the break in the mood.

"Brave Wolf, tell us some story; something you have never told us before."

"You both know all the stories I know."

"Then make something up, Brother. It will help to pass the time."

In the distance, muffled by the snowy stillness, they heard the howls of wolves. The three looked around the small shelter at each other. All felt respect and reverence for the great wolf—the Cheyennes called their scouts "wolves"—but fear, too. There were too many stories about wolves preying on starving, helpless people. Although their grandfather said most of the stories were untrue and told by people who were fearful, it was easy to believe such things out in the snow, away from the main camp.

"I will tell the story about the wolf." Brave Wolf spoke suddenly, aware that he should stem his siblings' rising fear.

Instantly, Aeneva and Coyote Boy focused their attention on their older brother, wanting to be diverted from the sounds of the howling wolves.

"There was a time many winters ago when a small band of Cheyennes was attacked by some Crows. Most of the Cheyennes were killed and three women and their children managed to escape. They hid in some trees next to a river and when the Crows left, they set off in search of other members of their band. They walked for days— frightened, tired, and hungry, but unable to stop for fear the Crows would attack them at any time. One night, they found shelter in a small cave and they slept quietly; all except one of the women. She was unable to sleep for she heard noises all around them. She wondered if it was the Crows following them. Finally she saw a large, dark shadow moving into the cave, and it was not until it got close to the small fires that she saw it was a large wolf. She was sure the animal was there to kill her, but she was unable to find the strength to be scared. But the animal came no closer. Instead, he sat down by the fire, his yellow eyes staring into those of the woman. Finally she fell asleep.

"The next morning they started out again, and when

the other women and children saw the wolf they were frightened, but the woman told them not to be afraid. The wolf walked with them, off to one side, and when they stopped to rest, so did the wolf. Finally, the woman who had first seen the wolf spoke to him, as if he were a real person, and she said, 'Try to do something for us, Wolf. We and our children are starving.' The wolf looked at the woman for a moment, then rose up and trotted off toward the north. The women continued to rest, for their feet were sore and they were weak from lack of food. After a time the wolf came back, and they could see that his mouth and jaws were covered with blood. He turned his head and looked back toward the direction from which he had just come. The women stood up and the wolf trotted off, waiting and looking back at them, until they followed him. When they reached the top of a hill, they looked down and saw the carcass of a buffalo and all around it sat many wolves. The wolf loped off toward the carcass and the women followed quickly now. They looked at the other wolves, but the creatures did not move. All sat very still, not feeding on the carcass.

"When the women reached the dead buffalo, they drew their knives and immediately began eating the liver and the fat around the intestines. Then they cut off pieces of meat and made up packs and started on their way again. As soon as they had left the carcass, all the wolves fell upon it, growling and snarling at each other. The big wolf ate with the other wolves.

"The women traveled on until dark and then they stopped. The big wolf came again that night and slept by their fire. They camped near willows, and after making beds of grass and willows for each of them and their children, they made one for the wolf to sleep upon. Later in the night they heard a noise such as they had never heard

55

before. The women were frightened as the noise grew louder and the thing came closer. Soon the wolf let out a high howl, and wolves came from all directions. When the thing that was making the noise came very close, the wolves rushed toward it and began fighting it, and the women seized their children and ran away into the night. When they reached safety, they stopped to rest and found that the wolf had followed them.

"The woman spoke to him again and said, 'Take pity on us, oh, Great Wolf, and help us to find the trail of our people!' When she had finished, the wolf ran off and the women followed. Before long they saw him coming back with a big piece of dried meat in his mouth. The wolf stood and waited until they had eaten and he led them to an old camp where there were sticks standing on the ground, and on each stick hung a parfleche of meat. Relations of the women had left these things knowing that the women were lost and hoping that they might pass this way.

"Now the women had plenty of food so the wolf led them to water and there they built a shelter for themselves and the wolf. That night it snowed and in the morning the snow was above their ankles. Again the woman spoke to the wolf and asked him to go find their winter camp. Again he left but returned some time later, stopped, and looked back. The women were sure he had found something and they started in the direction from which the wolf had just come. On the point of a high hill he stopped, and when the women drew even with him, they looked down and saw a big Cheyenne camp on the river below. They went down to the camp, but the wolf remained on the hill. After they had eaten, the woman who had always talked to the wolf took him some meat. After he had eaten she said to him, 'Now you have brought us to the camp, you can go back to your own kind.' Later that evening the woman went back up on the hill to see if the wolf was still there, but he was gone. She saw his tracks going back the same way he had come.''

"Is that a true story, Brave Wolf, or did you make it up?'' Aeneva asked in the growing darkness, rubbing her hands together.

"What do you think, little Sister?''

"I think you made it up,'' Coyote Boy replied knowingly. "No wolf would do such a thing.''

"Have you known many wolves then, Brother?'' Brave Wolf asked.

"No, but it is not like a wolf to act so. It is only a good story to tell.''

"It is true, Coyote Boy. One of the children traveling with the women was our grandmother's mother. That is why she named her son, our great uncle, Brave Wolf.''

"I never before heard this story. I wonder why Grandmother never told me,'' Aeneva said curiously. "I only know of the time Grandmother was almost attacked by wolves.''

"Yes, but Grandmother always says that if she had been calm and made some noise to frighten them off, they probably would not have harmed her.''

Again the howls of the nearby wolves echoed in the trees and Aeneva and Coyote Boy looked at each other, each still not sure of the goodness of the animals. They heard Brave Wolf's voice in the ever-growing darkness.

"Do not be frightened; they will not harm us.'' Brave Wolf's voice held such authority that the two younger ones were surprised but also reassured. Perhaps he knew something they did not. It was said that a person who was named after an animal usually developed a kinship with it. There was a spiritual closeness between the animal and

57

the human, as if the human adopted some of the animal's traits. Whatever the reason, Coyote Boy and Aeneva were grateful to hear their older brother sound so reassured. It made the cold, the darkness, and the howling of the wolves much less frightening than they would have been.

The storm grew fearsome during the night and blew the branches off their small shelter. They worked quickly to repair the damage before their refuge was filled with the swirling, rapidly falling snow. Hokiyo and Wounded Eye remained in their own small shelter while the others patched theirs up and returned to its relative warmth. It was not until morning that they realized their horses had broken free during the storm. Now they were without their mounts, as well as the extra food that was in the packs.

"How much food do we have with us, Aeneva?" Brave Wolf asked his sister.

"I took out one of the larger parfleches. If we are careful we will have enough for a few days."

"When the snow stops we can hunt for some small game," Coyote Boy added confidently.

"When the snow stops, we must build a bigger and more sturdy shelter."

"I think we should try to walk out of here, Brave Wolf. It is important that we keep moving in this cold. If we just sit here, we will freeze to death."

"Not if we build another shelter or if we can find something around here. We will never make it if we try to walk out of here. The camp is far and the snow is deep. Look,"—he pointed up to the dense, gray clouds in the sky—"it will start to snow soon. How far do you think we could go? If we did walk, by the time we stopped we

58

would be so tired we would not care about a shelter. We would just sit down and fall asleep in the snow."

Aeneva and Coyote Boy exchanged looks.

"When Grandmother was caught in the snow when she was a young girl, she walked out. She did not stay and freeze to death," Coyote Boy protested.

"Grandmother was foolish and lucky. Grandfather has said so many times. Besides, she had no other choice. She and the women were already very cold and they could find very little shelter. It is different with us. We are four men and one girl. If we cannot find shelter, we will build one. *Haahe?*"

Coyote Boy started to say something further, but Aeneva interrupted him. "I agree with Brave Wolf. It is better that we stay here, Coyote Boy. If Grandfather and the others come looking for us they will find our horses. We must try to stay alive until then."

"I feel young and foolish. All we had to do was hunt some game. Instead, here we are, caught in a storm without our horses—"

"It was not our fault," Aeneva interrupted again, "and Brave Wolf did what he thought was right. He has kept us alive this long. I trust him to keep us alive until grandfather comes."

Coyote Boy looked over at his sister and brother and slowly nodded his head. "You have done well, Brother. Had I not thought so, I would not be here. I will forget my pride and do as you say. You are the oldest and, I hope, the wisest."

Brave Wolf laughed, putting his arms around Aeneva and Coyote Boy. "I am lucky to have you two for a brother and sister. Both brave and both loyal. Thank you." He looked up at the sky again. "Now is the time for us to look for another place. Hokiyo and Wounded

Eye will go together, you two will go together, and I will go alone. We will meet when I shoot the rifle once. Do not wander far and be sure to lay a trail that you can follow.''

"We have laid trail many times before, Brother. Do not worry. Aeneva and I will find a suitable shelter. Come, little Sister.''

Brave Wolf watched them as, Coyote Boy holding on to Aeneva, they trudged through the deep snow, and the elder brother had a small stabbing pain in his stomach. If something were to happen to them . . . No, he would not think that way. They were both experienced in the ways of the woods and they would do well.

He turned his attention to Hokiyo and Wounded Eye, sending them off in another direction with the same instructions he had given Aeneva and Coyote Boy. Now he was alone and it gave him a deep sense of foreboding. He did not like being responsible for others; he did not look forward to becoming a chief. He shivered slightly and pulled his heavy robe closer around his neck and face. He hoped he had made the right decision, but he knew he had not. He should have done what his mind had told him to at the beginning—he should have taken his brother and sister and the other two home; then he could have ridden out with another hunting party and searched for Spotted Feather and his party. Instead, because of the responsibility he had felt for them, he had endangered the lives of his brother, sister, and two others. He walked off in the deep snow, breaking branches as he moved into the woods, making sure he left a trail that was easy to find.

Brave Wolf heard movement in the woods. He moved silently among the trees and looked out into a clearing. A doe stood, pawing at the sparse grass under the snow.

The doe lifted her graceful head suddenly and her nostrils twitched. She turned her head as something moved from the trees; then she began running frantically around the clearing as the pack of wolves emerged. She tried desperately to escape into the trees, but the wolves were upon her in seconds, severing the tendons in her forelegs, and going for her neck. The pack was hungry and they snarled as they pulled meat from the carcass. Brave Wolf watched in fascination as they ate their fill and sat down in the snow to rest. When they had quieted, Brave Wolf stepped slowly out of the trees and walked toward the deer. They stared at him, surprised at first, then angry at this intrusion upon their kill. But Brave Wolf did not still his movement; he advanced slowly, eying the leader of the small pack. He had picked him out earlier; he was the wolf who sat back and let the others feed first.

Brave Wolf watched the leader as he neared the carcass, his rifle raised and ready to shoot. The others snarled, but instead of trying to attack him, they sat back on their haunches, eying him with their peculiar yellow eyes, wondering why this human animal would dare to come among them. Brave Wolf knew that they would be less apt to attack since they had eaten. Although they would still feel threatened by this intrusion upon their kill, their stomachs would be full and they would be less aggressive. He thought of the story of the woman and the wolf and he wasn't sure if he believed it; the old men and women of the camp told so many stories. But it was a good story and he wanted to believe that the wolf did help the women and children. As he knelt next to the carcass, taking out his knife to cut off pieces of fresh meat, he wasn't so sure that these wolves wouldn't attack him in an instant. He noticed that they kept looking to their leader, waiting for him to make a move toward the man.

The leader, a large gray-black wolf, got up and walked toward the carcass. He stood near it and eyed Brave Wolf warily as he cut off pieces of meat.

"*Haahe, moohtaa-honehe. E-Toneto. Na-haeana.* Greetings, black wolf. It is cold and I am hungry."

The wolf looked at him, its yellow eyes giving away nothing. Brave Wolf continued to cut at the meat and place it in his parfleche as he talked. "I will take only as much as I need; then I will go. I thank you for helping me, Cousin." Brave Wolf stood up and stepped slowly away from the carcass, constantly keeping his eyes on the leader. The black wolf did not move; only his great head turned to watch Brave Wolf walk away. Then, as if given a silent signal, the rest of the pack went back to the carcass to feast on the fresh meat, while the black wolf lay down, his yellow eyes looking in the direction that Brave Wolf had gone.

Aeneva and Coyote Boy stumbled on to the cave almost by accident. They had entered a sparsely forested ravine containing many rocks covered by snow. With their large sticks to support them, they plodded forward among the rocks and boulders, listening as the sounds echoed in the stillness. When they saw a thin sheet of icicles fall away from the side of some boulders, they began hitting at them with their sticks. They had found the entrance to a small cave. Aeneva started to walk inside, but Coyote Boy pulled her back.

"It would be best to wait. This might be the winter home of a bear and I for one would not like to be the one to wake him. I would feel better with Brave Wolf's gun."

"Yes, you are right. We will go back and get the others; we can send them in." They both laughed and ran back through the snow, their hopes renewed by their find.

They heard Brave Wolf's rifle shot as they hurried back to camp. They saw the smile on Brave Wolf's face as he entered their small camp.

"What are you so happy about, big Brother? Do not tell me you have spoken to the wolves and they are going to lead us out of here?" Coyote Boy asked playfully.

"Not quite, little Brother. But I have been with some wolves." He explained how he had obtained the fresh meat.

"You are crazy, Brother; I know it for sure now. To go among a pack of wolves that is feeding . . ." Coyote Boy shook his head in wonder.

"And they did not harm you?" Aeneva asked in wonder. "It is amazing, Brave Wolf. Do you suppose they know you are cousin to them."

"That is foolish!" Coyote Boy burst out. "I have seen many coyotes and not one has ever come up to speak to me. I think you are lucky they did not tear you to pieces, Brave Wolf."

"I think you are probably right, Brother," Brave Wolf admitted. "The only reason I attempted it was that I knew they had eaten and their stomachs would be full. I hoped they would be so surprised by my intrusion that they would not attack. I always kept my eyes on the leader in case he came at me."

"But he did not," Aeneva replied, her voice still full of awe.

"Aeneva, you are being foolish," Coyote Boy reiterated. "Now tell Brave Wolf of our find."

"We found a cave," Aeneva replied happily.

"That is wonderful. You both did well."

"Well, we did not go inside. That is your job, Brother. Since you are so good with the animals of the wild, you check to see if there is a bear using the cave for the winter. I, myself, do not have such confidence with animals."

"We will light a torch and check the cave to make sure it is safe." Brave Wolf turned his head. "Ah, Hokiyo and Wounded Eye. How have you fared?"

"We found these at least." They each held up a rabbit.

"Well, it seems we have all done well. We will need to gather some wood to dry for a fire. Break off some of the underbark of the tree trunks to burn also. We must hurry. It grows cold again."

Leaving a tall stick standing in the snow with an empty parfleche hung on it in case some of their people should come looking for them, they hurriedly departed from their small encampment. Brave Wolf, Wounded Eye, and Coyote Boy—in spite of his protests—investigated the cave and found it to be quite shallow and without any other life, human or animal. Although it was not large, it provided adequate room for all of them to stretch out, and it was small enough to contain the warmth from their bodies and the small fire. Hanging the rabbits up, they roasted the fresh meat over the open fire. Aeneva gathered snow in a small bowl and let it melt so they would have water, and when they were finished eating, they covered the entrance to the cave with large branches to keep out the drifts of snow. All of them slept soundly, aware of how good it felt to have their stomachs full and their bodies warm.

In the middle of the night Aeneva woke suddenly when she heard the sounds of the howling wolves close by; she heard Brave Wolf's voice come at her through the semidarkness.

"Do not be afraid, little Sister. I have talked with them. They will not hurt us."

Aeneva lay back down. She wondered about Brave

Wolf, if he had truly talked with the wolves. But even if he had not, his voice was enough to reassure her. When next she heard the howls in the night, she was more comforted than frightened.

CHAPTER IV

"Ah, I am getting too old for this, *Veho.*" Stalking Horse sat astride his mount, rubbing his hands together and looking around at the terrain.

"I know what you mean, *mon ami.* I, too, feel the cold to my very bones. But it is probably much colder for the young ones right now."

Stalking Horse nodded. "It was foolish of me to send them out. I knew the weather would not hold for long."

"It was not foolish. You gave them a chance to be men."

"And what of Aeneva, eh? Did I give her a chance to die young?"

"Bah, you give up on them too easily. They are young and strong; and even more than that, they have a great knowledge of the wilderness, passed on from you, Sun Dancer, me, all their relatives and friends. I am confident that they are well. They are smart children."

"But what of the others? What if they decided to split up? There is discord between Spotted Feather and Brave Wolf. Perhaps I was wrong to name Brave Wolf as the leader of the hunting party."

"You were not wrong. Spotted Feather is not as experienced as Brave Wolf. You did the right thing. *Venezvous.* We are wasting time."

"I am glad you did not go up to that cabin this winter,

Veho."

"I, too, *mon ami.* I, too."

Stalking Horse and Jean rode together, while the rest of the party rode behind. It didn't take them long to find the small encampment, although most of the racks were now covered by fresh snow. Stalking Horse and Jean discovered many broken branches that stuck out of the ground. The young ones had laid a trail that was easy for them to retrace.

"They have learned well." Jean nodded his head in approval.

"How do you know it was our children? Perhaps it was some of the others."

"No, no, not with this." Jean leaned down slightly and grabbed the parfleche from the stick in the ground. "You and I taught them this."

"They were here but found shelter elsewhere. I see trails going in different directions. Let us each take one."

"*Oui,* a good idea. They probably looked in several places for a better shelter. One trail will lead us to them."

Brave Wolf knocked the snow away from the entrance and looked out on a solid blanket of white snow.

"It is beautiful, is it not?" Aeneva was next to him, gazing out at the wondrous sight. "I do not understand how something so beautiful can be so frightening."

"It is the same with many things, little Sister. Do not let the beauty in things deceive you."

"You sound strange this morning, Brave Wolf. What troubles you?"

"I make no sense. My thoughts are wandering."

"You are worried for the others. It was not your fault."

Brave Wolf looked over at his sister and put his arm

around her. "You are so much like Grandmother; do you know that? You can read a person's thoughts just as she can; you know when someone is hurting or frightened."

"You give me too much credit, Brother. I can do those things, it is true, but only with the people that I love. I know you so well it is easy for me to tell when there is something wrong. Just as you know when there is something wrong with me."

"Perhaps."

"Grandmother says we are much like her and her brother, Brave Wolf, our great-uncle. She says that there is something stronger than blood between us. Perhaps it is just that we perceive many things the same way. It is almost as if we look through the same eyes sometimes."

Brave Wolf nodded, considering the statement. "Yes, it is somewhat strange, is it not? It would seem that Coyote Boy and I should be of a stronger bond."

"You both have a bond of a different kind which I will never know, just as he and I have a different bond."

"And what is that?"

"We are both the youngest, of course. We have always had to take orders from you, most of the time when we didn't want to; and many times it was us against you, our strong big brother."

"Yes, I remember too well the many tricks you two have played on me. I especially remember the time you led me into the sleeping bear's cave. I thought I would die a hundred deaths when I stumbled over the huge beast."

Aeneva laughed gleefully, the sound echoing throughout the small cave. "I have never seen you so scared, Brother."

"What are you two laughing about?" Coyote Boy stumbled over to his brother and sister, squatting on the ground next to them.

69

"I was just reminding our big brother of the time when we led him into the cave of the great sleeping bear."

"Yes; as I recall, our big brother was not so brave that day. I seem to remember that he ran from that cave as if the wind were at his back." Coyote Boy and Aeneva laughed, delighting in the response they had evoked from their brother. "You may be able to talk to wolves, Brother, but you haven't yet learned how to talk to bears."

Their laughter was interrupted by a high-pitched howling, similar to that of a wolf or coyote, but different because of the tone.

"*Otaha!*" Brave Wolf admonished his siblings. "Listen!"

Again the sound echoed in the stillness outside the cave and Brave Wolf nodded his head, not waiting to confer with his brother or sister. He cupped both hands around his mouth and imitated the sound, waiting a minute, then repeating it. They heard the other sound again; this time it was much closer. Brave Wolf continued his calls. Soon they were all waiting outside the cave, knowing that someone had come to help them.

"Look!" Aeneva cried suddenly, running over the blanket of snow. She saw her grandfather riding his old paint, his shoulders covered by a heavy buffalo robe, his lance held out. Aeneva stopped as he drew close. She looked up at him, seeing his proud old shoulders, erect as if he were still a youth, and his finely chiseled face that betrayed no emotion. But she could see in the depths of his black eyes the joy that he would not let show. She smiled as she walked up to his horse, patted the familiar animal on the neck. She looked up at Stalking Horse.

"*Na-meseme.* My grandfather," she said softly.

Stalking Horse looked down at his granddaughter

nodded his head slightly, then extended his arm. Aeneva took hold and swung up behind her grandfather, hugging the heavy robe. She pointed out the cave to him and they rode to the entrance, dismounting in front of her brothers, who were now joined by Hokiyo and Wounded Eye. Stalking Horse quickly assessed the situation and confronted Brave Wolf.

"Where are the others?"

"I do not know, Grandfather." Brave Wolf stood tall, his eyes never wavering from his grandfather's.

"You were responsible for them all. I trusted your judgment."

Brave Wolf started to respond but stopped, not knowing what to say in his own defense.

"It was not his fault, Grandfather," Coyote Boy stepped forward to defend his older brother. "Spotted Feather—"

Stalking Horse raised his hand. "I do not want to hear excuses. A chief does not make excuses; he decides one way or another."

"But, Grandfather, Brave Wolf did the best he could."

"I never knew you to fight your brother's battles for him, Coyote Boy." He turned his hard gaze on Brave Wolf. "And I never knew you to let him."

Coyote Boy started to protest again, but Brave Wolf pulled him back. "Grandfather is right, Brother. Do not make excuses for me. I did not react as a chief would react. I did not make the right decision."

"Yes, you did!" Aeneva stepped over to Brave Wolf, locking her arm through his, staring defiantly up at her grandfather.

"Do not, Aeneva," Brave Wolf implored, but Aeneva continued on.

"No; I will tell Grandfather, this stubborn old grand-

71

father of ours." There was a resounding silence all around them and Hokiyo and Wounded Eye withdrew into the cave, not wanting to see the wrath of Stalking Horse. Aeneva walked up to her grandfather and looked up at him, anger and defiance on her young face. "Brave Wolf did the right thing, Grandfather. When the storm began, he wanted us all to go back, but Spotted Feather objected. He said we were all cowards and that he was going on to find game to prove to the elders that he was not afraid. Hokiyo and Wounded Eye came with us; the rest went with Spotted Feather. As we were going back, the storm grew worse and we sought shelter under some trees. We stayed there one night and yesterday morning Brave Wolf said we should find a better shelter. While we were looking for a shelter, he found us fresh meat. He walked in among wolves, Grandfather, and cut some meat from their kill." Aeneva waited a moment, seeing the slight flicker of her grandfather's eyes, then she continued. "We discovered this cave and stayed the night. I awoke early this morning to find Brave Wolf looking out of the mouth of the cave. He was worried about the others, worried if he had done the right thing. I am sure if you had not come along, he would have gone after them." Aeneva felt a hand on her shoulder and turned. Brave Wolf looked at her, a solemn expression on his face.

"That is enough, Aeneva. You have said too much."

"No, I have not." She pulled herself away from Brave Wolf and walked still closer to her grandfather. "You are always so quick to condemn Brave Wolf, Grandfather. Why? Is it because he is not so quick to fight as the others, or that he has feelings that run very deep, feelings that we will never understand? Are you afraid he will not make a good warrior and not make you proud?"

"I think you have said enough, child." Stalking Horse spoke clearly and deeply.

"No. He is my brother and I will defend him with my life, even against you." She stood tall, her chest heaving with the weight of the robe and the anger of her words. "You should be proud of him, Grandfather."

"I am proud of him, Aeneva." He looked at each of his grandchildren. "I am proud of you all. Prouder than you will ever know." They all stood silent for a moment. Stalking Horse reached out and touched Aeneva's cheek. "Such a loyal sister. You are much like your grandmother." He looked over at Brave Wolf. "Your sister is right, Brave Wolf; I have been hard on you. Perhaps it is because you are the oldest and I want you to be the best. Perhaps it is because I want you to be strong enough to defend yourself as your sister just did for you."

"I do not need Aeneva to defend me. I did not make the right decision. A chief who makes the right decision does not have doubts."

"A wise chief always has doubts. It is not easy for a man to make a quick decision, especially when the lives of others depend on it." He looked up at the sky. "Come, we will search now while the storm has stopped."

"Where is *Naxane* Jean?" Aeneva asked, her eyes searching the trees around them.

"He is out looking for the others. Do not worry about Jean, he will find us and he will let us know if he finds them."

The young ones started to go back into the cave, but Stalking Horse caught Aeneva. She looked at her grandfather, no fear apparent in her eyes. "You are an insolent child. I should beat you for talking to me that

73

way."

"But you will not," Aeneva said softly, a slight smile curling up the corners of her mouth.

"How do you know that?"

"Because you know I am right. You expect Brave Wolf to be many things. Is that not true, Grandfather? You do not expect so much of Coyote Boy or me. But you know what Brave Wolf can be. You want him to be a great chief, a chief who will guide our people with wisdom as well as courage when you are gone."

Stalking Horse emitted a deep sigh, his eyes glancing at the whiteness that surrounded them. He watched as Brave Wolf and the others led their horses out and he waved them on, holding Aeneva's horse as they passed. "I see in your brother everything that is good for this small band of ours. He has the gentleness and wisdom of your great-uncle, the courage of your father, and he has the ability to be a much greater chief than I. So much in one so young," he said thoughtfully, almost sadly.

"Yet you are afraid, Grandfather. Why?"

"Because when it is his time to be chief, I will not be here to advise him. It will be the hardest time of all for him, much harder than it ever was for me."

"Why?" Aeneva asked hesitantly, although she thought she knew why.

"Because of the whites. Not only will we be fighting Indians, but he will have to contend with the white man."

"But I have heard that since I was a child. We have seen very few white men."

"You were in the white man's city and in the place where the soldiers live. Tell me they did not frighten you with all their weapons." He nodded his head, his gaze far away. "They will come, Aeneva, do not doubt it. They will come, just as Sweet Medicine said they would."

74

Aeneva, colder than she had felt moments before, pulled her robe closer around her. She swung up onto her pony and followed her grandfather through the trees, all the time wondering if someday Brave Wolf would face Trenton on a field of battle. Trenton was now one of those whites of whom her grandfather spoke and this thought chilled her even more than the cold snow possibly could.

By midday they had picked up the trail of Spotted Feather and the others. They found them shortly thereafter in a small but tight circle of trees. Spotted Feather was unusually silent as he stood up to great Stalking Horse.

"*Haahe, Vehoooh-oho.* Greetings, my chief."

"*Ne-toneto-mohta-he?* How are you?"

"*Na-pevo-mohta.* I am fine."

Stalking Horse nodded his head as he looked at Spotted Feather and the others, satisfied that they were all in good health. "You were all foolish, do you know that?" His voice was controlled when he spoke, but it held an edge of anger.

Spotted Feather and the others nodded, staring solemnly at their chief. "I do not know what to say—"

Stalking Horse held up his hand, stopping Spotted Feather from continuing. "I blamed Brave Wolf for your foolishness, Spotted Feather. He would not defend himself. He would only say that he had made the wrong decision by not staying with you."

Spotted Feather looked over at Brave Wolf, antagonism extremely apparent in his eyes. "We needed food," he replied curtly, speaking before Stalking Horse could. "He wanted to go back without it."

"Do you have food?" Stalking Horse continued to

75

stare at Spotted Feather, his voice still controlled but still hinting at the anger he felt.

"No. We were waiting for the storm to stop."

"I do not want excuses, Spotted Feather. I also told Brave Wolf that. If you have made a mistake, at least be honest enough to admit it."

"I did not make a mistake." Spotted Feather held Stalking Horse's angry gaze, refusing to back down from the chief.

"You have courage but no sense," Stalking Horse said softly, shaking his head in disgust. "Pack up your things. It will be a long time before you become a war chief."

"You are an old man," Spotted Feather snarled as Stalking Horse turned away. Immediately, all three grandchildren stepped forward, ready to defend their grandfather.

Spotted Feather eyed them all in disgust, his eyes finally coming to rest on Brave Wolf. "Will you have your brother and sister fight for you, Brave Wolf?" He nodded his head toward Stalking Horse. "Even the old man could put up a better fight than you."

Coyote Boy withdrew his knife, but Brave Wolf waved him back. He walked slowly forward, his eyes never leaving Spotted Feather. "You have gone too far, Spotted Feather. You not only insult my grandfather, but our chief. It is too much this time."

"I thought it would be," Spotted Feather replied knowingly, shrugging off his robe and withdrawing his knife.

"Do not do this, Brave Wolf." Stalking Horse walked to his grandson. "He has purposely provoked you. It is not important."

"It is important, Grandfather. He insulted you; for that he will pay." Brave Wolf's words were final and Stalking

Horse withdrew, pulling Aeneva and Coyote Boy back with him.

"You must understand, *hoovehe*. He is not only defending your honor; he is defending his own." Jean spoke softly to his friend.

Stalking Horse nodded. "I know that, Jean. I know."

Brave Wolf removed his robe and unsheathed his knife, facing Spotted Feather as if he were a dreaded enemy. Brave Wolf was tall and lean, much taller than Spotted Feather, but Spotted Feather was heavier and was known to be very deft with the knife. Brave Wolf had great respect for his opponent; they had fought many times before. He did not underestimate Spotted Feather's ability or his strength. The air was still and it was quiet all around them, except for an occasional animal sound. Snow fell to the ground from the trees above, and in the distance, a lone wolf howled. Brave Wolf felt his strength increase, as if the wolf had given him the extra courage that he felt he had lacked.

Spotted Feather feinted to the right, swiping his knife at Brave Wolf's belly. Brave Wolf jumped back and circled slowly around, always watching Spotted Feather. Again Spotted Feather lunged forward, his knife missing Brave Wolf's shoulder, but his weight knocked them both to the ground. They rolled around in the snow, their bodies leaving smooth places as they slid and tried to regain their footing. Brave Wolf was up first. Breathing hard, his knees bent in a crouch, he ran toward Spotted Feather and knocked him back down on the ground. Spotted Feather rolled to the side, just in time to be narrowly missed by Brave Wolf as he attempted to pounce on his adversary. Both got up quickly. Then Brave Wolf lunged at Spotted Feather, knocking him backward into a tree, pinning him on the ground; he held his knife above Spotted Feather's throat. They stared at each other, Spotted Feather's eyes betraying no sign of fear, only hatred.

"Kill me, Brave Wolf. Kill me!" Spotted Feather screamed.

Brave Wolf withdrew his knife and slowly shook his head. "No, I am not going to kill you, Spotted Feather. You will live on and you will always know that you owe me your life. That is the worst punishment you could receive." He put his knife back in its sheath and got up, walking away from Spotted Feather.

"I will owe you a life, Brave Wolf," Spotted Feather screamed, "but when my debt is paid, I will owe you nothing. Nothing!"

They all watched in silence as Spotted Feather picked up his knife and robe and walked alone to his horse. He rode out a few minutes later.

"He will not return to the band," Jean said quietly. "He has been disgraced."

"I am proud that you did not kill him, Brave Wolf." Stalking Horse turned to his grandson. "But this one worries me. He is not to be trusted. He will not forget what you have done to him."

"I think *naxane* is right, Grandfather. Spotted Feather will join one of the warrior societies. He will not return to our band."

"He worries me also, Brave Wolf." Aeneva walked up to her brother. "I have never trusted him. He was always full of deceit. You should have killed him."

Brave Wolf looked at his little sister; then shook his head, sure of the decision he had made. "No, it would not have been right to kill him. He is not my enemy."

"You are wrong, Brother." Coyote Boy spoke up. "He is your enemy as surely as the Crows are. As long as Spotted Feather lives, you will always have to look over your shoulder."

Brave Wolf looked at his younger brother, then in the direction in which Spotted Feather had ridden. He wanted to believe that people were good, but in his heart he knew that what Coyote Boy had said was true: as long as Spotted Feather was alive, he would have to look behind him. The thought was a heavy one to contemplate for one so young.

"I hear you have been chosen as a soldier by the Dog Men." Sun Dancer spoke softly as she handed the plants to Aeneva to put in the basket.

"Yes," Aeneva replied quietly, shaking the dirt from the plants before placing them in the basket.

"It is quite an honor, Aeneva. You will accept, of course."

Aeneva continued to stare at the plants in Sun Dancer's basket, smelling some of them, feeling the texture of others, acting as if she hadn't heard Sun Dancer. "I think I will not accept, Grandmother," she said finally, sitting back on her haunches, wiping her hands on her skirt.

Sun Dancer stopped for a moment, putting her root-digger down. "Why not?"

"Because I do not want to be a soldier girl, a girl who is treated with great honor and as one who will bring the warriors great luck in fighting."

"But it is an honor."

"I know that, Grandmother, but it is not enough for me. I am not playing at being a warrior; I will be a great warrior one day. Why is it no one believes me?"

Sun Dancer reached up, pushed the strands of hair back from her face, and nodded wearily. "I believe you, child. I always have."

"Then why do you wish for me to become a soldier

79

girl? It is not something I wish to do."

"I was hoping that it would be enough. In my heart I knew it would not be, but I was hoping just the same."

"Why, Grandmother? Why you of all people? You have always been the one who has understood me the best."

"Yes, and because of it I have always worried for you the most. I do not underestimate your abilities, Aeneva. I have watched you for many years now. I have seen the way you ride a horse, the way you throw a lance and fight with a knife, the way you are able to wrestle with the boys. I know how you saved your brothers and grandfather. I know all this."

"Yet you are against my being a warrior. Why?"

"If you would open your mind and your heart for a moment, child, you would see why. I lost my brother, Brave Wolf, when I was still young. I loved him so. He was all that was good and honorable; much like your own brother." She hesitated for a moment, letting her words penetrate Aeneva's mind. "Then there was my friend, Laughing Bird. He was much like a brother to me." Sun Dancer took a deep breath before continuing. "Your parents died needlessly. When your grandfather brought you and your brothers back I swore to myself that I would protect all three of you with my life and every bit of magic that I knew. I wanted you three to live long lives, without bitterness and hatred and war. But I knew early on that there was nothing I could do to protect you from those experiences, just as there is nothing any parent can do to prevent the loved child from traveling a certain road. I knew all I could do was to love you and give you the product of my years of living. I could not stop you or your brothers from traveling your own roads."

Aeneva reached out and took Sun Dancer's hand, holding it in both of hers, staring at the brown leathered skin callused from years of hard work. But it was still a gentle, pretty hand. "I love you, Grandmother. I do not mean to make you worry so. Sometimes I do try to interest myself in other things, but always my mind goes back to thoughts of war. I see the boys racing or wrestling or shooting at targets with their arrows, and always I think I can do as well as they. Perhaps it is a sickness inside of me, Grandmother. Some kind of sickness for which there is no cure."

Sun Dancer smiled slightly, squeezing Aeneva's hands. "I suppose in a way it is a sickness; it is something that is a part of you, even if you do not want it to be."

"You understand then?"

"I did not always want to be a healer, child. There was a time when I had visions of my own and they scared me so that I never wanted to have another one. Many times when I would treat the sick with Horn, the old healer, I did not want to be there. I often thought of hunting with my brother or with Laughing Bird, or of playing at the river, or of riding my pony. But always I came back to the healing because it was inside of me. Horn knew it and later, I knew it also."

"I feel that I have caused you and Grandfather much sorrow," Aeneva said suddenly. "I know it has not been easy for you to have a granddaughter such as I. I know how the people talk about me. If you and Grandfather were not so important to this band, I would have been shunned long ago."

"You are different, yes," Sun Dancer agreed, "but you have never caused us sorrow or shame. You are different, just as I was different. Constantly, I asked my father why I was so different, why I liked to play with the

81

boys and not do girl chores, and he said I would change in time. He said I would change into a woman without knowing it and then I would like being a woman.''

"And do you, Grandmother? Do you like being a woman?"

Sun Dancer knew what Aeneva meant. "Do you mean, do I like being a woman in the kind of society in which we live? I can only answer that I know no other. I am luckier than most, Aeneva. I have lived with a man for many summers who has treated me like a partner, and I have my healing. I heal both men and women; there are no barriers for me there. You have been to the white world. Do you think it is better there? Would you like to live in one of the white man's lodges, dress in the strange clothes that the women dress in, wear the funny things they wear on their heads, put your feet into those moccasins Jean calls boots? Who am I to judge if I am better or worse off than anyone else? I only know that I have had sorrow in my life and I have also had great happiness. You and your brothers are a great source of that happiness. I could not bear it if anything happened to you or them.''

"I understand, Grandmother," Aeneva replied solemnly. "I will tell you something that I have never told anyone, not even Brave Wolf."

Sun Dancer raised her eyebrows, knowing that Aeneva shared everything with her brother. "What is that?"

"I wish that I could find a man like Grandfather. If I did perhaps . . .'' Her voice trailed off, and she looked down at the ground, suddenly ashamed of her admission.

"What of Trenton? You care deeply for him, do you not?"

"Trenton is a white man," Aeneva replied harshly, much too harshly.

"He is only half-white, Aeneva. He is also half-Indian."

"The white blood runs stronger in him than does the Indian blood. He will never return."

"What if he does?"

"He will not."

"You hope that he will not and then you will not have to face a decision; is that not so?" Sun Dancer asked pointedly, her eyes never leaving Aeneva's.

"That is not so. Even if he did return, we might not get along. It is not written that we will be together, Grandmother."

You are wrong, my Granddaughter, thought Sun Dancer, for I have seen the vision. You two will be together. "Then you have already made your decision. You will seek your medicine, become a warrior, and devote yourself to the life of a warrior, forsaking everyone and everything else in your life."

"No, I would never forsake you and Grandfather, or my brothers."

"But you would forsake Trenton, for he is the one who poses the only threat to you."

"No!"

"I may be old, Granddaughter, but I am not yet feeble of mind. You cannot fool this old woman."

Angrily, Aeneva stood up, thrusting Sun Dancer's basket at her. "I do not wish to speak anymore of Trenton. He is no longer a part of my life."

"As you wish," Sun Dancer replied lightly, picking up her root-digger and thrusting it sharply into the ground. "Just remember this, if he ever returns, you will not dishonor yourself by going with him. Go on your way now." Sun Dancer waved Aeneva away before she could reply. She waited for a moment, then looked up at the tall girl who walked away with such strength and dignity. She would make a good warrior; there was no doubt of it. And it was for that reason that Sun Dancer prayed to all the spirits, as well as Heammawihio himself, that Trenton would return and take Aeneva away. She knew it was the only chance her granddaughter had of living a long and peaceful life. She knew, too, that Trenton was the only man who could live with Aeneva and love her the way she was, for the strengths she possessed, not in spite of them. It might be some time, but Trenton would return, and when he did, he would make Aeneva fall in love with him.

CHAPTER V

"It has come to my attention that you would make an excellent soldier, Mr. Hawkins," Colonel Wainwright told the young man seated in front of him. He sipped at the glass of whiskey and cocked his head to one side. "You know, son, you could do worse than to make a career out of the army."

"Yes, sir. I'm sure I could, but those weren't exactly my plans."

"What exactly are your plans, Mr. Hawkins?"

"I plan to scout for the army a little longer, sir, and then I don't really know."

"I've heard some stories about you, Mr. Hawkins. Some stories that disturb me greatly."

Trenton smiled inwardly; he knew what was coming. "Just what have you heard, sir?"

"Well, that you are looking for a man."

"That's true, sir."

"Are you going to kill him?"

"I won't know that until I talk to him, sir. There's something I have to find out from him."

"About your father?"

"Yes. I want to know why he murdered my father."

"The lieutenant said your father disobeyed orders."

"If my father disobeyed orders, it was for a good reason. He was the best damned scout you people ever had.''

"Yes, I've heard he was very good.'' Colonel Wainwright was silent for a moment, sipping at his glass of whiskey. "You know that Lydia cares a great deal for you, Trenton.'' He addressed the young man on a personal level for the first time. "I wouldn't want to see her hurt.''

"I don't plan to hurt Lydia, sir. She's a nice girl; I respect her.''

Colonel Wainwright smiled and slapped his hand down on the desk. "Good, that's what I like to hear. You're tired and you've had a long trip. After you've rested up, we'll talk some more about your commission into the army.''

Trenton stood up and extended his hand, knowing that it was no use arguing with Wainwright. "Thank you, sir.'' He walked out of the office and across the open space of the fort. He couldn't believe a man like Wainwright was in charge of all the men at Fort Union. The man had no conception of what it was like to deal with the Indians; indeed, he preferred to leave all that to Trenton.

"Trenton!''

Trenton turned around, watching as Lydia Wainwright walked toward him. She was young and pretty with blond curls and blue eyes; she was a typical white woman, but not particularly the type of woman he preferred. "Hello, Lydia. What are you doing out here? You might get some sun on that skin of yours.'' Lydia didn't notice the sarcastic note in Trenton's voice.

"Oh, I don't mind a little sun now and again.'' She put her arm through Trenton's and leaned up against him. "Why don't we take the buckboard and go somewhere for a picnic?''

Trenton shook his head. "I don't think your father

would approve."

"Daddy already said we could. You know he won't deny me anything."

"Yes, I know," Trenton responded dryly, pulling his arm away from Lydia's. "Sorry, Lydia, but I have other things to do right now. I want to ride out and scout the area a bit. I'm not sure what tribes are camped around here right now. I might as well find out where we stand with them."

"Oh, Trenton, please let me come along. I think it will be so exciting."

"You didn't think it was so exciting on the boat when those Cheyennes were so close to us."

"Well, that was different. Here we're in open land and we don't have to have them forced on us. I'd like to see them in their natural setting."

"Would you now?"

"Oh, don't get angry with me again. I know how you feel about the Indians. Lord knows, I've heard enough of your lectures on them."

"Don't forget I'm a half-breed, Lydia."

Lydia waved her hand in the air, impatient with Trenton. "I've told you before that makes no difference to me. You don't look Indian and you don't act Indian."

"But if I did look Indian, that would make a difference to you, wouldn't it?"

Lydia shrugged her shoulders playfully. "Maybe, but we don't have to worry about that. Come on, Trenton, let's not argue. I've packed a wonderful lunch and we can go off somewhere and be all alone. I remember a time when you would have done anything to be alone with me."

Trenton finally relented. "All right, Lydia, we'll have a picnic. I'll go hook up the buckboard. Meet you at the gates in fifteen minutes.''

Trenton drove the buckboard over the bumpy ground, enjoying Lydia's discomfiture. He hated traveling this way. A horse was not only more convenient, but much more comfortable. His mother's people had ridden horseback for so many years it was natural to them. Prior to the horse, they had walked everywhere, carrying their own things or putting them on dog-pulled travois. He thought of Lydia in an Indian camp; he knew she could never last long in that kind of life, just as Aeneva could not live in the white man's world. Aeneva. He was never able to get her out of his mind for long.

"You're awfully quiet." Lydia leaned close to Trenton, whispering in his ear. "Be sure to find us a nice secluded place. It's so warm I might want to take off my shoes and stockings." Lydia giggled shamelessly.

Trenton didn't even look at her; he was used to her games. Her father thought she was a sweet young thing, completely innocent, but Lydia was about as innocent as a rattlesnake. She had very deftly drawn Trenton into her web and he hadn't even known what had happened. She was the first woman he had ever had and he delighted in her light skin and beautiful hair, all the while trying to convince himself that he enjoyed being a white man. But Lydia's charm didn't last for long; as soon as she became too possessive, Trenton grew colder and colder. Now it was Lydia who was pursuing him with an almost unquenchable hunger.

"Look over there." Lydia pointed to a stand of trees. "That looks like a nice cool place."

Trenton pulled up the buckboard and helped Lydia down, taking out the basket of food. They walked into the trees and spread out a blanket, sitting down under the shade of the cottonwoods. No sooner had she set down her things, than Lydia was taking off her bonnet, her shoes, stockings, blouse, and skirt. Trenton noticed the way her full young breasts pushed out of the slip, and the way her light hair fell down over her shoulders. She lay down on her side, giving him an even better view.

"It's been a long time, Trenton. I've missed you. Why didn't you come to my cabin on the boat?"

"You know damned well why I didn't come to your cabin. You're the daughter of a colonel. You have a reputation to maintain."

"Only with other people; not with you." She reached out and touched his leg, running her fingers up and down the hard muscles of his thigh. "You're the strongest man I've ever known, Trenton."

"Stop it, Lydia," Trenton said impatiently, pushing her hand away and sitting up. "We can't do this anymore."

"What do you mean?"

"I mean, it's time you started looking around for a husband."

"I don't have to look; I've found him." Again she reached out for Trenton and again he pushed her away.

"Don't, Lydia. I think you're a nice girl, real nice, but I don't want to get married. Besides, your father wants you to marry an army man."

"If you wanted to marry me, Daddy could make you an officer tomorrow."

"I don't want to be an officer. I like being a scout."

"But you can't be a scout all of your life. You have to do something else."

"Why?"

Lydia sat up, moving next to Trenton and wrapping her arms around his. "Because you were meant for more than that. You're handsome and bright and you can do anything you want."

"Maybe what I want is to go back to my mother's people."

"The Indians?" Lydia asked incredulously. She thought for a moment, then looked at Trenton quizzically. "You knew that Indian girl on the boat, didn't you?"

Trenton nodded curtly.

"Where? Is she one of your people?"

"No. I am Arapaho; she is Cheyenne."

"She was rather pretty, for a savage."

Trenton looked over at Lydia, his blue eyes drilling into hers. "She is the most beautiful woman I have ever seen."

Lydia shrugged her shoulders and nodded her head. "You're in love with her, but she doesn't love you. I could tell by the way she looked at you. She was very hostile toward you."

"I don't want to talk about her," Trenton said angrily.

"Good, then let's talk about us and our future together."

"No,"—Trenton shook his head slowly—"let's not talk at all." He reached for Lydia and lay back down, pulling her on top of him. He forced her mouth down to his and kissed her firmly, almost angrily. Lydia moved against him and Trenton felt his desire mount, the anger again building inside of him. He would make love to this woman over and over again, using her body to sate the hunger and desire he had felt for so long now. He would use Lydia and anyone else it took to try to make him forget about Aeneva. She was like some kind of disease that he could not rid himself of; no matter where he went or whom he was with, he always saw her face.

"Oh, Trenton," Lydia cried out, wrapping her arms

around his neck as he covered her with his body. And while Lydia was consumed by her passion, she would never know that Trenton was really making love to another woman.

"I don't know how I'll ever explain these bruises to Mamma." Lydia giggled lightly, rubbing the sore places on her neck and breasts. "You really are a savage sometimes, Trenton."

"That's what excites you the most, Lydia, knowing that I'm part Indian. It's part of your fantasy." Watching in amusement as Lydia's face grew red, he chewed a piece of chicken.

"That's not so. I would never dream of doing that with an Indian."

"But it's all right to do it with an Indian who looks like a white man."

"You're cruel, Trenton Hawkins." Lydia turned away, buttoning up her blouse in a pretense of humility.

"Maybe, but I'm also right." He pulled Lydia's arm and she fell against him. She struggled, but he held her easily with one arm, pinning her to the ground. "You'd probably even like it if I painted my body and did an Indian war dance."

Lydia pulled away, pouting petulantly. "No man has ever spoken to me in that way. If I told my father—"

"If you told your father what? That we have been together more times than he could count? What do you think he'd do? I don't think he'd call it rape."

"But I could tell him it was rape; that you took me out here on the pretext of showing me the countryside, and then you took advantage of me." Lydia lowered her eyelashes. "Daddy would believe me over you anytime."

"Probably," Trenton replied impatiently, "but I don't

really care what he thinks. I won't be around long enough for it to matter much.'' He stood up, stretching his long frame, and looking up at the clear, blue sky. He turned when he felt Lydia's hand on his arm.

"You wouldn't really leave, would you, Trenton?"

"I told you before. I have something to do and when I do it, I'll go back to my mother's people.''

"Or to that girl?"

"Maybe.'' Trenton surprised himself by answering truthfully. "But that's still a long way off."

"Then I won't worry about it." Lydia started to pack the basket. She was about to speak when Trenton raised his hand, signaling her to be quiet. "What is it?" she whispered softly, standing close to him.

"Horses."

"Maybe they're our horses."

Trenton shook his head. "No.'' He looked around him and shoved Lydia toward some trees. "Get over there and be quiet until I tell you it's safe."

"But what is it?"

"I don't know. Just do as I say.'' Trenton quickly gathered up their things and hid them in the trees next to Lydia. Then he made his way around the trees to a place where he could see the open countryside. A small band of Indians was approaching; they looked like Sioux from their clothes and the markings on their horses. They had noticed the buckboard and horses. They were talking to each other and looking around them. One of them jumped from his mount and walked to the horses, bending over to check their legs and examine their general health. They were older horses—ones used primarily for pulling loads—but Trenton knew the Sioux would probably take them anyway. Even if they weren't strong enough to be ridden as mounts for their warriors, they could be used to pull travois or as a first horse for a young boy or girl.

The leader said something to the man on the ground and he looked around him. Two others dismounted and walked toward the picnic area. Trenton surveyed the situation quickly; there were seven braves and only one of him, and he had Lydia to think about. He made sure his rifle was loaded and he ran back the way he had come, keeping his eyes on the two Sioux scouts. It didn't take them long to find Lydia's boot prints in the soft dirt and her screams rang throughout the trees when they found her. The Sioux warriors laughed at her, fingering her clothes and her light-colored hair. The more they touched her, the more Lydia went into a frenzy.

"Trenton!" She screamed over and over again until one of the Sioux tired of her ramblings and gave her a sound smack on the mouth. She quieted, but only for a few minutes. Knowing all Indians' impatience with screaming of any kind, Trenton advanced cautiously into the clearing, leaving his rifle next to one of the trees.

"*Haahe,*" he addressed them in Cheyenne, knowing they wouldn't understand.

Both warriors turned immediately, their looks extremely hostile. Trenton held up his hand, raising his first two fingers and closing the rest. It was the sign for friends. The warriors looked at each other, then back at Trenton, nodding slowly, indicating that he could continue.

"*Ne-tsehese-nestse-he?* Do you speak Cheyenne?"

One of the Sioux nodded. "*Na-tseskeoh-ohe-tsehese-neste.* I talk Cheyenne a little," he replied, handing Lydia to the other Sioux and approaching Trenton.

"*E-pevaoh-ohe,*" Trenton replied nodding, keeping his eyes on the man who approached him.

"*Tosaoh-oha ne-hesta-he?* Where do you come

93

from?'' the Sioux asked Trenton.

Trenton pointed back in the direction of the fort. *"Menaoh-ohe.* The fort.''

"Mohta-he notaxe-veoh-ohoh-ohe? You are a soldier?'' The Sioux asked, eying Trenton's buckskin clothes and his moccasins.

Trenton shook his head vehemently. *"Hovaoh-ohahane. Na—Hetane-voh-ohe.''*

The Sioux looked at Trenton, this time pointing to his hair.

"Tsehe-heto. Veho.''

The Sioux nodded; he understood that Trenton's father was a white man who had taken an Indian wife. He gestured to Lydia. *"Heoh-ohe?* The woman?''

Trenton pressed his fist to his chest. "She is mine.'' He thought for a moment. *"Moh-ohehe-noh-ohame?* You want the horses?'' Trenton quickly changed the subject from Lydia.

The Sioux shrugged his shoulders. *"E-maha-kahaneotse.* They are tired.'' Again he looked back at Lydia.

Trenton knew the Sioux was waiting for something else, to be offered some kind of gift. He remembered the blanket and tablecloth that Lydia had brought. He went to the tree and retrieved them, as well as the basket which contained coffee, sugar, fresh rolls, and blackberry preserves. He handed the things to the Sioux, startling the man with the utensils that went along with it. The other Sioux let go of Lydia and walked forward, peeking into the basket. They pulled out the various items and were particularly intrigued by the utensils.

Trenton stepped forward, confronting the two men. *"Mohe?''*

The Sioux looked at each other and nodded; delighted

94

with their new gifts, they walked off without giving Trenton or Lydia a second glance.

"Come on." Trenton pulled Lydia with him through the trees. He followed his same path back to the buckboard and watched as the warriors showed their gifts. The leader didn't seem too impressed, but after a few minutes of haggling, he settled on a spoon and the tablecloth. The Sioux mounted their horses and they rode off.

"How dare you give those savages my mother's best basket and her tablecloth. Couldn't you have given them your gun or something?"

"I suppose I could have; and they could have used it to kill me, and taken you along with them."

"Oh God," Lydia said dramatically. "I can imagine what they would have done to me."

"Yes, I'm sure you can," Trenton replied sarcastically. "The hell with your mother's things, Lydia, at least we're alive, aren't we?"

"Yes, you're right. You were very brave to do what you did." She walked up next to him, standing on tiptoe to kiss him on the cheek. "I'll be sure and tell Daddy what you did."

"Don't be dramatic, Lydia. We were just lucky that I could converse with them. If they had been in the mood to kill us, they would have." He grabbed her arm and dragged her along after him to the buckboard. He lifted her up and after checking the surrounding area to make sure there weren't any Sioux following them, climbed up after her.

"You didn't mean what you said awhile back, did you?" Lydia asked sheepishly.

"I said a lot of things today."

"You said that after you do whatever it is you have to do, you'll return to your mother's people. You wouldn't

95

really do that, would you?''

Trenton looked out at the open countryside around him and immediately knew the answer to Lydia's question; but he also knew that he could never explain it to her. How could he explain to someone like Lydia what it is to live out in the open spaces under the clear skies, hunting for food only when one needs it, fighting only to defend oneself, loving because one wants to love and not because one is forced into it?

"Trenton, you're daydreaming again."

Trenton looked over at Lydia and smiled nonchalantly. She was a pretty girl, a nice girl really, but not the girl with whom he would choose to spend the rest of his life. "Sorry. I'll just feel a lot better when I have you back at the fort."

"I understand," Lydia said softly, laying her head on Trenton's shoulder.

Trenton tensed up slightly at the feel of Lydia's head on his shoulder and her hand on his arm. How could he tell her she would never understand him or what he was about? No white man or white woman could ever understand him; he knew that now. He would never find peace again until he returned to his own people, or those of Aeneva. His Indian blood ran thicker in him than his white blood. And when he found Lieut. Robert W. Williamson and made him pay for murdering his father, he would return to Aeneva and never leave her again.

Trenton threw the tin cup across the small jail cell; it hit the bars with a loud clank. He couldn't believe that Lydia had actually done it; she had actually told her father that Trenton had raped her. When Colonel Wainwright confronted him with it, Trenton denied it.

"You'll marry her, of course," the colonel had said to

Trenton.

"I have no intention of marrying your daughter, sir," Trenton had replied bitterly. "I think you should know a little bit more about this 'rape.' "

"What do you mean?"

"I mean, your daughter and I—"

Colonel Wainwright had held up his hand. "I don't want to hear any more of this. Lydia said you'd react this way, trying to cover for yourself. You have two choices, Mr. Hawkins: either you marry my daughter or you rot in jail. It's your decision."

"Some decision," Trenton muttered to himself as he recalled standing in Wainwright's office and being dragged off by three guards. As far as he could reckon, that had been over three weeks ago, and he'd not heard a thing from either Lydia or her father. He pulled himself up to the small barred window that looked out on the inside of the fort. Activity went on as usual, no one caring that he might be locked up in a God-awful place forever. He looked up at the cloud-strewn sky and he longed to be out riding, feeling the freedom that he'd always taken so much for granted. He'd heard stories of Indians who'd been taken captive and put into jail; most of them died from the incarceration, not caring to eat or drink, wanting only to be set free. Many of them had killed themselves by hanging or bashing their heads against the walls. He could well understand their need to be free.

"Thinking of getting out that way, Hawkins?" The jailer laughed through the bars.

Trenton jumped down, confronting his jailer. "Hey, Mercy, how much does this army pay you?"

The corporal, expecting to be verbally attacked as he always was by Trenton, was surprised by the question. "Not much more than you I expect. Why?"

"Have you ever thought of getting yourself a large sum of money and building a little spread out west somewhere?" Trenton walked to the bars of the cell and looked thoughtfully at Corporal Mercy.

"'Course, who hasn't thought of doing that? You got any ideas where I can get this money, Hawkins?"

Trenton looked around him, making sure there was no one else listening; he motioned for Mercy to come closer to the bars. "I know where some money is buried."

Mercy looked at him, shaking his head. "If you know where some money is buried, why the hell are you in there and not out west someplace?"

"Because I messed up. If I hadn't got involved with Wainwright's daughter, I'd be on my way right now."

"What money are you talking about?" Mercy was suddenly interested.

"A few years ago some gang robbed a train in Missouri and decided to hide out west for a while. While they were traveling this way, they were ambushed by some Sioux renegades who took the money and buried it, not knowing what to do with it. They were more interested in the men's guns and rifles."

"Yeah, well what happened to the money?"

"Well, as far as I know, it's still buried up around the Black Hills."

"Hell, that's Cheyenne country. I ain't traveling up there."

"My mother was Arapaho; the Cheyennes are like brothers to us."

"Is that a fact?" Mercy asked, casually stroking his beard. "You never did tell me how you found out about the money."

"When my mother died a few years ago, she told me about it. The Sioux renegades had joined up with some

Arapahos and the word eventually spread through the tribe.''

"Well how do you know that one of them ain't gone and dug it up?''

"They have no need for money, Mercy. What could they do with it anyway? Besides, my mother made sure that that wouldn't happen.''

"How'd she do that?''

"She found the money and buried it in another place.''

Mercy smiled. "Smart woman, your ma.''

"Very smart. Well, Mercy, are you interested?''

"I'm interested, but I'm going to have to think on it some, boy. Not only can I be kicked out of the army; I can be shot for deserting. Let me do some thinking.''

Trenton nodded, watching as the older man limped slowly out and closed the heavy wooden door that led to the jail cells. Trenton knew that he would do more than think about it; he would do it. That there was no buried money in the hills was something poor Mercy would find out after Trenton had escaped. The important thing was that he had a chance to get out of this hole.

Trenton heard Lydia's voice in the room outside the cells and he turned over in his bunk to face the wall. He'd make her suffer, just as she'd made him suffer. He heard Mercy's keys in the lock and the heavy wooden door squeaked open. Lydia said a few words to Mercy and the door shut again. He heard her standing by the cell door; she was getting up enough courage to talk to him. "Trenton? Trenton, are you awake?''

Trenton remained motionless, staring at the wall, waiting for Lydia's next words.

Her voice was louder this time. "Trenton? Please, wake up, Trenton.'' When he didn't move, Lydia took a tin cup and rattled it against the bars. "Damn you, Trenton Hawkins. Wake up!"

Trenton smiled to himself and slowly turned over, pulling the blanket down from his body. He sat up, running his hands through his long hair and stretching his arms out in front of him. "I was wondering how long it would take before you came, Lydia."

"I hate you for this, Trenton. You've made a fool and laughingstock out of me in front of this whole fort."

"You did that yourself when you told your father your lies."

"I thought you'd marry me. Was that so terrible?"

"Wouldn't it be better if a man married you because he wanted to, Lydia? Anyway, I'm too young to be married."

"You're older than I am and I'm seventeen. Most people our age are married with children."

"I'm not most people." He stood up and walked over to the bars, his blue eyes staring at her. "I told you before I won't be forced into marrying you. I'll stay in here until I die; nobody forces me to do anything I don't want to do, Lydia."

"So I see," Lydia responded somewhat anxiously. She reached through the bars and touched him, smiling gently. "You look so tired and thin, and you need a good shave. Why don't you forget this foolishness and let me make you a good supper? You'll feel better after that."

"You mean I'll feel more like marrying you?"

"Damn you, Trenton, why do you make it sound so terrible? I'd make you a good wife. We've already proven that we're compatible."

"Just because we've made love a few times, doesn't make us compatible. You'd be ruining your own life as well as mine, Lydia. I wasn't meant to marry and stay in

100

one place. I'd go crazy living in a house. Maybe it's the Indian in me, but I'm a lot happier living out in the open and wandering from place to place. I don't think that's the kind of life you had hoped for."

"I'd hoped that—"

"You hoped that I would join the army and be just like your father. Well, I can't do that, Lydia. That's not me."

"Trenton." Lydia reached through the bars and grabbed his shirt, fear suddenly evident on her face. "Trenton, I'm pregnant. I'm going to have your child."

Trenton stared at her. Seeing the fear and apprehension in her eyes, he knew she wasn't lying. This was something totally different, something he hadn't even contemplated. It wouldn't bother him to leave Lydia after they'd made love a few times, but to leave her with a child to take care of, his child, that was something else. He wrapped his fingers around the bars, leaning his head against them. He couldn't leave her to face the humiliation alone; it had to do with honor. Honor. There was that word that was so fiercely ingrained in him by his Indian mother and white father. An honorable man would not leave a woman, a girl, all alone with a child. He felt Lydia's hand on his, and when he looked up, he saw the tears coursing down her checks.

"I'm sorry, Trenton. I truly am. I didn't mean for this to happen."

"It's not all your fault. I did have something to do with it."

"What are we going to do? If Daddy finds out, he'll make me go away somewhere to have the baby and give it away. I couldn't bear to do that, Trenton. I couldn't let someone else have our baby."

Trenton nodded slowly. "You won't have to."

Lydia straightened up, wiping the tears from her

cheeks. "You were right, you know. I don't want you to marry me because of this. I just want your help. Once I have the baby, Daddy will have to let me keep it. It'll be his grandchild. Will you help me, Trenton?"

"Of course I'll help."

Lydia smiled then, reaching up and touching Trenton's cheek. "You are good, you know. I was going to let you out of here tonight anyway, even if you'd said you wouldn't marry me. I couldn't make you suffer any more for my stubbornness."

"I think we should go away, Lydia. We can go to St. Louis. You liked it there, didn't you?" Lydia nodded slightly. "When the baby comes, we can come back here and tell your father that we're married and the baby is ours."

"You want to marry me? Why? Do you feel sorry for me?"

"I feel a sense of responsibility toward you. It was just as much my fault as it was yours."

"But you won't be happy married; you just said so." Lydia shook her head fiercely. "No, Trenton, we won't get married. All I need is your help until the baby comes. Once he or she is here, Daddy won't turn his back on me. I can even make up some story about being married to some young officer who got killed."

"And you don't think your father will think it strange that we both disappeared on the same night?"

"I'll leave after you escape; then he'll never know. We have to do it this way, Trenton. Daddy already wants to hang you after what I've told him. If he finds out I'm going to have your baby, he'll kill you for sure."

"I'll be a deserter anyway. What does it matter?" Trenton shook his head. "Let's just tell him the truth. He's a reasonable man."

102

"No, Trenton, I know him. He'll never listen to reason. He'll have you hung and me sent off somewhere. He would never stand the disgrace to his good name." She looked at Trenton, her small face set and determined. "I'll accept your help, Trenton, but I won't marry you. After the baby comes, we'll come back here and I'll explain to Daddy everything you've done for me. You can also tell him that you met my husband."

"There are records, Lydia. It would be a simple thing for your father to find out if you were actually married."

"Well, I'll worry about that when the time comes."

"I know a better way. Marry me. I'll use a different name. Something like Lieut. James Youngston. When your father checks, he'll see that you really were married."

"And he'll also see that this Lieutenant Youngston wasn't killed, never even existed. No, Trenton, we'll do it my way or we won't do it at all." She reached through the bars and took hold of his hand. "Please, for once, let me do the right thing. Just give me your protection and after that, you'll be free to go. For once I know I'm doing the right thing."

Trenton nodded, knowing it would do no good to argue with Lydia at this point. But he already knew that he would marry her and give his child a name. It was the least he could do for them.

"Are you all right, Trenton? Did you hear what I said?" Lydia tugged at Trenton's arm until he looked at her. "Please don't worry; everything will turn out all right. You'll see. As soon as the baby is born, you can go back to your mother's people and I'll return to mine."

Trenton looked at her again, although this time he didn't really see her. He was thinking of the land where he grew up, the friends he had known, the young girl whom he had befriended and with whom he had fallen so deeply in love one summer long ago when he was so young and life seemed so simple. He knew then that he would never see Aeneva or his land again, and he felt an emptiness deep inside of him; one that he knew would never again be filled.

CHAPTER VI

Trenton looked at Lydia as she lay sleeping next to him, her stomach large and swollen, her once-happy face now tired and drawn. Things had not turned out quite the way either of them had planned. Once they reached St. Louis, they realized that there wasn't much either of them could do. Although Lydia was well-educated, Trenton didn't want her working while she was pregnant, especially as a governess to some rich child. So it was up to him to support them both and he realized for the first time in his life that he was quite out of his element. He couldn't take any scouting jobs which would take him away from Lydia, so he eventually found work on the docks, loading the boats that went upriver. It was grueling work, starting at sunup and ending at sundown, and the pay was minimal. Still, they were able to get by. They were trying to save enough to pay for a doctor when Lydia was ready to deliver, and then Trenton wanted to buy a farm somewhere. Although Trenton was sure Lydia had other plans for their future, she had agreed.

As Trenton had known she would, Lydia gave in to his demand that she marry him, so they were married under the name of Lt. and Mrs. James Youngston. It had been a simple ceremony; Trenton had made the ring from some silver from his necklace. Neither of them was happy, but they both pretended; they were just two young people trying to make the best of an impossible situation.

Trenton looked up at the ceiling and felt a stabbing pain in his chest. He rose from the bed and looked out the small window. He hated being inside all of the time; he felt that he was constantly a prisoner. He looked around the small bedroom and shook his head, wondering how the hell he had gotten himself into this mess. Here he was, nineteen years old, living in a two-room shack with a woman he didn't love, who was going to have his baby. None of it made sense. He'd never even found Lieutenant Williamson and probably wouldn't now. He leaned his head against the dirty glass of the window and looked at the lights of the town. He hated it here; hated the city, hated the place he lived in, hated being responsible for Lydia and a child who wasn't even born yet. And most of all, he hated not being free.

"Trenton? Are you all right?" Lydia tried to sit up, but could not. "You're not sick again, are you?"

Trenton walked back to the bed. He had promised himself that he wouldn't make Lydia suffer for his own mistakes. He reached out and took her hand. "I'm fine, just restless. I guess the noise gets to me sometimes."

Lydia nodded. "I know. It seems the drunks don't even get started until normal people go to bed." She held out her hands and he helped her to sit up, propping the pillows behind her. "There's something else, Trenton. What is it?"

"It's nothing, really."

"Are you sorry you married me? I told you before; as soon as the baby comes, you can just take me back to Daddy. No one will know."

"I will know, Lydia. That wouldn't make me much of a man, would it?"

"Oh, Trenton, I feel so badly about it all. I know how

106

I've ruined your life. I know how you loathe it here. I know."

"It's all right; it won't be for long. As soon as we've saved a little money, we'll move away from here and find a place of our own. A place where we can raise our child in the fresh air, away from all this filth."

Lydia smiled, her face lighting up suddenly. "That would be nice. Could I have a flower garden? I love flowers. And we could grow our own vegetables. I'd like that, Trenton. I really would."

"Good. Once we're out of here, everything will be different. You'll see."

Lydia looked at him, nodding slightly, not quite so convinced as Trenton would have liked.

"You do believe me, don't you, Lydia?"

"Of course I do." She leaned over and kissed his cheek. "Now, let's try to get some sleep. You have to be up in just a few hours. You need your rest."

Trenton nodded and climbed into bed, putting his arm around Lydia as she laid her head on his chest. It will be better when we move to the country, Trenton tried to convince himself. He closed his eyes. In his mind there was a picture of the wide, open prairie. He was riding his horse faster than the wind, and beside him was Aeneva, her long dark hair blowing out behind her, her brown eyes laughing with joy. Again the stabbing pain returned and Trenton opened his eyes to the darkness that filled the room and seemed to permeate his very soul.

"Hey, Youngston, help me with these crates, will ya?"

Trenton walked over to Carl Forbes, the foreman of the dock crew. Carl was a large, crude, loud-mouthed man, but he paid a man for an honest day's work, and right now that was important to Trenton.

"I hear your wife's about to bust any day now." Carl laughed crudely, grabbing one side of a large crate filled with furniture.

"Yeah, any day now," Trenton concurred, ignoring Carl's jibe.

"I bet she's real pretty when she ain't got no kid inside her." Carl looked across the top of the crate at Trenton, spitting out some tobacco juice.

Trenton met the other man's intent gaze. "Pretty enough." He picked up his side of the crate, waiting for Carl to do the same.

They were making their way up the gangplank of the boat when Carl spoke again. "I seen your wife and think she's real pretty. If you ever get tired of her and you'd like to make some extra money—"

Trenton dropped his side of the crate, knocking Carl sideways down the gangplank. Trenton didn't wait for Carl to get up; he was on him in a second, his large hunting knife drawn and poised at Carl's throat. "I've taken a lot from you because I figured it was part of the job, but insults about my wife aren't. I don't like you; I never have. But I do my work and I stay out of your way. If you ever insult my wife around me again, I'll slit your throat and hang you upside down to bleed like a dead animal. Understand?" He pressed the point of his knife into Carl's throat until the latter quickly nodded his head, his eyes bulging. Trenton stood up and sheathed his knife. He extended his hand to Carl and helped him up. "I think we have some crates to load, don't we?"

Carl nodded dumbly, following Trenton back up the gangplank to the crate. He stared venomously at the men who had stopped their work to watch, and soon it was as if nothing had happened. Except that Carl Forbes was the kind of man who could never forget being humiliated by another man. He spit out some more tobacco juice, wiped the back of his hand across his mouth, and swore to himself that Trenton would pay and pay dearly for what he'd done to him that day.

Trenton seldom drank, but this night he felt as if he needed a shot of whiskey. The fight with Forbes had left a bitter taste in his mouth the entire day. He drank a shot of whiskey, ordered two more and took them to one of the few uncrowded tables in a corner of the dark, smoke-filled room. Sitting down, he ignored the stares of the other men who had been on the dock that day and seen the way he'd taken down Carl Forbes. He knew he'd have something of a reputation now, and that was something he didn't need.

"Want some company, boy?"

Trenton recognized the voice and looked up, a genuine smile appearing on his face. "Sure. Sit down, Joe." Joe was a huge black man who had befriended Trenton from the first day he'd started working on the docks. Perhaps he'd recognized that Trenton was different, just as Joe himself was. Joe had been born a slave on a plantation in Mississippi but had been given his freedom by his master years earlier. At forty years of age, Joe Spaniel had found himself a free man. Joe was one of the few men Trenton truly envied. Joe had suffered more than anyone could possibly know and no matter what he did from now on in his life, he would be a free man. He really knew what freedom meant. Trenton handed Joe one of the whiskey glasses. "I'd be happy if you'd share this with me, Joe. I'm not much of a drinker."

"Never seen you in here much, boy." Joe smiled, showing large white teeth. "But then maybe I'd be getting drunk if I'd done what you'd done to Carl Forbes today. Yessir, that was something." Joe drank down the whiskey and slammed the glass on the table. "Never seen anybody take down old Carl that way. I thought his eyes were gonna jump right outta his head."

Trenton smiled slightly, shaking his head. "It was a stupid thing for me to do. I've just made myself a real enemy."

"You can handle him, from what I saw today."

"I could've killed him and left him there and it wouldn't have bothered me one bit." Trenton drank down his whiskey and looked over at Joe. "He said some things about my wife."

"Then you probably should have killed him."

"What do you mean?"

"I mean, I've worked for Forbes for a while now and I seen the way he looks at women. He's been arrested lotsa times for molesting women, but he always seems to get off. It's his rich boss. Knows no one else on the docks can make men work as well as Carl."

"What the hell does he want with my wife? I didn't know he'd even seen her."

Joe shrugged his massive shoulders. "Hell, who knows, boy? All I'm saying is watch out for Forbes; he's a dangerous man."

Trenton nodded. "You want some more whiskey, Joe? I'm buying."

Joe put his hand on Trenton's. "No, I'm buying. You need to save every penny you make." Joe stood up and walked to the bar, returning with a bottle of cheap whiskey. He poured some into each of their glasses. He picked his up and clanked it against Trenton's. "Here's to a brave man."

Trenton looked at Joe across the rim of the glass and

drank down the whiskey, hating the taste and the way it burned his throat and insides, but liking the way it made him feel. "I'm not brave, Joe. I just reacted, that's all."

"Yeah, well I seen Carl say worse things to men who have never lifted a hand against him. I say you're brave or"—Joe took a sip of the whiskey—"you got damned good instincts."

"What do you mean?"

"I mean I ain't seen many men who handle a knife the way you do. The ones I seen were either trappers or Indians. From the way you dress, I'd say you could be either."

Trenton lowered his eyes, moving his glass around on the table. "My father was a trapper and a scout, my mother an Arapaho. I lived with her people until just a few years ago."

Joe nodded. "I figured as much. But what you doing here, boy, in a hole like this?"

"It's a long story," Trenton said wearily, pouring himself another shot of whiskey.

"I got lotsa time," Joe replied firmly. "I been here almost two years now and ain't made no friends. I found it easier to stay away from people and avoid trouble."

"Why me?"

"I sensed something different in you from the day you came to the docks looking for work. You were young, but you had a certain confidence that I'd only seen in older men. I figured you'd been on your own for a while."

Trenton didn't reply. Instead, he started to pour himself another drink, but Joe's hand stilled him.

"You're no drinker, boy. Let it be. The stuff's bad for you anyway."

Trenton looked up at Joe and nodded, unable to resist the sincerity and goodness that shone from his eyes. Be-

111

fore he realized it, he found himself telling Joe all about his life and how he had wound up in St. Louis with Lydia.

Joe whistled loudly, shaking his head. "For a smart boy, you sure did a dumb thing."

"Yeah, I know."

"Well, I'd say that if you plan to stay with her and raise your kid, then you better get the hell out of here. This ain't no place to raise a family unless you have money."

"I don't have any money, Joe. Why do you think I stay at the docks?"

"I got a little saved up. My master was real generous. . . ."

Trenton held up his hand. "No, I won't take your money. Thanks anyway."

"Well, then, we got to think of another way, a faster way for you to make money." Joe thought for a moment, rubbing his chin. "You ever gambled?"

"Not much. Every time I ever played, I lost."

"Well, maybe you need some lessons."

"No, I'm not going to get into any poker games. Too many men get killed during those things."

"I'll be there to make sure you're all right. Can you think of any other way to make some fast money?"

Trenton shook his head. "If I could, I wouldn't be here."

"Well, then, I'm gonna make a gambling man out of you, boy. But even after you learn, you're still gonna act like a dumb kid. That's how you'll get all those men to bet their money."

"I don't know, Joe—"

"Look, boy, you need some quick money and this is the only way, unless of course you want to rob a bank."

"Where did you learn to gamble? I thought you were a

slave.''

Joe smiled, his grin lighting up his entire face. ''I was a slave all right, but for the last ten years of my bondage, I was a manservant to the young master, who happened to be one of the best Mississippi gamblers around. He practiced on me, every day, and I learned to play against him. I learned all the tricks so he wouldn't be fooled when he was at the gaming tables.''

Trenton smiled finally. ''Well, you are full of surprises. I'll bet you can even read.''

''I can read and write, but people around here don't want no niggers who can read and write. They just want niggers who can work.''

Trenton cocked his head slightly, pointing an accusing finger at Joe. ''You've been planning this all along, haven't you? You've been waiting for some dumb white kid like me to come along so you could train him and make yourself some money.'' Trenton laughed appreciatively, shaking his head in disbelief. ''I've got to hand it to you, Joe; you put on a pretty good act. If I didn't know any better, I'd think you're just a big, dumb nigger.''

Joe smiled and nodded his head. ''That's exactly what I want everyone to think.''

''Why did you pick me? Did I look that stupid?''

''I could see you wanted to get out of here. I could see it in the way you look up at the sky every minute of the day. You're more a slave than I ever was, boy.''

Trenton lowered his head, his eyes avoiding Joe's. ''It's funny you should say that, because the first time I looked at you I thought to myself you were the freest man I'd ever seen.''

''It's all up here, boy.'' Joe pointed to his head. ''If you tell yourself you're a slave, you begin to believe it and then you start to go crazy. But if you tell yourself you're free, no matter where you are or what you do, you begin to believe you really are free. Then no man can make you feel otherwise.''

"I'd like to take you to my mother's people sometime, Joe. They'd like you. You'd fit right in.''

"I'd like that, boy, but first I'd like to buy myself some fancy clothes and do some traveling.''

"Well, when do these lessons begin?''

Joe laughed, extending his hand to Trenton. "Right now. The first lesson is to look at a man's eyes. A man's eyes will always give him away or tell you if he's honest.''

"Hell, I already know that lesson. Do you think I would have let you sit down here if I hadn't already studied your eyes?'' Trenton watched Joe's look of surprise; then they both laughed, shook hands, and drank to their new partnership.

From the bedroom Lydia listened to Trenton and Joe as they went about their nightly lessons. The first time Trenton brought Joe Spaniel home, Lydia was shocked. She had been raised in eastern schools and taught that black people were beneath her dignity, although she wasn't always sure she believed it. Still, it was somewhat of a shock when the huge black man walked through the door that one night a few weeks ago. Lydia had a second shock when she found out what a gentlemen Joe was and how conversant he was on so many subjects. She found she was looking forward to his nightly visits; he always seemed to have some interesting bit of information to share, as well as a food staple which he knew the young people could use. In fact, she found she was looking on Joe as somewhat of a substitute father. She was able to talk to him about Trenton, and one night in a fit of crying

114

and guilt, she had told Joe the truth. Joe had not judged or condemned her; he had only told her she had to forget the past and look to the future, just as Trenton was.

Lydia lay in bed, smiling as she heard the laughter of the two men. They genuinely enjoyed each other; they were like father and son, brothers, dear friends. She knew Trenton filled a void in Joe's life also. They all needed each other.

"You're doing good, boy." Joe slapped Trenton on the back. "By this time next month, we'll be making ourselves some money."

Trenton spread out the cards in one fluid motion; then flipped them back over and put them together. He shuffled them quickly and expertly and dealt five cards to himself and to Joe. He fanned the cards out close to his face, taking special pains not to reveal any emotion. Joe knew him well enough by now to read him. If he could fool Joe, he could fool a table full of strangers. He glanced down at the cards in his hand, then across the table at Joe. It was a good hand—three aces, a king, and an eight. Joe's eyes met his across the table.

"I'll bet two hundred dollars," Joe said confidently, placing two match sticks out in the middle of the table.

Trenton placed two match sticks next to Joe's. "How many cards do you want?"

Joe mulled it over a few minutes, shaking his head up and down. Trenton smiled to himself, knowing that Joe was using one of the tricks he had taught Trenton. Whenever the situation warranted it, take your time and make the other players wait; they might think your hand is so good you can't decide what to throw away.

"How many cards, Joe?" Trenton acted impatient, although he was playing along with his friend.

"Well now, I think I'll take myself two cards," Joe responded slowly, carefully taking two cards from his hand and putting them down on the table.

Trenton dealt Joe two cards, discarded his king and eight, and dealt himself two. Trenton picked up the cards. It was difficult to maintain his composure. He drew two queens; a full house, aces high. Trenton was as excited as if he were in a real poker game.

Joe made a low sound, then placed five match sticks in the middle of the table. "I'll raise five hundred dollars."

Trenton put his cards together, put five sticks next to Joe's, then placed five more. "I'll see your five and raise you five."

Joe nodded and placed five more sticks out. "I call."

Trenton slowly fanned his cards out for Joe to see; then he looked up, unable to contain his smile. "Full house, aces and queens."

"That's good, boy, real good," Joe admitted, laying down his cards, "but not good enough." Joe had a heart flush. He laughed when he looked up and saw the downcast look on Trenton's face. "Don't ever be too sure of yourself, boy. Always assume the other guy has the better hand and you have to bluff him to win."

"I don't know if I'm ready for this, Joe."

"You're ready. I wasn't sure how to play it for a while. I knew you were confident and had something mighty good. I just got lucky with my cards. I drew two hearts. If I hadn't drawn them, I wouldn't have had anything."

"When do we start?"

"Why not try a few of the smaller games down on the docks this week? If you do well enough there, we'll talk about going into some of the other places."

"But as soon as we make enough, we're gone. I want to get Lydia out of here as soon as possible. She hasn't been looking well lately."

"It's best to stay here close to a doctor then, just in case something goes wrong."

Trenton glanced in the direction of the bedroom. "Nothing can go wrong, Joe. Lydia's counting on this baby; she's pinned all her hopes on it."

"It's not good to pin all your hopes on just one thing, boy. That's a heavy burden for a little baby to carry."

"I know, Joe. I keep telling myself things will get better when we get out of here. They have to, for all our sakes."

Joe nodded silently, looking across the table at the boy of whom he had grown so fond, and whom he so desperately wanted to help. If Lady Luck would be kind to them, they could be out of St. Louis in a couple of months and on their way west to a nice piece of land and a farm. Then maybe, just maybe, they'd have a chance.

Joe slapped Trenton on the back, laughing and counting the money again for the third time. "I can't believe it; two hundred and sixty-eight dollars. Whew!"

"And half of it's yours, Joe."

"Boy, you coulda fooled me in there. You seemed like the biggest, dumbest kid I ever set eyes on. Those guys were sharpening their teeth for the kill; they were sure they had you. You were smart to make it seem like luck that you won. If any of them had suspected how really good you are, they'd have been all over you."

"And where would you have been?"

"Right there, of course."

Trenton laughed and they walked along the dingy streets by the docks until they came to Trenton's place. "Come in with me, Joe. Lydia will want to hear all about it."

"No, you two need some time together."

"Come on."

"O.K., just for a minute."

They waited outside for Lydia to open the door, but when she didn't respond, Trenton knocked again. He always made her lock and bar the door.

"Lydia," Trenton yelled, banging on the door. He looked at Joe and ran around to the bedroom window, knowing it would be covered. He rapped on it softly at first, then much more loudly; but still there was no response. He ran back to the front door, but Joe shook his head.

"I'm going to break the window." Trenton located a large rock and hit it against the window. The thin glass broke easily and Trenton reached through and lifted the window up. He crawled inside the dark room, fumbling his way around. He felt his way to the stove and located the box of matches. He lit a lamp, turned it up, and walked to the bedroom. Lydia was not in the room and the bed was unmade. He rushed back to the main room; she was not there either. Lydia was nowhere in the house. Trenton unbarred the front door and let Joe inside. "She's not here."

Joe looked around. The place looked as neat and tidy as ever, but Lydia was nowhere to be found. "Where the hell could she be at this time of night?"

"Nowhere. She has no friends. She'd never go out this time of night by herself."

"What about the baby? Maybe she walked to the doctor's herself."

"Joe," Trenton said thoughtfully, looking slowly around the room. "The door was barred from the inside and the window was locked. How the hell could she have gotten out and then barred the door and locked the window?"

"She could've locked the window first and then climbed out of it."

"But why? For what reason? Besides, Lydia couldn't even fit through that window in her condition. What the hell is going on here?"

Joe walked into the bedroom and came back out again. "I think we should check with the doctor just in case; then we'll take it from there."

"I'm telling you, Joe, she's not at the doctor's."

"Just come on, boy. Let's find out for ourselves."

Trenton nodded silently, unable to still the sick feeling that was growing inside of him. He followed Joe out the door and into the main part of town. Something was bothering him, something at the back of his mind, but he kept on walking, hoping against hope that Lydia was at the doctor's.

They hurried to the doctor's house at the outer edge of town. Trenton paced up and down waiting for someone to answer the door, but a light came on and the doctor's wife spoke from behind the closed door.

"Who is it?"

"It's Jim Youngston, ma'am. I'm looking for my wife. I thought maybe she came here tonight."

A minute passed and the door opened. Dr. Clinton's wife was gray and dour-looking, but she was efficient and compassionate. The latter aspect of her character always showed when she saw Trenton and Lydia. She and her husband had been good to them, charging what amounted to a token fee, knowing they couldn't afford to pay the doctor's normal fee. She eyed Joe suspiciously for a second, then waved both of the men in. "The doctor's sleeping right now, Mr. Youngston. Is there something I can help you with?"

"Yes, ma'am. I came home from work and couldn't

find Lydia. I know it's near her time and I was afraid the baby had come. I thought she might be here.''

"No. Lydia isn't due for her checkup until next week. We haven't seen her since the last time she was here.''

Trenton looked over at Joe, his face expressing his fear. "You're sure, Mrs. Clinton? I can't think of any other place she'd go.''

Mrs. Clinton put her hand on Trenton's arm. "I'm sorry, dear boy, but Lydia hasn't been here. Is there anything I can do?''

"No, no, I just have to find her. Something's happened.''

"When you do find her, if anything is wrong, bring her right here. I'll tell Dr. Clinton all about it.''

"Yes, thank you, ma'am. Sorry for your trouble.'' They walked into the street and Trenton raked his fingers through his hair. "Where the hell is she, Joe?''

"You're sure she has no friends she visits when you're working? She might be visiting one of them right now.''

"No, she's kept to herself the entire time we've been here. And why the hell would she be visiting this late?''

"Maybe the baby started coming.''

"If that were true, then someone would've notified the doctor.'' Trenton looked up and down the street. "Let's go back to my place and see if she's back. If she isn't, I don't know what the hell to do.''

"Take it easy, boy. We'll find her. Just take it easy.''

Carl Forbes sat on the chair across the room, drinking from the half-empty whiskey bottle and staring at Lydia, who was bound, gagged, and lying terrified on his filthy cot. Carl was not one to forget that another man had humiliated him, especially over such a stupid thing as a woman. He hadn't really wanted to take Lydia while she was still pregnant, but he figured it would torment the Youngston kid more to wonder if his wife and child were both safe. He laughed to himself and took another swig of whiskey, dribbling some of it down his chin.

Lydia watched him as any trapped animal watched the hunter who was about to close in for the kill. She huddled closer to the wall as Carl approached, whimpering slightly. Carl sat on the edge of the cot, reached down to touch Lydia's soft blond curls. She instantly recoiled, but Carl grabbed her hair and held firm, stroking it and wrapping it around his finger.

"You sure is a pretty little thing," he said gruffly, running his fingers over her neck and the smooth skin of her shoulders. He ran his fingers down to her full, tender breasts, and Lydia cried out as he squeezed them, clearly reveling in making her suffer. When his hand went down to her stomach, Lydia drew farther back, crying out behind the dirty gag in her mouth. She struggled against the rope that bound her hands, trying to move away from the monster who wanted to hurt her.

Carl was undaunted by Lydia's protest and he placed both hands on her huge stomach, rubbing it and running his fingers all around it. "I never seen a woman like this before," he said drunkenly, reaching down to pull up the skirts of Lydia's dress. She screamed out in pain and horror at the thought of this repulsive man touching her; and with a strength that came from deep inside of her, she moved against him, knocking him to the floor. She tried to sit up, but Carl was already up on the cot, pinning her against it.

"That wasn't a nice thing to do, lady," he said, his face only inches from hers, his breath wretched and stinking. Quickly, he pulled the gag from her mouth and before she could scream or react, his mouth was on hers, smashing her lips, bruising them, making her wish she were dead. His full weight was on top of her now and no matter how much she tried to push him off, he wouldn't budge, seeming to delight in molesting a pregnant woman. Lydia knew then he wouldn't stop at kisses and fondling. She felt him against her belly and knew it was inevitable. Clamping her teeth down on Carl's lips, she would not let go. She tasted the salt of his blood, but she still wouldn't let go, not until he struck her against the side of the head.

"Nobody does that to Carl Forbes and gets away with it," he cried angrily, slapping her again until she began to cry. He ripped the bodice of her dress and buried his face between her breasts, moving against her, punishing her.

Lydia felt the first wave of pain flood over her and she screamed involuntarily, bringing her knees up toward her belly. She breathed heavily, knowing what was about to happen.

"What the hell is wrong with you, woman? You scream like that again, I'll beat the hell out of you."

"I can't help it. It's the baby."

Carl moved to one side of Lydia, looking down at her, studying her to see if she was lying. When the next wave of pain overcame her, he could see by the look on her face that she wasn't lying. He rapidly untied her, letting her grab her knees until the pain passed.

"Please, the doctor. Can you get the doctor?" Lydia looked up at him, her eyes clouded in pain.

"Are you crazy? I ain't bringing no doctor out here. He'll know what I done."

"I won't say anything, I promise. Just please bring the doctor here."

"I'm sorry, lady, but I can't do that. You're on your own now." Carl stood up, taking a quick look around the room. He'd had it with St. Louis anyhow. He threw a few things into a bag, along with the two bottles of whiskey he had left, and the little money he had made gambling that night. He looked at Lydia once more, wishing she weren't ready to have the baby. But he wasn't about to stay and face her angry husband, not with the way he handled a knife.

"Please, help me," Lydia screamed in anguish, but Carl didn't even look backward as he went out the door.

Lydia waited until the contraction passed and she sat up, knowing the only chance she and the baby had was to get to someone who could help. Carl lived across the river from town in a little shack. She had to find some way to get back across the river and into town. She had to find Trenton. She got up and started across the room. The pains were not too bad yet; she could walk for a while. Trenton had told her that Indian women worked almost up until the time they had their babies. That gave her strength, that and knowing she would soon find Trenton.

She went out the door and down the embankment to the river. It was a dark night and she slid along the slimy bank, falling a few times before she reached the edge of the water. There was no way she could get across to the other side without a boat. She couldn't swim in her condition; or could she? She walked along the bank, hoping to see some kind of boat or raft, anything that might take her across the river. A few yards from the path to the house, she heard voices, male voices. One of them was deep, like Carl Forbes's, and in her terror she walked into the water, wading out until she could no longer touch bottom. She intended to stay in the water only until the men passed by, but the current in the river moved her out, in spite of her efforts to stay where she was.

Pain engulfed her as another contraction came; she

rolled onto her back, trying to ride with the pain and the current of the river. When the contraction passed, she turned back to her stomach and continued swimming to the opposite bank. Parts of this river were impossibly wide, she knew. She had seen them when she had traveled on the steamer with Trenton. But she also knew that this part of the river was not too wide for a person to swim if she had to; she tried not to think of what a burden she was carrying.

As each contraction came, Lydia rode out the pain and returned to her small strokes, exhaustion steadily overtaking her. Her breathing was labored and sounds seemed magnified to her. She saw the lights of the city and she knew how deceptive they were; they were far away. Still, it was comforting to know they were there, to know that somewhere over there, Trenton would be waiting to help her.

The contractions were closer together now and Lydia knew that the more she tensed up, the worse they would be. She tried everything she knew, every way she knew how to make herself relax. She thought again of the many things Trenton had told her about his Indian mother, and of the ways the Indians had of stoically facing pain. They concentrated on one thing only and forced all other things, especially the pain, outside their focus. Right now, Lydia's total focus was on making it alive to the other shore of the river. She wanted to show Trenton she was strong enough to survive, that she was courageous enough to face a situation alone and come through it safely. She breathed deeply, rested a moment, and pressed onward, centering her total attention on the lights across the river. They would guide her to safety.

CHAPTER VII

Trenton wanted to search every place in St. Louis until Joe convinced him they should sit down and think it through. Something had happened, something planned, and they had to figure out who had planned it.

"What about her father? You said he was real possessive."

"He wouldn't have gone to the trouble of locking the door and window from the inside. If her father had been here, I would have known about it. He would have come straight to me."

"Well, who else then? Is there anybody who disliked Lydia or you . . . ?" Joe stopped before he finished the sentence, his eyes meeting Trenton's across the table. He saw how the boy's light blue eyes suddenly turned cold and dark.

"Carl Forbes."

"I don't know, boy—"

"You told me he never forgets. Well, this is his way of getting back at me, through Lydia."

"But why go to all the trouble? If he wanted her, all he had to do was come in and take her."

"To stall us, to give himself more time." Trenton slammed his fist down on the table and stood up. "Damnit, why didn't I see it before? He's the only one who could have done it."

125

Joe stood up, too, lifting his rifle from the table. "I think you're right, boy."

"You stay here, Joe. I want to do this alone."

"I ain't letting you go alone. You might need someone to help you with Lydia. This is no time to be proud."

Trenton nodded and walked to the door, waiting for Joe.

"What about your rifle, boy?"

"Don't need a rifle."

Joe looked at Trenton and saw the cold hatred in the boy's eyes; it was the same look he had had in them the day he had threatened Carl Forbes. "Let's go then."

They ran down the alleys to the dock, stealing one of the rowboats which was tied up there. Joe knew where Forbes lived; he had heard the stories of the women Forbes took across the river to his shack. Trenton rowed like a demon, heaving and breathing deeply, not letting up even when his arms felt ready to burst. Joe knew better than to offer his help.

Joe considered the dark bank ahead of them, scanning it, trying to remember where Carl Forbes had his filthy shack. He knew it was up the bank somewhere behind the trees. He had rowed Carl home one night when the latter was too drunk to walk. Joe had seen the disgusting place Carl called home, and he grew sick inside thinking that Lydia might be there with that man.

"Over that way, I think." Joe pointed, and Trenton eased up on the oars, turning the boat to the right as they approached the shore. He rowed parallel to it until Joe held up his hand. "Wait now, I think this is close to the spot. Damn, I wish I could see better."

"This is close enough." Trenton's voice came out of the darkness. He lifted the oars into the boat and let it drift in to shore. Trenton jumped out, pulling the boat onto the low bank.

Joe jumped out after him, looking up the embankment, shaking his head. "I've been here once before and that was at night. I can't tell for sure if this is it." He turned around and looked across the river. He remembered that Carl's shack was almost directly across the river from "The Bull's Mouth," one of the taverns on the dock. "This must be about right. Let's go on up and take a look."

They climbed the embankment, slipping on the wet, muddy soil. When they got to the top, they looked under the trees, but they couldn't see anything.

Joe looked back across the river, then back at the trees. "I think it's this way."

Trenton followed in the darkness behind Joe, trying to keep his thoughts from Lydia and what she must be suffering at the hands of Carl Forbes. He stumbled into Joe's broad back when the big man stopped suddenly. "There it is. You can barely see it. He's got the lights off."

Trenton strained his eyes to see in the darkness and in a few seconds he was able to make out the outline of the shack. He started forward, but Joe jerked him back.

"Slowly, boy. You're an Indian; you're supposed to know how to be quiet. If he's in there, he'll be waiting for us."

"All right." Trenton walked slowly, more confidently, his moccasin-covered feet making no sound on the moist ground. He was completely alert, his body ready for any movement, his eyes and brain clear. He reached the side of the shack, leaning against it, waiting for Joe. They noticed there were no windows, only a burlap-covered opening which was used as a door. Trenton moved to the high wooden steps; they were meant to keep out unwanted intruders like snakes and men. He

127

leaned down and applied pressure to the bottom step, seeing if it would make any noise when he stepped on it. The step creaked slightly. He turned back to Joe. "I'm going up. You stay down here and keep your eyes open. I don't trust the bastard." Trenton carefully placed one foot on the bottom step. He placed his other foot up on the edge of the next step and eased his way to the top of the porch. When he stepped toward the door the old wood groaned with his weight. Quickly drawing his knife, he stood motionless, standing poised and waiting for Forbes to run out the door. When there was no such movement, he moved cautiously forward to the side of the door, listening for any sound from within. He craned his neck forward, trying to hear Lydia's breathing or the drunken snores of Forbes, but there were no sounds. He stepped inside, quickly jumping to the side of the door in a reflexive movement, but he knew that the room was empty. Lydia was not here; neither was Carl Forbes. He called to Joe, and the big black man ran up the stairs and into the shack.

"I can't see nothing," Joe said while he stumbled around in the darkness.

"It doesn't matter. No one is here."

"There must be a lantern somewhere around here." Joe moved forward and bumped right into the table, his hand reaching out and locating the lamp. He reached into his pocket for some matches and lit the lamp. The orange glow gave the room an even more sinister look. Both men looked around the small, dirty room, their eyes alighting on the cot next to the wall. Trenton walked over to it, lifting up Lydia's shawl from the rumpled blanket.

"She was here," Trenton said angrily, "but where is she now?"

"I'd like to know where he is, too," Joe added. "If

they're still together.''

"What makes you think they're not?''

"Maybe he got scared and left her. You never know with scum like Forbes.''

Trenton walked over to Joe and took the lamp from him. "Let's go outside and see if we can find any tracks. Maybe we can tell something.''

They proceeded outside and looked around. It took Trenton only minutes to distinguish Forbes's footprints from his and Joe's and he followed them for a distance to establish that he had gone off alone. Shortly after that, he located Lydia's prints going off in the other direction. He and Joe followed the prints away from the shack, down the embankment to the river; but they abruptly stopped. "Where the hell did she disappear to?'' Trenton looked up and down the bank with the lantern. "Do you suppose there was a boat here?''

"If I know Forbes, he took the only boat and got away.''

"Where did Lydia go?'' Trenton looked at Joe in the eerie glow of the lantern light, seeing the fear and apprehension in his friend's eyes. "Joe?''

Joe shook his head, placing a hand on Trenton's shoulder. "I figure it like this, boy. Forbes tried to molest Lydia, but something scared him off and he ran away. When he left, Lydia ran out and down here. She knew she had to get away and, if there was no boat, the only way she could get to the other side would be to swim. Fear makes people do things that otherwise might seem impossible.''

"Hell, Joe, she couldn't swim in her condition.'' Trenton shook his head rapidly. "No, she found a boat. I'm sure of it.''

"Forbes had the only boat over here, boy.''

"Maybe Lydia got to it first."

"And maybe she didn't."

"Why are you talking like this, Joe? Goddamn it! She's all right; I know she is."

Joe stepped forward, taking Trenton firmly by both shoulders. "Listen, boy, the only thing we can do is get back to our boat and search this river. Then we can go back across and see if Lydia did make it over there. If she did, chances are she made it to the doctor. If she didn't, then we can come back here and search when it's light. C'mon, now."

Trenton shook his head, looking around him as he followed Joe along the bank back to their boat. He was sure Lydia was hiding somewhere and that they'd find her in the morning. He looked out to the river and he got a sudden chill. He knew there was no way in hell that she could have survived a swim in that cold water in her condition; she wouldn't have even tried it. "Joe," he said softly, stopping on the bank.

Joe stopped and walked back to Trenton. "What is it, boy?"

"You take the boat and go back across. I'm going to stay here, just in case."

Joe patted Trenton on the shoulder. "I'll be back as soon as it's light. You take care now."

Trenton nodded and walked up the bank, looking for any signs of Lydia's footprints. He prayed that he would find some sign. He couldn't face the possibility that she had tried to swim that river alone under impossible conditions. He wasn't sure he could face the consequences.

Lydia dragged herself onto the opposite bank, unable to move as the contraction tensed her body and her wet clothing caused her to shiver almost uncontrollably.

130

When the contraction subsided, she crawled up the bank. Having rested at the top, she stood up, and started to walk along the dock. She knew it was dangerous here at night, but she was no longer afraid. She had made it away from Carl Forbes, and she had made the swim across the river alone. She would be all right now. She stopped and leaned against a building in an alley when the next contraction came, her breathing growing more labored, her legs getting weaker with every step. She forced herself to keep moving, to focus her attention on getting to the doctor's house. She heard voices and she ran between two buildings, waiting until the men passed by; then she continued on her way. She stayed in the alleys and behind the buildings, afraid that she would be stopped if she walked through the main part of the city. At one point, her legs almost collapsed and she leaned against the side of a building for a long time before she got enough strength to continue.

"Let's go, Lydia," she said to herself. "You are strong enough. Do something right for once in your life. Come on." She started walking again and, before she realized it, she had come out on the main street that led to Dr. Clinton's house. She was half-walking, half-running now, her breath coming in great gasps. She saw the doctor's house and she ran through the gate, banging on the door without surcease until a light came on inside. Lydia leaned on the door and almost fell inside when Mrs. Clinton opened it.

"Why, Lydia, my dear. What in God's name?" Mrs. Clinton screamed for her husband as Lydia fell against her, collapsing in her arms. "Raymond, hurry yourself down here. It's an emergency."

Raymond Clinton was down the stairs in seconds and together he and his wife managed to carry Lydia into his

131

examining room. "Get some blankets, Jesse," he said to his wife, quickly stripping the cold wet clothes from Lydia and checking her for any superficial cuts or bruises. When Jesse returned with the blankets, he covered Lydia and turned to Jesse. "Start rubbing her hands and feet; get some circulation going in them." He removed the stethoscope from his bag and listened to Lydia's heart; then he placed it on her stomach. "Her contractions are close together. She'll deliver soon."

"What if she doesn't wake up, Raymond?"

"We'll have to wake her up."

"But what if we can't?"

"Then I'll have to deliver the baby myself, if I can. Make some coffee, Jesse. She'll need something to warm her up." Raymond Clinton turned back to Lydia; he lifted the lid of each of her eyes and looked into them. He slapped her cheeks, trying to rouse her. "Come on, Lydia. Wake up, girl. Wake up." Lydia moaned slightly as a contraction racked her small body and Raymond Clinton tried without success to rouse her from her deep sleep. Jesse returned and Raymond turned to her, his face wearing a doubtful expression. "She's in shock; I don't know when she'll wake up."

"The baby?"

The doctor shook his head. "I don't know if I can save it." Lydia moaned again and Dr. Clinton approached her, talking to her softly, coaxing her out of her sleep. "Come on now, Lydia, wake up. You must wake up now."

Lydia mumbled something and then her eyes began to flutter open. She looked first at Mrs. Clinton, then at the doctor. "Where is Trenton? Please, I need to talk to Trenton."

"Trenton?"

"My husband."

"You relax now, Lydia. Your husband will be here real soon. Don't you worry."

Lydia tried to sit up, gasping with pain as she did so. "Please, Doctor, I must talk to Trenton. There are things I have to tell him."

"All right, all right, my dear. Jesse will find him. You just concentrate on taking care of the baby who wants so desperately to be born."

Lydia nodded, closing her eyes and relaxing. Dr. Clinton took Jesse off to one side. "I don't know who Trenton is, but find her husband. Send Jack out to look for him."

Jesse nodded. Wrapping her shawl tightly around her shoulders, she stepped out of the room and carrying a lantern, she walked out the back door of their house to the small stable. She rapped on the door of the stable, calling out loudly. "Jack, Jack, are you out here?"

Minutes later, an old, thin man appeared at the stable door, squinting at the light of the lantern. "That you, missus?"

"Yes, Jack. I have an errand for you. It's extremely important. A woman's life may depend on it."

Jack stood up straight now, tucking in his wrinkled shirt and dusting off the hay from his pants. "You can count on me, missus."

"I knew I could, Jack."

Joe was leaving Trenton's and Lydia's house when he heard a voice call to him out of the darkness. His hand tensed on the rifle in his arms.

"Hey, mister, you a friend of James Youngston?"

Joe looked in the direction of the voice. "Who's talking? I don't talk to voices in the dark."

133

Jack stepped into the dim light of the Youngstons' small house, his stubbly gray beard sparkling in the light. "My name is Jack. I work for Doc Clinton. He says I'm to look for Mr. Youngston or a big black man named Joe."

"I'm Joe."

"Mrs. Youngston is at Doc's place. She's real sick. Doc wants you to find Mr. Youngston real fast."

Joe nodded, reaching into his pocket and handing Jack a few coins. "Here's for your trouble, Jack. Thanks. Thanks a lot. Tell the doc I'll get Mr. Youngston there as soon as I can."

Jack looked appreciatively at the coins in his hand, his mouth watering at the thought of the drinks they would buy. "Thank you, Joe."

Grabbing a lantern from the house, Joe ran down to the docks and jumped into the small boat. Dipping the oars into the water, he rowed quickly, his muscular arms making swift, cutting strokes in the water. He reached the opposite shore after what seemed like an eternity, jumped out of the boat, and headed up the embankment. He swung the lantern around, looking for Trenton's tracks. The moccasin prints were easy to locate. Joe followed them at least a quarter of a mile downriver before they went up away from the river into the dark trees and undergrowth. He swung the lamp around, looking for the footprints, but he could not find them. Trenton had come into the trees somewhere and virtually disappeared.

Joe put the lamp down, cupping his hands around his mouth. "Trenton! Hey, boy, where are you?" He glanced around him, waiting for a reply; then repeated the call. Joe continued to call every few minutes, waiting for Trenton to reply, knowing that it would be smarter to remain in one place rather than go around in circles looking for him.

"Hello, Joe." Trenton stepped out of the darkness behind Joe, nearly causing the big black man to fall off the log he was sitting on.

Joe jumped up. "Ain't anybody ever taught you no manners? You don't come up behind people like that. You liked to scare me to death."

"Sorry. Did you find her?"

"No, but I know where she is. She's at Doc Clinton's. Somehow she made it across the river. The doc wants you to come now."

"How is she?"

"I don't know. I just know she's real sick and she needs you right now."

Trenton nodded, picking up Joe's lantern and handing it to him. They ran down the embankment, following the shoreline until they found the rowboat. Joe started to row, but Trenton waved him away. "I need something to calm me down."

They didn't speak as they rowed across the dark river, just listened to the slosh of the water against the boat. When they reached the other side, they jumped out and started running toward Dr. Clinton's house on the main street. They reached the end of the street and ran into Doc Clinton's yard. Trenton banged on the door, not waiting for Mrs. Clinton to open it as he had done before. He charged through the salon and into the doctor's office, colliding with Jesse Clinton as she started out.

"Oh, I'm sorry, Mrs. Clinton."

"It's all right, James." She gently but firmly took his arm. "Lydia's over here. Come on." She led him over to the table where Lydia was breathing deeply and crying out occasionally from the pain. Trenton looked at the doctor, then down at Lydia's pale face. He touched her

135

cheek softly, stroking it several times before he spoke.

"Lydia, it's Trenton. Can you open your eyes?"

Lydia strained to open her eyes, the normal blue clarity of them now clouded by pain and confusion. She managed a weak smile, but it faded as pain contracted her body. When the pain passed, she lifted up her hand. "I'm glad you're here. The baby is coming."

"I know." Trenton smiled, wiping the beads of sweat from Lydia's face. "I want to help you. I'll stay here with you."

Lydia smiled then. "You are so good, Trenton. You will take care of him, won't you?"

"Take care of who, Lydia?"

"Our son. We're going to have a son."

"You're going to take care of him, too. But I'll help all I can; don't you worry."

"Trenton . . ." Lydia started to speak again, but her words were cut off as she clutched her stomach.

"Breathe, Lydia," Dr. Clinton advised her firmly. "That's right. Don't fight it, dear." He turned to Trenton, motioning him to the corner of the room. "Will it bother you to stay in here? I think it will help her to know you're here."

"No, I'll stay. How is she, Doc? Will she be all right?"

"I don't know. Aside from the fact that she's about ready to deliver the baby, she could be coming down with pneumonia. When she came here, she was soaking wet and close to freezing. Her fever is up." He shook his head negatively. "I don't know, James. She's not a strong girl anyway. I just don't know."

"Trenton?" Lydia was frantic now, and Trenton ran to her side.

"I'm here, Lydia. It's all right."

"Promise me you'll take good care of our son. Please promise me."

"Lydia . . ."

"Promise me, Trenton!" Her voice was raised in a fevered pitch.

Trenton bent his head close to hers. "I promise you, Lydia. I will take care of our son."

Lydia nodded and seeming somewhat satisfied, closed her eyes for the moment. "Trenton, will you name him Nathan? That was my grandfather's name."

"Yes, I'll name him Nathan. Lydia, you have to concentrate on getting well now."

"Oh, Trenton." Lydia smiled indulgently, grasping tightly onto his hand as she endured another contraction. "Don't you understand? I'm going to die. But don't worry; I'm not afraid. I know you'll take care of him."

Trenton laid his head down next to Lydia's. "God, I'm sorry, Lydia. I'm so sorry."

"Don't be sorry. None of it was your fault; don't you see that? I am being punished for being so bad. You did your best to make me happy."

"But I didn't take care of you. If I had been there tonight—"

"It wouldn't have mattered, Trenton; don't you see? It was meant to be. Now you can—" Lydia stopped; a piercing scream broke from her. Trenton stood up abruptly, looking over at the doctor.

Dr. Clinton bent over Lydia, moving his stethoscope around, pressing down on her abdomen with his hands. "All right, Lydia, it's time now. You are going to have to push with all your might. Your child is ready to be born." He looked over at Trenton. "Talk to her, encourage her any way you can."

Trenton nodded and moved closer to Lydia, holding on

137

to her hand.

The next two hours were a blur to Trenton; they passed in a haze of Lydia's pain and his confusion. Dr. Clinton constantly barked out orders to his wife or to Trenton, and Lydia cried and screamed, sometimes pushing Trenton away. When it was over and Lydia had delivered their son, Trenton declined to hold him, instead going to Lydia's side. She looked up at him, but her eyes were uncomprehending. She started to say something, but shook her head. When Dr. Clinton held the baby up for Lydia to see, she smiled, looked over at Trenton, and shut her eyes. She never opened them again.

Trenton walked from the room, ignoring Dr. and Mrs. Clinton as they implored him to take his son. He walked past Joe and outside, where he sat down on the porch steps. He looked at the sky; funny how the stars seemed so far away. Tears came to his eyes, tears he hadn't felt since his father had died. He hadn't loved Lydia, but he had respected her courage and strength at the end. If he'd never dallied with her in the first place, she would probably be alive right now. . . .

"No use you blaming yourself, boy." Joe sat down beside Trenton on the step, holding the tiny bundle which was Nathan. "You got other things to think about now—namely, him." Joe gently handed Nathan to him and Trenton reluctantly took the baby in his arms. "You're all he's got in this big ol' world, boy. You gonna deny him that?"

Trenton looked down at the baby in his arms, the wet blond hair and the puckered features of the child seemed utterly unreal to Trenton. Nathan gurgled contentedly and Trenton smiled in spite of himself.

"He's got your Indian blood in him; no doubt about it." Joe leaned over and looked at the baby. "No crying for this one. He'll just wait his turn.''

Trenton reached out a tentative finger and the baby immediately grasped hold, trying desperately to stick it into his mouth. ''I think he's hungry.''

''Good guessing. If I was you, I'd get myself back in there and find out what to do.''

''What about Lydia?''

''Lydia's gone now, but your son is here. He's all that matters now.''

Trenton hugged the precious bundle even closer as he stood up. Before he went back into the house, he hesitated, looking over at the older man.

Joe sensed his hesitation. ''What is it, boy?''

''I'm scared, Joe. I don't think I've ever been this scared of anything in my life.''

''Well, if it's any comfort to you, I felt the same way when I got my freedom. My whole life I had been told what to do and then suddenly, there I was on my own, able to make my own decisions. But I did it. And you can do it; you been doing it for a long time now.''

''But I didn't have a son to take care of then.''

''Well, if you'll let me, I'd like to help. I don't got nowhere else to go.''

''What about all those nice clothes you wanted to buy and the places you wanted to see?''

''I can still do that someday. But right now,''—he reached over and touched the baby's cheek—''I want to help out with this little guy. Just to make sure you don't drop him on his head or something.''

''Well, then, if you're going to stay with us, you ought to be a godfather at least.'' He lifted up the baby so Joe could see him even better. ''Nathan Joseph, meet your godfather, Joe.''

Joe reached out and took the baby. He held him close,

as if he were whispering a secret. "You don't know it yet, little Nathan, but you got yourself one fine daddy. You're a lucky little boy." He hugged the baby to him and extended one large hand to Trenton. "Thanks, boy. That's about the nicest thing anyone's ever done for me."

Trenton grasped Joe's hand and shook it firmly. "Yeah, well, I'm being selfish. He and I are going to need you, Joe. I hope you'll stay with us for a while."

"You know I will. At least until I know you can raise him on your own."

"That's a deal," Trenton replied lightly, more lightly than he had intended. He shook his head, leaning against the porch railing. "I still can't believe she's dead. If I had only been there tonight."

"I told you before, boy, you can't be thinking that way now."

Trenton nodded in resignation. "I know you're right, but I'll always wonder if she would be alive right now if she had never met me."

"She wanted to meet you, boy. You couldn't have avoided it."

"What do you mean?"

"She wanted you and she got you. It's that simple."

"How do you know?"

"She told me, even more than you did. She told me she trapped you into this marriage. She knew you'd feel guilty enough to marry her. Lydia was not as innocent as you think."

"I don't believe it."

"Don't, but it's the truth. Those were her words."

Trenton pressed his forehead against the pole, closing his eyes to the thoughts that tried to invade his mind. Was it true? Had Lydia planned the whole thing, knowing that he would eventually marry her? It still seemed inconceivable; and now that she was dead, it seemed disloyal.

"I see you still have doubts, boy. Well, maybe this will convince you. Her father knew the whole time you were here; he even knew when you left. In fact, he gave her his blessing. He didn't want a grandchild around early to clutter up his untarnished reputation, as Lydia put it. If you don't believe me, boy, write him. You have to anyway, to tell him about his daughter."

"No!" Trenton slammed his fist against the railing, unable to believe that Lydia had deceived him so willingly. He had come to respect her for her honesty and the courage she had shown in leaving her father—and without any money. He turned to Joe. "She wasn't going to stay with me, was she?"

Joe shrugged his shoulders noncommittally, poking a large finger at the baby in his arms. "Don't know. Could be she was waiting' to see how much money we made gambling."

"I don't understand why she told you all this, knowing how close you and I are."

"Confession's good for the soul, boy. Don't you know that? Whatever else she had done, she did care for you— even loved you, I think. She didn't want to ruin your life. She knew deep down inside you still loved that Indian girl."

Trenton turned abruptly, staring at Joe as if he'd been punched in the stomach. Aeneva. For the first time in too long, he was able to think about her without pushing her out of his mind. "So, she was going to take Nathan and go back to her family, just as she said she was."

"I think so. She wasn't lying about that."

Trenton shook his head in disbelief, walking over to Joe and taking Nathan from him. "I can't imagine not having my son now. It would have been so strange if she'd taken him away from me—''

"Well, he's right here and you're the only person responsible for him, besides me, that is. So, let's get ourselves back in that house and find out how to feed this little one. He's been patient long enough. You'll be wanting to make arrangements for Lydia, too.''

Trenton agreed, pressing his son to his chest. It was an incredible feeling holding the infant; it made him feel strong and weak at the same time. He hoped he would never do anything to hurt the boy. Trenton promised himself Nathan would always be cared for and loved. His son would never feel alone in this world. Never. Nathan Joseph Hawkins would grow up feeling secure.

Trenton lifted the baby up and kissed him softly on one cheek. He held his son high above him, offering him up to the heavens as so many other Indian fathers had before him. "Oh, Great Father, look down upon this small and innocent child with favor. Grant that he will be healthy and that he will have respect for his elders, and grant that he will be a truly honorable person. And please, Great Father, grant that this son of mine will always know the love that I feel for him at this moment. Let him always be a part of me." Trenton held Nathan up for a second longer and walked into the house. Somehow, he felt calmed now that his son had been blessed by the Great Father. There was enough of Trenton's mother in him to make him believe that a child should walk on the right path from the beginning. With his help, Nathan would always choose the right path.

CHAPTER VIII

Aeneva watched in anguish as Brave Wolf hung from the rope which pulled at the skin on his chest. She had followed her brother and grandfather up into the mountains to see Brave Wolf's sacrifice, and now she wished she had not come. Facing east, Brave Wolf stood motionless when Stalking Horse ran a knife through the skin on either side of his chest and passed a skewer through each hole. Attached to each end of the skewers were deerskin strings attached to a leather rope, which in turn attached to a pole that Stalking Horse had planted in the ground. Aeneva covered her mouth when her grandfather lifted Brave Wolf up and drew him back to see if the rope was tight. He told Brave Wolf to walk up and back four times, walk to the right and back four times, to the left and back four times, until he had completed a half-circle. The ceremonial pipe was at the end of the quarter-circle to the right and it was there that Brave Wolf would smoke it three times during the day. All the time Brave Wolf walked, he leaned back on the rope, trying to tear the skewers through the skin of his breast. Aeneva watched her grandfather as he gave Brave Wolf his instructions and when he had done so and tested the rope once more, he started down the mountain. He would return again at sundown to cut the skin across each skewer if the skin had not broken. Aeneva watched her grandfather walk slowly down the mountain and was startled to see him stop and look at Brave Wolf; she could see the pain in his eyes. This had not been easy for him either.

Aeneva focused her attention on her brother, watching as he pulled back on the rope. She could see the skin pull out from his breast, but still it would not tear. Brave Wolf continued to try to rip the skin that covered the skewers, proving to the Great Father that he was indeed worthy.

Brave Wolf had been greatly affected by the fight with Spotted Feather; Aeneva had seen the change come over him. He had not felt himself worthy enough to be a warrior, and he felt he had to prove something to himself and to Stalking Horse. He doubted himself, and a warrior could not live that way. He knew that the only way he could respect himself and perhaps gain the respect of the Maiyun and the Great Father was to sacrifice himself. There was nothing more precious that a man could sacrifice than his own blood; perhaps the Great Father would see this and take pity upon him, and guide him on the right path.

Tears stung Aeneva's eyes as she watched her brother. She turned away, resting her back against a boulder. She didn't want to watch his pain and suffering any longer; it was now between him and the Great Father. Quietly, fighting the urge to look back at her brother, Aeneva left her hiding place and descended the mountain. She could not understand why he wanted to do this; it was not required of a warrior. But Brave Wolf felt he was not a true warrior and he needed to prove to himself that he possessed the courage it took to endure this self-torture.

"Have you seen enough, Granddaughter?" Stalking Horse stepped from behind some rocks and walked up to Aeneva. "I knew you would not stay long."

"Grandfather, I . . ." Aeneva shook her head, not

knowing what to say. "Do you suppose the Great Father will be angry with Brave Wolf because of me? If it is so, then I will go up there and—"

"No, child, the Great Father will not be angry with Brave Wolf. He will see that Brave Wolf has a sister who loves him deeply and cares only that he doesn't suffer needlessly."

Aeneva lowered her head. "Thank you, Grandfather. You did not tell Brave Wolf that I was there?"

"No, he did not need to worry about you also. It will be difficult enough for him."

"Why is he doing it, Grandfather? I do not understand. Brave Wolf has always been the one who never sought to gain anyone's favor, even yours."

"I know, child, but I think he now feels that he must prove something to himself and to me." Stalking Horse nodded his head. "Yes, I feel I am a great part of this."

"Because of what happened in the winter? This was many moons ago and you told Brave Wolf that you had misjudged him."

"It makes no difference. Inside, he feels that I do not trust him. He feels that he must prove to me what a man he is, that he is in great favor with the Maiyun and the Great Father." Stalking Horse saw the accusation in her eyes. "I tried to talk him out of it, Aeneva. He would not listen to me."

"He did not believe you. He believes that you want him to be a great warrior who will count many coups on the enemy. You have made him expect too much of himself, Grandfather." Aeneva turned away and continued walking.

"You are right, Aeneva. I wanted Brave Wolf to be more than any boy could be. I did expect too much."

Aeneva stopped, her voice soft. "But you do not expect too much now? Now you will accept him as he is?"

"Yes."

"Then tell him that, Grandfather. Make him stop this foolishness. Convince him that he is worthy and good the way he is."

"I tried, Aeneva, but he would not listen. This is something he must do. To stop him now, would be to make him doubt himself forever. Do you not see that?"

Aeneva saw the pain and sadness in her grandfather's eyes and realizing that she had spoken to him as no other person would dare to speak to him she touched his arm. "You are right. I do see that."

"But you are still angry with me."

"I am not angry, Grandfather. I just want Brave Wolf back the way he was. He was not so serious then; he always saw the laughter in things. He always made me see the laughter."

"People change, child. They grow up."

"A person can grow up and still laugh; is that not so, Grandfather?" Aeneva looked up at her grandfather, the yellow specks in her eyes reflecting the sunlight, her face young and untouched.

Stalking Horse touched Aeneva's cheek, suddenly drawing her to him. He hugged her fiercely, loving her with a passion he had not thought possible. With the exceptions of Sun Dancer and his own children, his grandchildren had filled him with more love and joy than any man had a right to receive in a lifetime. "Yes, a person can grow up and still laugh, child. Look at Jean; do you know anyone who laughs more than he?"

Aeneva smiled as she thought of the long silver hair and beard of Jean. Indeed, she could not think of any grown-up person who enjoyed life more than her uncle. "Well then, perhaps Brave Wolf will see that he can be a

146

good warrior and still laugh at other things. Do you think so, Grandfather?"

"I hope so, Aeneva. I hope so with all my heart."

"Brave Wolf will try to break the skin of his chest; I know he will." Aeneva was referring to the fact that a man was more favorably looked upon by the spirits if he managed to break the skin from the skewers, rather than have them cut for him at the end of the day.

"Yes, he will be down before I go up to get him. If he has to rip the skin down his chest, he will break through."

"The skin is so tough, Grandfather; not many have been able to do it."

"Yes, but I am now learning that your brother can do anything he is set upon doing."

"Even if it maims and scars him."

"He will be scarred, but not maimed. It was devised only to inflict torture, not to disable." He looked at Aeneva. "You surprise me, child. You want to be a warrior. Why does this practice offend you so?"

"Because I do not believe I need to torture myself to prove to the spirits or anyone my worth as a warrior. I will be judged on my ability only."

"Does it frighten you?"

"Pain does not frighten me, Grandfather. I am not afraid of pain or death. But I do not believe in torturing the body that houses my spirit. It is barbaric. I do not understand many of our customs, Grandfather."

"Now you sound like your grandmother. She questioned just about every custom we had when we were young, and we had many more to abide by than you have now."

Aeneva grinned impishly. "Did she give her father much trouble?"

"She gave him nothing but trouble. That is why he consented to let her marry me. Then I was responsible and he no longer had to worry."

"But you worried, did you not?"

"Constantly. She wanted to learn how to fight, so I taught her how to fight. She already rode well and she handled a knife like a man, but she always wanted to be better." Stalking Horse looked beyond Aeneva to a time only he remembered. "She was so very beautiful and so full of life. Everyone fought to be around her. She was the very meaning of life itself."

"You loved her very much."

"I still love her very much, child. We change, our bodies betray us and grow older, our minds feebler, but our feelings do not change. She has not just been my woman, she has been my partner in life. We have shared everything." He nodded his approval. "That is how it should be. That is how it should be for you, Aeneva."

"I told you many times, Grandfather,"—Aeneva tried to make her voice sound light—"I will never marry. I will dedicate myself to my family and my tribe."

"That is not enough."

"How do you know?"

"I know, child, because I have shared most of my life with another person. It is not good to be alone. Do not fool yourself into believing that it is good, or you will always be alone and one day you will find that it is too late to change. For once, listen to an older voice, Aeneva."

Aeneva started to reply, but was cut off by her grandfather's sudden exit. He walked away from her, leaving her alone with her thoughts and his words. She bent down and picked up a large rock, hurling it through the air. It landed on a large boulder and bounced from it to the ground. She bent over to pick up another rock and smiled in spite of her mood. She recalled the time when she and Trenton had tried to stay hidden from Brave Wolf and Coyote Boy for one entire day. Many times she had almost given their cover away, but Trenton had always managed to lay a false trail so they could get away. It had been wonderful for them—she a girl, he a half-breed—to fool two Cheyenne boys. She knew even then that she loved Trenton. She threw another rock and it soared through the air, landing far ahead of her in a puff of dust on the ground. She wondered where Trenton was now and if he ever thought of coming back here. It had all been so long ago; she wondered if he even thought of her at all.

She sighed deeply and looked up at the clear sky. She heard the distinctive sound of an eagle screeching. She shielded her eyes from the sun and soon found the eagle, flapping his great wings furiously, gliding easily as he looked down at the earth below for something to eat. He circled high above Aeneva, craning his head to look down at her. Aeneva laughed with pure delight and yelled up at the large bird. *"Netse!"* she screamed out, waiting for some sign from the bird. He screeched loudly and circled above her again and she saw something float down from the sky. She chased after it and caught it before it hit the ground. It was one of the eagle's tailfeathers, a large dark feather trimmed in snowy white. Aeneva touched it to her cheek and waved to the eagle, shouting up at him. *"Ne-aoh-ohese netse."* The eagle circled her again and soared high, his piercing shriek echoing in the air. Aeneva knew it was a sign; she knew then that Trenton would return. When he had left that summer long ago, she had seen an eagle that had called to her, much as this one had called. Now the eagle had reappeared to tell her that Trenton would soon return.

149

Suddenly she felt joyous, as if she had found her own medicine, her own power. She thought her father must have felt much the same way on that mountaintop so long ago before she had been born, when he had gone to seek his medicine. He had stayed up there for many nights and had seen nothing except the vision of a snake, the snake with the rattles, and he knew it was a bad sign. Soon afterward, an eagle appeared above and plummeted down, taking the snake in his mouth and soaring into the air. The eagle left a golden tailfeather and that had been her father's medicine. Perhaps her father would be proud that she had also had a sign from an eagle.

Aeneva tucked the tailfeather safely into one of her braids and started running across the prairie, her arms flung out open to the world. She felt truly free and happy for the first time in a long while and she knew part of the reason was Trenton. She didn't know when, but she knew he would soon return. Perhaps things would not be the same between them, but they might find that they still cared deeply for each other. Whatever the outcome of their meeting, Aeneva was eager to see him. Contrary to what her grandfather believed, she, too, did not want to spend the rest of her life alone.

Sun Dancer cried out, waking Stalking Horse from his sleep. He knew without asking that she had had one of her dream visions, and he waited for her to tell him about it. She began to shiver and he covered her with a robe. These were the times that frightened her the most. In these dream visions, she had seen the death of her brother; and she had known something terrible would happen to Little Flower and Young Eagle; she had also known of Trenton. He smoothed the long hair away from her face and pulled her to him, comforting her as he was so used to doing. "Are you all right, Wife?"

Sun Dancer did not look at him. She leaned forward, covering her face with her hands. Stalking Horse could hear her trying to stifle the painful cries that tore at her. He touched her shoulder firmly. "Sun Dancer, what is it?"

Sun Dancer shook her head, pulling away from Stalking Horse and lying down on their robes. She turned away from him. "I do not want to talk now, Stalking Horse."

Stalking Horse lay back down, his thoughts going quietly through his head. She always told him everything. Possibly, this vision was far worse than anything she had seen. Perhaps she had foreseen the death of Brave Wolf or Coyote Boy, or even Aeneva. Aeneva. Stalking Horse's stomach bunched into a tense knot and he pulled Sun Dancer toward him. "Is it Aeneva? Surely, the Great Father would not take her from us so soon. Not her."

Sun Dancer looked up at her husband and tears filled her dark eyes. She reached up and gently touched his face, the handsome craggy face that so instilled her with pride and love. Even now, after all the summers and winters they had spent together, she still thought him the most beautiful man she had ever seen. "No, husband, it is not Aeneva or one of the boys."

"Is it you then? Did you see. . . ?"

Sun Dancer put her fingers on Stalking Horse's lips. "No, it is not me. You know that would not frighten me anyway. I am ready to die. The only sadness I would hold would be at leaving you so soon."

"Then who was it? You did have a vision, did you not?" Stalking Horse hesitated for a moment and seeing the look on Sun Dancer's face, he knew. He pulled her to him, enclosing her in the secure circle of his arms, breathing in the smell of her hair and her skin, breathing in her very existence. "It was I you saw." It was a simple statement, made without fear or accusation. He felt the faint nod of Sun Dancer's head beneath his chin and he hugged her even tighter. He had always hoped it would be this way; he had always wanted to die before she. She was the stronger; she could exist without him. He knew he could not exist without her. "Do not be sad; I am not afraid to die either."

"I am not ready for you to die, Stalking Horse. I will not let you go."

"You cannot prevent it, Sun Dancer."

"No," she cried out in anguish, holding on to him with all her strength. "I love you with all my being. If I were left alone without you—"

"You would go on; you must go on. You must see that our grandchildren have a good life. When that is done, you can join me in Seyan. You will travel the Hanging Road and I will be there to meet you. Do not be sad. We will see your parents and Brave Wolf, Little Flower and Young Eagle, Laughing Bird—"

"I do not wish to hear any more. Do not tell me of the people I will see in Seyan. I want only to be with you. I am selfish."

"You have never been selfish, but you knew it would be like this. Horn said you would live a long life and accomplish many things. You have many things left to do. We will be together soon enough."

Sun Dancer sat up, wiping the tears from her face. "Why must you always see the truth in things? Why must you always be right?"

Stalking Horse laughed, running his hand down the length of her hair. "You make me feel like a god, Wife. Perhaps that is why I have stayed with you all this time."

Sun Dancer turned, the familiar arrogant expression on her face. "A god, no. You are only a man."

"Does that disappoint you?"

"I would not want to love a god."

"Well then, we are in agreement. Now, let us not talk of this any more tonight. Do not think so much about this, Sun Dancer. I could live a very long time and you could grow tired of me by then and push me on my way."

Sun Dancer smiled, laying her head on his chest. "I do love you, Stalking Horse." She held on to him, trying to still the tears that began to flow. Her vision had told her something else: it had also told her that Jean would die with Stalking Horse. Not only would she lose her husband, she would lose the best friend she had in the world.

"It will be all right; do not worry," Stalking Horse said calmly and soothingly, as if reading her mind.

Sun Dancer nodded, trying to placate Stalking Horse, but she would not be all right. She would constantly worry about Stalking Horse whenever he left the camp. As he said, he could live many more summers, or he might die tomorrow; this part of the future, she did not know. She had to hold on to the thought that Stalking Horse and Jean would live much longer and when the time came for them to die, she would follow along after them. She could not imagine life on earth without either one of them.

In the spring, Stalking Horse's band met a large part of the Northern Cheyenne tribe for the Sun Dance. This was a great social occasion and a time of reacquaintance for relatives and friends who had been apart for a long time. After the Sun Dance, the tribe dispersed and each band went its own way. Stalking Horse's band migrated farther west into the Black Hills and beyond to follow the buffalo.

The Cheyenne tribe had now split into two distinct groups: the Northern Cheyenne, who settled down along the North Platte, Big Horn, Powder, and Yellowstone rivers; and the Southern Cheyenne who settled along the Arkansas, Platte, and Republican rivers as well as along Sand Creek and Badge Creek. Like the other Plains Indians, they were nomadic and they followed their main source of food, the buffalo, whenever it migrated. It was also important that they try to avoid contact with the white man, who seemed to follow the Cheyennes and other tribes doggedly, wherever they went. It was getting so that there was very little sacred land left anymore. Sweet Medicine's predictions had been much too accurate.

The land that Stalking Horse's band chose to live on this summer was close to the hills for coolness, but also close to the river for water. The women erected their lodges near the river, but when the buffalo were nearby, they followed the hunters. The tedious task of butchering the buffalo and packing the meat on a travois was accomplished by the women, aided by some of the girls. The older women were busy making pemmican and jerky for hunting trips and for the winter, as well as drying currants and vegetables.

When the summers grew too hot, the band moved the lodges upriver, higher into the hills, where the trees brought coolness and shade.

Aeneva was now old enough to join the others in the hunt. She was sixteen summers old—tall and strong, and an extremely able hunter with lance or bow. She had ridden with her brothers and grandfather since she was small, and where she had once felt fear and awe of the huge beasts now she felt respect. She rode alongside one

154

large bull and drew close with her horse, careful to avoid the sharp horns of the animal in case he should turn and gore her mount. When she had ridden close enough, she drew back her throwing arm and thrust the lance hard into the animal's side, aiming for the heart. The buffalo grunted and stumbled, falling on its forelegs, then toppling over. Aeneva nimbly jumped from her horse, approached the animal from its blind side, pulled out her lance, and thrust it in again to make sure the bull did not suffer. He had not; her first throw had been a true aim and had taken the animal down immediately. She knelt down and with her big hunting knife, began to butcher the animal, cutting out the pieces of meat the women would carry back to camp. She had retrieved the meat many times herself, and now, as a hunter, she made it a practice to butcher as much of the animal as she could before she went on to the next. It made the job that much easier for the women.

Aeneva wiped her bloodied hands on the ground and sheathed her knife, before swinging up on her horse. For a moment she watched Brave Wolf and Coyote Boy go after a large bull. Brave Wolf singled him out of the herd and Coyote Boy was waiting for him when he turned. It was safer to work a large bull with two men. Aeneva turned her horse and galloped out toward the scattered herd. She noticed riders in the distance and stopped, squinting her eyes, trying to see who they were. Then she heard a horse beside her and glanced over as Coyote Boy pulled up.

"You saw them also?"

"Who are they? Look at the dust; Indians would not be riding like that out here. They know not to scare the buffalo."

Coyote Boy cupped his hands around his mouth and

made a loud call, the sound of alarm. The hunters who heard him stopped; the others who didn't were soon alerted. The hunters grouped together, Stalking Horse and some of the other war chiefs at the front. Stalking Horse watched the thick cloud of dust that surrounded the oncoming riders and he made his decision. "Aeneva," he yelled, "go back and warn the village. Have the women and old people be ready."

Aeneva turned her horse and galloped back to camp, not turning back to see what was happening. She rode into the camp yelling, screaming at anyone who would listen. "We are being attacked; make ready. Get your weapons and get inside the lodges." Aeneva cantered her horse to her grandparents' lodge and jumped off before the horse stopped. She found Sun Dancer outside the lodge, dressing some hides.

"What is it, Aeneva? You ride in here like the wind—"

"Quickly, Grandmother. Riders are coming. Grandfather wants you all to gather your weapons and make ready." Aeneva helped her grandmother up. "Please hurry, Grandmother."

Sun Dancer thought of her vision. "Stalking Horse—"

"He is fine. Please, you and the others protect yourselves." Aeneva started back to her horse.

"Where are you going, Aeneva?"

"Back to fight, Grandmother. I must be with my brothers and grandfather." She swung deftly to her horse's back and jerked on his halter, heading back toward the hunters. When Aeneva reached the hunters, they were divided into groups. Stalking Horse had arranged to protect the front of the camp with some of the strongest and most able warriors, while placing another farther out from the camp. The other group was strung out behind the now-

156

alert herd of buffalo. Aeneva rode to the foremost group; she spotted her grandfather out in the lead, his lance poised and ready. He owned a rifle that Jean had given him years before, but he was a warrior of the old days and was still used to the lance. Aeneva rode up next to him, meeting his gaze unwaveringly, daring him to challenge her. She held the lance he had made for her in her right hand. He could not stop her from fighting.

Their horses stamped the ground impatiently. The nearby herd of buffalo snorted and pawed at the earth; they lifted their noses to the wind, sensing something that did not belong. The buffalo lived in harmony with the Indians, knowing instinctively that the Indians were not their enemies. But they did not know this strange new smell.

It did not take long before the hunters recognized the blue uniforms of the soldiers. Stalking Horse glanced at his granddaughter, conscious of the fact that he could lose her. He looked back at the men who guarded the village, recognizing Brave Wolf and Coyote Boy as they sat in front of the others, willing to give their lives for the women, children, and old ones of the band. He turned his gaze back toward the soldiers. He did not know their intent; he hoped it was peaceful, but his instincts told him it was not. His warriors knew that if he raised his hand, it would be a sign to fight; he prayed to all the gods above that he would not have to give that signal.

When they were about a half-mile away, the soldiers turned abruptly toward the herd of buffalo, and divided into two columns. Stalking Horse knew then that the soldiers had come to move the herd out of Cheyenne land. He could not permit this to happen; without the buffalo the Cheyennes would cease to exist. He lifted his hand, pointing to the herd, motioning his warriors to try to move them away before the soldiers reached them. The warriors in front of the camp did not move; they would guard the village until it was safe.

Aeneva rode alongside her grandfather, heading out toward the leaders in the herd, trying to turn them. The buffalo were now excited and began to run in several directions. The Cheyennes surrounded them, herding in the strays whenever they tried to leave. The herd reacted instinctively and turned, stampeding farther into Cheyenne land. Aeneva smiled to herself, knowing that it would now be impossible for the soldiers to turn the herd. Then the soldiers fired their rifles at the buffalo. The Cheyennes tried to keep the herd together, but the sound of the gunfire terrified them and they scattered. Aeneva glanced ahead, watching as a group of soldiers descended on them. She put her lance in its holder and pulled out her rifle. Shots sounded behind her and she tried to find her grandfather in the band of warriors. She heard a yell and turned to her right, surprised to see a soldier riding toward her. She pulled her horse up, aimed her rifle and fired; the soldier fell from his horse, hitting the ground with a thump. She started to ride away, but another soldier came at her. He fired at her and a bullet passed close to her shoulder, but Aeneva recovered quickly and fired at the man, knocking him from his horse.

"Aeneva!" She heard her grandfather's voice and turned. He was waving her to follow. She kneed her horse and they rode toward the warriors who now had most of the herd running away from the soldiers. The other Cheyennes who were guarding the village now rode forward to encircle the unsuspecting cavalry. The soldiers fired out of fear but the Cheyennes kept clear, waiting for the white men to exhaust their supply of ammunition. The soldiers were trapped and after some futile attempts at fighting, they threw down their arms and held up their hands in surrender.

Stalking Horse approached the white men, holding his lance across his horse's neck, his look one of pure disdain. He stopped his horse in front of the lead soldier, eying him suspiciously for a moment before he spoke.

"You are on our land," he said simply, but the words had their desired effect. The soldiers looked at each other, surprised that a Cheyenne could speak such good English.

One of the scouts walked out in front of the others, dusting his hat against his thigh in a nervous gesture. "We're after them buffalo, same as you, chief."

"You were not after the buffalo, white man," he said with disdain. "You were trying to run them off our land. There is a difference."

"You don't own all them animals, you know, chief. All you Indians seem to think them buffalo is special."

"We understand each other, white man. That is something I do not think you or I could ever do." Stalking Horse looked past the scout to the others who were anxiously waiting. "Why did you not hunt the animals you needed? We understand the need for food."

"We wanted to have the herd closer to us."

"You do not understand, white man. Just because you make the herd go with you one day, it does not mean they will be there the next. They go where they will. We have always followed them; they do not follow us."

"Well, we figure different. We white men go after what we want. We figured we could bring most of that herd back with us and corral them."

Stalking Horse was puzzled. He looked behind him, waving at Aeneva. He spoke to her, explaining that he did not understand what the scout had said.

"He means they would put the buffalo in pens, Grandfather. They would not be free to roam the prairie."

"That's right, little girl."

Aeneva stared at the white man. She spoke slowly, her voice betraying little of the anger she felt. "I am not a little girl, *Veho,* and you should remember that you are on our land, surrounded by our people." She smiled then, clearly enjoying the man's discomfiture.

The man ignored Aeneva and looked again at Stalking Horse. "You have women fighting for you now, chief?"

"She is a warrior," Stalking Horse replied, surprised at the anger he felt inside.

"A warrior?" The white man turned, laughing at the men around him. "Did you fellas hear that? She is a warrior. Would you be willing to fight me, warrior?" He looked at Aeneva.

Stalking Horse started to speak, but Aeneva leaned close to him. "Please, Grandfather, let me do this. You cannot always fight my battles for me."

"There will be no fighting," Stalking Horse said with finality.

"Grandfather, if I were a man, you would not stand in the way. Please, this is my honor. I am not afraid."

"I know you are not afraid, Aeneva." He looked down at the belligerent white man and thought of his granddaughter facing this man; it did not seem right. Clearly, she was no match for the man physically; he was taller, heavier, and probably stronger. But Stalking Horse knew from experience that skill was much more important than physical stature and if his granddaughter possessed one thing, it was skill in the ways of the warrior. With a subtle nod of his head he allowed Aeneva to have her way and he and the others backed their horses up.

Aeneva did not move. She looked at the white man,

160

speaking clearly and calmly. Her voice held no fear. "How do you wish to fight, white man? Guns, knife, lance? You name the weapon."

The scout laughed, turning around to the men for support; they didn't laugh with him. "You aren't serious, girl. I could kill you in a second and then your whole tribe'd be on us. I ain't that stupid."

"We are a people of honor, *Veho,* and we keep our word. If you should kill me, you and your people would go free."

"Is that so, chief?" The scout looked past Aeneva to Stalking Horse for confirmation.

Stalking Horse nodded. "It is so."

"Well, then . . ." The man smiled as he pulled a large knife from his boot. "I think I'd like to fight you with my knife. That is, if you're not afraid."

Aeneva dismounted, looking up to see Brave Wolf and Coyote Boy ride silently forward. She considered both of them and nodded, grateful that they did not try to stand in for her. They understood how important this was to her sense of honor and duty as a warrior. It was time she stood up for herself. She unsheathed her knife and cautiously approached the white man. Her knife was much smaller than the white man's, but the blade was long, thin, and extremely sharp. Brave Wolf had made the knife for her when she had turned fourteen summers. He had made the handle to conform to her grip and it fit perfectly in her hand. She tried to remember all of the things her brothers and grandfather had told her about fighting hand-to-hand: approach slowly, let the enemy make the first move, never take your eyes from him, and do not think so much that your instincts are slowed.

"I never killed me a woman before," the man said cruelly, obviously relishing what he thought would be an easy task. He circled around Aeneva, tossing his knife from hand to hand, trying to make her nervous, trying to make her lose her concentration; but Aeneva remained calm, used to the games the man was playing, knowing that soon he would grow impatient and attack. The advantage was with him, she knew, because of his size, and it was up to her to be fast and agile, to keep away from him until she was able to get close enough to use her knife. With a deep growl the white man charged Aeneva, his knife held low, aimed at her belly. Aeneva easily dodged to the side, turning and steadying herself for the man to come at her again. The white man came again, swiping at her with his knife, moving it back and forth across her chest and stomach, trying to inflict some damage. But Aeneva, agile and able to back away from the weapon, kept her eyes on the man's every move. She was conscious of the pain in her shoulders and arms from the tension, but all her thoughts were focused on the man in front of her. He again charged at her with renewed fervor, this time cutting at her left arm with his knife. Aeneva felt the searing pain, but didn't look at it; she kept her eyes fastened on the enemy. Soon it would be her turn to attack.

''Does it hurt, little girl? It should; this here's a big knife.''

Aeneva didn't reply. She advanced toward the man this time, using herself as bait. He didn't disappoint her. He ran at her again, but this time Aeneva was ready. She threw her knife at him before he made it halfway to her; he stared at her in mute surprise, dropping his own knife as his hands went to the one which was now embedded in his stomach. He fell to his knees, then onto his stomach, groaning. Aeneva picked up his knife and walked over to him. She started to bend down next to him, but her grandfather's voice stopped her.

"Leave him, Aeneva."

Aeneva stood up and faced her grandfather, afraid that she had disgraced him, but she realized that it had been a subtle warning to her. As a child she had been taught never to go near wounded animals because they were the most dangerous, her grandfather now warned her to be wary of this man. "It is all right, Grandfather." She took the man by the shoulder and turned him over. He was bleeding from the wound and his eyes were dazed. She pulled her knife from his belly and walked over to one of the other white men. "He is still alive; I have seen many of our warriors recover from a stomach wound." She started to walk away, but stopped, turning back to the white men. "Do not come on our land again. If you need food, find buffalo elsewhere. They are plentiful now, but they will not be if you do what you tried to do today." She walked over to her horse and swung up, waiting for her grandfather to signal them to go. Stalking Horse looked at the white men for a moment, then raised his hand, and he and the other warriors rode back to the village.

"Are you all right, Granddaughter?" Stalking Horse looked at Aeneva's bleeding arm.

"I am well, Grandfather, thank you. And thank you for letting me fight. It was important to me. I hope I did not disgrace you."

"You fought well. The man was so big I was afraid if he got you down—"

"I know. I was not going to give him the chance."

"Well done, Sister." Coyote Boy slapped Aeneva's leg. "You learned your lessons well."

"Thank you, Brother."

She waited for Brave Wolf to ride up and when he did

163

not, she fell behind until he caught up with her. "Do you think I learned the lessons well, Brother?"

"Too well," Brave Wolf replied hostilely.

"You are angry with me. Why?"

"You should not have done that."

"Why? Because I am a woman?"

"You are only a girl, Aeneva. A girl. You could have been killed."

"But I was not. I knew what to do."

"You were lucky."

"It was not luck that made me win that fight; it was skill."

"Do not fool yourself into believing that, little Sister. The man was much larger than you and he knew the ways of the knife well. You were lucky and he was impatient. That is all."

"Why are you talking this way, Brave Wolf? I do not understand you of late. You are so serious about everything. I cannot please you; no one can."

"I do not ask you to please me, Aeneva. I only ask you to do what I have asked of you since you were small."

"And what is that?"

"To give up this foolish notion of becoming a warrior."

"It is not a foolish notion. I *am* a warrior. I fought today with the rest of you. You did not seem to think I was so foolish then, or when I killed many buffalo during the hunt."

"Hunting is one thing; fighting is another. I cannot believe Grandfather let you fight that man."

"Grandfather understands."

"Grandfather understands nothing." Brave Wolf kneed his horse and rode on ahead, leaving Aeneva to wonder at his words. She rode up next to Coyote Boy.

164

"Why does Brave Wolf have so much anger in him? I do not know him anymore."

"Our brother has much on his mind lately. Do not worry yourself with it, little Sister. He has many things to work through."

"You are sure he is not angry with me? I cannot seem to please him anymore."

"It is not you, Aeneva; he is the same way with me. We would do best to leave him alone. It is difficult being the eldest. Much rests on his shoulders."

"Yes," Aeneva agreed, "I understand." But she was not sure she did. There was something more that she did not know about, something Brave Wolf and Coyote Boy were not telling her. They had never kept secrets from her before and she would not let them begin now. She would find out what was bothering Brave Wolf and she would help him if she could.

CHAPTER IX

Jean and Stalking Horse sat high up on the mountain, looking out at the vast prairie and the deep orange glow of the setting sun. Stalking Horse puffed deeply on the pipe, then passed it to Jean, who puffed on it and passed it back to Stalking Horse. So it would go until it was empty. They had performed this ritual many times, in many different places, but always it was the same. They spoke little during these times, their friendship a deep and unbreakable bond which allowed them to be just as they were without having to explain. But this night would be different; this night there would be much conversation.

"What is it, *mon ami?* You are troubled this day."

"Yes, *hoovehe,* I have had much on my mind of late."

"Aeneva?"

"Aeneva and Brave Wolf."

"That is not all."

"It is Sun Dancer; I am worried about her."

"Is she ill?" Jean asked in alarm.

"No, but she has had a vision."

"She has seen death?"

"Yes, she has seen my death," Stalking Horse replied without emotion.

"No," Jean said softly, his voice, contrary to that of his friend, full of emotion.

"Why are you so surprised, old friend? Do you forget

that I am an old man?''

"If you are an old man, then I am older. I have been on this wretched earth longer than you.''

"Yes, but you seem younger than I. That has always puzzled me.''

"I am not responsible for so many people as you are, *hoovehe*. I am free to come and go as I please. You are bound by duty and honor.''

"I suppose that is part of it, but you have always been different, Jean. You have always been able to laugh more easily.''

"Thanks to you, *hoovehe*. You have made my life easy. I have been able to call your village my home for many years now; but when I like, I go to my cabin in the mountains or to the cities.'' Jean waved his hand impatiently. "We did not come up here to talk about me. You said Sun Dancer saw a death vision?''

"Yes, she saw me. She would not explain it, but she said that she saw me die.''

"She is upset of course.''

"She has not been the same since. Every time I leave her, she looks at me with pleading eyes as if begging me not to go. She thinks every time I leave her, I will be killed.''

"Can't you see how difficult this must be for her? You have always been the one constant in her life. There have been many births and deaths, but you have always been there for her. It must be difficult for her to contemplate a life without you.''

"She is strong; she will be fine.''

"You are glad, aren't you?''

"What do you mean?'' Stalking Horse looked at him in surprise.

"You are glad that you will die first. You couldn't face

168

life without her.''

"You have always seen through my words, *Veho*. I should never have made you my blood brother that day so long ago; you seem to believe you are truly Cheyenne.''

"I am truly Cheyenne.'' Jean looked out at the wide expanse of prairie below them and spread his hands. "We are lucky to live at this time, *hoovehe*. It will be different when your grandchildren are grown.''

"Yes, it is already changing rapidly.''

"What of Aeneva? She is proving to be a warrior of great ability, is she not?''

"Much to my dismay. It seems she will not be turned from this path which she seeks to follow.''

"Aeneva is special, like her grandmother.''

"Yes, but I do not want her to be special in this way. She is getting to be known now. Word is spreading throughout our tribe and others that we have a woman warrior. And the white men have seen her three times; they seem to think it even more strange.''

Jean nodded. "Yes, I wouldn't be surprised if they were out to capture her.''

"Capture her? Why?''

"Some of these white men have a strange way about them. When they do not understand people or animals, they wish to kill them or lock them up.''

"Do you know this to be true—that they want to capture my granddaughter?''

"No, *hoovehe*, I am only guessing.''

"But you can find out. I want to know.''

"I will find out for you. I will make a trip to the fort. I will find out about the woman warrior.''

"I wish the white boy would come back.''

"I think he will. He cares for Aeneva; I could see that on the boat.''

"But why is he not here? Why has he not come back for her?"

"He has to follow his own path, just as Aeneva has to follow hers. Hopefully their paths will cross someday."

"Perhaps he has tasted too much of the white man's life and will never return."

"I don't think so; I think Trenton Hawkins will return."

"Perhaps." Stalking Horse nodded, looking off into the distance. "Have you talked with Brave Wolf of late?"

"No, but I have heard that the Dog Warriors want him to join them. Is it true?"

"Yes."

"You do not want him to join them?"

"There is no need. He will one day be a great chief; there is no need for him to be with those crazy young men."

"Perhaps he feels a need to be crazy, *hoovehe*. Brave Wolf, too, must seek his own path. But in the end, it will be the right one."

"I hope that is so." Stalking Horse patted Jean on the shoulder, an uncharacteristic gesture on his part.

"What is it, *hoovehe?*"

"Will you take care of Sun Dancer when I am gone? It will make it easier for me."

Jean reached out and grasped Stalking Horse's arm, squeezing it tightly. "You know that I will give my life for her."

"I know that and I will rest easier in Seyan while I am waiting for you two to join me. But remember, *Veho,* I will be watching you. Take no liberties."

"Me? Why, old friend, you insult me by speaking so," Jean said in a mocking tone.

170

"You probably cannot wait until I am gone to have her to yourself."

Jean stroked his beard thoughtfully. "I will miss you, it is true; but to have Sun Dancer all to myself—"

"I have changed my mind," Stalking Horse stated definitively as he stood up.

"About what?"

"I will not die after all. I will wait until you die and then I will follow. I do not trust you alone with my wife."

Jean's laughter echoed down the hills, filling both the men with a gaiety that they had not felt in a long time. One thing was certain—whoever died first, the other would feel truly alone. They were not only friends and blood brothers, they were brothers of the soul. It was a tie that could not be broken, not in this life or the next.

Aeneva listened to her grandfather with quiet intensity as he spoke. She nodded her head occasionally, knowing what she must do. When he was finished she sat quietly for a time, letting her thoughts settle into some order.

"Do you understand what I just said, Aeneva?"

"I understand, Grandfather."

"Why are you so silent? Do you wish to say something?"

"There is nothing to say, Grandfather."

"I want to know how you feel, Aeneva."

"It does not matter how I feel, Grandfather. What is most important is that I do not place our people in any more danger. I will do what has to be done."

"You will give up your life as a warrior?"

"Yes," she replied solemnly but without self-pity.

"You can still hunt; we do not always war."

"It does not matter," Aeneva said matter-of-factly. She stood up, looking down at her grandfather. "You are most worried about the white soldiers? You did not speak of the Crows or any other tribes. Am I permitted to fight against them?''

Stalking Horse was silent, contemplating Aeneva's question. ''Many of the tribes trade with the whites; word will spread.''

''I understand.''

''Aeneva, I hope you do understand. I know what this means to you.''

''No, I do not think you do understand what this means. I do not think anyone does.''

Stalking Horse called out after Aeneva, but she did not respond. He had not expected her to react so calmly. But she was his granddaughter and she would do the honorable thing. He only wished there were another way. He was now beginning to understand how much being a warrior meant to her. She had worked hard to prove she was as skilled and proficient as most of the men. He thought for a moment—it was not like Aeneva to take things so lightly. She was like her grandmother and would voice her opinion on any matter; he had learned that long ago. This gave Stalking Horse cause for concern because he realized that if Aeneva were to give up the one thing she loved the most to protect her people, she would probably go off on her own. He could not let this happen. He got up and strode out of the lodge, intent on finding another way to keep Aeneva with them and to let her keep her honor.

Aeneva was sitting alone in the woods when she saw the riders draw near to the village. From her vantage point she was able to see the entire village, as well as anyone who approached it. It was late and the moon was high. Aeneva had been alone since earlier in the day when her grandfather had told her what Jean had found out. She had thought about it the entire day and most of the night, contemplating what her life would be like if she had to marry and have children like all of the other women. She was different from them, she knew; not better, just different. Just as they would not be suited to the warrior's life, she would not be suited to the life of a wife and mother.

Aeneva was able to see the movement in the distance as the moon shone down on the wide expanse of prairie. There were many men on horseback approaching the village. She strained her eyes in the semidarkness and was able to tell that they were Crow warriors. She quietly stood up and scrambled back through the woods, entering the village from behind. She had to warn her people before the Crows attacked. She ran through the trees, falling once and quickly getting back up on her feet, bumping into tree branches and bushes that were in her way. She waded across the stream and climbed up the opposite bank, screaming as loudly as she could, *"Ooetane, Ooetane!"* She yelled the word "Crow" while running through the village, slapping against lodge doors. By the time she reached the middle of the camp, gunshots were sounding and there were screams all around. Aeneva ran to her grandparents' lodge, pushing inside to look for her rifle. Her grandmother was sitting by the lodge door, fear evident on her face.

"Are you all right, Grandmother?" Aeneva asked, bending down and touching Sun Dancer.

"I am fine, Aeneva. Where have you been?"

"I will tell you later. Now I must help. I saw the Crows and came back to warn the village."

Sun Dancer watched as Aeneva ran to her backrest and pulled out her rifle. She came back and knelt at the flap of

173

the lodge, peering outside. "What are you doing?"

"I am guarding you, Grandmother."

"I do not need to be guarded by my own granddaughter. Go somewhere else where you will be needed," Sun Dancer replied indignantly.

"I am needed here."

"You are not needed here, Aeneva. I never needed you to guard me before; please do not insult me by insisting that I need your help now."

"But Grandfather said—"

"Grandfather said you were to keep out of sight of the white soldiers; he did not say you were to stay hidden if you were needed to help protect your people. Now go."

Aeneva kissed Sun Dancer on the cheek and ran out the lodge door. The camp was in pandemonium; women were screaming and running with their children to the stream for safety; men and boys were preparing to fight. Aeneva moved steadily from one lodge to another, wary of any Crow warrior who might come into sight. She was aware that she had not actually seen any Crows; she had heard gunshots and seen her people running scared, but where were the Crows? What were they trying to do? It was then she thought of all the women and children unguarded and alone at the stream. If she had been able to make her way around the village unnoticed, so, too, might have the Crows. They might have used a few for decoys at the entrance to the camp, firing shots and creating havoc, while the brunt of the raiding party planned to wait for the women and children at the stream, knowing they would go there for safety.

Aeneva reversed direction, looking for some of the men, but almost all of them were guarding the entrance to the camp. She raced back the way she had come, circling around close to the trees to give her cover while she looked down at the stream. She couldn't see into the woods, but she knew the Crows were over there waiting for the women and children.

"*Ooetane, Ooetane!*" she shouted, yelling for the women and children to come back into the village. She dashed down the embankment and waited, helping small children and mothers with babies. She heard some of the women wail and saw movement from across the stream. Crows were coming out of the woods, wading into the stream and pulling women and children across with them. Aeneva raised her rifle and fired, killing a Crow who was dragging two small children with him. She felt strong hands on her and, turning in the tight grasp, faced a Crow warrior. He hit her across the jaw and she was unable to get away from him or raise her rifle. He tried to pull the rifle from her hands, but she held on to it, using her weight to push him backward into the water. Aeneva fell on top of the Crow, unable to gain her footing in the water. Her face was against his shoulder and she bit into him, tasting the salty blood as it flowed into her mouth. The Crow howled in anger and struck at her, but he had released his hold enough to allow Aeneva some freedom. She raised her rifle enough to jam the butt into his ribs and then lethally, into his throat. She stood up, watching the confusion all around her. Another woman screamed and Aeneva raised her rifle to shoot, but she was unable to see. Instead, she ran toward the sound, swinging her rifle across the back of a Crow's head, knocking him into the water. She helped many of the women up the bank and was relieved when she saw Brave Wolf and some of the others running into the stream, chasing the Crows back into the woods. She looked around her, waiting to see if there were any more Crows, but they had disappeared into the woods at the sight of the Cheyenne men,

175

taking as many of the women and children as they could. Rubbing her sore jaw and finally feeling the chill from her wet dress she sat down on the bank.

"I see you have done it again, little Sister." Brave Wolf sat down next to Aeneva, turning her face toward him. Are you all right?"

Aeneva shrugged his hand away. "I am fine. What does it matter to you?"

"Do not act childish, Aeneva. I love you and I worry about you."

"You talk to me of acting childish? You, who have always known the right path to follow, who have always been the best at everything he has ever done, who has always been loved by everyone. You, my brother, have been acting like a child of late," she stood up, brushing some of the dirt from her dress.

"You acted well, Aeneva. I am proud of you," Brave Wolf's words sounded so welcome after such a long silence.

"Grandfather told me I am not to fight anymore. Did you know that?"

"He would never tell you to do that."

"I made the decision; he said my fighting could endanger our people. I had not intended to fight tonight, Brave Wolf. I wanted to keep my word."

"You had no choice tonight. You defended yourself and your people."

"I fear it will always be so. I will never be satisfied with anything else." Her voice was soft now, full of sadness. "I cannot stay here."

Brave Wolf stood up now, putting his hands on Aeneva's shoulders. "Do not speak so, Sister. You are tired; it is always hard to think after one has fought and killed another. Things will look clearer tomorrow."

"They will look the same tomorrow, Brave Wolf. I cannot stay with my people any longer."

"Promise me you will not go until I have talked to Grandfather. You must promise me, Aeneva."

Aeneva was silent, refusing to answer. "I cannot promise you that, Brave Wolf."

"Promise me on your word as a warrior."

"All right, I promise."

"Good, I will talk to Grandfather tomorrow."

"Do not ask him to change his mind; he is right to ask me not to fight."

"I would not ask him to change his mind, but perhaps he has another idea. Do not be so stubborn."

"I am not stubborn."

"You are as stubborn as I am foolish, and all the spirits above know how foolish I have been lately."

Aeneva smiled then, wrapping her arms around Brave Wolf and hugging him close. "Then I suppose I am a little stubborn."

"Do not worry, little Sister. We will find a way for you to remain a warrior and remain with your people."

"I don't know why I didn't think of it before," mused Jean. "She's tall enough. With pants and a shirt and paint on her face, she'd pass for a man."

"Yes, it is a good idea," Stalking Horse agreed avidly. But will Aeneva agree?"

"Aeneva will agree to anything that will allow her to remain a warrior," Brave Wolf added.

"I think you should ask Aeneva." Sun Dancer interrupted the men, joining the conversation while mixing up one of her medicines.

"Grandmother is right. Aeneva may not agree at all. She is stubborn."

"That she is, boy." Jean laughed. "But I think she'll go along with it. She doesn't want to leave us any more than we want her to leave."

"Bring your sister to us, Brave Wolf," Stalking Horse ordered his grandson.

Aeneva entered the lodge a few minutes later and looked at the men in the circle. Stalking Horse motioned for her to sit on his right. "What do you want, Grandfather?"

"Would it offend you to dress as a man?"

Aeneva looked at Stalking Horse, then at Jean and her brothers in confusion. Finally she looked over at her grandmother and back at Stalking Horse. "I do not understand."

"Would it offend you to dress in the clothes of a man when we go on a hunt or if we raid?"

"I have never dressed in the clothing of a man before. Surely you do not mean a breechcloth. . . ." Aeneva's eyes grew wide.

Stalking Horse suppressed a laugh. "No, you would wear the pants that we wear in the winter, and a shirt like ours. You would look much like a man."

Aeneva looked at everyone again, seeing that it was no joke. "Why? Why do you want me to dress this way?"

"If you're dressed like a man, people will think you're a man. You're tall like many of the men and in men's clothes you could pass. Your face will be a problem though."

"What do you mean, *naxane?*"

"He means that you are too pretty to pass for a man," Sun Dancer replied. She walked over to the circle. "What these men are trying to tell you, Granddaughter, is that if you want to be a warrior, you must dress as one. Then no whites will ever know that a young girl is fighting their men. Their pride will not be hurt and they will not seek revenge on our people.''

"I see," mused Aeneva. "If I dress and act like a man, then I can fight. If I dress like a woman, then I can no longer be a warrior."

"Is it not better than denying yourself what you want most?"

"You are being stubborn again, Sister. Does it really matter how you dress?"

Aeneva stood up, her face flushed with anger. "Would you dress as a woman to fight?" She didn't wait for their reply. "I know that you would not, just as I will not dress as a man. I will no longer fight; I do not want to endanger the lives of my people. I know you have all tried to do the right thing and I thank you for it. But I will live my life my own way." She looked back at Sun Dancer, backed out of the circle, and left the lodge.

All four men stared after her, shocked expressions on their faces.

"Did you really expect her to go along with you?" Sun Dancer asked them. "She is so proud. Just because she does not seek the traditional role as a wife and mother does not mean she is not proud to be a woman. You men seem to think she would be glad to give up her identity to fight as a man; you do not know her so well, I think. She is proud to be a woman and she will never hide the fact."

Jean, stroking his beard thoughtfully, peered over at Stalking Horse. "As usual, Sun Dancer speaks the truth. We thought we were helping Aeneva, but I think we have made her feel more unwanted. She cannot even feel at home among her own people."

"You are right, Jean; we have made a mistake."

"I will talk to her." Brave Wolf stood up. "Forgive me, Grandfather, but I think we would be foolish to force

Aeneva. She will either stay here and be unhappy or she will leave. Either way we will lose her.'' He looked at Jean. ''Are you so sure the white soldiers are that interested in her?''

''I only told your grandfather what I heard. The soldiers have other matters on their minds; the Sioux have been giving them problems. They will not have time to think about Aeneva.''

''Then what does it matter? Our men do not resent her; they realize her skill. If we happen to fight white soldiers again, we will just have to hope that Aeneva is not involved. It is not right, Grandfather. We are treating her as if she has done something terrible when all she has done is fight, just like one of us. You saw what she did last night; she saved many of the women and children from being captured or killed by the Crows.''

''He is right, Husband. If it had been a man instead of Aeneva, we would have sung his praises. We treat her as if she had done nothing special.''

Stalking Horse held up his hands. ''All right, all right. I can see I do not have a chance against you all.''

''You will tell her she can remain a warrior?'' Brave Wolf asked hopefully.

''I will ask her if she will honor us by remaining one of our warriors. Your grandmother is right; many times Aeneva has come to our aid and little has been said about it. This time, something will be said.''

Aeneva sat silently, still amazed that she had been invited to sit in on the war council. Her grandfather had sung her praises in public and had asked the war council if she could sit in while they made their plans to bring back their women and children from the Crows. No one had disagreed with her grandfather; she had been accepted by all.

She was unusually awed by the circle of men. There was her grandfather, and there were three elder council chiefs, numerous war chiefs, and outstanding young warriors such as Brave Wolf and Coyote Boy who would soon be war chiefs. She still couldn't believe she was here.

"What do you think, Aeneva?" Aeneva jerked her eyes around when she heard her grandfather address her. All eyes were on her and she felt uncharacteristically timid. "If there is a chance, even the slightest chance that any of our women or children are alive, we should try to bring them back. The Crows did not do this just to take lives; this was also for humiliation. They want to take as many Cheyenne women and children as they can and raise them to fight against their own people."

There was a small murmur of voices as the men conferred with each other and Stalking Horse spoke again. "I believe my granddaughter makes a good point. Some of you will remember when she was just a baby, she and her mother were taken by the Crows. When she came back to us, she was more Crow than Cheyenne."

"Then let us form our raiding party and go. We should not waste any more time."

"I agree with you, Broken Buck," Stalking Horse replied, and he proceeded to name the men who would travel into Crow country. "I think Aeneva should travel with them also. Not only is she an able warrior, as we all know, but she speaks the Crow tongue well."

Everyone agreed and plans were hastily made for their departure. Aeneva joined in the general discussion this time, unafraid to voice her opinion. She looked up once and caught her grandfather's eyes and she smiled; that smile told it all. Stalking Horse knew that he had done the

181

right thing. He had a granddaughter who was a warrior and it was time he got used to it.

Jean looked over at Aeneva. "Are you ready, girl? You sure you want to do this?"

"I am ready, *naxane*. It is the best way."

Jean nodded, tying Aeneva's hands behind her back and grabbing her horse's reins. She looked dirty and tired enough to have been traveling as a captive; he only hoped the Crows would believe it. They had been riding in Crow territory for over two weeks and had discovered nothing. Then Jean had gone into one of the Crow camps to trade and had learned that there was another band of Crows camping along the Yellowstone; it was said that they had Cheyenne women and children with them. Jean and Aeneva had decided it would be a good idea to use her as a captive whom Jean wanted to trade to the Crows for supplies. While she was in the camp, she could learn if the Cheyenne women were there and where they were kept. Jean could leave and return at night with the Cheyenne raiding party.

"Are you frightened, little one?"

Aeneva looked over at Jean and smiled; he still called her "little one" as if she were the tiny little girl he used to toss into the air. "I am more frightened for you, *naxane*. You have traded with the Crows for so many summers without danger; now word will spread among them that you are not to be trusted."

Jean shrugged, showing little concern. "*C'est la vie*, eh? It does not matter now. I will not be trading for much longer. I am too old to make those long trips. I find I enjoy sitting around the village, visiting, making things with my knife, playing with the children."

"And loving the women?"

"Watch your tongue, girl; you are too young to speak of such things to me," Jean replied, a definite twinkle in his eye.

"*Naxane*," Aeneva said softly, feeling a sudden tenderness for this white man who was as close to her as her own grandfather, "I find I am a little frightened. Perhaps if you kissed me on both cheeks as you taught Grandmother to do, I would again find my courage." Aeneva pressed her knees into her horse's side and her mount stopped immediately.

Jean leaned over, took Aeneva's face in his large hands, and kissed her on either cheek. He looked at her a moment, his eyes slightly moist. "You are a good girl, Aeneva. But remember that fighting is not all there is to this life. There must be something more."

"I will remember, *naxane*. Thank you." She kissed him back and smiled.

Jean straightened up and cleared his throat. "Well, if you are to be my captive, look a little more unhappy. They will wonder why we are bestowing kisses on each other as if we were family."

"Yes, *naxane*. Thank you for everything you have always given to me and my brothers. Thank you for loving us and caring for us as only a true uncle would do."

Jean held up his hand. "Enough! I cannot take any more of your compliments. I am not used to this from you, girl. Usually I suffer a tongue-lashing from you."

Aeneva laughed, but stopped suddenly as she looked ahead. "There are riders, *naxane*." She strained to see. "Crows?"

"I imagine, girl. Now remember you hate me and don't be afraid to show it. Our lives will depend on it."

"They will never guess you are my uncle," Aeneva said softly, digging her heels into her horse. The horse pulled away sharply and the reins came out of Jean's hands.

"Come back here. Come back here, girl," Jean yelled behind her, riding at full speed to keep up with her.

Aeneva lay low against her horse's back, holding on as tightly as she could with her legs. When she was halfway between Jean and the Crows she loosened her hold with her legs and slipped to the side of her horse, falling onto the hard ground. She rolled over a few times before stopping and she grunted from the pain she felt throughout her body. She made a feeble attempt to get up and start running. She saw the Crows riding toward her now and Jean coming from the other direction. She hadn't run very far when she was scooped up by strong arms and tossed over the front of a horse. She tried to look up, but every time she lifted her head the man shoved it back down. The horse stopped and she heard Jean's voice speaking in Crow.

"The girl is my captive; I want her back."

The Crow warrior pulled Aeneva's head up by one braid, examining her face. "She is Cheyenne?"

"Yes. I am interested in trading her for supplies."

The Crow grunted and ran his hands along Aeneva's body, feeling the strength there. "This one is strong; she could do much work."

"She works as well as two men if you can keep her from trying to kill you," Jean protested.

The Crows laughed loudly and the Crow who had Aeneva on his horse pushed her to the ground. She landed in a heap, spitting at him and cursing him in Cheyenne. Again the Crows laughed loudly and the warrior asked, "What does she say?"

"She says your mother mates with buffalos," Jean translated.

The Crows laughed at the warrior and he, too,

laughed. "I like this one; she has much spirit. I could use another wife. Perhaps I will take her." He nodded to Jean. "Come, white man, we will talk."

Jean jumped down from his horse, carrying a length of rope. He approached Aeneva, but she kicked out at him, shrieking and spitting every time he got close. They put on a show for the Crows, who enjoyed watching Jean trying to tame the spirited woman. Eventually, Jean got the rope around Aeneva's waist and mounted his horse, pulling her along after him. He looked over at the Crow warrior who was interested in Aeneva. "I don't think you know what you're getting yourself into, friend. This one is a wildcat. I will be glad to get rid of her."

The Crow looked back at Aeneva, his face thoughtful. "You just do not know the way to handle women, white man. I will have her broken in a day."

Jean looked at the man and nodded, not doubting him for a second. He could well imagine the way he "broke" his women. He did not intend to leave Aeneva with this man for even half a day; it could prove to be fatal.

By the time they reached the Crow camp it was late afternoon. They had ridden well over six miles and Aeneva looked tired and sore, although her spirit was still intact. She tried to run away from Jean as he pulled the rope off her, but the Crow warrior walked over and hit her on the side of the head, knocking her to the ground. Aeneva lay still for a moment, dizzy from the blow. She looked up at the man and at Jean; she got up to her feet and spit in the Crow warrior's face. He raised his hand again, but this time Jean caught it in an iron grip before it landed.

"She is still my property, friend. We have not come to terms yet. When we have decided on a price, then you can do anything you want to the wench."

The Crow looked as if he were going to turn on Jean

for a second, but he nodded his head in agreement and walked away. Jean yanked Aeneva's arm and pulled her along after him. One of the Crow women led them to a small lodge where Jean was to stay. As a captive, Aeneva would have to be tied up outside the lodge and allowed to sleep inside only at night if Jean permitted her. Jean gently shoved Aeneva to the ground, tying her hands loosely to a stake. "Are you all right? I was afraid the bastard would knock your head off."

"I am all right, but my head is throbbing. The man is strong. I do not think I would like to be with him very long."

"Well, we will have to find out where the women are very soon. He wants you for his wife and he will make you mind him any way he can."

"Make the trade as soon as possible. Perhaps you can ask if there are other Cheyenne women you could trade for. Say that you have a special liking for them."

"That is a good idea." Jean stood up. "You rest now; you had a long walk. I will return when I find something out."

Aeneva nodded and instantly closed her eyes, not caring about the ropes that bound her wrists. All she wanted to do was sleep. She had never walked so far or so fast in her life and her head hurt more than she would tell Jean. She had a bad feeling about this. The Crow warrior was an evil one; she could see it. She had a feeling he would not let her go very easily.

Jean looked at two of the Cheyenne women that the Crow warrior, Black Fox, brought to him. Jean recognized them instantly: Laliya, the daughter of Standing Bear; and Flying Bird, the wife of Gray Beard. He looked at them as if he had never seen them before, motioning

186

them to step forward so he could examine their legs and hands, as if they were pieces of horseflesh to be bought and traded. "They are not as good to look at as the other, but they seem more docile," Jean said offhandedly. "Are they good workers?"

"They are strong and they are silent. They do as they are told."

"Good, I like that." Jean considered them a moment. "They are handsome women, the Cheyennes. You must agree, Crooked Teeth, or you would not have so many in your camp."

"Cheyenne women are handsome, but they also smell because they have lived with Cheyenne men." He laughed loudly, waiting for Jean to join in.

Jean laughed uproariously, his hand aching to smash the Crow in the face. "You are right, Crooked Teeth. It takes much time for the smell to go away."

"So, white man, you like these women? It is a good trade, two women for one."

"Ah, but the one woman, she is something, no? If I were many years younger, I, myself, would keep her. But, I am too old for taming women. I like them already tame when I buy them."

Crooked Teeth slapped Jean on the back. "I understand. I, too, weary of it. But this one, I think she will be a real challenge."

"She will be more than that, my friend."

After they made the trade, Jean and Crooked Teeth smoked and ate and they retired to their lodges to sleep. Jean would bring Aeneva to Crooked Teeth in the morning.

"You have made the trade?" Aeneva asked him as he sat down next to her.

"Yes. We smoked and ate and now we are to sleep.

When I awaken, I will take you to him.''

"Did you get to see any of the women?"

"Laliya and Flying Bird. I am trading you for them."

"Very good, Uncle."

"Not so good, Aeneva. I don't like the thought of leaving you with that animal for even a few hours."

"I will be all right, Uncle; do not worry. When you have the women, you can find out where the others are. Then you can return with our men."

"I am worried, Aeneva. The man seeks to do you harm."

"He will not have enough time, Uncle. Please, do not worry. I will be fine."

'I hope so, little girl. I would never forgive myself if anything happened to you.''

Aeneva tried to lift her head, but she could not. For the first time in her life, she felt completely helpless. Jean was right—Crooked Teeth wanted to harm her and he was doing a good job of it. Already he had whipped her, beaten her with his fists, and pushed her face into the dirt until she felt the grains between her teeth. She could smell Crooked Teeth's rotten breath and she turned her face away from his, trying to breathe in some fresh air. Crooked Teeth pulled her face back, holding it between his hands, forcing her to look up at him.

"I have a surprise for you, girl. Your friend, the Frenchman, is still here."

Aeneva felt her stomach lurch; she knew something had gone wrong. "What do you mean?"

"One of my men recognized him. He saw him in your camp the night we raided it. You and he were sent here to trap us. I am sure there are other Cheyenne pigs waiting out there for us. Is that right, girl?"

"I do not know what you are talking about." Aeneva tried to calm the fear inside her, but she recoiled when she saw the fist coming toward her. She cried out, unable to stop herself. She didn't want to break down in front of this man; she didn't want to give him the satisfaction. "I have never seen the Frenchman before."

"You are lying. I do not like my women to lie to me." He ripped Aeneva's dress from her. His eyes scanned her body and face, and he removed his knife from its sheath on his thigh. He shifted the point across Aeneva's face, waving it in front of each eye and resting it on her chin. He moved it slowly from her chin, down her throat, to her chest. Aeneva tried not to move; she held her breath. She felt the sharp point of the knife as it cut into her flesh. Crooked Teeth was only trying to scare her now; the real torture would come later. The knife traced a line down her chest, between her breasts to the skin of her belly. He stuck the point in her belly and Aeneva closed her eyes, readying herself for the blade to go all the way in; it did not. She felt Crooked Teeth's weight on top of her and she felt his breath next to her face. "You are brave, girl. I admire that. I will keep you alive because of it. For a while at least." Crooked Teeth raped Aeneva while still holding the knife at her throat. When he was through, he tied her hands and feet, staking her to a pole in his lodge so she couldn't move. He stood over her, adjusting his breechcloth and resheathing his knife. "I will let you see the Frenchman soon. But I want him to suffer first."

Aeneva watched him as he walked out of the lodge and she turned her head away, closing her eyes to the fear and the pain. Tears filled her eyes and she began to cry for the first time since she was a small girl. For the first time in many years, she was completely helpless and all her skill and training could do nothing to save her or Jean.

CHAPTER X

Jean lifted his head from his chest, a simple gesture but one that at the moment took a monumental effort. He had to hand it to the Crows; not only had they made him suffer, they had done it in very little time. They didn't want to linger around and wait for Stalking Horse and his men to attack, so they tortured Jean, found out nothing, broke camp, and left in the middle of the night. He tugged at the bindings which held him to the cross-poles, wishing that the leather would not tighten with every movement. His body was blistered from the hot sticks they had poked all over him, and his limbs were stretched to the very limit on the poles. Crooked Teeth had derived particular pleasure from cutting pieces of Jean's body off with his knife. As near as he could remember, he'd lost almost three toes, five fingers and his left ear lobe. The pain didn't matter now; he only wanted it to end. But he had to stay alive long enough to tell Stalking Horse where they had gone. He had heard Crooked Teeth tell some of his men to pack up and head for their site in the hills. It was beyond the trees and the river in a place called Turtle Creek. Crooked Teeth was not taking any chances; he wouldn't be taken by surprise.

Jean heard a sound, a loud cry, and he was shocked to realize that it was he, as his head fell back against the pole. Crooked Teeth had taken part of Jean's scalp, and the exposed flesh was tender. Although a white man's scalp was not as valuable as another Indian's, it would still be something of a prize to have the scalp lock of light-haired white man. Crooked Teeth held the bloodied scalp in front of Jean's face and screamed, delighting in his act. Jean looked at Crooked Teeth, and in spite of the blinding pain, he smiled. That smile cost him a broken jaw.

He knew he was dying; he felt the life draining out of him as every minute went by. He wanted so desperately to help Aeneva, but she had been taken away and he was able to do nothing. Both of them were helpless to assist each other; and both of them would suffer for it.

The morning sun beat down on his half-naked body, causing the blisters and the wound in his scalp to seem on fire. He heard noises, but couldn't make out what they were. Nothing was clear to him; everything was a circle of pain. He heard birds above him and he didn't have to look up to know that vultures, smelling imminent death, were circling and waiting, just biding their time for the moment when he died. "I am sorry, Aeneva. Forgive me, Stalking Horse and Sun Dancer. Forgive me." His head fell forward on his chest and there was no more movement.

"Look, Grandfather, over there." Coyote Boy pointed to something in the distance.

"What is it? Can you see?"

Stalking Horse didn't have to wait to be told; he knew that it was his friend, his brother, hanging there. He urged his mount into a gallop and arrived first, jumping from his horse before it stopped. He ran to Jean, took out his knife, and cut the bindings that held him, catching Jean as he fell limply into his arms. Tears stung his eyes as he carried the thin frame of his friend and placed him gently on the ground.

"Bring me water," he cried to his grandsons as they rode up. Stalking Horse held a drinking vessel to Jean's lips, pouring some of the water over his face and body.

"Is he alive?" Coyote Boy asked tentatively.

Stalking Horse nodded. "He is alive. Barely." He looked up at his grandsons. "Make something so we can get him out of the sun."

While Brave Wolf, Coyote Boy, and some of the others constructed a makeshift lean-to, Stalking Horse shielded Jean from the sun with a blanket held over his face. He continued to moisten Jean's lips with water and rub it over his body.

"It is ready, Grandfather." Brave Wolf reached down and helped Stalking Horse carry Jean to the lean-to, laying him on a soft robe.

"Leave us," he ordered the young men. "Go look for your sister. Try to see what direction they went. We will wait for you here."

"I will stay," Brave Wolf protested.

Stalking Horse waved him away. "Do not argue with me, boy; I do not need your protection. When you find out which way your sister has gone, you can return for me and your uncle. Go now."

The younger men of the party rode off in the direction of the Crow camp, but Stalking Horse did not watch them go. He continued to nurse his friend, talking to him of the times they had spent together. He talked as if nothing were wrong, as if Jean would recover at any minute. Stalking Horse recalled the time so long ago when Jean had saved his life. They had been hunting and had been attacked by a grizzly bear. Stalking Horse had been badly hurt by the animal, and Jean had made a travois and pulled him on it across the prairie for almost three days.

"It is good to see your face, old friend." Jean's voice was almost a whisper.

Stalking Horse looked down at Jean, incapable of believing his friend had suffered so much. He held the drinking vessel to Jean's mouth. "That is enough for now; more will make you sick."

"Sick? Does it matter?" Jean asked with a grim smile on his face.

"It matters. I will take you home."

"Do not fool yourself, *hoovehe*. I will not make it."

"Then I will still take you home," Stalking Horse replied solemnly, holding on to his friend.

"I knew you would come; I tried to stay alive long enough. Damned Crows; who would've ever thought they'd finish me off." He tried to sit up, but yelled out. "*Sacré bleu!* My head feels as if it is on fire."

"They have taken your hair, *Veho*."

"You do not have to tell me that!" Jean cried out, laughing as he did so.

Stalking Horse could not control himself and he, too, laughed, shaking his head. "It is like you to laugh, even when you know you are going to die."

"Better to laugh than to cry, no?" Jean reached out for Stalking Horse's arm. "Help me to sit up, old friend; I want to look out at the world when I die. And I have things to tell you."

Stalking Horse held Jean against him so he could sit up. "Aeneva?"

"She has been taken by a Crow named Crooked Teeth, a mean bastard."

"He did this to you?"

"*Oui,* so you must find Aeneva as soon as you can."

"Do you know where they went, Jean?"

194

"I overheard Crooked Teeth tell one of his men to pack up, that they were going back to their camp up in the hills, beyond the trees and the river, to a place called Turtle Creek. That is all I know."

"It is enough. You rest now."

"I do not want to rest. In a short while I will be resting for all eternity. I want to talk now."

"You always want to talk, *Veho*."

"It is the beauty of me, no?" Jean flashed a brilliant smile that made his broken jaw ache. His eyes were suddenly serious. "Tell Sun Dancer that I love her. She was the world to me for a very long time. If you had not been my blood brother, I would have killed you and taken her away."

"Do you think I did not know that? I never trusted you, *Veho*."

Jean grinned, reaching up to hold his jaw. "She was beautiful, wasn't she? Aeneva is so much like her." His face filled with pain. "You must find Aeneva. I am sorry I failed you, my friend."

"You did not fail; you could do nothing. We will find Aeneva. Do not worry yourself. She is strong and she will survive until we can find her."

Jean shook his head anxiously. "I do not know, *mon ami*. This one is cruel. He enjoys causing pain."

Stalking Horse's expression hardened. "Do not worry, *hoovehe*. We will find Aeneva and I will see that this Crooked Teeth pays for what he has done to both of you."

"It is not like you to talk revenge, Stalking Horse."

Stalking Horse looked down at Jean. "I remember a time when you saved my life. You did not know me well then, but you risked your life for mine. There was also the time that you saved Sun Dancer. I owe you, *hoovehe*.

I owe you much more than I can ever repay."

"Then do not talk of revenge. Just get Aeneva back."

"I am not talking about revenge; I am talking about blood. You are the only brother I have ever had; you were closer to me than a true brother could be. No one does this to my brother and lives. Crooked Teeth will pay dearly for his cruelty."

Jean saw there was no point in arguing and he didn't feel up to it. He coughed and he had difficulty breathing. One of his lungs had been injured when Crooked Teeth had beaten him. He coughed again; this time little spittles of blood came out. He looked up at Stalking Horse and saw the pain there, as well as the love, and he nodded his head, smiling. "It is all right, old friend. It is better this way. Rather I than you or Sun Dancer. I will be waiting for you two in Seyan. I hope I go to Seyan."

"You will be there, *Veho*. You will be there hunting buffalo, trapping beaver, and chasing women. You will be having a good time while I must work hard here on earth."

Jean laughed and started to cough, holding on to Stalking Horse's arm. "Good-by, old friend. *Ne-sta-va-hose-voomatse.*" He closed his eyes and his head fell against Stalking Horse's chest, a slight smile still on his face.

Stalking Horse wiped the blood from Jean's mouth and nodded, tears streaming down his face. "Yes, I will see you again, my friend. May your trip be a good one."

Trenton and Joe rode into the village during the day. It was almost fall and the women were busily preparing skins, robes, and clothes for the winter, as well as drying meat, vegetables, and fruits for their winter stock. Ever since they had left Missouri, Joe was constantly amazed by the beauty and openness of the land.

"I thought I knew freedom, but I never really knew it till now."

"Now you know why my people love their land so."

It had been a natural decision for Trenton to seek out Stalking Horse's band rather than his mother's people, for he felt closest to Aeneva and her family. He couldn't wait for Aeneva and Sun Dancer to see Nathan; he hoped they'd be proud he'd given up his quest for revenge and set upon building a new life for himself and his son.

"Those things are even bigger than the pictures," Joe said in an awe-struck voice as he pointed to the buffalo that grazed nearby.

"Big but peaceful. They have always lived side by side with the Indians; they seem to know they are hunted out of necessity, not cruelty."

Joe nodded at the lodges in the distance. "How do you know that's the village of Stalking Horse?"

"We've tried most of the places they hunt and they haven't been there. It's easy if you follow the buffalo. If that's not Stalking Horse's band, they can probably tell me where he is now. The bands all meet in the early summer. Even though they travel separately most of the year, they are able to communicate with each other."

When Trenton and Joe reached the outskirts of the village, they were approached by some Cheyennes who wanted to know who they were and what they wanted. When Trenton spoke to them in Cheyenne, telling them he was a friend of Stalking Horse and Sun Dancer, he was escorted into the village and taken to Sun Dancer's lodge. He carried Nathan in a backpack, much the same way Indian women carried their babies in cradleboards. He found it much easier to ride, while Nathan slept most of the time.

"I'll wait here," Joe said apprehensively, looking all

around him. He reached up, took the straps of the back-pack from Trenton's shoulder, and held Nathan in his arms. "You go visit with your friend. Nate and I will stay out here in the sunshine."

"I'll be back soon." Trenton walked to the lodge door and spoke loudly. "*Haahe*, Sun Dancer. *Na-hoh-ohe-hoh-ohtse*. I have come to visit."

"*Nevaahe taoh-ohtohe?*"

Trenton smiled happily; Sun Dancer sounded as warm and friendly as he had remembered. He walked through the lodge door. Sun Dancer was at the back of the lodge. "It is Trenton, Sun Dancer."

She stood up, looking toward him. "Trenton?" She walked forward, a bright smile spreading across her still-beautiful and youthful face. She held out her hands and Trenton took them. "It is you, Trenton. I knew you would return."

Trenton pulled Sun Dancer to him, hugging her, realizing what a special woman she was and how much she had affected his life. "You are still as beautiful as I remember."

Sun Dancer waved her hand at him, smiling girlishly. "Ah, Trenton, you have not changed. You still have a way with words. You did, even as a young boy."

"I spoke honestly as a yong boy; my mother and father taught me that."

"So the words you spoke to Aeneva were true?"

"I did not lie to her; I always intended to come back here to her. But things happened, things that changed my life." He breathed deeply, looking away from Sun Dancer for the first time.

Sun Dancer reached up and touched Trenton's face, forcing him to look at her. "Sometimes things happen which are beyond our control."

198

"You always saw things that other people did not. You are so special, Sun Dancer."

"It is good to see you, Trenton. Your words are kind to these old ears. But come,"—she waved him over to a backrest—"sit down and we will talk. I think you have many things you would like to tell me."

"More than I care to admit." Trenton shook his head impatiently. "I have been very foolish, Sun Dancer. I will tell you about it and you can see for yourself." Trenton related the details of the last five years of his life, omitting nothing, even his relationship with Lydia. He described their life in St. Louis and everything that had happened there. The only time his face showed signs of brightness was when he talked of his son or Joe.

"Where is your son, Trenton? And this friend of yours?"

"They are waiting outside. I wanted to speak to you alone first. I wanted to see if we would be welcome."

"Now you are being foolish; you are always welcome here. Bring them in; I am anxious to meet them both."

"In a moment, Sun Dancer. I want to ask you about Aeneva."

"What about Aeneva?"

"How is she? Is she married? Does she hate me?"

"Why would she hate you? She was hurt when you did not return, but she did not waste her time. She is doing what she has always wanted to do; she is a warrior."

"You are serious?"

"I am very serious. She has already fought in many battles and proven herself to be very able."

"You don't seem surprised."

"I have seen her all of these years, Trenton; I knew it would happen. She was different even as a child; she had no fear of anything. She is still the same way."

"Has she married?"

"She says she will never marry. She wants only to devote herself to being a warrior."

"Where is she, Sun Dancer? I must speak to her."

"She is not here, Trenton. She has been gone for over a moon now. She is on a raiding party with her brothers and grandfather. They have gone into Crow country to try to get back some of our women."

"You are still at it with the Crows?"

"It seems it will never end with them. We hate each other so much and I do not really know why. I often remember what my father told me once about this bitterness between our people." She paused as if trying to recall her father's exact words. "He said that we are not bad people and they are not bad people, but we fight each other because we have done it for so long, we know no other way. We think of the Crows as being such terrible people, but we Cheyennes have also done terrible things to them."

"I am beginning to realize how much I have missed you, Sun Dancer. Your words come like a fresh breeze on a hot day."

Sun Dancer smiled, shaking her finger at Trenton. "Your words may work on me, but you will have a more difficult time with Aeneva. Her anger will not subside so easily."

"There is no reason that it should; she has a right to be angry at me."

"Enough of this for now. I am anxious to meet your son and your friend. Bring them to me."

While Trenton and Joe were working on their second helping of food, Sun Dancer rocked back and forth on the robe, holding Nathan in her arms. She sang softly to him, touching him lightly on the head and cheek. She smiled and looked up at Trenton. "He is a beautiful child, Trenton. He is so much like you."

"He is a good boy. We have ridden hundreds of miles on horseback and he hasn't given us any problems. I am lucky to have him."

"Yes, you are." Sun Dancer touched the baby; then directed her next question to Joe. "And you, Joe, what do you think of Trenton's son?"

"I think he's going to be about the luckiest boy alive—with a father like him and friends like us to care for him." Joe smiled brightly, hoping that Sun Dancer would not take offense.

"I think you are right, Joe. He is a lucky boy. Have you had enough to eat? You have both traveled a long way."

"I'm fine, thank you, ma'am," Joe replied formally.

"You can call me Sun Dancer. I do not know what Trenton has told you about me, but I am not as important as you think. I am just an old woman who tries to heal people if she can."

"Well, just the same, ma'am, I think you're more than that. I can see just by the way you look."

Sun Dancer looked at Joe, then over at Trenton. "I see that you and your friend both have a gift with words." They all laughed and Sun Dancer laid Nathan on the robe next to her. "I will have a lodge prepared for you two so you can rest. We will talk more later. Leave this one with me so we can become acquainted," she said gently, looking down at Nathan.

"We don't need a lodge, Sun Dancer—"

"Do not argue, Trenton. You will be here for a time and you will need a suitable lodging. Finish your food."

"That's some lady." Joe whistled after Sun Dancer left.

"Yes, she's more of a lady than any I've ever met."

"She must've been a real beauty."

"My father says she was the most beautiful woman he'd ever seen. He called her his Indian princess."

"I can see why. What about the granddaughter?"

"She's not here. I'm going to wait until she comes back. You don't have to stay, Joe. With some of the money we made gambling, you can travel anywhere you like."

"I kind of like it here right now. I think I'll stay for a while. These people don't seem to notice the color of my skin too much."

"I was hoping you'd stay. But anytime you're ready to leave—"

"I'll let you know, boy. Don't worry."

"Your friend is a good hunter," Sun Dancer said, looking out to the herd of buffalo.

"Yes, I think Joe would like to become a Cheyenne. He seems to be right at home here."

"Like another man I know."

"How is Jean?" Trenton asked cautiously, realizing that he was not around.

"I do not know."

"Where is he?"

"He is with Stalking Horse and the others."

"Then he is all right."

"I cannot be sure of that, Trenton. I have had certain feelings for days now."

"What kind of feelings?"

Sun Dancer took her eyes away from the hunters and went back to her digging. "Do you remember that I had visions—I was able to 'see' certain things?"

"Yes."

"I had a dream-vision some time ago. I saw Jean and Stalking Horse killed in it. I do not know when it will be, but I have had strange feelings about Jean for days; I know that something is wrong."

"You think that he is hurt?"

"Or worse." Sun Dancer pulled out a plant. Having examined the roots, she put it into her basket.

"What about Stalking Horse?"

"I have had no such feelings. He is well; I am sure of it."

Trenton knelt down next to Sun Dancer. "Do you want me to try to find them, Sun Dancer?"

"I cannot ask you to do that."

"You did not ask. I'd like to help if I can."

"You may not be able to help, Trenton."

"But maybe I can. You must tell me everything about the Crows who raided your camp and where Stalking Horse had planned to go."

"You do not have to do this."

"I want to do it; I want to help you in any way that I can. If Jean is hurt, I can bring him back here while they continue their search. I'll set out in the morning."

"Does this have anything to do with Aeneva?"

"I am anxious to see Aeneva, but I want to ease your mind also. You will be crazy if they don't come back for a long time and you don't know whether—"

"Jean is alive or dead."

"Yes. You will take care of Nathan for me?"

"I will watch him like he is one of my own."

"He already is one of your own." Trenton took the root digger from Sun Dancer and pushed it into the ground.

"I do not need your help, Trenton." Sun Dancer reached for the digger but Trenton refused to give it back.''

"I want to help you. You tell me what to dig and I will dig it for you.''

"I am not that old.''

"I didn't say you were old; I said I wanted to help you. It's not often that I volunteer to help a woman.''

"I will take your help. And later you can help me scrape hides.''

Trenton looked over at Sun Dancer, shaking his head. "You are cunning, Sun Dancer. I'll bet Stalking Horse didn't have a chance against you.''

"What do you mean?''

"You know what I mean. I only hope Aeneva isn't as smart as you.''

"She is smarter.''

"Then I haven't got a chance.''

"It doesn't displease you?''

"We will have to wait and see, Sun Dancer. Aeneva and I have changed a lot.''

"You have both changed, but your feelings are still the same.''

"You are sure?''

"I am sure.'' She grabbed the digger from Trenton and stood up. "That is enough. Come, we have many skins to scrape.''

Trenton stood up, putting his arm around Sun Dancer. "Now I know why my father was so in love with you.''

"Your father was in love with me?''

"He told me that he dreamed about you all the time. He said you were the most beautiful woman he'd ever seen, an Indian princess.''

"Your father was very kind. Just like you. But I have had enough of your sweet words, Trenton. We have work to do.''

Sun Dancer was holding Nathan and singing to him. She was about to talk with him when she heard people yelling in the camp. She started forward and a runner came to her, telling her that Stalking Horse was back. She looked for Trenton, but couldn't find him. She hurried to the entrance to the camp from which she saw riders in the distance and the travois that Stalking Horse pulled behind him. She also saw Jean's riderless mount. She held Nathan tightly in her arms, as if holding him so would assure her that nothing was wrong. She knew it was not so. She watched the sadness in Stalking Horse's eyes as he rode up.

He stopped, looking down at her. He saw the baby.

"That is a white baby."

"He is Trenton's son." Her eyes went back to the travois behind Stalking Horse's horse. "It is Jean?"

Stalking Horse nodded, anger and bitterness suddenly replacing sadness in his eyes. "He was tortured by the Crows. The same Crows who have Aeneva."

"No." Sun Dancer shut her eyes to the words. She had lost her son and daughter to the Crows; she could not lose Aeneva also.

"*Haahe*, Stalking Horse." Trenton ran to where Stalking Horse and Sun Dancer stood, immediately sensing that something was wrong.

"Trenton. It is good to see you."

"And you, Stalking Horse." His eyes now went to the travois.

"It is Jean," Sun Dancer said sadly, handing Nathan to Trenton.

"The Crows tortured him."

"I'm sorry, Stalking Horse." He watched as Sun Dancer walked to the robe-covered travois.

"That is not all, boy." Stalking Horse dismounted and stood next to Trenton. "They have taken Aeneva." Stalking Horse watched as Trenton's eyes showed first dismay, then anger.

"When?"

"It has been eight days now. Her brothers are looking for her."

"Do you know where they've taken her?"

"Beyond the river that the whites call the Yellowstone, to a place called Turtle Creek."

"Do you know how many are in the band?"

"It is a small band now, but they could be joining a larger one at this new place."

"I know that area. I traveled there for the army making maps. I know where many of the Crow encampments are."

"You will look for her?" Stalking Horse asked hopefully.

Trenton reached out and pressed Stalking Horse's shoulder. "I will find her, Stalking Horse. I will bring her back." He walked over to Sun Dancer who was sitting silently by Jean's body. He knelt down next to her. "I am sorry about Jean, Sun Dancer. I know that you loved him like a brother."

"Yes," Sun Dancer replied softly.

"We cannot bring him back, but I promise you that I will bring Aeneva back. I promise you that." He kissed her on the cheek and walked back to Stalking Horse. "I will leave as soon as I pack."

Stalking Horse walked over to Sun Dancer, helping her up. "Come, Sun Dancer, there is nothing we can do for him now."

"What they did to his body—"

"Do not think about it; the pain is over for him now."

"Did he talk at the end?"

"He talked and he laughed."

"He laughed?"

"He said it was better to laugh than to cry."

"What else did he say?"

"He said to tell you that he loved you and that you were his world for a long time. He thought you were so beautiful."

Sun Dancer looked up at Stalking Horse, her lips trembling and tears clouding her eyes. "He was the beautiful one; his heart was big enough for five people."

"He was not afraid, Sun Dancer. He said he was glad it was this way; he wanted to die before you or I. He said he would meet us in Seyan."

"He will have a good time there," Sun Dancer agreed, unable to contain a smile.

"That is what I told him and he laughed. Sun Dancer,"—Stalking Horse took Sun Dancer's shoulders—"I must go back. I must kill the man who did this to Jean. Do you understand?"

"I understand, Stalking Horse. I understand." She leaned forward, resting her head on her husband's chest, letting the tears flow freely now. Not only did she understand Stalking Horse's need to kill the man who had done this to Jean, she also understood that he would not return alive. She held on to him, wishing that she could die with him, but knowing that she would have to go on for a time without him, and that time on earth would seem like an eternity.

Sun Dancer and Stalking Horse prepared Jean's body with great care. Sun Dancer dressed him in his best clothes and wrapped him in the robe she had made for him so many years before. He loved the robe and had re-

207

fused to let her make a new one for him. Jean had not been a warrior, but he had always carried an old Kentucky rifle with him and the hunting knife that he had used to skin the thousands of beaver he trapped. He had had many books, but he had asked Sun Dancer and Stalking Horse to keep them and give them to their grandchildren. He still had the lance and shield which Stalking Horse had given him all the years before when he had saved Stalking Horse's life. Jean had loved the mountains and the mountains would be his burial ground; so Sun Dancer and Stalking Horse made a quiet, solemn journey to the mountains Jean loved so dearly. Stalking Horse built the scaffold next to Jean's cabin, placing all of his personal possessions around him. They wrapped him tightly in another robe and placed him on the scaffold, hanging the shield and lance in front. Although there was still sadness in their hearts, Stalking Horse and Sun Dancer knew that Jean's spirit had already found the trail where the footprints all pointed the same way and that he had followed the Hanging Road to Seyan, where he had already met his relatives and friends. Stalking Horse sang a song and he and Sun Dancer both prayed to the Great Spirit that Jean might have a safe journey.

"Good-by, old friend." Stalking Horse waved to the scaffold as he mounted his horse.

Sun Dancer looked at Stalking Horse and smiled slightly. "We will be with you soon, Jean." She leaned over and took Stalking Horse's hand and they rode slowly down the mountain together.

Trenton swung down from his horse and walked to the fire pit. He moved the ashes around with his fingers. "They were here this morning."

"How are you sure it's them?" Joe asked, dismounting from his horse.

"There's a difference between Indian ponies. Since they don't wear shoes, they have distinct prints and you can always tell how many there are. Stalking Horse told me there were ten other Cheyennes besides Brave Wolf and Coyote Boy. It's them."

"How do you know they were here this morning?" Joe motioned to the fire.

"The ashes are still warm. It means they were here within the last few hours."

"It sounds pretty hopeless to me, boy. You can't even find the Cheyennes who are looking for the Crows who kidnapped this girl. From what you told me about how much they hate each other, the girl might not even be alive."

"You don't know her, Joe. She'll be alive. She has too much spirit."

"Even the most spirited horse can be broken, boy. And if the horse won't be broken, it'll die."

Trenton looked at Joe, a shocked expression on his face. He started to protest that Aeneva wouldn't die, but the more he thought about it, the more truth he saw in it. Aeneva was like a spirited horse and if she couldn't be free, she would rather be dead. He swung up on his horse and turned to the north. "Let's go, Joe. I'm going to find her."

"I hope you do, boy. I hope you do."

Aeneva tugged at the ropes that bound her, but as always, they were too tight for her to wriggle her hands even slightly. She looked over at Crooked Teeth and his three wives, the anger inside her intensifying as she did so. She hated them all, but she especially hated Crooked Teeth. The man had abused and humiliated her in the

209

worst ways and he seemed to derive continual pleasure out of it. She strained angrily at the ropes, but still they didn't budge. She lay down on the hard ground of the lodge, curling up for warmth. She was not provided with robe or blanket and the only reason Crooked Teeth permitted her to sleep inside the lodge was to make sure she didn't try to escape. She had already tried twice to escape and both times had been caught and badly beaten. She was sure some of her ribs were cracked from Crooked Teeth's last beating, but she didn't want to let him know of any more weak spots; she had already provided him with too many.

She tried to empty her mind of her angry thoughts, but she could not; she kept remembering Jean as she had last seen him tortured and dying. Her eyes overflowed with tears. Jean had smiled at her through his pain and he had given her the courage to go on when she had thought she would give up. She often considered killing herself; she knew that if she could not escape Crooked Teeth, she would be dead. But she would try to escape because she wanted a chance to seek her own revenge on Crooked Teeth. She heard grunting sounds in the lodge and knew that Crooked Teeth was taking one of his wives. She tried to close her ears to the sounds, but they seemed to reverberate throughout her brain. The man was a pig and he was insatiable in his lust for Aeneva and his wives. Aeneva tried not to think too much about this part of her captivity; for although she was a skilled and experienced warrior and hunter, she had known nothing of men or the physical act of love. She had been so sure that one day she and Trenton would be together. . . . But that was not to be; if things went according to Crooked Teeth's plan, she would never seen Trenton again.

The sounds in the lodge finally stopped and Aeneva

knew she was safe until the next night. Crooked Teeth would wait until then before he decided which wife he would use. She forced herself to clear her mind of all things which would deter her from her purpose—survival and eventual escape. She had to focus all of her positive energy into being strong and cunning and somehow finding a way to escape Crooked Teeth. Then, when she was free and had time to become strong again, she would plan with relish how she would kill Crooked Teeth. There could be no sweeter revenge for her now.

CHAPTER XI

Trenton found the band of Crooked Teeth quite unexpectedly. He had been looking for Brave Wolf and the rest of the Cheyenne raiding party, but had found other tracks. The moccasin prints were different from the ones he had been following and one thing was easy to detect—the Crows were leading a captive on a rope. It had to be Aeneva. Trenton couldn't believe that Crooked Teeth would leave such an easy trail to follow, but Crooked Teeth had no idea that Jean had overheard him say where he was going; Crooked Teeth made the additional mistake of assuming Jean would die quickly from the torture. It was a fatal mistake to underestimate the strength and courage of the Frenchman.

In spite of Aeneva's having to travel on foot, Crooked Teeth kept a good pace. Aeneva would either keep up or she would be dragged; Trenton had seen the practice before. His own people had once done it to some Kiowa women they had captured. Trenton's real concern was to keep close to the Crows without being spotted.

"What about your friends? What if you get the girl out and they don't know about it?" Joe asked as he handed Trenton some dried beef. They were resting in the heat of the day, waiting again until night fell before they continued tracking.

"Aeneva comes first. Once I get her out, I can try to

find Brave Wolf and the others.'' He shook his head, trying to concentrate. ''I don't understand where the hell they are. We were following them for days and suddenly lost them and found the Crows. It doesn't make any sense.''

''Maybe the Crows found them first.''

''No, we would've seen some signs of a fight. Dead bodies at least. The Crows wouldn't have buried the bodies of Cheyennes; if anything, they would've mutilated them and left them for the birds and animals.''

''Maybe they spotted the Crows and went another way. Maybe they're waiting for them up ahead somewhere.''

''God, I hope so. We could use some help. If we do find those Crows, I don't know how the hell I'm going to get in there and get Aeneva out without getting caught.''

''Maybe I should go; they wouldn't be able to see me at night.''

Trenton laughed. ''Good thought, but as heavy-footed as you are, you'd warn them before you even got off your horse.''

''Well, how else you going to do it, boy? They ain't gonna just let you walk in there and take her out. We already seen how much they like white men.''

''No, but a true Indian can't resist a good trade. I've got to think of something that Crooked Teeth can't resist.''

''What about guns? You said they're always looking for guns.''

''Yes, but I'm thinking about something even more irresistible to a man like Crooked Teeth.''

''Like what?''

''Like Cheyennes.''

Joe sat forward, his dark eyes drilling into Trenton's.

"I don't like the way you're talking, boy. You wouldn't tell them where your Cheyenne friends are?"

"How could he resist Stalking Horse's two grandsons? He's had his granddaughter . . ." He stopped. "I've got to find Brave Wolf."

"Well, I'm glad to know you're going to tell him about your little plan. For a while there I was afraid you were going to sacrifice them for the girl."

"The thought had entered my mind," Trenton replied honestly, "but Aeneva wouldn't want it that way. And I couldn't do that to my friends."

"Sounds to me like we've got a hard ride ahead of us."

"I've got to figure out where the hell they went, Joe. If we can't pick up their trail, I don't know what we're going to do."

"If anybody can do it, boy, you can."

"I hope so." Trenton stood up and walked his horse. "Let's get started while it's still light. I want to see if I can pick up their trail."

Trenton tried to think as Brave Wolf would. Brave Wolf would know that Crooked Teeth was expecting him to follow and probably had backriders checking to see if the Cheyennes were pursuing him. So Brave Wolf had done just that for a time. Then he had stopped abruptly, making Crooked Teeth think he had given up. But Trenton knew that Brave Wolf would never give up looking for his little sister. Brave Wolf had probably chosen an alternate route to get to Crooked Teeth's other encampment. The problem that faced Trenton was how to figure out which route.

He and Joe rode on through the night, trying to get as deep into Crow territory as they could. There was always the possibility that they would be spied by another band of Crows and attacked before they could do anything.

215

Trenton tried to make sure that didn't happen. He used every bit of knowledge his father, Jean, and his mother's people had taught him about tracking. He would need all of it if he were to find Brave Wolf and Aeneva.

Trenton picked up Brave Wolf's trail again two days after he had lost it. As he had thought he might, Brave Wolf had traveled northeast, circling around Crooked Teeth's band. He was obviously trying to reach the area where Crooked Teeth was headed in order to try to cut him off. Trenton was sure Brave Wolf was traveling much the same way he and Joe were—resting during the heat of the day, doing most of the riding in the early morning, late afternoon, and night. They were too deep into Crow territory now to risk being attacked.

"Well, what do you think?" Joe looked down at Trenton, who was kneeling on the ground examining tracks.

"I think we're real close. These are the freshest tracks I've seen; the outline of the hoof has hardly been disturbed. We should find them by tomorrow if we're lucky."

They were lucky. By riding straight through that day and all through the night, they came upon Brave Wolf's camp at dawn. The Cheyennes were still sleeping. Trenton saw the two guards; he cupped his hands around his mouth and out came the surprisingly lifelike howl of a wolf. Both guards turned toward the howl and they saw Trenton. Their weary horses stopped, heads hanging low, the riders made the peace sign and asked for Brave Wolf. Brave Wolf came immediately.

"We knew we were being followed, but we could not lose whoever it was that was following us. We were sure it was not the Crows; we knew we had lost them. Of course it would be you, Swiftly Running Deer, you who were always the best tracker. *Naxane* said you were good

216

like your father.''

Trenton laughed. He swung down from his horse and walked forward to embrace Brave Wolf. "It is good to see you, Brave Wolf. I'm just sorry it's like this.''

"You know about *naxane?*''

"And Aeneva. That's why I'm here. I had the Crows trailed; I was right behind them. Then I thought of a plan.'' He turned around and motioned Joe down. "This is my friend, Joe. He is also like a brother to me.''

Brave Wolf extended his hand and Joe took it. "You are welcome here, friend of Swiftly Running Deer. Now, let us talk further about this plan of yours.''

They walked back into the small camp. While they sat eating dried beef and fruit, Trenton told Brave Wolf, Coyote Boy, and the others of his plan.

"How do you know this Crooked Teeth will believe you? You saw what he did to *naxane*. He has no great love for white men.''

"I know; Joe already asked me that. But I think Crooked Teeth hates you and your people so much, that he would jump at a chance to get back at you.''

"Why should he let Aeneva go? He could just get the information from you, kill you, and come for us.'' Brave Wolf shook his head. "I do not like it, Trenton. This one is a bad one; he cannot be trusted.''

"What if you suggest a trade?'' Joe asked. All eyes turned to him. "What if you tell him Brave Wolf has some Crow women and boys whom he's willing to trade for Aeneva? Maybe he'd go for that.''

"He might,'' Trenton said thoughtfully.

"I have a better trade.'' Coyote Boy spoke up. "What if you offer him one of Aeneva's brothers, grandson of Stalking Horse. He could not refuse.''

"No!'' Brave Wolf replied sharply. "I will not let you

sacrifice yourself. We will find another way.''

"I would gladly give my life for Aeneva's, Brother. I am not afraid to die at the hands of the Crows.''

"I know you are not afraid, Brother, but we cannot risk your life. If there is a chance we can get Aeneva out alive without risking your life, that is how we must do it.''

"I do not understand you, Brave Wolf. It is a risk just to be here. What more risk is there in my offering to trade myself for Aeneva? I am sorry; you cannot refuse me in this.''

Brave Wolf looked at his brother angrily, but Trenton interrupted him before he spoke. "I think I speak for Brave Wolf when I say enough lives have been lost already—Jean's, those of innocent Cheyenne women, and possibly Aeneva's. It would be painful for Brave Wolf and for your grandparents to lose two grandchildren.''

Coyote Boy was silent, looking first at Trenton, then at his brother. "I understand my brother's love for me, Trenton, but what kind of man would I be if I sat here and did nothing to help my sister? She may be strong and a skilled warrior, but she is still only a young girl. In the hands of a man like Crooked Teeth . . .'' He stood up, kicking his foot at the ground in frustration. "I cannot bear the thought of what he has done to her.''

Trenton stood up, placing his hand on Coyote Boy's shoulder. "Nor can I, my friend. That is why we are all here.''

Coyote Boy sighed heavily and nodded his head. He sat back down in the small circle. "All right, I will listen to your plan.''

"Good.'' Trenton slapped him on the back and sat down next to him. "I think both Joe and Coyote Boy have the right idea. Crooked Teeth might be rotten to the core, but he will probably be willing to trade for some of his own people, especially women and young children he knows could someday grow up to be Cheyennes. But to make it irresistible, I can tell him that Aeneva's brothers are the ones who are holding the women captive. I can tell him you have two of the women and one of the boys with you and as soon as you see Aeneva is alive and well, you will trade them for her."

"I still do not like it, Trenton. Crooked Teeth could turn on you as easily as he did on *naxane* and that would be the end of you and Aeneva."

"That's a risk I'm willing to take," Trenton replied calmly. "I want to help her as much as you do, but I think I have a better chance. Crooked Teeth may torture and kill me, but I don't think so. I think he's the kind of man who's greedy. What better honor for him than to get back some of the women and children of his tribe, as well as to capture their Cheyenne captors?"

"I think Trenton is right," Brave Wolf agreed.

"What do you think, Coyote Boy?"

"It does not seem to matter what I think. You two will do your own planning."

"Forgive me, my friend, if I have intruded into where I do not belong, but my love for Aeneva is too great to permit me to sit and do nothing. I do not mean to challenge your manhood." Trenton spoke with honesty and sincerity.

Coyote Boy shrugged in frustration. "You were always good with the words, Trenton. I would rather fight you with weapons than with words."

Trenton laughed and extended his arm. Coyote Boy grasped his forearm and Trenton did the same. "Thank you, Coyote Boy, you have a generous heart."

"I know how much you care for Aeneva or I would not

let you do it. Now, let us discuss this plan of yours."

Trenton waited for Crooked Teeth's band. He easily picked up their trail again. They slowed their pace considerably, confident that they weren't being followed. Aeneva was still being led on the rope; he could see her tracks well behind one of the horses. Trenton found them the third night out and rode on, waiting for them the next day along the river where he knew they had to stop for water. He waited impatiently, knowing that soon he would see Aeneva, praying that she was not badly hurt. As his thoughts tumbled furiously around in his head, he heard the whinnying of horses and he looked up. He recognized Crooked Teeth immediately—a large, stocky man sitting astride a beautiful black horse. His body bore the scars of his many battles and his face was just as scarred. When he stopped, rifle aimed at Trenton's chest, and opened his mouth to speak, Trenton saw why he had been given his name. All of the man's teeth were crooked and misshapen, giving him a ghastly, frightening appearance.

Trenton stood up slowly, careful not to take his eyes away from the man in front of him. He held up his hands, indicating that he wanted to parley. Crooked Teeth kept the gun pointed at Trenton, not moving, not responding to his request. Trenton didn't speak again, but waited patiently; he knew it was part of the game. Crooked Teeth was sizing him up.

"What do you want to talk of, white man?" Crooked Teeth asked, speaking in Crow.

"I speak only a few words in the Crow tongue, but I speak some Cheyenne and Arapaho. I can also use my hands to speak. Will you understand me?" Crooked Teeth barely nodded and Trenton continued. "I have come for the Cheyenne girl, the granddaughter of Stalking Horse."

Crooked Teeth showed no change in expression. "I know of no such girl."

"I have heard you have taken her for your wife."

"You have heard wrong, white man," Crooked Teeth sneered, raising his rifle to Trenton's head.

"I have been sent here by the girl's brothers. They have some Crow women and children. They are willing to trade them for their sister."

"That is all?" Crooked Teeth seemed completely uninterested.

"They said to tell you they have ten Crow boys who are quickly becoming Cheyenne. They said they now have ten more Cheyennes to fight against the Crows." Trenton had finally gotten to Crooked Teeth. There was a subtle change of expression.

"What else?"

Trenton steeled himself. "They said to tell you your women are not so good to look at, but they know how to please Cheyenne men."

Crooked Teeth raised the rifle as if he were going to fire at Trenton, but he lowered it, narrowing his black eyes. "Where are these Cheyenne dogs?"

"They are near, waiting for your reply."

"I do not like you, white man. I could easily kill you and find them myself."

"That would be unwise, Crooked Teeth, for the Cheyennes are well-hidden and will kill your women and children if you come for them. They expect me to bring your answer within the day."

"Ah!" Crooked Teeth raised his rifle and shouted. He stared menacingly at Trenton, then turned, issuing some orders to one of his men.

Trenton stood without moving, not wanting to provoke Crooked Teeth any more than he already had. He waited, hoping that the war chief would fall for the bait and send Trenton back to the Cheyennes with news that he was willing to trade. While Trenton waited, Crooked Teeth disappeared. His people dismounted, walking to the river and watering their horses. Minutes passed before Crooked Teeth appeared again. He approached with a rope in his hand, the other end tied around Aeneva's waist. When Trenton saw Aeneva, it took all the self-control he possessed for him not to rush forward and slit Crooked Teeth's throat. Aeneva stared at Trenton through tired, glazed eyes, her face and jaw swollen and discolored, her body bruised and thin. Her hands were tied behind her. Her long braids were tangled and dirty, her dress torn and ragged, her moccasins worn almost completely through. She started to speak, but looked at Crooked Teeth and stopped, lowering her head. Trenton could not believe this was the same proud, fearless young woman he had known.

"Is this the girl of whom you speak?" Crooked Teeth asked loudly, yanking up Aeneva's chin.

"She is the one."

"Look at her, white man; why would anyone want to trade so much for her?" He laughed then, pushing Aeneva forward and yanking back on the rope. She lost her balance and fell down. She didn't look up at Trenton.

Trenton stepped forward, trying desperately to keep his temper in check. He reached down and gently helped Aeneva to her feet, taking the rope from around her waist. "You have been very stupid, Crooked Teeth," Trenton said in Crow so that Crooked Teeth would not misunderstand him.

Crooked Teeth started forward, taking his knife from

222

his belt. "You will die for that, white man."

"I do not think so. If you kill me, you will have lost the chance to save many of your people. You would be greatly dishonored if you did that."

Crooked Teeth reached out for Aeneva and jerked her toward him. "The girl is my property; do not touch her again."

"You would be wise to treat her kindly, Crooked Teeth, for if she looks any worse than she does now, her brothers will kill your women and children anyway. They want their sister back alive and in good health. She is no good to them if she is crippled or near death." He tried to keep any emotion from his voice, but it was hard when he looked at Aeneva.

"I have not yet decided to trade her. How do I even know that you tell me the truth? You may have been sent here to trick me, just as the other white man was."

"If I wanted to trick you, I would have waited with the Cheyennes and ambushed you. You forget I was here first; we knew where you were."

Crooked Teeth seemed somewhat disconcerted. "I must have time to think."

"While you think, Crooked Teeth, I would like time alone with the girl."

"Why?"

"I want to talk to her; I want to make sure she is well. I must be able to tell her brothers that she is unharmed."

Crooked Teeth looked as though he would object, but he pushed Aeneva toward Trenton. Trenton caught her in his arms and was leading her toward one of the trees when Crooked Teeth spoke out behind them. "Do not leave the riverbank with her or you will both be shot."

Trenton didn't acknowledge Crooked Teeth's warning, but led Aeneva to a secluded place by the river. He sat her down and walked to his horse, removing his water vessel. He squatted next to Aeneva and lifted the vessel to her lips. She shook her head at first, but as her lips touched the water, she drank greedily. Trenton poured water into his hands and gently wiped the dirt from her face, trying to control the trembling that seized him as he looked at her bruised and battered faced. Aeneva leaned her back against the trunk of the tree, closing her eyes and visibly relaxing. Trenton unsheathed his knife and cut the rope which bound her hands. Her wrists were bleeding and raw from constant abrasion. Trenton poured water over them, rubbing them as gently as he could. Aeneva didn't move or speak; she lay completely still, resting her head against the tree trunk.

"Aeneva." Trenton spoke softly, touching her bruised face. "I will get you out of here; he will not touch you again."

Aeneva didn't respond, but Trenton was shocked to see tears rolling down her cheeks. He knew she must be feeling humiliated; and to someone who prided herself on being strong and competent, what Crooked Teeth had done to her was the greatest of all humiliations.

"Aeneva, it's all right."

Aeneva jerked her head away, finally opening her eyes and scowling at Trenton. "Go away. There is nothing you can do to help me."

"I am going to get you out of here. Brave Wolf and Coyote Boy are waiting out there. If I fail, they will come for you."

Fear clouded her face and she sat forward, reaching for Trenton's arm. "No, you must go. You do not know what he is like. You should have seen what he did to Jean."

"I saw."

224

"Then you must convince my brothers to return home; they cannot take me away from Crooked Teeth. He has too many men and he is planning to rendezvous with two other bands when we reach the mountains."

"He'll never reach the mountains, Aeneva. He is going to trade you to me."

Aeneva shook her head, her eyes pleading. "Please, Trenton, just go. He will not trade with you; he will kill me before he will let me go. Do not risk your life for me."

"I am doing this for me, too, Aeneva." He reached up and drew her head to his chest, stroking her hair. "I've waited for this moment for a long time now. We will be together again."

"No." Aeneva pulled away. "I do not want you to touch me." Again her eyes filled with tears; her reaction totally disconcerted and touched Trenton.

"Why, because he has touched you?"

"He has done more than touch me, Trenton. He has treated me worse than he treats his dogs."

"That doesn't matter."

"But it does. I cannot come to you now. Not now, not ever." She started to stand up, but stumbled and fell against Trenton. He wrapped his arms around her, holding her so she couldn't move. "Do not do this, Trenton. Let me go."

"I'll never let you go, Aeneva. I love you."

She looked up at him, her lips quivering slightly. "You do not love me, Trenton. You love a young girl you remember from a summer long ago. I am not that girl anymore."

"That is enough talk, white man." Crooked Teeth's voice intruded on their private moment. "Tell the Cheyennes that I am not interested in trading with them." He

225

walked over and yanked Aeneva away from Trenton.

"Then you and all your band will die," Trenton responded coldly. "How many children have you in your band, Crooked Teeth? Or don't they matter to you?"

"Leave now, white man, before I decide to kill you myself."

Trenton slid his hand down to his knife, letting it hang loosely. "I would gladly fight you, Crooked Teeth. But you are probably out of practice; you seem to be more used to fighting women."

Crooked Teeth's nostrils flared. He reached for his knife, but Aeneva stepped between him and Trenton.

"No, Trenton. Tell my brothers I do not wish to go with them. Tell them to go back home. Please." Her eyes pleaded silently with Trenton and he did not argue.

"I will go now, Crooked Teeth, but we will meet again." Trenton walked to his horse and swung up. "You are a foolish man. The Cheyennes will not leave without their sister."

"Then tell them to come meet with me. I will talk only to them."

Trenton laughed harshly. "Do you expect them to walk into your trap? Once they are in your camp, you can kill them and be done with it. It is easy to see you care nothing for your own people or you would be willing to talk of trading for them."

Trenton turned his horse, but Crooked Teeth stood in his way. "Come back tomorrow when the sun rises. I will have my answer by then."

Trenton nodded, looked once more at Aeneva, and rode away. Aeneva watched him, trying to keep her emotions in check. She didn't want Crooked Teeth to even guess that she cared for Trenton. Crooked Teeth walked up to her, staring at her with cold, emotionless eyes.

"You like that white man?"

Aeneva shook her head, hardening herself for what she knew would soon come.

"I think you lie, girl. And you will be punished." He jerked on one of her braids and dragged her after him. He barked orders and Aeneva was lashed to a tree, her dress ripped from her back. "They will have my answer in the morning." Crooked Teeth lifted his rope and tied several knots in it. When he was satisfied, he walked up behind Aeneva and whispered cruelly, "They will have my answer when they find your body hanging on this tree tomorrow." He stepped back and whipped the knotted rope against Aeneva's back; she grunted, the force of the blow knocking her face against the bark of the tree. She knew she would not survive this, but it did not matter. She just prayed Trenton would not try to rescue her; she could not bear the thought of him being tortured. She could accept her own death but she could not accept Trenton's.

Trenton crawled through the darkness, his belly sliding along the cool earth. He felt with his hands, careful to avoid brush and twigs that might snap and arouse suspicion. He came back before dark and saw what Crooked Teeth had done to Aeneva; he hoped she would somehow use that incredible inner strength to survive until he could get to her. He stopped and listened to the sounds of the forest and the river, making sure there were no other noises that didn't belong. He knew that Joe, Brave Wolf, Coyote Boy, and the others were out there somewhere, some close to him, some wading their way across the river. He expected Aeneva to be heavily guarded, but it didn't matter; he would do anything to get her away from Crooked Teeth. If he couldn't get by the guards, he would wait for the Cheyennes to attack, and in the ensuing melee, he would get Aeneva out.

He heard a movement near the clearing by the river and he stopped, removing his knife and lying completely still. Someone was walking back and forth, obviously expecting the Cheyennes to come in that way. Trenton crawled the rest of the way to the clearing and paused behind a trunk of thick pine. The fresh smell of the trees assaulted his senses and he was aware of the dry, brittle needles beneath him. He watched with practiced eyes as the guard sauntered across the clearing, checking for anything suspicious. Trenton reached around on the ground for something to throw. He found a rock, waited until the guard passed by him, and threw the rock to his left. The guard turned immediately, walking toward the trees to investigate. Trenton crawled out into the clearing and came up behind the man, choking off any sound with his arm at the man's throat, and ending his life quickly with a knife to his heart. Dragging the body into the trees, he waited. He knew there would be a guard across the river and he hoped that one of the Cheyennes would reach him soon. He scanned the clearing; to his right was the place where Aeneva was tied. Her body was still and unmoving, hanging limply from the ropes which bound her. He stole behind the trees until he reached her, hastily cutting the ropes and catching her as she fell. He carried her out of the clearing and back into the woods as quietly as he could. The rest would be up to his friends; his only concern now was Aeneva.

He placed her over his shoulder and walked through the trees, ducking low branches and limbs. He worked his way back to his horse and lifted Aeneva across the saddle, while he swung up behind her. He dug his knees in sharply and his horse turned, walking quietly out of the area. He rode slowly, still taking care to keep the sound to a minimum in case the Cheyennes had not yet reached Crooked Teeth. When he was far enough away, he urged his mount into a gallop and headed for the safety of the camp the Cheyennes had chosen.

Trenton dismounted and led his horse back into the rocks. He lifted Aeneva down and carried her to one of the robes which had been prepared. At hand were the bear grease and medicines that Sun Dancer always sent with the warriors. He laid Aeneva on her stomach and washed the dried blood from her back. Crooked Teeth had used a knotted rope; Trenton had seen it done before. It left deep tears in the skin and if beaten hard and long enough, a person could die from it. Next Trenton applied the bear grease combined with some of Sun Dancer's healing plants. Then he stripped the filthy dress from her and removed the worn moccasins. He washed her as much as he could and he covered her with another robe, careful to leave her back exposed to the air. Sun Dancer had told him once that one of the best ways to heal a wound was to expose it to the air. He lay next to her and waited. He refused to believe she wouldn't survive; it was something he would not let himself think about.

Brave Wolf and Coyote Boy waited until the second guard had been taken out and they were sure Trenton had rescued Aeneva. Then they stole into the Crow camp and were soon joined by Joe and the others in their raiding party. One of the men went to the horses, soothing them in a calm voice, while Brave Wolf and Coyote Boy threw scraps of dried meat to the snarling camp dogs to keep them from barking. Coyote Boy had wanted to go into the camp and kill as many people as he could find, but Brave Wolf argued against it.

"We only want Crooked Teeth, Brother. He is the one

who has done this to our sister."

"But the others are Crows, Brave Wolf. They are just as bad."

"No," Brave Wolf had replied firmly. "We take Crooked Teeth and our women, and we leave."

Coyote Boy had finally agreed to go along with his brother's order, but inside him was a fire that burned hotly and deeply. He knew the only way it could be put out would be to kill as many Crows as he could, to make them pay for what Aeneva and Jean had endured.

They were making a dangerous approach to an enemy camp so they were all careful. Because the Crows traveled each day, they had not erected lodges but were sleeping out in the open on their robes. They could be awakened at the slightest unfamiliar sound.

Trenton gave Brave Wolf a description of Crooked Teeth, but it was going to be difficult trying to find him at night. The only thing they could do was check each man for the scarred face and body that Trenton described. The Cheyennes moved silently through the Crow camp, checking each man to find Crooked Teeth, while others looked for Laliya and Flying Bird. Suddenly a baby cried and a woman sat up, reaching out for her child. She saw the movement in the camp and screamed, throwing herself over her baby. The Cheyennes were now forced to fight and they were far outnumbered by the Crows. Brave Wolf called to his men to head for the woods, knowing that it was not cowardice to take them away from a sure slaughter. He had been taught by his grandfather that you killed only when necessary; you did not slaughter innocent people because of revenge.

The Cheyennes made it to the woods, but Brave Wolf couldn't find his brother. He ordered the others on while he returned to look for Coyote Boy. Coyote Boy was near the edge of the woods, protecting Laliya and Flying Bird from two Crows, fending them all off with aggressive knife swipes. Brave Wolf joined him and together they fought off the Crows, took the women, and ran through the woods to the clearing on the other side and to their waiting horses. Their only advantage was that the Crows would not be able to follow because the Cheyennes had taken their horses. Although Crooked Teeth had escaped their assault, they had at least taken his horses and some of his Cheyenne captives. He would not soon forget that.

Brave Wolf and Coyote Boy rode swiftly to catch up to the other members of the raiding party. They heard shouts behind them and they both turned.

"Someone will suffer Crooked Teeth's wrath this night," Brave Wolf told Coyote Boy.

"I wish it were he who was suffering ours."

"Never mind, Brother. Aeneva is safe; nothing is more important than that."

"I know, Brave Wolf; I love her as you do. It is because of that love that I want Crooked Teeth to suffer as she did and as *naxane* did."

"I understand, Brother, but do not let this hate consume you. You must be strong for Aeneva."

"You are right," Coyote Boy conceded. "But tell me one thing, Brother. Do men like Crooked Teeth ever pay for their cruelty?"

"Perhaps not in this life, but he will pay, Brother. He will pay."

They built a travois for Aeneva and strapped her to it. It was important for them to leave Crow territory as soon as possible. Crooked Teeth would let other Crow bands know what had happened and they would all be searching for the Cheyennes. Brave Wolf planned to travel south until they ran into the North Platte, and they would follow it to the east when they reached the South Platte, the place where Stalking Horse intended to winter his band. Many of the Cheyennes had broken off from the northern bands and migrated south, so Stalking Horse wanted to spend one winter there to see if it was the kind of place to which his people could adapt. When Brave Wolf told Trenton of his plans, Trenton was silent and somber.

"What is it, my friend? You do not agree with my plan?"

"I have something to ask you, Brave Wolf. Something very important."

"You can ask me anything. If it were not for you, we would not have our sister back."

"I want to take Aeneva away for a while, until she heals."

"Away?" Brave Wolf asked, startled. "Where?"

"To the mountains of the Black Hills, where Jean lived. I want to take Aeneva to his cabin for the winter so she can heal."

"She can heal among her own people," Brave Wolf snapped.

"I know that, Brave Wolf, but it is not just the physical healing I am talking about. She needs to find her inner strength again before she goes back to her people. I know her; she could not live with the humiliation if her people, especially you and your grandparents, saw her this way. She needs to find her pride again."

Brave Wolf was silent; quite clearly he had not considered this possibility. "I will have to discuss it with my brother."

Trenton rode slowly, thinking of how Aeneva would react when she discovered she was alone for the winter with him. She would not take it well; of that he was sure.

"How you doin', boy?"

Trenton shook his head. "Not well, Joe. I didn't expect her to be this bad."

"You said she was strong; she'll pull through."

"A person can be only so strong. You said it yourself, Joe."

"Ah, hell, what do I know?" Joe looked behind him. "Here come your friends. I hope they give you the answer you want to hear."

Coyote Boy and Brave Wolf rode up to Trenton, each looking over at him. Trenton could not keep from smiling. "You both look as though you'd like to string me up by my thumbs."

"It is not an unpleasant thought," Coyote Boy quipped. "I think there is truth in what you have told Brave Wolf. I know my sister and she would not like her people to see her as she is now. She is much too proud for her own good."

"You will let me take her?" He looked at both young men.

"You must promise only to care for her," Brave Wolf warned. "Do not let your feelings get out of control as she heals and her beauty returns."

"Do I hear right? You two don't trust me with your sister?"

"We trust you with her life," Coyote Boy responded seriously. Then more lightly, "It is only with her chastity that we do not trust you."

Trenton shrugged and nodded his head. "You may be right; I don't even know if I can be trusted."

"I am not worried." Brave Wolf spoke confidently. "When Aeneva is well enough for you to even consider such things, she will be strong enough to fight you off. I do not envy you, my friend. You will have your hands

233

full.''

"Especially when she wakes up and finds you have kidnapped her and there is nothing she can do about it.'' Coyote Boy and Brave Wolf both chuckled, slapping Trenton on the back as if they knew a joke and he did not.

The more Trenton thought about it the more he knew he was right. Aeneva might resent him for having taken her away from her family, but she would need the time to grow strong again. She was so ashamed, so afraid, so humiliated; it would kill her to have her family see her that way. He hoped he had made the right decision, but if he hadn't, he was going to follow through with it anyway. Not just for Aeneva's sake, but for his own.

Crooked Teeth yelled until his throat was hoarse; he had given his orders and anyone who didn't comply would suffer the consequences. Most of the men were out gathering stray horses or any wild ones they might encounter, while Crooked Teeth sat thinking. It would take a good day before they gathered up enough horses to continue. In the meantime, he would send a few of the men with the women to rendezvous with the other Crow bands. He, on the other hand, would pick up the trail of the Cheyennes. He would follow them until he found them and until he got the girl back. After he got her back, he would make her suffer even more than she could imagine; then he would kill her. And he would go for her brothers and the white man who had come into his camp. The white man would suffer greatly, just as the other had; he, Crooked Teeth, would see to it that the man didn't die for many, many days. He would beg for mercy and Crooked Teeth would show him none.

One of his wives approached him with a bowl of food and he knocked it from her hands, sending the woman running away in tears. Crooked Teeth was not in the mood to eat; he had only one thing on his mind. He would search as long as it took him, but eventually he would find the Cheyennes and the white man. They would rue the day they had ever heard of the Crow war chief, Crooked Teeth.

CHAPTER XII

Trenton stopped and pulled his thick robe closer around his shoulders. He had chopped and stacked enough wood to last them for at least a month. Periodically, knowing that winter was not far off, he would stop and look up at the blue-gray sky. The cold wind blew at his long hair, lifting it from his neck and invading the comforting warmth of his body. He found himself stopping in the course of the day to occasionally glance at the scaffold which stood close to the cabin. The wind blew the feathers on the shield and lance and whipped the robe which was wrapped around Jean's body. Trenton found himself talking to Jean, as if he could hear him. He felt as if Jean were bestowing his blessing on them, as if Jean were happy the cabin was being used by people who cared for these mountains as he had cared for them.

He checked the racks next to the house to see if the meat was drying properly. Soon there would be little sun; winter would have set in for good. He turned the racks so the meat would dry on all sides. He checked the traps he had set in the woods near the cabin. Only two rabbits today, but that was good enough; Aeneva would have fresh stew. The dried meat would serve them later when they were unable to go outside for food.

Aeneva was beginning to recover physically, but she spoke very little. Although he was out of her life, the

237

presence of Crooked Teeth still loomed heavily in her mind. Trenton didn't know exactly what Crooked Teeth had done to Aeneva, but he could guess. And he had to figure out the best way to reach her without losing her. Again the wind howled and as he looked up at Jean's scaffold, Trenton nodded slightly.

"I know you are watching me right now, Jean, and I know you would tell me to do what is right. I hope I am doing the right thing." He swung the ax into the chopping block and left it there. Picking up a stack of wood, he walked to the door of the cabin, pushed it open with his shoulder, and walked to the big fireplace in order to stack the wood next to the rest. He glanced over at Aeneva, but she was still asleep; she would sleep for a long time. It was part of the healing process.

As Trenton walked over to the kitchen table, he shoved the door shut, and picking up a cup, went over to the fireplace. He poured himself a cup of coffee and returned to the table, sweetening it with some of the precious sugar which Jean had kept available. He sat down in one of the large chairs which Jean had made and he looked around the room. There was a lot of history here. Jean had built the cabin with his own hands over forty years ago. He had made all of the furniture as well: the heavy round table, the kitchen chairs, the dressers, the cabinet, and the two bunks. In this room many of the great trappers and mountain men had sat and talked, including Ira Trenton, after whom Trenton was named, and his own father, Jim Hawkins. And Stalking Horse and Sun Dancer had been here when they were young; Jean had brought Sun Dancer here when she had been sick with the cholera, and he had nursed her back to health. Here, too, was where Aeneva's parents, Young Eagle and Little Flower, had discovered their love; it was where they had decided they

238

could never leave each other. Eventually, they had gone away together to fulfill that love. From their love had come Brave Wolf, Coyote Boy, and Aeneva. Aeneva. He looked over at her, wishing that she would awaken and speak to him. During the times when she was awake, she seemed to resent him and what he had done or perhaps, for what he had seen. He, more than anyone else, saw what Crooked Teeth had made her suffer and that was something she would never forget. He heard a sound and noticed that Aeneva was staring at him. Her brown eyes reflected the flames and it gave them a strange yellowish color. He walked over to her and knelt down, smiling broadly.

"You look better every day. Are you hungry?"

She watched him with those strange eyes. "Why did you bring me here?" Her voice was barely audible.

Trenton sat down, never losing sight of her eyes. "I wanted to help you."

"Why? Why did you come back?"

"I told you why."

Aeneva turned her head away and stared into the fire. "It would have been better if you had never come back."

"You mean it would've been better if I'd never seen what Crooked Teeth had done to you. Why don't you be honest with me, Aeneva?"

"You had no right to come in there. You should have stayed in your white world with your white woman."

"I had every right to come in there after you. I promised your grandparents that I would bring you back to them and I will."

"I do not want to go back. I cannot face them."

"You are acting foolish, Aeneva. Your grandparents and your brothers don't care what Crooked Teeth did to you."

"I care and I cannot live with it."

"What are you going to do, give up? Are you going to kill yourself? Here." Trenton reached down and pulled out his knife. "Use this; it'll be faster."

Aeneva reached out and knocked the knife from Trenton's hand. "Leave me alone, Trenton."

"For a while, Aeneva; I'll leave you alone for a while." He stood up and walked back to the table, sitting down and picking up the coffee cup. A subtle smile played around the corners of his mouth. It was the first emotion other than complete apathy that she had shown since they had been up here. Anger, it was a good sign; it meant she was beginning to care. If she cared about something enough to get angry, then she would care enough to get well.

Aeneva felt Crooked Teeth's hands on her body. She tried to resist him, but he beat her over and over again until her entire body ached. The more she resisted, the more she was beaten. She smelled his rotting breath and heard the vulgar sounds he made as he abused her. She tried not to cry, but she couldn't stop herself. He always hurt her, always debased her; she had never experienced anything like it. All of her life she had been loved and encouraged to do what she wanted. She considered herself a warrior, a skilled and competent person with weapons and horses, but none of that had done any good with Crooked Teeth. He always kept her tied up and he always had the advantage; none of her skill had been able to help her or Jean. She fought again, but again she was beaten. Nothing mattered anymore; all of the fight was out of her. There was no reason to live. Suddenly, she saw Trenton; he had come to take her away. He stood in front of her, trying to protect her from Crooked Teeth, but Crooked Teeth took his lance and plunged it into Trenton's heart. She heard him grunt as the lance went in and she saw the blood spurt from the wound. She cried out and tried to catch him as he fell, but Crooked Teeth dragged her away, leaving Trenton to die alone. She tried to run back, but Crooked Teeth wouldn't let her. She called out to him, hoping he would hear her. "Trenton! Trenton!" She screamed and the sound echoed in her ears. She heard breathing and realized it was her own. She felt arms holding her, gentle arms, kind arms, and she opened her eyes.

"Trenton." She looked up at his rumpled blond hair and almost laughed. He was alive and he was beautiful.

"Are you all right? You were dreaming."

Aeneva didn't seem to hear him. "When I first saw you, I thought you were the most beautiful thing I had ever seen. You had dark skin, almost as dark as mine; yet you had hair the color of corn and eyes the color of the sky." She shook her head in awe. "I had seen *naxane,* of course, but you were the first white person I ever really saw. And you were so beautiful. And so strong and fast. Your mother named you well when she named you Swiftly Running Deer."

Trenton smiled and stroked Aeneva's cheek lightly. "I think you're still dreaming. The woman is not supposed to call the man beautiful."

"But you are."

"You should rest." He helped her lie down and he covered her. "Don't be afraid; I'm here with you."

"Crooked Teeth killed you in my dream. You do not think it was a dream-vision, do you?" she asked apprehensively.

"You were only being plagued by Crooked Teeth's demons. Soon they will all depart and be replaced by good spirits. I am going to live a long life; I must, I have a son

241

to take care of now.'' Seeing the look on Aeneva's face, Trenton regretted his words as soon as he had said them.

"Son? You have a son? You did not tell me." She seemed confused. "You are married then, to the white woman? I do not understand."

"I will tell you all about it when you are ready to hear. My wife is dead, but I do have a son. Your grandmother is taking care of him until we return."

Aeneva nodded, still seeming unsure. "And your son, does he have hair the color of corn and eyes the color of the sky?"

"Yes. But you will see for yourself when we return."

Aeneva turned on her side. "I am tired now, Trenton. Thank you." She closed her eyes; not to sleep, he knew, but to shut him out.

The news of his marriage had been too much for her to hear; somehow he would make her understand how it had happened. But he wasn't sure he could make her understand when he still wasn't sure himself how it had happened.

He felt warm when he thought of her words. To her, indeed, to most Indians, there was not a great distinction between a man and a woman being called beautiful. A person was either beautiful or not; it did not matter if that person were a man or a woman.

Trenton stretched out on his robe, suddenly feeling more at peace with himself than he had for a long time. Aeneva had finally spoken to him and even though it would take a long time, he felt they would eventually find their way to each other. And there was his son. He had an incredible need to get back to Nathan; he hoped he never had to leave him again. Things were going well and he felt that perhaps the Great Father was smiling down on them, wishing them well.

Crooked Teeth found the spot where the trail separated and he looked up into the ominous mountains. It would be crazy to go up into them now, just when winter was almost upon them. But he knew that that was where the white man had taken the girl. The tracks showed a travois being pulled by one lead horse. The other was the white man's horse, and there were two other horses. The tracks were the same. His men wouldn't want to go into the mountains in the dead of winter; they would be scared and they would ask him to wait until spring. But he could not wait until spring. As long as it was winter, he knew they would be up there, alone and trapped. Nothing gave him greater joy than the thought of finding those two alone. The Cheyennes could wait; the man and woman could not. He held up his hand and led his men toward the mountains, offering them no chance to disagree with him. Any man who rode with Crooked Teeth learned to do whatever Crooked Teeth desired. To do any less invited death.

Crooked Teeth rode hard, knowing that it was possible to make it up the mountains before the first heavy snows. After he had disposed of the white man and the girl, they would wait out the winter until it was time to seek the Cheyennes, the brothers of the girl. Crooked Teeth had never known defeat at the hands of an enemy and he did not intend to start now.

They were sitting eating stew one night when Aeneva put down her bowl and faced Trenton. "Tell me about your wife."

"What do you want to know?"

"Was she the same white woman I saw you with in the city?"

"Yes."

"You loved her even then?"

"I didn't love her, Aeneva."

"Why did you marry?"

"Even now it's hard for me to figure out what happened." He stirred his stew a few times and, setting the bowl down, proceeded to relate the whole story to Aeneva. "I was a dumb, stupid kid, wise in the ways of the land but ignorant in the ways of people. Especially white people."

"At least she gave you a son. What is his name?"

"Nathan Joseph."

"It is a good name. Have you thought of an Indian name for him yet?"

"No."

"Well, perhaps when he is bigger." She smiled at Trenton, her eyes sparkling brilliantly. "Do you remember when we were children and you saved me from Gray Fox? You almost killed him."

"He took the game of war too seriously; he could have hurt you badly."

"You were ferocious; that is what Brave Wolf said. I did not understand the word then, but *naxane* explained it to me. He said it was like a mother bear fighting to save her cubs or a man fighting to save the woman he loved." She blushed slightly at the last.

"Yes, I remember. I would have killed him if you hadn't stopped me."

"You were like that when you came into Crooked Teeth's camp. There was no fear in your eyes, only anger. You would have given your life for mine."

"Yes."

"Why, Trenton?"

"Why do you think?"

244

"I think you care about me and my family, but you have not seen us for so long. Why risk your own life, especially when you have a son to care for?"

"Because I have loved you from the first moment I saw you. I loved your spirit and your courage."

"I told you before, you loved a girl who existed a long time ago. She does not exist anymore; she is dead."

"She is not dead; she has only changed."

"She no longer has her spirit or her courage. She has been cowed."

"I don't believe that."

"It is true." She pulled the robe up to her chin, a sure sign that she was about to shut him out, but Trenton moved next to her.

"Don't do this, Aeneva. You have to give yourself time. You suffered a great deal when you were with Crooked Teeth; most women wouldn't have survived it."

"What good is it to survive if you have no honor left, Trenton? What is there without honor?" She turned away from him again and Trenton saw that there wasn't any point in pursuing the conversation. How could he explain to her that through love she could again find honor; but she would have to find that out for herself.

Crooked Teeth lost the trail but it didn't matter. He had heard of the cabin that the white trapper had had in these mountains. Everyone had heard of it. He had allowed many men, white and Indian to stay in it. The cabin was where the white boy would take the girl; it was the only place.

He warmed his hands by the fire and pulled his robe around his shoulders. they would wait out the storm in this cave and afterward they would push on. He knew the general area of the cabin; it would not take him long to find it. They could not get away; they would be caught, just like two animals in a trap. And he would be the hunter waiting to put them to their deaths.

Aeneva looked at the pictures and laughed. It was the laugh of a young, happy girl. "I saw these in the city with *naxane*. How do the women get these things on? Surely they cannot breathe in them."

Trenton looked at the laced corsets and nodded his head. "They wear them and they pull them as tightly as they can."

"Why do they put themselves through such torture?"

"They want to have small waists. It is stylish."

"Stylish? What is stylish?"

"Well, many of your women wear beads in their braids, or feathers. That is a certain style. White women have certain hair styles and certain styles of dress, just as you do."

"But I would die in something like this."

"You don't need something like that; you are small enough without it. By the nature of the way you live, you are strong and slim. Many of the richer white women do nothing but sit around and talk and eat and drink tea."

"Grandmother told me that once; it is such a strange custom. Do they not get bored with all that sitting around?"

"I suppose some of them do. But not all white women are like that. Many of them are well educated and have good jobs. Some teach, write, and sing."

"Sing?"

"In the white world, people who sing well, or play a musical instrument well, are paid to perform in front of others. It is their job."

Aeneva shook her head in confusion. "I am not sure I

understand."

"It doesn't matter anyway. It's just important for you to know that not all white women are like the ones in these books."

"Was your wife one of the good ones?"

"Yes, I think deep down inside she was good. It just took her too long to find it out."

"I did not say it before, Trenton, but I am sorry that she is dead. It must have caused you great pain."

"I blame myself for her death, but if Lydia had lived, I'm not sure we would have stayed together. Joe told me she had planned to leave me."

"Why?"

"Because she had trapped me into the marriage, she thought she would repay me by letting me go."

"She was good."

"Yes." He was silent, studying his hands for a time. He looked over at Aeneva's hands and pulled one of them toward him. She attempted to pull it away, but he held it firm and looked at it. There were small marks in the palms that he hadn't noticed before. "Was there no end to the man's cruelty?" he asked angrily.

"I dropped his food bowl one night. He took a stick from the fire and held it to the palms of my hands. He said I would appreciate my hands more and make sure never to drop his food bowl again."

Trenton angrily slammed his fist down on the table, knocking the coffee cup and book from it. "I should've killed him when I had the chance. After I got you, I should've gone back."

"It does not matter now. We are free of him."

"You will never be free of him, Aeneva; don't you see that?" He stood up and paced around the room. "I see the fear in your eyes when you hear a loud noise or when you have a bad dream. Sometimes I watch you when you're thinking and I can see that he has invaded your very soul. You can only be free of him if he is dead.''

"I do not like to hear you talk like that, Trenton. The last time you talked of seeking revenge, I did not see you for many summers.'' She walked to him, taking his hands. "It does not matter now. I am free of him; it will just take me some time to rid my mind of him. You were right; I am strong and I will be all right again. You have done much to see to that.''

Trenton lifted her hands and opened them, looking again at their scarred palms. He kissed them tenderly. "No one will ever hurt you again, Aeneva. Ever.'' He pulled her to him, hugging her fiercely. He felt her stiffen in his arms. "I'm sorry.''

Aeneva reached up and stroked his cheek "Do not be sorry; do not ever be sorry.'' She walked to her robe and lay down. The openness was suddenly over between them. Whenever he felt as if he was getting close, she closed the door. He leaned back against the fireplace and shut his eyes. It was going to be a long winter.

"You're crazy, Aeneva. You'll freeze to death out here.''

"I do not care. I must have a bath; I cannot wait until spring.''

"I can heat some water in the cabin and you can wash yourself in there.''

"It is not the same. I want to get my entire body wet and I want to wash my hair.''

"You won't be able to stay in it that long.''

"*Naxane* told me he was able to bathe in the stream in the wintertime. He said it was very good for his blood.''

"I still think you're crazy. Here.'' He handed her the

248

soap that Jean had kept in the cabin, as well as a blanket. "I'm going to wait here to make sure you're all right."

"I will be fine; you do not need to wait for me."

"I'm not leaving you out here alone."

"Go check your traps. By the time you are finished, I will be finished. I cannot take a bath knowing you are standing there looking at me."

"I've already seen you take a bath."

"When?"

"That summer. I followed you down to the river and watched you."

"I trusted you; I thought you were my friend."

"I was your friend, but I still wanted to watch you bathe."

Aeneva picked up a ball of snow and threw it at Trenton's face, then ran down the stream bank, turning around and sticking her tongue out at him. Trenton smiled and bent down. He gathered a large ball of snow, patting it together until it was hard; then he threw it. It landed right in the middle of Aeneva's back, knocking her off balance. She slipped on the icy bank and landed on her rear end. She turned around and looked up at him. Trenton cupped his hands around his mouth and called out, "Have a good bath," and he headed into the woods to check his traps. He hadn't felt so good in a long time.

Aeneva washed her hair from the stream bank, wetting it, soaping it, and speedily rinsing the soap in the icy water. She was sure her head was frozen by the time she was finished. She swiftly took off the heavy robe and stepped into the icy water. She went slowly at first, and sat down to her shoulders, emitting a loud yell. She hastily soaped herself down, rinsed, and climbed up the bank. As she wrapped the blanket around her and reached for her robe, she heard a noise behind her; she turned around. "Is that you, Trenton? Were you watching me again?" She waited for a moment, but when there was no reply, she hurried up the bank. The air quickly chilled her and she pulled the robe tightly around her body. She felt clean for the first time in weeks and she couldn't wait to dry off by the fire in the cabin. There was another noise behind her and she stopped, her heart pounding in her chest. Slowly, she turned her head, but there was nothing. Shadows fell in the dark woods and she imagined that she saw evil spirits following her. A sudden terror overwhelmed her and she tore through the woods, running straight into Trenton.

"Are you all right?"

"Yes, oh, yes." She laid her head against his chest. "I thought I heard things out there. I thought I was being followed."

Trenton's eyes looked over the top of Aeneva's head and into the woods. "Let's go back to the cabin before you get completely frozen. It's all right now. There are always sounds in these woods." He put his arm around her and led her back toward the cabin.

While Trenton skinned the rabbits he had caught, Aeneva dried herself in front of the fire. She stood close to the flames until her skin felt hot to the touch, and she combed her hair with her fingers until it was dry. She had no clothing of her own, so she dressed in one of Trenton's shirts and a pair of his pants. The pants were much too large and the shirt hung well down her thighs, but they were clean and comfortable. She made some coffee and she added some of the dried vegetables to the soup she had started before she had gone for her bath. The door opened and Trenton walked in, holding fresh rabbit meat. Walking over to the pot, he dropped it in. He walked out and cleaned his hands in the snow. When he came back, he put the bar over the door—Aeneva had never known him to do that before—and he took down the two rifles and made sure they were loaded.

He turned to her then, and smiled. "Your mother named you well."

"Why do you say that?"

"She named you after the winter because that is when you were born. You went out and took a bath in freezing water and you came back looking more beautiful than the first ray of spring sunshine."

Aeneva shook her head, smiling slightly. "Such pretty words, Trenton."

"They're true."

"Thank you." She looked at the rifles on the table. "Why did you take them down and bolt the door?"

"It's always best to be prepared."

"For what?"

"For anything. You said you thought you heard sounds in the woods. I want to make sure we are prepared in case the sounds are people."

"What people?" Aeneva asked in alarm.

Trenton walked to her, his look of confidence calming her instantly. "Jean said that sometimes mountain men or trappers stopped by for food—even some Indians. Don't worry, you probably heard an animal anyway."

"Or I was imagining that evil spirits were out to get me. I seem to be afraid of my own shadow these days."

"You just need time to recover. When the spring comes and you see your family again, you will feel differently."

Aeneva didn't reply but walked to the fire. "I dreamed that Crooked Teeth was following me. Do you think it is possible he knows where we are?"

251

"How could he know. He didn't have horses to follow us for at least a day. By that time we were well away from there."

"But maybe he tracked us and he knows we are up here."

"Why? Why would he do that? It's winter now; he'd be crazy to come into these mountains now."

"You do not know him as I do, Trenton. He *is* crazy. The man is unlike anyone I have ever known."

"Aeneva, Crooked Teeth is not here. No one knows where we are except your family. You have to stop this; soon you'll be imagining he's watching your every move."

Aeneva turned away and walked across the room. How could she tell Trenton that that is exactly how she had felt in the woods—as if someone were watching her every move. She felt Trenton's hands on her shoulders and was suddenly comforted.

"Even if he does come here, I won't let him touch you again. I promise you that with my life."

"No!" Aeneva turned in Trenton's arms and laid her head against his chest. "Do not say that, ever. I would never want you to give your life for mine."

Resting his chin on her head, Trenton stroked her long silky hair. "Don't worry; I don't plan to die soon. I have too much to live for."

"But if Crooked Teeth should—"

"That's enough about Crooked Teeth; let's not let him spoil our good stew. Come on." They sat down by the warm fire and ate their stew while the cold wind howled outside the cabin. Aeneva refused to listen to it and to the warning she thought she heard it carry. She would not live her life in constant fear of the unknown. She would not.

Crooked Teeth smiled; he had seen the fear on Aeneva's face as she had run through the woods. It would have been easy to have taken her then, but he had decided to take his time with this. It would give him more pleasure to see her imagining things, to keep her wondering if there really was someone watching her. He tucked himself into the burrow of the tree and rubbed his hands together. His men had been complaining; they were cold and hungry. They wanted to go into the cabin soon. Crooked Teeth told them it would be very soon. He also told them that they were Crow warriors and strong and tough enough to stand a few nights in the snow with little food. That quieted them for the time being.

He looked up through the top of the trees and saw the smoke from the chimney as it drifted overhead. It would be a welcome warmth, but it would be even more welcome because he had had to wait for it, just as he would have to wait a few more days for Aeneva. But it would be worth it.

Aeneva pushed the cards from the table in one angry swipe. "This is a silly game; I do not want to play anymore."

"You're not concentrating. It would help pass the time."

"I do not want to pass the time, I want to be out of here. I feel as though I am locked in a cage in this place. Why did you bring me up here?" She got up from the table and stomped across the room to the fire.

Trenton sighed and bent down to pick up the cards. When he was finished, he dealt them all out to himself and began playing solitaire. He needed something to pass the time. He and Aeneva were beginning to get on each other's nerves.

"What are you playing now?" Aeneva stood behind him, looking over his shoulder.

"It's solitaire. You can play it by yourself."

"I am sorry, Trenton, I did not mean to throw the cards all over the floor. It is just . . ." Aeneva was interrupted by a loud thumping sound against the side of the cabin. She stared at Trenton, her eyes wide and full of fear.

Trenton stood up, putting his finger to his lips. He took the rifle from the mantel and walked to the door. He leaned his ear against it and listened. Again there was a noise; this time it was against the front door. He reached for his robe.

"No." Aeneva grabbed at his arm. "Do not go out there. You can see nothing. Whoever it is will be waiting for you. You will be at a disadvantage." When Trenton hesitated she put her hands on his arms. "Please. Please, do not go out there."

Trenton dropped his robe to the floor and put his arm around Aeneva, holding his rifle in the other hand. They waited in silence for a long time, but there were no more sounds. Trenton put the rifle on the table and led Aeneva to the fire.

"What do you think it was, Trenton? Do you think it was someone trying to get in?"

"If someone were trying to get in here, he would've kept trying." He shook his head. "No, I think it was an animal trying to get in out of the cold."

"What kind of animal would make that kind of noise?"

"I don't know, Aeneva. Maybe one of the horses got out of the lean-to. I should check."

"Please wait until tomorrow. Do not go out tonight."

"All right." He took Aeneva's hand and rubbed it. It

felt cold in spite of the warm fire. "Don't worry. Everything will be all right." As Trenton wrapped his arms around her, he couldn't quite convince himself of the fact. Those sounds were not made by any animal, he knew, and if the sounds weren't made by animals, they had to be made by people. But what people would be crazy enough to be up in these mountains at this time? A chill went through him and he tried to suppress it from Aeneva. He knew as certainly as he had ever known anything in his life—Crooked Teeth was out there and ready to get revenge.

"Are you all right, Trenton? You keep shivering."

"I'm fine. I just keep thinking how cold it must be outside. I'm glad we're in here instead of out there." But he really wished they were outside because out there they might have a chance. In the cabin they were like elk caught in the pit, ready to be slaughtered. If only there were someplace, someplace he could hide Aeneva when Crooked Teeth came for them. A thought suddenly intruded. He remembered something Jean had told him many years ago. As much as the Frenchman had loved the mountains and this cabin, he didn't completely trust everyone. Under one of the bunks he had built a trap door from which he could escape. He said it always made him feel as though he wasn't completely trapped. Crooked Teeth would have no idea there was a door because Jean had always stacked his wood in this area, leaving enough room between the wall of the cabin and the woodpile.

Trenton breathed more easily now. When Aeneva was asleep, he would test the door to make sure it still worked, and when Crooked Teeth finally decided to break into the cabin, Trenton would send Aeneva out the trap door with a rifle. She wouldn't want to leave him, he knew, but if he kept the cabin door barred long enough and he shot at Crooked Teeth's men from the window next to the door, it would give Aeneva enough time to get out. She could hide there, concealed by the high woodpile for as long as she needed to hide. Then when she felt she could get away, she could steal the horses and ride off, leaving Crooked Teeth and his men without any mounts.

"What are you thinking about? You keep staring into the fire."

"Nothing. I was just thinking about when we were kids. What a good fighter you were even then. That will never change, Aeneva. You will always fight to save yourself or others whom you love. You must believe that." Aeneva looked at him, a puzzled expression on her face, but Trenton wouldn't allow her to answer. "Come on. It's time for bed. You need your rest."

Trenton waited for well over an hour to make sure that Aeneva was really asleep. He walked to the bunk and slid underneath, groping along the edges for the door until he finally found it. He pushed at it gently, but it didn't budge, then he leaned on it, forcing his weight against it. It hadn't been opened in a long time, possibly years, and it was sticking fast. Trenton finally sensed a slight give and pushed harder against the door until he became aware of the cold rush of air on his face. He pushed it all the way open and slipped his head and upper body outside. He waited for a moment until his eyes became accustomed to the darkness, and he viewed his hiding place. He looked up and saw the tall woodpile. He would have to squeeze in order to fit his entire length into the small space, but it was adequate for someone who was fighting for his life; and someone who was getting wood from the pile would never even see the space behind it. Jean had planned well.

Letting the trap door down slowly, Trenton backed his way into the cabin. He cut a piece of leather fringe from his shirt and lifted the door, placing the leather underneath. He pulled on the leather and was able to draw the door tightly shut again. He felt much more secure about Aeneva. At least now he knew there was a way for her to escape. He hauled himself from underneath the cot and started to get up, but saw with surprise, that Aeneva was sitting cross-legged on the cot staring at him.

"Aeneva. I thought you were asleep."

"Yes, I know. I learned very well in Crooked Teeth's camp how to feign sleep. What were you doing, Trenton?"

"Doing?" Trenton rubbed his hands on his thighs; he felt like a kid who had been caught with his hand in the candy jar.

"What were you doing under there? I watched you. Half of your body disappeared and then appeared again. What is under there?"

Trenton sat down next to Aeneva. "It's a trap door to the outside, by the woodpile. Jean told me about it a long time ago."

"Why would Jean put a door there? It is a silly place for a door, no?"

"No, it is a clever place for a door. No one would think to look under the bunk for a door. Besides, Jean planned the woodpile around it. He left a space just large enough for a grown man or woman to fit into, and the woodpile is so tall that no one would ever suspect that there's a hiding place behind it."

"You still haven't answered my question, Trenton."

"What question?"

"Stop treating me like a sick child. I am not sick and I am not a child. Why did Jean build the door?"

"Because he didn't want to be trapped inside here in case someone was trying to break in. He said there were always crazy mountain men and trappers running around."

"And Indians," Aeneva responded solemnly.

"Yes, and Indians. I won't lie to you anymore, Aeneva. I think you're right; I think Crooked Teeth is out there just waiting for the right time to break in."

"I knew it. I knew it when I was coming back from the stream. He was watching me."

"Probably. Watching and waiting."

"Yes, that sounds like him. He delights in torture of the mind also."

"What do you mean?"

"Often he would tell me that my family had forgotten about me and adopted another daughter. Over and over again he told me this and after a while I began to believe him. Deep down inside I knew it wasn't true, yet my mind dwelt on it constantly. It was almost worse than the physical torture."

Trenton looked at her and reached out for her hand, sensing that she wanted to say more. "What else?"

"He knew how scared I was of him physically. No matter how many times he took me, it was always like the first time. He took great pleasure in watching me at night, making me wonder if he was going to take me that night. Many times he would not, but I spent many sleepless nights wondering if he would take me." She squeezed Trenton's hand and managed a weak smile. "As much as I trust you, and I trust you with my life, Trenton, you are no match for Crooked Teeth. He is cruel and evil; he is not possessed of an earthly soul."

"I don't believe that and neither do you. He is as human as you or I and that means he, too, has weaknesses. I will find a way to get to him, Aeneva. You and I will call upon the Maiyun and the Great Father to help us, to send us brave and good spirits to fight off the evil spirits of Crooked Teeth. We will pray to them and we will remain strong; we must. If you let your fear overcome you now, then you will most certainly die."

"How you must despise my weakness. I feel such shame."

"Don't, Aeneva. You know what I feel for you. I don't despise anything about you. It's you who despises the weakness in yourself, or what you see as a weakness. By enduring what you did and feeling as you now feel, you've only proved to me that you're more human. It will pass. You come from strong, honorable blood, Aeneva. Soon you will be strong again and you will feel the fear fade away. But it's important that you don't give in to that fear now, especially not now. Crooked Teeth is out there and he is waiting for us. If ever you needed to overcome your fear it is now."

"I will try to make you proud of me, Trenton," Aeneva said softly as she leaned against him, seeking the warmth and comfort of his body.

"I am already proud of you, Aeneva." He reached for her face, kissed her gently and fleetingly. For the first time she did not pull away, but Trenton did. Now was not the right time. After he had taken care of Crooked Teeth there would be plenty of time for loving Aeneva; hopefully they would have their whole lives.

CHAPTER XIII

Trenton checked his traps, trying to act as if nothing had changed. But everything had changed. Every nerve in his body was charged and ready to act; he knew he was being watched wherever he went. He whistled gaily as he reset the traps and took the dead animals back to the front of the cabin. He only caught three rabbits; there should have been many more. He assumed that Crooked Teeth and his men had raided his traps a few times and then re-set them, not wanting Trenton to think that anything out of the ordinary had happened. When he had finished skinning and butchering the animals, he went to the woodpile and walking around all sides of it to try to get a look at the small crawl space, gathered some logs in his arms. He couldn't see anything and again he started to whistle. Crooked Teeth might get him, but he would never get Aeneva.

He walked back to the front door and kicked at it three times. "Aeneva, let me in." The door opened slowly and Aeneva let him in. Trenton went back outside to check on the horses and to make sure they had something to eat. He noticed round mounds in the snow next to the horses and smiled, shaking his head. Some of Crooked Teeth's men must have gotten too cold out in the woods; Crooked Teeth wouldn't be happy if he knew they'd come in here and risked being seen. When he was through with the horses, he picked up the fresh meat and started into the house, turning and looking back into the woods as he did so. He thought he saw a slight movement behind one of the trees, but he didn't acknowledge it and he went inside. Aeneva barred the door behind him.

"Did you see anything?"

"I thought I saw something move in the trees, but I couldn't be sure. Also, I saw prints in the snow by the horses. Some of his men must've slept in the lean-to last night."

"You were foolish to go out there."

"I would be more foolish to stay in here and hide. If he thinks we even suspect he's out there, he'll set the damned place on fire if he has to. No, I want him to think we don't suspect a thing. That's the only chance we have."

"How long do you think it will be before—"

"I think it'll be soon. His men are getting restless and he can't keep putting them off. I'd say it'll be tonight or tomorrow night."

"Tonight?" Aeneva asked anxiously. "No, he cannot come tonight. I cannot handle this, Trenton. You were wrong about me; I have no courage left."

"I know that's not true. Don't let him do this to you. Just remember that you are a good fighter, a good warrior. If something happens and you can't use the rifle, fight him with your knife, kick him, scratch at his eyes. Do anything to fight him."

"I tried that before and you saw what happened."

"No, it was different before. Before, you were a prisoner in his camp and tied up like a dog. This time you'll have a chance to fight. And you can fight, Aeneva. You've been doing it since you were born that cold winter long ago."

Aeneva breathed deeply and nodded her head. "All right. What do we do? Do we just wait for him?"

"No, we're going to practice."

"Practice?"

"I want to prove to you that you haven't lost your instinct to survive." He took out his knife and handed it to her; he picked up his rifle from the table. "Pretend I'm Crooked Teeth and I'm here to kill you. But before I kill you, I plan to torture you like I did before. Just think about it a minute. Think how you felt the first time he hurt you. Think how you fought back." Trenton watched her for a moment, and without warning, lunged toward her, swinging his rifle at her arm. Aeneva moved quickly, instinctively circling around and facing Trenton. "Good, that's good. Don't forget, I'm stronger and bigger and I'll try to tackle you if I can. Remember you will have to strike first and you must make it count." He circled around the room, watching her watching him. He waited for a few minutes until he was sure she had stopped thinking of him as Crooked Teeth and he charged toward her, his rifle held in front of him in a defensive position to ward off any strikes by the knife. He knocked Aeneva against the wall, but she bent down and recovered quickly, turning, holding the knife up, ready to throw at him. She had a clear shot at his chest. She stood tensed, the knife clenched in her fist, her breathing coming in heavy gasps. Trenton put the rifle down and walked to her, taking the knife away. "That was very good. You would have had the first strike. But remember, Crooked Teeth will probably have his robe on; you can't throw for his chest. You'll have to aim for his neck or face." He saw the panic in her eyes and drew her to him. "It's all right; you did well."

"I was ready to throw it at you. I could have hurt

you.''

"You wouldn't hurt me; you couldn't." He put his hands on her face and lifted it up. "*Ne-mehotatse*, Aeneva." He kissed her deeply, tasting the soft sweetness of her lips. She was stiff and unyielding at first, but she soon gave in to his demanding but gentle kiss. It was a wonderful sensation to her and she leaned her body in to his, putting her arms around his waist. This kissing was a wonderful thing, as *Naxane* Jean had often told her it was. It was one custom the whites had that she liked.

Trenton held her, rubbing his cheek against her hair and kissing the line of her neck and throat. "We should stop," he murmured against her ear.

"Why should we stop?"

"Because I promised your brothers that I would take care of you."

"You are taking care of me. You are taking very good care of me." She laughed and put her arms around his neck, lifting her mouth for another kiss. "I like this kissing, Trenton. It gives me great pleasure. Is it the same for you?"

"More than you know," he replied hoarsely, almost crushing her against him. He started to lift her in his arms but he was interrupted by a loud thump on the door. He stopped, immediately crossing the room and reaching for his rifle. "Get the one from the mantel," he told Aeneva quietly. He grabbed the box of shells from the table. The thumping at the door continued in measured beats until the door began to shake on its leather hinges. "They have a ram of some sort; they'll be in here in minutes," he told Aeneva. He grabbed her arm and drew her to the bunk. "I want you out of here now."

"I will not leave you, Trenton."

"Damn it, Aeneva, this isn't the time to get heroic.

Get the hell out of here and let me handle this. Now!'' He shoved her down on the floor and made sure she was under the bunk. ''Now push against the wall until it moves. Hurry.''

Aeneva did as she was told and pressed the wall until it opened. She started to say something to Trenton, but he shoved her out, making sure she didn't have a chance to protest. He thrust her robe, rifle, and a box of shells out after her. ''Stay there. If you don't hear from me, wait until you can steal the horse and get the hell out of here.''

''Trenton—''

''Damn it, Aeneva, just do as I say. I have to know that you'll be all right. Promise me you'll do as I say.''

''I promise.''

''All right.'' He pulled the trap door, making sure it was flush with the rest of the wall. He loaded his rifle, waiting for Crooked Teeth and his men to come in. He overturned the table and knelt behind it, putting the rifle barrel over the top. He thought about Aeneva; he knew the fear she must be experiencing right now. He wanted to follow her outside, but he could not. He had to make sure Crooked Teeth was killed; the man could not be permitted to live. If he did, he would somehow track Aeneva down until he finally killed her.

The sound of the ram against the door echoed throughout the room until the heavy door fell inward, landing with a crash on the floor. Trenton peered around the side of the table. There was no movement. He knew Crooked Teeth would wait; he wouldn't run into a well-lit room. He would wait and Trenton would have to be on his constant guard. Crooked Teeth would send some of his men to harrass Trenton until they wore him down; and when he was ready, Crooked Teeth would come for Trenton himself. Trenton attempted to relax, to lessen the tension in his body. It was important that he be ready for Crooked Teeth or his men, but it was also important that he be relaxed enough to respond with confidence and skill.

There was a sound outside the door, a slight crackling of snow. Someone was walking around the door waiting for the right moment to rush Trenton. He kept watch around the side of the table, pulling the rifle barrel down from the top of the table and laying it across one of the legs for support. He knew the first attack would come soon. There was a war cry and a sudden flurry of movement in the door. A robed figure charged in and considered the room for a second. Spying the table, he lifted his rifle and began shooting. Trenton took careful aim and fired once, knocking the Crow to the floor. He shot him in the head; he was taking no chances.

One down. He didn't know how many were out there; he didn't know how many would follow Crooked Teeth up into the mountains, but he had to assume the worst. He had to assume there were at least ten or fifteen more like this one out there. He put another shell into his rifle and readied himself again. They would wait longer this time, try to make him feel secure; and when they thought him least aware, they would rush him. But Trenton had one advantage—they didn't know he'd been raised as an Arapaho and that he knew their games and tricks as well as anyone. He had developed his patience over the years and he could wait them out as long as he had to, as long as it took to kill Crooked Teeth.

There was another movement in the door frame. Before Trenton shot, the man threw a lance into the table. Trenton, looking around the table, saw the jagged black lines on the lance, the dark eagle feathers hanging on the end. It had to be Crooked Teeth's lance; he was reminding Trenton that he was still there. While Trenton looked at the lance, shots came from either side of the door and splintered the wood around his face. He jerked his head back and waited; he couldn't afford to waste any shots and lose the time reloading. He had to make every shot count.

Wrapping her robe around her, Aeneva pulled her knees to her chest. She held on to the rifle, making sure the box of shells was within reach. She heard the first shots and jumped. She knew Trenton didn't have a chance. He had only one rifle against possibly ten. They could rush him and that would be the end of him. She heard more shots and she realized that as long as she heard them, Trenton was still alive. She had to think of a way to help him; she couldn't stay hidden in this dark place letting Trenton fight her fight for her. She had to come to his aid, but first she must find the courage to face Crooked Teeth.

She wrapped her arms around her knees and rocked back and forth. She sang softly to herself, a song about courage and bravery and honor. She said the words over and over again, hoping that she would grow stronger from saying the words. She remembered Coyote Boy's favorite song: "My friends, only stones stay on this earth forever. Use your best ability." It meant that a person should fight and not be afraid to die; this was what she had to do. She sang the song again: "Aeneva, only stones stay on this earth forever. Use your best ability." She nodded to herself, knowing what she had to do. Trenton was willing to die for her; she had to be willing to do the same for him. She could do no less.

Crooked Teeth sat in the cold snow, unusually patient. He would make the white man wait another hour before he sent in his men. Waiting was the worst part for the white man; he didn't know when or how Crooked Teeth's men would attack next. But Crooked Teeth had been surprised by the man's effectiveness. He was always alert and ready, but it could not last. Soon he would make a mistake. And that was when Crooked Teeth would go in himself.

Crooked Teeth was troubled by one thing—the girl. She didn't seem to be in the cabin or the man had her well hidden. She was hidden somewhere, but where? Both of them couldn't fit behind that table. She was probably along the same wall as the door, frightened, terrified. He laughed derisively in the cold, dark night as he thought about how she had fought when he had first taken her. "I am a warrior!" she had protested; and she had tried to fight him, but it had done no good, just as it would do no good now. He nodded to two of his men to go toward the cabin. They moved silently in the night, one on either side of the open door. They waited and watched, each taking a look inside the cabin; there was no movement. There were loud yells and the two Crows rushed into the cabin, firing their rifles at the table. Then Crooked Teeth sent in the rest of his men; it was time to seize the enemy.

Shots were fired from inside and Crooked Teeth moved to a place where he could see. He heard one of his men cry out, then another, then he saw the white man stand up behind the table, swinging the rifle at the remaining Crows. His men were told to take the man alive, so they converged on him, without getting close enough to be hurt. Trenton swung out wildly with his rifle, but the Crows, although close enough not to let him get away, stood well back. Trenton stood still, withdrawing his knife. They would have to fight him now. He advanced, his knife held in front, clearly signifying that he was ready to die. The Crows let him move forward, but as he got to the door he was stopped by the evil presence of Crooked Teeth, who stood with his rifle aimed at Trenton.

"So, white man, we meet again."

Trenton didn't betray any emotion; he knew he had to act fast before he was killed. He lifted his arm and threw his knife at Crooked Teeth. Crooked Teeth fired his gun, at the same time moving to the side. Trenton's knife landed in the wood beside the Crow chief's head.

Crooked Teeth walked over to Trenton and nodded at his men to pick him up. In spite of the bullet wound in his shoulder, they dragged Trenton to his feet. "Now," Crooked Teeth said as he looked around the room, "tell me where the girl is."

"She's not here," Trenton responded forcefully, "and you'll never find her."

Crooked Teeth stared at Trenton and without warning struck him across the face with the butt of his rifle. "I will find her, and when I do you will both be sorry." He screamed at his men to tie Trenton up and he searched the cabin.

He had not seen her come out and as far as he knew, there was no other way out of the cabin. She had to be there somewhere.

Trenton wriggled his hands against the rope, but knew it was useless. His shoulder was throbbing and he could feel the blood pouring down his arm. He tried to move his jaw around, but it felt as though it were broken. He looked up at Crooked Teeth and he knew he was in for a great deal of suffering. But it didn't matter; all that mattered was that Aeneva was safe.

"What are you smiling about?" Crooked Teeth stood over Trenton, his look menacing.

"You won't find her. She's probably back with her people by now."

"What do you mean? She did not leave this cabin. We watched!"

"You thought you watched."

Crooked Teeth kicked Trenton in the stomach, knocking him backward. He pulled him up by his shirt and stared into his face. "Tell me what you mean."

"You did not see her leave the cabin; yet she is not here. Perhaps she is magic and found her own way out. She is probably working her medicine on you right now." Trenton saw the flicker of doubt in Crooked Teeth's eyes and especially in those of his men. "When she told you she was a warrior she told you the truth. She has very strong medicine; she will not forget what you did to her." Trenton glanced at the men around him.

Crooked Teeth saw the doubt in the eyes of his men and he lifted his hand in a defiant gesture. "You lie, white man. If she had such strong medicine, she would have used it long ago."

"Good medicine, strong medicine, sometimes takes a long while to work, Crooked Teeth. If you know of her grandfather, Stalking Horse, then you know that his wife is Sun Dancer, a great Cheyenne healer and medicine maker. She also has dream visions." Crooked Teeth was now interested. In spite of the Crow's great outward show of strength and courage, Trenton had gotten to him where all Indians were vulnerable—medicine and spirits. The longer he could keep Crooked Teeth talking, the better chance Aeneva would have of getting away.

"The girl's grandmother, I have heard of her."

"Yes, and I'm surprised you were so foolish to have treated the girl the way you did. Her grandmother will not forget that."

"The girl is my enemy, just as all Cheyennes are my enemy."

"It makes no difference to Sun Dancer. You have hurt and defiled something she holds dearer than life itself."

"Her granddaughter?"

Trenton nodded ominously, looking slowly around the room at all of the men. "I saw Sun Dancer before I left. She took me into her medicine lodge. She sang songs and said many prayers and chants, and she made a colored smoke. It was in that smoke that she saw the vision."

"What did she see?" One of the other Crows walked up.

"She saw her granddaughter being tortured and she saw the man who did it to her." Trenton looked at Crooked Teeth. "It was she who sent me after you, Crooked Teeth. She knew who you were and where you would be. That is why I was waiting for you that day."

Crooked Teeth slammed his rifle down on the wood floor. "I do not believe you, white man. You lie!"

"If that is what you want to believe—"

Crooked Teeth yelled and took out his knife, jumping on Trenton and sticking the knife at his throat. "I will kill you now."

"No, Crooked Teeth," the warrior who had walked up shouted at Crooked Teeth, shoving him away from Trenton. He faced the war chief with his rifle, pointing it at the chief's head. "I want to hear what the white man has to say." He looked at the other Crows who surrounded Crooked Teeth. "We want to hear."

"You cannot believe what this white coward says. He will do anything to save his life."

"He does not seem afraid to die, Crooked Teeth. You have waited this long to kill him, you can wait a little longer."

"Sun Dancer told me to offer a trade for her grand-daughter. If you accepted, she would do nothing. If you refused, she would realize that you had little honor and her medicine would work well on you."

"You lie!" Crooked Teeth struck out at Trenton again, but was was pulled back by his men. He looked around at them. "You cannot believe the ramblings of an old Chey-enne woman."

"A Cheyenne healer and medicine woman, Crooked Teeth. One who has been known to deal with Crows hon-orably. Continue, white man."

"She told me if you refused the offer, I would have to steal Aeneva. She said that we would get away and that we would go to the mountains and that you would follow us here. She said. . . ." Trenton hesitated deliberately, making Crooked Teeth wait.

"What did she say, white man?"

"She said that Crooked Teeth would not leave these mountains alive."

Crooked Teeth lunged forward, his knife sinking into Trenton's stomach before he was dragged away by his men. "You lie, you lie!"

The other Crow warrior motioned for the men to hold Crooked Teeth; he knelt down next to Trenton. The knife had entered in the muscle of the abdomen. "You will live," the Crow said casually, examining Trenton's rifle wound. "You are losing much blood from this wound."

"It doesn't matter," Trenton whispered, the pain obvi-ous in his face and eyes.

The Crow spoke softly. "Did the Cheyenne woman see anything else? Did she speak about Crooked Teeth's men?"

Trenton shook his head, closing his eyes momentarily, then opening them again. "She only saw that Crooked

272

Teeth would die here. He was the one she was using her medicine on.''

The Crow warrior nodded and reached around his neck, pulling out the small leather bag from inside his shirt. He cut Trenton's shirt open and sprinkled the contents of the bag onto the wounds. Trenton grimaced, but made no sound. The Crow spoke again. ''I have no fight with the girl or her grandmother. Not all Crows are like him.'' He nodded toward Crooked Teeth. He sprinkled some more of the contents of the bag on Trenton's wounds. ''It is not the same as the Cheyenne healer's, but it is good. It was made by my mother.'' He walked outside, grabbed a handful of snow, and placed some over each wound. ''The bleeding should stop soon.''

''Thank you.'' Trenton spoke in halting Crow. ''What is your name?''

''My name is Long Knife.''

''You are a good man, Long Knife. I will not forget what you have done.''

Long Knife stood up, shrugging slightly. ''You did nothing to me; neither did the girl.'' He turned to the men who were holding Crooked Teeth. ''Let him go.''

The men backed away as Crooked Teeth flailed his arms at them. ''You will die for this, Long Knife.'' He stood up and moved toward Long Knife.

''I do not wish to kill you, Crooked Teeth,'' Long Knife replied in a low voice, withdrawing his knife and watching Crooked Teeth. ''There is no reason to kill the white man; I was foolish to listen to you.''

''You were foolish to go against me.'' Crooked Teeth lunged forward, but a shot fired at his feet stopped him. He turned toward the door; Aeneva was standing there, the rifle held in her hands. ''You!'' he cried out.

''Yes, Crooked Teeth, it is I. Drop the knife.'' Aeneva

273

waited until he did so and she looked at Trenton lying on the floor. Her eyes went to Long Knife. "Is he alive?"

"Yes."

Aeneva nodded. "I have no fight with you or the others. My fight is with Crooked Teeth."

Long Knife motioned to the others. "We will go." He and the other Crows started toward the door and Aeneva moved to the side. "You have much courage to come back here and face him. Why?"

She kept her rifle pointed at Crooked Teeth. "I must prove to myself that he did not defeat me. He did not give me the chance to fight before; I am giving myself the chance now."

"Good luck to you, Cheyenne woman. You will need it."

Aeneva did not turn as Long Knife and the other Crows walked out of the cabin; she kept her eyes on Crooked Teeth. He stood still, his evil eyes drilling into Aeneva's. "It will be different this time," she said slowly, walking around the perimeter of the room, always keeping her rifle aimed at Crooked Teeth.

"What are you talking about?" he asked indignantly.

"You will not torture me this time. This time we will be equals."

"Equals?" Crooked Teeth laughed. "You are stupid, girl."

"I do not think so," Aeneva responded calmly, squeezing the trigger of the rifle. The shot sounded and Crooked Teeth looked down at his right arm. He lifted his hand and looked at the blood. Aeneva watched him a moment then squeezed the trigger again, this time shooting him in the left thigh. The pain was equalized now; his right arm would be difficult to lift and his left leg would slow his movement. She threw the rifle down on the floor with a loud clatter and unsheathed her knife.

"Aeneva, don't do it," Trenton cried, but Aeneva ignored him.

"We are even now, Crooked Teeth. Pick up your knife."

Crooked Teeth rubbed his left thigh. "Why did you shoot me? We are not equals if I am wounded."

"You forget that I am still suffering wounds myself. Both of my arms are weak and I am unable to move as quickly as I used to. I think that makes us even." Her expression hardened. "Pick up the knife, Crooked Teeth, and let us see what a true coward you are."

Crooked Teeth wasted no more time. He bent over and picked up the knife with his right hand, grimacing as he did so.

"Does it hurt, Crooked Teeth? I hope so," Aeneva said harshly, moving slowly to the side.

"You will die for this," Crooked Teeth screamed and ran toward Aeneva, missing her with a wild swipe of his knife. As he turned, she slashed his side.

"You tried to kill me once before, but you could not. You are a weak man, Crooked Teeth, one who preys on women and children. You do not know what it is like to fight with honor." A wild expression appeared on his face and his lips trembled. She stilled the fear inside of her and forced herself to watch him. She eyed the blood as it poured from his wounds. She had been lucky; he had taken off his robe. It might not have been so easy otherwise. Crooked Teeth's war cry resounded again as he ran across the cabin, slashing his knife at the air next to her. He turned quickly and was upon her, knocking her over. Aeneva rolled away from him, coming to her feet and holding her knife in front. Crooked Teeth was losing a lot of blood, but he seemed to be driven by some evil force

275

that would not allow him to stop. He attacked again but this time Aeneva had prepared herself; she moved back and swiped out at him with her knife. He jumped backward and lost his balance, falling over one of the chairs. Aeneva was on him, her knife at his throat, her knee on the hand that held his knife. "You are evil, Crooked Teeth. You have no soul."

Crooked Teeth glowered at her with a crooked, malevolent smile, and spat in her face. Aeneva drew the knife sharply across his throat, listening to him as he choked on his own blood. His body jerked and his head fell to the side. Aeneva stared at him, unable to believe that he was actually dead. So, Trenton was right; he was only a man after all. She wiped the blood from her knife and resheathed it. She stood up, still staring at Crooked Teeth's body. She put her hands under his arms and dragged his body out into the woods, then ran back to the cabin and Trenton. She knelt next to him, checking his wounds. She looked at the medicine that had been applied to his wounds and she put her nose next to it, trying to smell it.

"The Crow said it was good medicine. His mother made it." Trenton looked at Aeneva with glazed eyes.

"The Crow helped you?"

"He saved my life. Remember that, Aeneva."

"What, that one Crow is good?"

"No, that not all Crows are bad." He attempted to sit up, but he fell back against the floor. "I won't be able to fix the door for a while."

"Do not worry about the door; I will find a way to fix it." She found a robe and covered Trenton. She pushed the hair back from his forehead; he was hot, in spite of the cold temperature. "The Crow was right; it is good medicine. The bleeding has stopped." She pressed the flesh around the bullet wound and Trenton flinched. "I will have to take the bullet out.''

"Take it out," Trenton said matter-of-factly.

"It will be painful."

"You don't have to tell me, Aeneva." Trenton tried to smile. "Just do what you have to do."

"All right." Aeneva walked to the fire and stuck the blade of her knife into it, holding it there until it glowed orange. She walked back to Trenton and knelt next to him. She began to perspire and she wiped her palms on her clothes.

"Go ahead," Trenton urged calmly.

Aeneva stuck the point of the knife into the wound. Trenton groaned. Beads of sweat broke out over his face and trickled down. As Aeneva poked and explored with her knife and fingers, Trenton stilled his mind and body against the incredible pain. When Aeneva was through she cleaned the wound, applied a poultice, and carefully covered Trenton with a robe. She touched Trenton's hot face; he had fallen asleep from exhaustion.

It began to snow again and the wind blew through the open cabin. Walking to the door, which was lying on the floor, Aeneva tried to lift it up; it was solid. She dragged a chair over and lifted the door as far as she could, placing it on the chair. She lined the bottom up with the base of the door frame and lifted it up the rest of the way, pulling the bottom out a little way so the door was balanced against the frame. She located the hammer and nails and hammered the leather hinges to the door frame; she opened and closed the door several times, pleased with herself that she had done it. She put more wood on the fire and lay down next to Trenton. His face was flushed and Aeneva placed a cool hand on his cheek. She rubbed it gently, fingering the swollen bruise on his jaw. She stood up and went outside to fill a bowl with snow, then placed some of it on his jaw, and rubbed the rest all over his face to cool him down. After a while, she placed the bowl to the side and covered herself again with the robe.

Aeneva took a deep breath and closed her eyes. For the first time in months, she would be able to rest easy. Crooked Teeth was dead and he could not hurt her again. Thanks to Trenton, she had found the strength to face her fear and deal with it. She would never be able to repay him for what he had done for her, but she would try. She looked over at him and smiled; she would try.

CHAPTER XIV

It took William Wainwright almost a full year and a half to track down his grandson, but he finally did it with the aid of a Crow tracker named Long Nose. He had read the letter Trenton wrote him and reread the letters Lydia had written him before her death, but he still blamed Trenton for Lydia's death. It seemed improbable—indeed, impossible—that his sweet Lydia could do any of the things she had described to him in her letters. He was sure that she'd written the letters because Trenton had ordered her to. Then the letter came from Trenton saying that Lydia had died in childbirth, leaving a son—a grandson, Nathan Joseph, and that Trenton was taking him to Cheyenne country to be raised by savages. No grandson of his was going to be raised that way.

It took him a long time, but he finally found someone who was not afraid to track Trenton Hawkins. Long Nose worked for the army and had no loyalty to any tribe, including his own. He had murdered someone in his own tribe and was now an outcast. For the right money he would track anyone. When Wainwright had lost Trenton's trail in Cheyenne and Arapaho country, it was Long Nose who had picked it up again. It was also Long Nose who had been able to find out that the child, Nathan Hawkins, was alone with a band of Cheyennes led by Stalking Horse.

"Good work, Long Nose. You'll have a bonus for this." Colonel Wainwright slapped the Crow on the back. "It should be easy now."

"Not so easy," the tracker replied. "Stalking Horse very strong, very powerful. If we do something to hurt him, whole Cheyenne tribe will come after us."

"We're not going to do anything to hurt him; all we're going to do is go in there and get my grandson. He belongs to me."

"We must be careful. I do not care how many Cheyennes I hurt, but I know from all the years they have fought with my people, they will not give up looking for you or the boy until they have found you both. They do not suffer defeat easily."

"They won't find me or the boy. Besides, the Cheyennes aren't like other tribes; they're afraid of us. They seldom come into our towns or cities."

"You are wrong, soldier man," Long Nose replied cuttingly. "The Cheyennes are afraid of nothing or no one. They do not go into your cities because they do not think you people are worthy." Long Nose stared at Wainwright for a moment, then walked silently away.

"Insolent son of a bitch," Wainwright muttered to himself. "We'll just see how brave the Cheyennes are."

Although outwardly disdaining Long Nose's knowledge of the land and people, Wainwright finally deferred to the Crow's superior knowledge. He was smart enough and had been a soldier long enough to know when he was out of his element. So Wainwright and Long Nose planned how they would get the child out with as little bloodshed as possible. The Cheyennes would have reason enough to come after them because of the kidnapping, but if the soldiers killed some of their people, they would be even more tenacious about hunting them down.

280

They decided to wait until spring, when the majority of the Cheyenne men would be out hunting and the women would be spread around the camp doing various jobs. It would be easy enough to spot the white-haired child and go in after him.

"But how will we get in there without anyone spotting us?"

"I will dress as a Cheyenne and ride into the camp. No one will expect it."

"But you told me yourself you look much different from the Cheyennes. Even your skin is darker."

"Yes, but they will not know that until I am close enough to grab the white child. By then it will be too late. Once I have the child, no one will risk hurting him to shoot at me. They will follow, but they will only attack when they think it is safe."

"Good. I agree to the plan."

Long Nose looked up at the colonel and slowly shook his head. "You have no choice but to agree to the plan, soldier man." And with that Long Nose rode off, promising to return when the time was right.

Wainwright looked out the window of his office at the snow on the ground. There were five, perhaps six more weeks of winter left. He wasn't sure he could wait that long, but he had no choice. If he wanted to see his grandson he had to be patient and wait it out. Once he had the boy, there would be nothing Trenton Hawkins could do. If he came after the boy, Wainwright would kill him or hang him for desertion, whichever was the most convenient at the time. Whichever he chose to do, it was a sure thing that Trenton Hawkins would never live long enough to see his son grow up.

Aeneva checked the horses and reset the traps; then she

wandered down by the stream and sat down. She looked up at the sky and noticed tiny patches of blue as the clouds raced by. She smiled, knowing that it wouldn't be long before they could go home. She looked down at the stream. The wind blew slightly, making a whistling sound, and she thought she could actually hear voices of a time past, when her parents and Jean were here. Jean had told her of the time her mother had fallen into the stream with her robe on and almost drowned until her father had saved her. Young Eagle had been angry with Little Flower and had almost beaten her. It was then he knew he was in love with her; but it was a forbidden love.

Aeneva sighed. Her mother and father were tormented by the fact that they had been raised as brother and sister. Although there was no actual blood tie, the taboo on such a relationship was a great one. But eventually they defied everyone, including their own parents, and left the band to live on their own and raise their children. Tears came to Aeneva's eyes as she thought of her mother, when, all alone and with a small baby, she was kidnapped by a Crow warrior. She and her mother had lived with the Crows for over two winters before they were finally found by her father and grandfather. When her father and mother had found each other again, it was only for a short time. They went back to the place where they had had their children, and it was there they both had been murdered by Crows. Aeneva slammed her fists into the cold snow; tears of anger, frustration, and loss streamed down her face. Her parents had never had a chance in life. Never.

"What are you thinking about?" Trenton walked up behind Aeneva and sat down next to her. She turned her face away, trying to wipe away the tears. He pulled her face toward his. "Why are you crying?"

"I am not crying!" She shrugged his hand away and sniffled slightly, trying to keep her nose from running. Trenton had a most uncommonly bad sense of timing, she thought indignantly.

"If you're not crying, then what exactly is it you're doing?"

"It is none of your business what I am doing. Just leave me alone." She started to stand up, but Trenton yanked her back down.

"Wait; I won't bother you anymore."

Aeneva glared over at him and settled down again, staring out at the frozen stream. "You should not be out here. You are not completely healed."

"I need exercise."

"You need to get well."

"I got lonely."

"Go talk to the horses then," Aeneva snapped.

"Tell me, Aeneva, who is the woman who lies with me every night and kisses me with such tenderness?"

"I was only comforting you."

"Do you comfort all wounded men that way?"

"Stop it! You have always known how to make me angry, Trenton."

"I know." He reached out and caressed her cheek. "You're cold. Come into the cabin."

"No."

"Why not?"

"Because I feel uncomfortable in there. There is not enough room."

"Ah, I think I understand. Because I am getting stronger, there isn't enough room for you to stay away from me. When I was weak, it was all right for you to lie next to me and kiss me because I couldn't do anything back. But now that I am strong, you're afraid I'll do

283

something—"

"Stop!" Again Aeneva started to stand up, but Trenton grabbed her robe and she fell to the ground. He pushed her back into the snow and put his weight atop her, forcing her to be still.

"Why are you so afraid of me? I won't hurt you."

"I am not afraid of you." She tried to push him away, but he pressed harder. "Let me go, Trenton."

"No, not until you talk to me. I saw the change in you begin a few days ago. Before, you were ready to—"

"Before, you were going to die."

"But now that I'm going to live everything is changed."

"Yes."

"Oh, Aeneva," he said softly, covering her mouth with his, denying the fact that she tried to move her mouth away, waiting until her lips moved against his. She sighed softly and he rolled away, quickly getting to his feet.

"What are you doing?" she asked, totally surprised.

"I don't want to force you to do anything against your will." He slapped his arms together. "I'm cold. I'll see you back at the cabin."

"You, you *veho!*" Aeneva screamed vehemently, gathering together a ball of snow and throwing it at Trenton's back. She missed and it sailed by him. He laughed and ran through the woods back to the cabin. Aeneva fumed for a few minutes until she, too, began to smile. She wondered if her parents had loved each other the way she loved Trenton. He was right, she was afraid; but not of him, only of the unknown. She didn't want to find him again only to lose him. She found a stick and broke through some of the ice to the water. She quickly stripped off her clothes and washed, steeling herself against the freezing cold. She wanted to cleanse herself, make herself as pure as she could for him. She lowered her hair into the water, rinsing it quickly. She was shivering now, but she wouldn't stop. She had no one else to help prepare her for her marriage bed, so she would do it herself. She rubbed pieces of snow over her body until she was shivering uncontrollably; she wanted to feel she had purified herself. When she could control the shivering no longer she threw on her robe and ran barefooted through the snow, holding her moccasins and dress in her arms. Her teeth chattered and her head felt frozen. When she reached the door her fingers wouldn't work to open it and she banged on it with her fists. When Trenton wouldn't come she called to him; he finally came to the door. Aeneva fell against him, shivering, her teeth chattering.

"What in the hell have you done?" He carried her to the fire, settling her down next to it, and immediately began rubbing her feet and legs, hands and arms. He removed her robe and covered her with one of the warmer robes which was lying on the floor. As her shivering subsided and she started to relax, Trenton forced her to drink some hot coffee. "What did you do?"

"I took a bath," she chattered between clenched teeth.

"Why?"

"For you." She sipped at the coffee, wrapping her hands around the hot tin.

"For me? What in the hell are you talking about?"

"I was trying to purify myself for you."

"Aeneva, what are you talking about?" But as soon as he asked, Trenton knew what she meant. It was the most important thing for a Cheyenne woman to come to her marriage bed pure, untouched by any man; it was the best thing she could offer her man. But because Crooked Teeth had taken Aeneva, she felt that she was impure.

She endured her own purification ceremony to make herself worthy of Trenton. He shook his head and reached out, pulling her into the circle of his arms. "You didn't have to make yourself pure for me, Aeneva. I already see you as pure, untouched by any man."

"But we both know that is not so," she replied quietly, moving her face against his chest. "Crooked Teeth made me do so many things."

"I don't want to hear about them."

"You are ashamed, as I am."

"I am not ashamed, Aeneva." He lifted her face, kissing her softly. "Crooked Teeth is dead and all that he did to you is dead. You must forget it and think of us."

"It is all I think of. It frightens me."

"Why?"

"Because I do not know the future."

"None of us knows the future. We must hope that our lives will be long and happy; that is all we can hope for."

"I must ask something of you, Trenton. Think before you answer me."

"Go on."

"I must ask you never to leave me. If you did, I am not sure I could ever take you back."

"Why would I want to leave you?" He bent down and kissed her, but Aeneva pulled away.

"Please, Trenton; this is important to me. This is all I ask of you. Promise me you will never leave me."

Trenton nodded solemnly. "I promise that I will never leave you, Aeneva. Never." He took her face in his hands and stared at her a long while. "Now I have something to ask of you."

"What is it?"

"I want you to know that if something should happen and we get separated—"

"But you just promised you would never leave me."

Trenton placed a finger over Aeneva's mouth. "I said I would never leave you and I meant it. But sometimes things happen and people are forced to be apart for a time. If that happens to us, believe that I will always come back to you."

"No." Aeneva moved away and turned her head. "You will leave me again."

"I told you I would come back to you and I did."

"After you took another woman as your wife. If she had not died, you would not be here now." She turned to face him. "Is that not so?"

"That is not so. I didn't love Lydia; I married her because I felt obligated. Even if she had lived, we wouldn't have stayed together for long."

"You cannot say that for sure."

"But I can. All the time I was with her, I was thinking of you. Always."

"You have always confused me with your words, Trenton. Even when we were children."

"I'm not trying to confuse you; I'm telling you the truth. I promise you I will never leave you and I mean it, but if something should happen to separate us, believe that I will come to you again, no matter where you are. Tell me you belive me, Aeneva."

Aeneva could not resist the clear blue eyes that spoke with such honesty. "I do believe you, Trenton." She leaned forward and put her arms around him. "I am ready now," she said solemnly.

Trenton laughed and held Aeneva away from him. "You sound as if you are going to the gallows."

"I do not understand. What is this 'gallows'?"

"You sound as if you are going to be tortured." He touched the wrinkle that appeared on her forehead. "But

287

then it was torture for you, wasn't it?'' He lifted her chin and touched his lips to hers, moving them gently against hers. He stopped.

''What is it?''

''I forgot.'' Trenton opened the small buckskin bag that hung around his neck and shook the contents into the palm of his hand. Among the herbs and medicines was a bright gold band. He took it out, placed the medicine back into the bag, and wiped it off with his shirt. He took Aeneva's left hand and placed the ring on it. ''With this ring, I thee wed. I, Trenton, take you, Aeneva, for my wife.''

Aeneva stared at Trenton and down at the gold band. ''I, Aeneva, take you, Trenton, for my husband. I will love you, care for you, and I will always believe in you.'' She took his hand and kissed it. ''I think we are married now.''

''Yes, I think so,'' Trenton replied softly, leaning forward and pushing her robe away. He ran his hands along her shoulders and down her arms, his eyes never leaving her face. ''I knew you would be this beautiful. When we were children and I first saw you, I knew you would grow up to look like this.''

''The light from the fire is not much and it can hide many things.''

''Come, Aeneva, I have never known you to be humble.''

''I am not being humble; I just do not think of myself as beautiful. My grandmother and my mother were beautiful.''

''And so are you. You are each different but each beautiful.''

''*Naxane* Jean said you were a poet. What does that mean?''

288

"It means I am good with words." Trenton smiled, reaching out for Aeneva. "Ah, my wife. I can't believe it." He kissed her, running his hands along the smooth skin of her naked body. She was now warmed by the fire and her long hair hung in wet trails down to her waist. She shut her eyes as Trenton ran his hands over her body, enjoying the sensations he stirred in her but also frightened by what would come next. Her only experience with a man had been a violent, abusive one, and it was difficult for her to put that from her mind. "I love you, Aeneva. *Ne-mehotatse.*" He kissed her, touching and exploring her young body. But when he undressed and it came time for the actual physical act, Aeneva pushed him away, turning onto her side.

"I am sorry Trenton. I feel such shame."

"It's all right. It will just take time, that's all."

"I thought it would be easy with you, you are so different from him."

"It doesn't matter. In time you will forget him and everything he did to you."

"I hope you are right, Trenton." I pray with all my heart that you are right, she thought to herself.

The next few weeks passed slowly for Trenton and Aeneva. They were thrown together in close quarters, unable to go out except for short periods during the days, and their tempers were beginning to flair. Trenton could think of nothing but making love to Aeneva; having her so close but being unable to touch her was like the most horrible of tortures. For Aeneva, it was also a torture. Although she desired Trenton and wished with all her heart to love him as a woman should, she was still overwhelmed by the fear that had stopped her the first night they had tried to make love. She found it rather strange that she, a woman warrior, a woman who was afraid of no one and who had no fear of fighting, was afraid of such a natural physical act. But for her it wasn't natural. Crooked Teeth had seen to that. Not only had he made sure that she found the act of physical love disgusting, he had made sure that she was ruined for any man in the future. Every night she steeled herself against the fear that overcame her and many times she went to Trenton, but each time she came away scared, ashamed, and angry with herself. She could also see how it was affecting Trenton. He was growing more surly every day, becoming impatient and rude. Many times he would stomp out of the small cabin whether it was snowing or not.

"What are you making?" Aeneva watched Trenton as he carved on a piece of wood.

"I don't know yet. I'm just keeping my hands busy."

"Perhaps you could make a flute for Nathan. I'm sure he would like that."

"I don't need you to tell me what my son likes, Aeneva."

"You do know how to be cruel, Trenton." Aeneva spoke softly as, grabbing her robe, she walked to the door. She pulled the gold band from her finger and threw it at Trenton. "Perhaps we should dissolve this marriage before it has begun."

Trenton watched her as she walked out of the cabin, disgusted with himself but unable to do anything about it. He felt as if he should have gotten through to her by now and he couldn't figure out why he was unable to. What had Crooked Teeth done to her that had made her so afraid? What had he done to ruin the act of physical love for her for the rest of her life? He started to get up, but thought better of it. Aeneva needed time to think and so did he. He picked up his mother's ring from the floor and rolled it around in his hand. She had given it to him before she died, asking that he give it to his wife when he married. The ring had been his grandmother's, Grandma Hawkins', and before she had died, she had asked his father to give it to his wife. Trenton laughed out loud, wondering what his grandmother would have thought if she had known two Indian women had worn the ring. He knew one thing for sure, no one would wear the ring but Aeneva; even Lydia had not worn it.

As he reached for his knife and the piece of wood, he heard the howling of wolves close by. "Damn!" he yelled, jumping up, grabbing his rifle and robe, and heading out the door. The horses were whinnying and bumping each other in their lean-to, and Trenton stopped for a moment to comfort them. "Whoa now, whoa there. It's all right. It's all right." When the horses had quieted, Trenton followed Aeneva's tracks into the woods. The wolves howled again, quite close this time, and Trenton fired up into the trees, the sound echoing through the still air. The howling immediately stopped and Trenton cupped his hands around his mouth. "Aeneva, Aeneva. Are you all right?" When there was no answer, Trenton continued to follow her tracks deeper into the woods. He heard sounds around him and he knew the wolves were watching him, waiting and wondering. He fired the rifle again and he called out Aeneva's name. He easily followed her tracks into a clearing and looked around. The tracks suddenly ended a few feet ahead of him. How could she have just disappeared? He walked slowly forward, looking all around the clearing, stopping just before he fell into the trap. It was an old pit that Jean had used years before to catch deer, elk, or wild mountain sheep. They would scamper unknowingly through the clearing and fall right into the pit breaking their legs or their necks. Jean finally quit using the trap because so many of the animals suffered for so long before he was able to get to them.

"Aeneva, are you all right?" Trenton could barely see her in the deep hole. He was afraid she had broken an arm or leg.

"I am all right. Why were you firing your rifle?"

"Wolves. Didn't you hear them?"

"Yes, they smelled me in here. They will be angry with you for getting me out."

"Let them be angry then." Trenton looked around him. He would have to run back to the cabin for some rope if he couldn't find a branch long and thick enough to pull Aeneva out. He walked around, checking some of the branches that were lying on the ground. He checked several until he found one to his liking. He walked back to the hole and stuck it down inside. "Grab onto this and try to climb out while I pull."

"Why don't you just run back to the cabin and get some rope?"

"Don't argue with me now. Just grab onto the branch."

Aeneva reached up and grabbed onto the branch, trying to climb up the inside of the hole as Trenton pulled. Every time she started to climb, her feet slipped and she fell back down. "The sides are too slick. I can't get a foothold. You'll have to go back for the rope."

"Damn!" Trenton threw the branch to the outside of the hole. "All right, I'm going back, but you keep the rifle. Stand to the side while I throw it down. I'm throwing down some bullets too."

"No, you'll need it in case—"

"Just listen to me for once, Aeneva. The wolves aren't going to follow me when they have you trapped here. If they get too close, fire at them and let them know you're alive."

"All right, Trenton. Just go."

Trenton retraced his steps through the clearing and the woods, running into low branches and knocking off chunks of snow as he did so. The run back to the cabin seemed interminable; all he could think of was Aeneva trapped in that hole. When he reached the cabin, he ran inside and got the other rifle, loaded it, and got the rope from the lean-to. As he ran back toward Aeneva he heard the wolves and two shots. He hurried faster, reminding himself that wolves did not attack unless they are hungry. But that only made him feel worse because he knew for sure that these wolves were hungry. He sprinted through the woods and finally saw the clearing and in it, a large pack of wolves surrounding the pit. He shot at them, yelling and screaming at the top of his lungs. They scattered slightly and he fired again until they finally ran off into the woods. He knelt down by the hole, dropping the rope down to Aeneva. "You're all right?"

"Yes," she said anxiously, taking the rope and tying it around her waist. She reached for the rifle and tucked it underneath her arm. "All right, Trenton, you can pull."

Trenton wrapped the rope once around his waist and held it in both hands. He backed up in the snow, easily pulling Aeneva from the pit. He ran to her, pulling off the rope, and taking her hand. "Come on, let's get out of here." They ran back to the cabin, stopping only once to fire off a shot when they thought they heard something in the woods around them. When they were safely inside the cabin, Trenton walked to Aeneva and took her into his arms.

"Don't ever do that to me again."

"I am sorry. I was angry."

"You had a right to be. I shouldn't have said what I did before."

"It is not your fault, it is my fault. I cannot be a good wife to you, Trenton. It is not possible."

"Don't say that. I don't believe it."

"It is true. We have tried, but I am too frightened."

"But what are you frightened of? He cannot hurt you anymore, Aeneva. And I will not hurt you."

"I know that."

"Then what is it?"

She turned away from him, dropping her robe on the floor. "No matter how good or gentle you are, you are still a man, a man who will use me the same way Crooked Teeth did."

"I don't want to use you, I want to make love to you. There is a difference."

Aeneva shook her head. "No, it is all the same. I swore to myself that if I ever got away from Crooked Teeth, I would never let that happen to me again."

"What is it you want from me, Aeneva? You want me to share your robe and live with you, but you don't want me to touch you? Is that it?"

Aeneva walked toward the fire. "I don't know."

"Answer me!" Trenton jerked her around. "Tell me the truth for once. You owe me that at least."

"Yes, I want you, but not in the way you want me." Her voice trembled slightly and she could no longer meet his eyes which had suddenly grown cold.

"Oh, I see. You knew it all this time, but you waited until now to tell me. Why? Why, damn it?"

"Because I hoped that I would change. I hoped that it would be different with you. I was wrong."

"Yes, so was I," he replied angrily, throwing a coffee tin across the room. "Goddamn you, Aeneva, I've never known you to back away from anything—even Crooked Teeth. You finally faced him and you won. Why won't you try with this? Why won't you try for us?''

''I have tried. I can do no more,'' she said finally, walking across the room and picking up the coffee tin.

''All right, we'll leave it for now, but you'll change your mind, Aeneva. You will want me.'' He stomped across the room and sat down at the table, picking up his knife and the piece of wood.

I already do want you, my love, Aeneva thought to herself, wondering solemnly what would become of them.

The wind whipped at the door, shaking it on its loose hinges and whistling through the cabin. Aeneva sat up, aware of the sudden darkness. The fire was barely smoldering; only a few embers glowed. She started to get up to put more wood on the fire, but she was rooted to the spot, suddenly too terrified to move. The fear, the terror, came back to her as it hadn't for a long time now.

''Aeneva?'' She heard his voice out of the darkness and she sighed deeply, moving closer to him. She snuggled against him, laying her head on his chest. His arm came around her and she felt the security of his presence. ''Did you have a dream?''

''The darkness woke me up. The wind must have blown out the fire. Listen,'' she said softly, her head turning slightly, ''you can hear it sing. Grandmother once told me that many of the old people believe that when the wind whistles, it is really the spirits of the dead talking.''

''Do you believe that?''

''No, not when it is warm and the sun is shining; but when it is dark and I am frightened . . .''

His hand stroked her bare shoulder. ''I knew you were

frightened; I could sense it. Were you thinking of Crooked Teeth again?''

"For a moment when I first woke up, I forgot that he was dead. I forgot that there is nothing to be frightened of anymore.''

"It will take time; I know that now.''

"It seems as if it has been long enough.''

"Not so long." He pulled her closer, moving his head up her throat. "This is the first time you've let me hold you in a long while.''

"I want to be strong; I am trying.''

"You can still be strong and let a man love you." He raised himself up on his elbow and stared down at her in the semidarkness. He touched her face lightly and bent down to kiss her. She responded willingly but with some hesitation. Trenton sensed it and pulled away, taking her hand in his. "There is nothing wrong with having feelings, Aeneva. It does not make you weak.''

"Now you sound like my grandmother.''

"Your grandmother is a wise woman.''

"Yes, and she has it in her mind that you are the only man for me. She thinks you will tame me." Her face moved closer to his. "Will you try to tame me?''

"I don't want to tame you; I only want to love you." He reached for her, but she sat up.

"Does it bother you that another man has had me?''

"What?''

"You know what Crooked Teeth did to me, how he used me. Does it bother you? I am so different now, Trenton.''

"I am different also, Aeneva. Does it bother you that I was married to Lydia?''

Aeneva's eyes sought him out in the pale light of the coals. "Yes, it does bother me. But it does not bother me enough to want to let you go."

"Then you know how I feel." He reached for her hands, squeezing them tightly as he spoke. "Sometimes I think about what Crooked Teeth did to you and it eats away at me, not because you come to me as any less of a woman, but because I couldn't do anything to help you. That makes me feel very weak."

"You could do nothing; you did not even know where I was."

Trenton sighed and nodded his head. "It seems we've missed each other too often in the past few years. I won't let us be apart again." He kissed her deeply. "I never stopped thinking about you all the years we were apart. Even with Lydia—"

"You told me before."

"But I want you to understand and I don't think you do. I felt I had to find the man who murdered my father, but I had it in my mind all the time to come back here to you. Even after I married Lydia, I knew deep down inside we would be together again."

"I also knew that we would be together again; it was meant to be." She reached up and touched his face, running her fingers lovingly over his features. "I want more than anything in this world to love you, Trenton. I do." She got up on her knees and leaned against him, kissing him deeply. His arms came around her, stroking her back and hips. But just as they got started Trenton pushed away.

"That's enough of that. A man can only take so much."

"How much can a man take?"

"That's not funny, Aeneva; now lie down and go to sleep."

"I don't want to sleep; I don't want to try to escape

297

anymore. I want to learn about love. I want you to teach me.''

Trenton groaned and shook his head. ''We've been through this before and one of us winds up getting angry. Let's just wait awhile longer until you're sure you're ready.''

''Oh, you are stubborn, Trenton.'' Aeneva sighed impatiently, pulling the robe away from him and climbing on top of him. ''What do I have to do to make you understand that I am ready. I don't want to wait any longer.''

Trenton looked up at the woman sitting astride him and he had to smile. It was just like her to finally decide she was ready and to take the initiative. ''All right, Wife; for once I won't argue with you.'' He put his arms around her and pulled her down to him, kissing her deeply, savoring the softness of her lips and the taste of her mouth. He wound his fingers through the dark mass of her hair and felt for the first time the way her body moved against his. His hands moved down her back to her buttocks and thighs and back up again to encircle her in a tight embrace; then he rolled her onto her back. His mouth moved from her lips to her neck and throat and down to her breasts. Her skin was soft and moist and he savored its very texture. He touched, explored, and kissed her until his excitement and need had grown to grand proportions and he could no longer contain it. He was gentle with her and held himself in check, afraid that he would hurt her in some way. But she surprised him—instead of being frightened she grew as excited and consumed as he by their mutual need. She held on to him tightly, crying out at the end. She buried her face in his chest until she stopped crying.

''Are you all right?'' He brushed the wet and tangled hair back from her face. ''Did I hurt you?''

Aeneva shook her head. "You did not hurt me, Trenton. I cried because it was so different. It was never like that with him. I am crying because I am happy."

"God, I'm glad. I was so afraid I had hurt you."

"Now that I know what it's like, I'm sorry for everything I put you through. I feel so foolish."

"Don't blame yourself, I haven't been easy to live with lately. But it's over now."

"I love you, Trenton," Aeneva said softly as if just wanting to hear herself say the words. She sighed contentedly and laid her head on his chest, closing her eyes. It wasn't long before she was asleep and breathing evenly.

Trenton lay awake for some time, holding Aeneva and thinking about what their life together might be like. He felt a twinge of guilt over Lydia, feeling sorry that she hadn't known what it was like to be truly loved by a man as Aeneva now knew. He had made love to Lydia, but he had never loved her.

He kissed Aeneva's head and closed his eyes. He hadn't felt so totally at peace with himself since he had been a young boy and his father had brought him his own pony. He remembered the feeling he had had when he was out alone riding his pony, the wind against his face, no one or nothing stopping him. That was how he felt now with Aeneva by his side; he felt as if the whole world was there for him to conquer. But all he really wanted to do was to take care of Aeneva, her family, and Nathan. He finally understood why his father had been such a happy man. He had had a good woman, a son, and he had been able to live with nature in such a way that he enjoyed it and took advantage of all it had to offer, but he never destroyed it or took it for granted. He had lived at one with nature, in harmony. That was what Trenton would try to do; that was all he wanted.

Colonel Wainwright counted the weeks until spring. He knew the army would never condone his personal vendetta against Trenton Hawkins, so in spite of Lydia's letters, he renewed the desertion charge against Trenton, and he made it known that a certain band of Cheyennes was hiding Trenton and protecting him. By the time he got through with Trenton Hawkins, there would be nothing left of him.

By late April, there were sightings of various Indian bands coming down from the mountains. Wainwright ordered Long Nose to look out for Stalking Horse's band.

"They will not be there yet."

"Why? Others have been seen."

"Most of them are starving and have come down to look for food. Stalking Horse's band is not starving."

"How do you know that?"

"They have never starved before. Wherever he takes them, it is to a place that provides them with enough food for the winter. He will not be down for at least another three weeks."

Again Wainwright deferred to Long Nose's vaster knowledge and again he waited. Almost four weeks later it was Long Nose who came to him.

"It is time for us to go. They will be coming down now, following the buffalo herds."

"How many men do you want?"

"You, I, and ten others. You and they will stay back while I go into their camp. If something goes wrong you will leave."

"Ten? I'm not going into hostile Indian country with just ten men."

"You do what you want, soldier man, but stay away

from me. The Cheyennes will smell you before you even get within range of their camp. The less men you bring, the more chance we'll have of getting the boy."

"All right, all right, I'll do as you say. But shouldn't we do something to make sure you get into that camp?"

"What?"

"Perhaps my men and I could create a diversion of some kind." At the blank expression on Long Nose's face, Wainwright explained. "If my men and I rode outside where the men were hunting, perhaps we could stampede some of the buffalo; that would keep them busy enough to stay away from camp. You could go in, get the boy, and meet us somewhere."

Long Nose thought for a moment. "Yes, I think that could work. You are beginning to think like an Indian," Long Nose replied seriously and then laughed.

Wainwright bristled at the thought of being compared to an Indian, but he let it pass. The most important thing now was to get his grandson back; then he could wait for Trenton Hawkins to fall into his trap. Only when Hawkins was dead, only then, could he go on with his life.

CHAPTER XV

Sun Dancer laughed as she watched Nathan run around the camp, his soft blond hair hanging almost to his shoulders, his skin already dark from the sun. He was a beautiful child, much like his father, and he was bright. Everyone in the camp loved him and found an excuse to play with him. No one resented his presence; he was thought of as one of them. Sun Dancer scraped the flesh off the hide and stopped for a moment, resting back on her haunches. She hated this work; she had always hated it. She recalled how she had always tried to get out of it when she was a girl, but her mother always had made her do it; although she recalled times when her mother had let her ride her horse or go to the river for a swim. Those had been such wonderful days. She closed her eyes and she felt the warm sun and the light breeze of those carefree days; she recalled the feeling she had had in her stomach when first she had seen Stalking Horse dive into the river. It was a feeling that had never gone away. She took a deep breath and continued with her work. She was doing too much daydreaming lately. If she wasn't careful, they would put her out to graze with the old horses who were good for nothing but eating grass and carrying supplies.

Gunshots resounded in the air and Sun Dancer looked up. She glanced in the direction of the sound and instantly she looked for Nathan. She saw him in the distance, running as fast as his stocky little legs could carry him. "Nathan! Nathan, come back here," she screamed, and she stood up and ran after him. When she saw the rider, she knew he wasn't a Cheyenne; she knew also that he was going to take Nathan. "Nathan!" She screamed again, and this time the boy turned around, somehow sensing the urgency in her voice. "Come back, Nathan. Come here," she said gently while withdrawing her knife. Nathan's laughter filled the still afternoon air and she was helpless to do anything as the rider rode up to the boy, bent down and picked him up. "No!" Sun Dancer screamed, running after them. The rider turned for a moment to look at the old woman who ran after him so furiously, and he was off, riding into the distance. Sun Dancer watched as the man rode to the east. She saw the men who had fired the shots around the herd leave and follow the lone rider who had been dressed as a Cheyenne, but who wasn't a Cheyenne.

Sun Dancer heard hoofbeats and she saw some of the hunters ride in to check on the women and children of the camp. She thought Stalking Horse would be among them, but when she looked up, he was not among the men who had ridden in. Joe rode up to her and dismounted, putting his strong arms around her.

"Stalking Horse has been shot. We were afraid to move him."

"Let me get my things," Sun Dancer replied, running to her lodge and fetching the things she would need. When she came back, Joe had her horse waiting for her. He helped her up. "He is bad?" She glanced over at Joe and saw him nod.

"Where is Nathan?" Joe asked suddenly.

"Oh, God," Sun Dancer replied in anguish. "They have taken him."

304

"Who has taken him?"

"A man dressed up as a Cheyenne rode into camp and took him and he rode off to the east."

"You say he wasn't a Cheyenne?"

"He was a Crow. I know that. And the men who were fighting against you rode off in the same direction."

"Damn! That means it was Wainwright. Trenton was right."

"Who is Wainwright?"

"Nathan's grandfather. He's a soldier and Trenton had a feeling that he might come after the boy someday. So this was all planned just to get Nate out of there. The bastard."

"I am sorry, Joe. It is my fault he is gone. I did not watch him closely enough."

"Don't say that, Sun Dancer. I've watched that boy enough times to know you can't keep him from doing anything. He wanders anywhere he wants to. You can't blame yourself. There was nothing any of us could do. If he didn't get Nate this time, he would've gotten him another time."

"What will we do?"

"Trenton will be back soon. I'll wait for him. He'll know what to do." He placed a hand on her arm. "There he is."

Sun Dancer jumped down from her horse and ran to her husband. She knew before she examined his wounds that he was dying. He had been shot in the chest and stomach and he was bleeding profusely. He didn't open his eyes when he said, "It took you long enough."

Sun Dancer smiled through her tears. "Old age has slowed me down considerably, my Husband. I am not the young girl I used to be." She started to work on the wounds, but Stalking Horse took her hand and brought it

305

to his mouth and kissed it.

"Do not trouble yourself, Wife; it will do no good. My time has come."

"Do not say that, Stalking Horse. Please." Sun Dancer again began to examine the wounds.

"Did you not hear me the first time?" He opened his eyes; they were slightly glazed. "Send the others away. I do not want them around when I die."

Sun Dancer obeyed, sending the others back to camp. She sat down on the ground, taking Stalking Horse's hand in hers. "I am so angry with you."

"Why now?"

"Because I told you long ago I do not want to exist in this life without you. You are leaving me alone."

"You still have things to do in this lifetime. I am through. I have done enough."

"How can you say that? How can you leave me?" she asked angrily, letting go of his hand.

Stalking Horse coughed and then laughed, taking Sun Dancer's hand. "You have not changed in all this time, woman. You are still stubborn and still so beautiful. Even this day pales next to you."

"Always the words, you were always good with the words, Stalking Horse. How can I live without you?" She laid her head on his chest.

Stalking Horse's hand came up to her head and stroked it lightly; he felt her tears as they fell onto his chest. "Do not cry, Sun Dancer. We should rejoice. What a life we have had together."

"I am selfish then, because I want more of my life with you."

"It is time for me to go. I am old and I have grown weak. It is not good for a warrior to be weak. There is no honor in that."

306

"Honor, that was always important to you."

"It must be so if a man is to be a man." He coughed violently, spasms racking his chest. He opened his eyes and squinted against the sun. "I picked a good day to die."

"You did not pick it; it was picked for you," Sun Dancer replied softly, staring into his face.

"Do not be so precise. The fact is, I am dying and it is time."

"I will join you soon, my Husband. As soon as my work here is through."

"I will be waiting for you, Wife. I will be easy to find—I will be the most handsome warrior, riding on the fastest of all horses, waiting for the most beautiful of all women."

"Oh, Stalking Horse," Sun Dancer cried, unable to stifle the sobs that began deep down inside of her. "You have been the love of my life, my strength, my courage. Through you I have learned the meaning of honor."

"Those are fine words, Wife, much too fine. . . ." Stalking Horse began coughing and he grasped his stomach as spasms racked his body. Sun Dancer watched helplessly, holding on to him and finally, holding his head in her lap. "This is not good. I wanted it to be quick. I did not want you to see me like this."

"I am glad I have had this time with you. I would have been angry if you had gone quickly and not let me say good-by."

Stalking Horse closed his eyes, muttering something inaudible. He rested for a few moments while Sun Dancer held him; then he opened his eyes again. "Do not grieve for me, Sun Dancer, for I have been lucky in my lifetime. Do what you must do here; make sure Aeneva and her brothers are well, then come to me. I will be waiting."

He closed his eyes again, attempting to cough, but not having the strength. He opened his eyes once more and looked up at Sun Dancer; he smiled. She smiled back and lowered her face next to his, resting her cheek against his. "I love you, Sun Dancer, I . . ." He could not speak anymore. He saw her face against the sunlight; he reached up and touched it once more and his hand fell limply to his side.

"I love you, too, Stalking Horse. I love you, too, my Husband." She cradled his head in her lap and began rocking back and forth, singing as she would to a baby. It was not a song of death and mourning, but one of life and living—Stalking Horse wouldn't have wanted her to grieve openly over him. She saw riders coming in the distance and she knew it was time to tell them. She looked down at Stalking Horse once more and smiled. He was right; they had had quite a life together, a life to be proud of and to rejoice in. "Soon, my Husband, we will be together soon." She held him for the last time while the warm sun shone on them both.

Sun Dancer stepped back from the scaffolding and she felt proud. It was a fine scaffold, built by Coyote Boy and Brave Wolf, and it was decorated with Stalking Horse's finest things. Although he had wanted his personal things to go to his grandsons and Aeneva, the boys had decided that Stalking Horse's weapons should be buried with him, for no one would ever use them as their grandfather had.

Sun Dancer washed Stalking Horse and dressed him in his finest shirt and leggings. She put on his ceremonial headdress, made from the tailfeathers of eagles, and she wrapped him in the robe she had made for him. He was placed on the scaffold and wrapped in another robe which was tied around him. His quiver of arrows and his bow were placed next to him, as were the rifle Jean had given him and his favorite knife. His shield and lance were hung at the head of the scaffold. Sun Dancer made sure that the scaffold was wide enough to hold two people, for she wanted to lie next to Stalking Horse when it was her time to go.

There were many speeches, and tributes were given to Stalking Horse by many chiefs from many bands, but Sun Dancer would allow no mourning. Life was to go on as before, only now it would be without Stalking Horse.

Her life was especially empty without Nathan, but Joe saw to it that she was not alone. After he hunted with the men, he would help Sun Dancer with her chores and he would talk to her of his days as a slave.

"Was it terrible being owned by another man, Joe?"

"I didn't know any other kind of life. My mother and her mother before her were both slaves, so I was raised knowing that that was the only life for me. But I knew I was different from the rest."

"How did you know?"

"I knew it in here." Joe touched the place over his heart. "In here I was free no matter what they made me do. There were also the books."

"Books?"

"My master taught me how to read. I started reading about all the places in the world that I'd never seen and I promised myself that someday I'd see some of them."

"I saw a city once," Sun Dancer said thoughtfully as she recalled the time Pierre had kidnapped her and had taken her into the white man's town. "I did not like it. I never wanted to see another white man's city after that."

"You were treated badly?"

"It was not a good experience; but we were not talking about me. Tell me more about you, Joe. I am interested."

"Well, after I showed some interest in books, my master taught me many things such as numbers, English, history, geography and cards."

"Cards," Sun Dancer repeated thoughtfully. "I have heard of cards." She thought for a moment, then nodded her head. "Yes, I remember now, Jean used to play with the cards in his cabin. He used to put them on the table, place them on each other, then mess them up and throw them on the floor. Is that cards?"

Joe laughed deeply. "Yes, Sun Dancer, that is cards. God, you're wonderful. I can see why Trenton loves you so much."

At the mention of Trenton's name, Sun Dancer frowned. "When do you think they will be back? I am so worried about Nathan."

"Trenton will be here soon, I promise you. I'd go after Nate myself, but I know Trenton would want me to wait. The one thing we can be sure of is that Nate is safe. He's with his grandparents and they'll take good care of him."

"I suppose that is a good thing." Sun Dancer thought for a moment, then looked at Joe. "What will he do, Joe? Trenton has such a temper."

"I don't know."

"You must make sure that he thinks this out. I do not want him to act without thinking. He must not."

"He'll have to plan this one out in order to get into that fort."

"Is it possible for him to get Nathan back?"

"Sure it's possible. When that boy puts his mind to something, he gets it done. He'll get Nate back, don't you worry."

"I just wish they would get back. It has been such a long time. I have missed Aeneva so."

"They will be here soon. If I were a gambling man, I'd

say they'll be here within the week. What would you say?"

"I am not one to gamble," Sun Dancer said seriously, "but I think they will be here in three days' time."

Joe rubbed his chin. "I don't know as I should gamble with you. Trenton told me you could see into the future. For all I know, you've already seen when they'll be back."

"Well, if you are a gambling man, as you say, you will have to take that chance."

"Oh, you're a smart woman, Sun Dancer. Smart as they come. All right. What is the wager? What do we give up if we lose?"

"I will wager a winter robe for you, all hand-quilled of course."

"Um, that's a good one." Joe thought for a moment. "I have a big-bladed knife that would make scraping the flesh off those hides a lot easier. That's my wager." He extended his hand to a puzzled Sun Dancer. "I usually shake hands on a wager. It's a matter of honor, you see."

"Honor, yes, I see," she replied softly, recalling Stalking Horse's last words. "'There must be honor if a man is to be a man.'" She extended her hand to Joe and shook firmly. Before she died, she swore to herself, she must learn the true meaning of honor, and she would make Stalking Horse proud of her. Only then, could she go to him with her head held high.

Aeneva looked over at Trenton and smiled. They stopped their horses and looked out over the prairie now alive with wild wheat, grass, and wild flowers. Aeneva shut her eyes as the warm breeze blew across her face and hair and she breathed in the sweet air. She saw a small herd of buffalo grazing in the distance, the calves running playfully around their mothers.

"I did not think I could miss it so much."

"It is beautiful, isn't it?"

"I would die if I had to live in a white man's lodge."

"You lived in a white man's lodge all winter and you didn't die."

"I knew the spring would soon come and I would be free again. Was it terrible when you were in the prison?"

"I wasn't in it for too long, but it was pretty bad. I never before realized how accustomed I was to my freedom. When I was in there, I tried to imagine things like riding my horse out on the open prairie with the wind against my face, but I couldn't make them real. Nothing is real in prison except that you are alone and your freedom is lost."

"If I was ever put in one of those places I would kill myself. I could not stand to be put in a small place." Her voice shook slightly.

"You don't have to worry; you'll never be put in one of those places." He watched her as she stared out at the open land in front of her. "Are you all right?"

She nodded her head slightly, then turned to him, smiling brightly. "I am better than I have ever been. It is spring, we are going home, and I have you. I am a woman of great fortune."

"Yes, you are," Trenton agreed. "And don't you forget it."

"I will never forget it. Now, let us continue on our journey. I am anxious to see my family and your son."

"God, I'll bet Nathan's grown a foot since I last saw him."

"And he will be so happy to see you."

"After being with your grandmother, he may never want to see me again. Come on."

They rode for the next three days until they came upon a large herd of buffalo. They had passed many small bands of Indians—Sioux, Shoshoni, Ute—but they hadn't yet seen their own band. The morning of the fourth day Trenton saw some hunters working part of a herd and they soon discovered that they were Cheyennes. As soon as they rode into the herd, Aeneva spotted Brave Wolf and Coyote Boy. She kneed her horse when she spotted them and rode at a gallop until she was next to them.

"Brothers." She smiled brightly, leaning across her horse to embrace them both. "It is so good to see you both. You have grown."

"As have you, little Sister. You look almost like a woman."

"Your mouth has not grown any tamer since I have been gone, Coyote Boy."

"Our brother is right; you have changed, Aeneva. You look different. Pretty."

"Thank you, Brave Wolf. You both seem so surprised." She stopped when Trenton rode up beside her. He shook hands with Brave Wolf and Coyote Boy. "Has my husband not changed also?"

"Husband?"

"Yes, Brother, we are married. Do not act so surprised. You knew I had my mind set to it when we were children."

"Yes, but I did not think Trenton would let himself get caught." Coyote Boy shook his head ominously. "I wish you luck, my Brother, for you will need it with her."

"Yes, I know," Trenton replied, reaching out for Aeneva's hand. "It will be a challenge."

"Well, we must have a celebration tonight."

"I will tell Grandmother and Grandfather myself. They will be very happy."

"Wait, Aeneva."

"What is it, Brave Wolf?"

Brave Wolf looked first at Aeneva, then at Trenton. "Grandfather is dead."

"No," Aeneva responded blankly, "that cannot be. He was so strong."

"He did not die of disease, Sister. He was shot by white soldiers," Coyote Boy added bitterly.

"White soldiers came here? I can't believe it," Trenton asked.

"Yes, and that is not all, my Brother. While they were here, they took your son."

Trenton stared at Brave Wolf. Slowly, comprehension dawned on him and he could feel the anger begin to rise. "When?"

"Almost two moons. The soldiers came into the herd trying to stampede it and they shot at us. While we were trying to fight them, a Crow dressed up as one of us rode into camp and took your boy."

"These same soldiers killed Stalking Horse?"

"Yes. He did not live out the day."

"Jesus," Trenton muttered angrily. "Come, Aeneva, we must speak with your grandmother."

"We are sorry about your son, my Brother."

"Thank you, Brave Wolf. I am sorry about your grandfather. He was a great man, an honorable man."

Trenton and Aeneva rode slowly into the camp, each silent. Thinking of his own loss, Trenton knew that it was Lydia's father who had come for Nathan and he knew that he would leave as soon as possible to get the boy back. Suddenly he thought of Aeneva and he touched her arm. "I am sorry, Aeneva. I know how close you were to your grandfather."

Aeneva nodded her acknowledgement, but said nothing. She could think of nothing to say. It seemed impossible that her grandfather was dead; he who had taught her almost everything, he who had always been there, he who had indulged her and loved her. He had actually been her father, not her grandfather. She was saddened, not only by his death, but also by the knowledge that it would be difficult for her grandmother. Her grandparents had always been so close; theirs was a relationship like no other Aeneva had ever seen. She thought of all the times they had talked well into the night—he would seek Sun Dancer's advice on tribal matters; she would talk to him of sick patients or of people she couldn't help—and then they would laugh and love each other. Always the love was there.

"We are here, Aeneva." Trenton's deep voice invaded her thoughts and she looked up to see her grandfather's lodge. Tears stung her eyes, but she controlled them with an immense effort and jumped down from her horse. Trenton put his arm around her and she drew strength from him as they entered her grandmother's lodge.

"*Haahe,* Grandmother," she said as she entered the lodge. Sun Dancer was preparing medicines for the day's healings. At the sound of Aeneva's voice she stopped her work and looked up, a smile covering her face. She held out her arms to Aeneva and the two embraced.

"It is good to see you, Aeneva. I am glad you are home."

"It is good to be home, Grandmother." She kissed Sun Dancer on both cheeks, and she took her hands and squeezed them tightly. "Brave Wolf and Coyote Boy told me about Grandfather. I am so sorry."

"I, too, Sun Dancer." Trenton spoke and stepped forward. He embraced Sun Dancer. "Stalking Horse was an honorable man.''

"Yes, he was that.''

This must be a hard time for you, Grandmother. We of course, will move in with you.''

"Why would you want to do that?'' Sun Dancer spoke with genuine surprise.

Aeneva glanced over at Trenton. "I know it must be a lonely time for you.''

"It has been lonely, but my memories sustain me. Do not mourn for me, child, for I am not sad. Stalking Horse and I had much time together and soon we will be together forever.''

Aeneva stepped forward, startled. "What do you mean 'soon'?''

"Soon my work here on earth will be finished and I can rest.'' She reached out and stroked Aeneva's grief-stricken face. "Do not look so sad, my child. I am ready to leave this place, especially now that I know you are happy.''

"How did you know.''

"It is obvious to anyone. I knew long ago that you two would be together.''

"We are married, Grandmother. We performed our own ceremony. See here.'' She extended her left hand. "This was his grandmother's ring.''

"It is lovely.'' Sun Dancer smiled at them both. "You look so good together.'' She was suddenly solemn as she looked at Trenton. "I am so sorry about Nathan. It was my fault; he was with me and I could not get to him in time. These old legs failed me.''

"Do not blame yourself, Sun Dancer; you could do nothing. I know the man who did this thing and if he hadn't been able to get Nathan that day, he would've gotten him another day. It is I who should apologize to you.

316

If I had not brought my son here to stay with you, perhaps Stalking Horse would still be alive.''

"And if you had not brought your son to stay here, perhaps Aeneva would not be alive,'' she answered quickly. "You are right, Trenton, it does no good to place blame. Joe tells me this soldier is Nathan's grandfather. He says he will take good care of him.''

"I'm sure that he will, but that doesn't matter to me. Nathan's my son. I'll get him back and I'll make Wainwright pay for what he did to Stalking Horse.''

"No, Trenton, you must not do that.'' Sun Dancer squeezed Trenton's arm. "Stalking Horse would not want you seeking revenge for him.''

"It would not be for him; it would be for me,'' Trenton replied coldly.

"Grandmother is right, Trenton. You must not seek revenge against this man. You may never see your son again.''

"I won't endanger Nathan. I'll make sure he's safe; then I'll go after Wainwright.'' He looked at both women. "I'll let you both visit now. I want to talk to Joe.'' He walked back to Sun Dancer and kissed her on the cheek. "It is good to see you, Sun Dancer. I finally feel as if I've come home.'' He smiled over at Aeneva and left the lodge.

"Come, let us sit down while I prepare some of these medicines. I have two hunters to look after.''

"I will help you, Grandmother.''

"You look well, Aeneva,'' Sun Dancer said as she handed some plants to Aeneva to grind up. "I would say you look happy.''

"I am happy, Grandmother. Trenton is . . . well, he reminds me much of Grandfather. He has the same kind of wisdom. He is a good man.''

"It does not surprise me. And this terrible time you had with Crooked Teeth, are you over it now?"

"Yes, I think I am over it. There are still times when I wake up at night and I am frightened, but then I know that he can no longer hurt me or anyone else."

"He is dead?"

"Yes. He followed us up into the mountains. There were many times when I would walk through the woods and feel as though someone was watching me; it was him all the time. He finally grew impatient and broke in our door one night. *Naxane* Jean had made a small door in the wall below the bed, and Trenton made me go outside. He faced Crooked Teeth and his men alone."

"What did you do?"

"I was frightened, Grandmother, more frightened than I had ever been before. But when I heard the shots I knew I had to do something to help Trenton."

"And you went back inside."

"The door led to the woodpile outside the cabin so I was completely hidden. I climbed out of there, went quietly around the side of the cabin, and through the door."

"Trenton?"

"He was shot and stabbed; one of Crooked Teeth's men helped him. He said he had heard of you and that he had no quarrel with you or me. He and the others left me alone to fight Crooked Teeth."

"So there is honor among all men. This pleases me greatly."

"Yes, he said you had dealt fairly with the Crows in the past. Thanks to you, Grandmother, Trenton and I are alive."

"I had nothing to do with it; it was you two."

"Trenton would have died for me; he was prepared to

318

do that.''

"You sound surprised. Why?''

"I do not know; I suppose I did not expect it of a white man.''

"Have you learned so little in all your years, Aeneva? Do you not know the times Jean would have died for Stalking Horse or me? In fact, he did die to protect you.''

"I am sorry; I did not mean that. Perhaps I meant I was surprised that he loved me so much he would die for me.''

"You did not think it possible to be loved so?''

"Never. It confuses me.''

"It will always confuse you, Granddaughter. But it is a good confusion.''

"Grandmother, did you speak with Grandfather before he died? I would like to know that you were able to say good-by.''

"Yes, we spoke for quite a time. He said he had chosen a good day to die. I told him he had not chosen it, but that it had been chosen for him.'' She laughed at the words, then caught Aeneva's shocked expression. "Why do you look so surprised, Aeneva? Did you expect to find me with my hair cut off, my body slashed, and my cries and moans rending the air?'' She shook her head. "No, it would not do for our people to see the wife of Stalking Horse carrying on so. It is not—''

"Honorable?'' Aeneva interrupted.

"Yes. And it was Stalking Horse's wish that I not be sad my last days on this earth. Knowing that I will be with him soon makes it easy.''

"I admire you so, Grandmother.'' Aeneva reached out and took Sun Dancer's hand. "I wish I could be more like you.''

"You are a good girl, Aeneva. You have always let

your love for us shine through."

"You and Grandfather have been good to me and my brothers. We can never forget that."

"Just be happy in your life, Aeneva. Live it with honor and you will discover that you have no need to be like me. You will find that you are already an admirable person."

Aeneva looked down at the crushed leaves in the bowl and handed them to Sun Dancer. "I loved Grandfather so; I hope I did not disappoint him too much."

"He loved you very much. He wanted to know that you were well, but he will see that for himself. And he was never disappointed in you. His heart was full of you."

"Thank you, Grandmother," Aeneva said much too quickly, trying to hide the trembling in her voice. "What else can I help you with?"

"I do not need help. Go to Trenton. I am worried about him."

"Do not worry about Trenton; he will find a way to get his son back."

"I know he will get his son back; it is the other thing I am worried about. The last time he was consumed by vengeance, he was gone for a long time."

"He will not leave again; he has promised me."

"Aeneva, he will have to leave to get his son. Do not ask too much of him."

Aeneva picked up her grandmother's basket and stood up. "Come, I will help you. We can talk about Trenton later."

Sun Dancer watched Aeneva as she walked out the lodge door, hoping that the girl would not ask the impossible of Trenton and make him choose between her and his son. It was not a choice that any man could face lightly, and Sun Dancer hoped that Aeneva would see that there was no reason for Trenton to have to choose. If Aeneva would let him, he could have her and Nathan. She had to trust Trenton, as well as love him.

"He's at Fort Union, boy. I rode over there and checked it out myself. The word is, the old man is getting out of the army and going back east with his wife and Nate."

"I can't believe this, Joe. I can't believe he actually came into Cheyenne territory, killed one of their most honored chiefs, and then stole my son."

"Well he did it, boy, plain as day."

"Who was this Crow Sun Dancer was telling me about?"

"His name is Long Nose, an outcast from his own tribe. He's been a scout for the army for a couple years."

"I want him."

"And just how in hell do you plan to get him? Word's out on you, boy. You go anywhere near that fort and you'll be hung."

"But no one gave you a second look, did they, Joe?"

"Why is it since I've been with you, I've been shot at, chased by hostiles, been nursemaid to your kid, and I still ain't been anywhere?"

Trenton slapped him soundly on the back. "It's because I'm so lovable, that's why."

"Don't push it, kid."

"If you'll help me get Nate back, I'll give you all the money I have saved up and you can travel anywhere you want to. I promise you."

"Now don't go getting soft on me, boy. I'll help you get Nate back, you know that, and I'll also take your money. Now that you got yourself an Indian wife, I don't expect you'll have much need for money."

321

"I don't expect so."

"She's a pretty one, boy, and I hear from her brothers, real spunky."

"I'd call it more than spunk." He stopped, realizing suddenly that he'd be leaving Aeneva. "Listen, Joe, let's plan to leave early in the morning."

"You can't go with me, boy. That's crazy."

"I can travel with you, I just won't be seen in the fort with you. When you find Long Nose, you can bring him to me."

"Whatever you say."

Trenton put his arm around Joe's shoulders. "Thanks, Joe, you've been a good friend. I won't forget it."

"Yeah, yeah, be on your way now. You've got a new wife to be talking to."

"Yes, and she's not going to be very happy to hear that I'm leaving. I'll see you later."

"O.K., boy." Joe watched Trenton as he ambled off in the direction of Sun Dancer's lodge. It seemed as if he had grown in inches and in years as well. He was no longer the scared, indecisive young man whom he had first met; he was now a mature man with a man's responsibilities. And Joe didn't envy him one bit.

Trenton and Aeneva helped Sun Dancer the rest of that day, and in the evening they went for a walk on the starlit prairie. They held hands and walked as young lovers do, thinking their own thoughts but reveling in their love for each other.

"You are leaving tomorrow." Aeneva spoke simply. There was no anger in her voice.

"I must. Already too much time has passed since Nate's been gone. Joe found out that Wainwright is planning to take Nate and move back east somewhere."

"And you will follow him there?"

"If I have to. He is my son, Aeneva. I would do the same for you."

"I understand."

"Do you really?" He stopped and took her in his arms.

"Yes, I do understand. You left your son to search for me; it is only fair that you leave me to search for him."

"You aren't angry?"

"I have no right to be angry. I just wish I could help. Perhaps if I came along—"

"No!" Trenton replied adamantly. "I don't want to have to worry about you, too."

"But I can help."

"There isn't anything you can do except cause me extra worry. You stay here."

"Now you do not think I can take care of myself."

"That's not it, Aeneva. I know you can take care of yourself here, but it's different in the white world. People will treat you differently; they will look down upon you. I don't want you to have to go through that."

"I am strong enough to survive it."

"You just don't understand the way these men think. There are some good ones, but many are bad and hate Indians—any Indians. You won't be safe."

"But I want to help you, Trenton. Please let me help."

"You can help me when I get back with Nate. He'll need a mother."

"Of course I will help you then, but I want to help you now."

"No, Aeneva. There is nothing you can do. Just stay here and be safe." He put his arms around her and held her tightly. "It'll be good to know I have you to come back to," he murmured softly as he kissed her.

But even as Aeneva kissed him back, she knew she

323

would not wait for him here. She would follow him and she would do anything she could to help. It was not in her blood to wait quietly while others acted; she couldn't change her basic nature and she would not, even for Trenton.

As soon as Trenton and Joe rode off the next morning, Aeneva ran to her grandmother's lodge and started to pack some things. She ignored Sun Dancer's stares.

"I know you have something to say, Grandmother. What is it?"

"Why are you following him? He asked you not to."

"I want to help him."

"He does not want your help, child, can you not see that? This is something he must do for himself."

"But he is letting Joe help him."

"Joe will help him, but Trenton will get his son. It is a matter of—"

"Do not tell me it is a matter of honor, Grandmother. This has nothing to do with honor."

"What does it have to do with?"

"Trenton does not want me with him."

"Now you are acting as a child would."

Aeneva thought for a moment and stopped, sitting down on the floor of the lodge. "Yes, you are right." She buried her face in her hands.

"What is it, child? There is something else bothering you."

"I think I am with child, Grandmother." Her muffled voice came softly from her hands.

"Ah, now it makes sense." Sun Dancer walked to Aeneva and sat down next to her, taking one of her hands. "You were not quite prepared for this, were you? You did not think of motherhood when you thought of marriage.''

Aeneva nodded her head in agreement. "When I was with Crooked Teeth it was my constant fear that I would be with child by him. I knew if I had his child, I could never leave him.''

"But it is not his child you are carrying; it is Trenton's.''

"I am confused, Grandmother. I am feeling things I have never felt before.''

"Like you never want to be apart from Trenton because you are afraid you will never see him again?''

"Yes, yes, that is it. He thinks it is because I want to fight and that is what I thought also, but it is really because I am afraid for him.''

"You do not have to be afraid for him.''

"You know, Grandmother? You have seen?''

Sun Dancer nodded. "You will both live a long time, together.''

"Thank you for telling me, Grandmother. I know you do not usually speak of your visions. I know that they frighten you.''

"I have never been frightened by my visions of you. They have always been good.''

"And my brothers, have you had visions of them?''

"No, I do not have visions of everyone. I see only those whom the Maiyun choose for me to see.''

"Thank you, Grandmother, you have eased my mind.''

"You will stay?''

"Yes, I will stay. I fear the warrior in me is no longer there.''

"Do not be sad, child. My father once told me never to be sad about what we have lost, but to think of it as one phase of our life we have gone through, and that we are

325

now moving on to another. You will go through many and you must accept them all gracefully.''

''I do not know if I am ready to be a mother.''

''Do not forget that you will have two children to care for.'' She sighed contentedly. ''Perhaps I will be around awhile longer after all. I cannot leave you until I know that you and your husband and children are well. I suppose that is what Stalking Horse meant.''

''What do you mean?''

''He said that there were many things left for me to do on this earth yet. He especially would not want me to leave until you are well.''

''Grandmother, I have something to ask of you.'' Aeneva spoke seriously.

''What is it, child?''

''I want you to teach me about healing. I want to learn as much as I can. I would be proud to carry on for you. I know I would not do as well as you, but I do not want your vast knowledge to die with you. Grandfather would not like that and I would not like it.''

''Aeneva,'' Sun Dancer said quietly, her voice trembling with emotion. This was something she had not expected.

''Have I offended you, Grandmother?''

''Offended me?'' Sun Dancer spoke softly. ''You could not have given me a more precious gift. Healing comes easy to you, just as it did to me, but I did not think you had any interest in it.''

''I want to be able to help my people if it is possible. And I want my children and their children to know all about you and what you did.''

''I am overwhelmed, Aeneva.''

''Well, do not think, just because I am going to be a mother, that I will give up fighting. If I am needed, I will

326

fight alongside the men. But I do not think I would look very fearsome with a belly round with child.''

''Thank you for this, Aeneva. My heart is full and I know that your grandfather is looking down on you and nodding his head. 'I am not surprised she did this good thing,' he would say, 'for she is *my* granddaughter.' ''

Aeneva laughed. ''Let us see to those hunters now. I have learned much from you already, Grandmother. Trenton healed up well, do you not think?''

''Very well. As I said before, it comes easily to you. You will be a better healer than I.''

Aeneva turned, her eyes and expression almost reverent. ''No one can be a better healer than you, Grandmother. The best I can do is to carry on where you left off. That will be my greatest honor.''

Sun Dancer nodded and led the way out of the lodge. She could not recall a time when her heart felt so full. She smiled at Aeneva and looked up at the sky. Let me die on a day like today, she prayed silently to the Great Spirit, when my heart is full and my mind is at ease.

CHAPTER XVI

"Long Nose is nowhere around. He found himself a woman and went off somewhere. Guess he'll be back when he runs out of whiskey or when he tires of the woman."

"Now what?" Trenton stomped around the small campsite.

"I found something else out."

"What?"

"Nate and the grandmother are leaving for the east in two weeks."

"Two weeks? Well, I have to get him out of there before then."

"Or else we wait and steal him from the stagecoach."

"Stagecoach? You mean they're not going by river?"

"Going by stage to St. Louis and from there by train."

"Why not by boat?"

"I don't know. I wasn't able to find that out," Joe replied sarcastically.

"There must be a reason," Trenton replied seriously, unconscious of Joe's jibe. "He's gonna have Nate guarded and I'd think it'd be easier to guard him on a boat than a stagecoach. It doesn't make sense."

"Unless she's afraid of boats."

"It's possible I suppose." He shook his head. "No, there's a better reason than that. Wainwright's too smart.

Maybe he thinks I won't try anything on a stagecoach. Wait a minute . . . two weeks from now.'' Trenton calculated quickly. ''The payroll coach usually comes into the fort at that time.''

''So what does that mean? I'll tell you what it means, nothing. Look, boy, the lady's taking the boy out on the stagecoach because it leaves at that time. That's all. Ain't nothing else to do with it.''

''Yeah, maybe you're right. But if it is the payroll coach, it'll be well-guarded.

''C'mon, boy.''

''Do you know how many men will be guarding it?''

''Maybe I can find that out another day. I can't be seen walking around there every day asking questions. Somebody's gonna get suspicious.''

''All right, we'll wait a few days. Then you go back in there and find out what you can. Also find out the schedule for the riverboats.''

''You still ain't convinced, are you, boy?''

''I just want to check everything, that's all, Joe. He's the only son I have.''

''All right, all right.'' He reached into his shirt pocket and pulled out a deck of cards. ''You wouldn't care for some cards, would you?''

Trenton finally relaxed and smiled. ''If you're ready to lose, I'm ready to play.''

''Oh, listen to him. That's real fancy talk, boy, but let's just see how good your luck is.''

''Is there a chance I can get me a ticket on the stage going out of here in two weeks?'' Joe asked the man in the supply store.

''Don't know. I heard the colonel's wife is going out all alone. Don't expect he'll want anyone riding with her.''

"She going alone, is she?''

"No, taking her grandson back east. The colonel's getting out of the army soon. Ever been back east?''

"Yeah, but didn't like it much. I like the wide open spaces myself.''

"Well, I never been back there myself, but I don't expect I'd like it much either. Don't like lots of people.''

"Know what you mean.'' Joe nodded his head, pointing to some tobacco on the shelf, as well as some coffee and sugar.

"Will that be all?''

"That'll do it. Say, where can I find out about the riverboat schedules? If I can't get that stage out of here, guess I'll have to take the boat.''

"It's not a bad ride. Real slow in parts, but not too bad. They'll give you all the information you need down at the docks.''

Joe paid for his goods. "Thanks very much, mister; you been a real help.'' Joe walked out of the store and along the wooden sidewalk, stepping down and starting across the parade ground. He walked toward his horse; then he turned, hearing a child's voice call out to him. He saw Nathan with Wainwright and his wife and he turned his head away, trying to ignore the boy. He continued to walk toward his horse, but Wainwright shouted orders and soldiers appeared from nowhere, surrounding and detaining Joe.

Wainwright walked up to the black man, assessing him silently. "So, you know my grandson?''

"Ain't never seen that boy in my life, sir.''

Wainwright motioned for Nathan to come forward, his voice suddenly gentle. "Who is that man, Nathan? Do you know him?''

331

"Joe, Joe." Nathan spoke frantically, reaching ou
with his arms to the man he knew so well.

Joe turned away from Nathan, steeling himself agains
the boy's voice. "I told you I ain't never seen that boy be
fore."

"Well, I think you're lying."

"Think what you want," Joe replied curtly.

"Since I'm in charge here, I will think what I want
mister." He turned to his men. "Take him to the guard
house. I will be over to question him later." Wainwrigh
took the boy to his wife and stomped off toward th
guardhouse. Joe was just being locked up when Wain
wright threw open the wooden door that led to the cells
"All right, where the hell is he?" He made no attempt t
control his anger or the sound of his voice.

"Where's who?" Joe looked up blankly, a look he ha
perfected from all his years as a slave.

"Where's Trenton Hawkins? I know he's here some
where."

Joe rubbed his chin thoughtfully, then shrugged hi
shoulders. "Don't know no Trenton Hawkins. Knew
Jeb Hawkins once back in Louisiana—"

"Stop it, you fool. Don't you realize I can have you
hanged? Do you want to hang for him?" He wrapped hi
fingers around the bars and peered through at Joe. "I
you tell me where he is, I'll let you go."

"I'd be glad to tell you where he is, sir, if I knew who
he was."

"You're lying! He sent you here; I knew he did."

"Like I told you before, I don't know no Trento
Hawkins."

"How is it my grandson knows you then?"

"Never saw that boy before in my life. He just took
liking to me, that's all."

332

"You big dumb—"

"What?" Joe's eyes drilled into Wainwright's.

"I'll have it beaten out of you. Then you'll tell me where he is."

Joe was unmoved; he had been beaten so many times in his life that he was thoroughly unfazed by the threat. He leaned back on the cot and propped his legs up on the wall. "Do what you want, white man. In the meantime, I'm gonna take me a little nap."

Wainwright turned to the guard. "This man is to have nothing, no food or water, until I say so. Do you understand?"

"Yessir!"

"We'll see how long you decide to remain loyal," he said bitterly and strode out through the door.

Joe breathed a sigh of relief when Wainwright left. Now he had to think of a way to get out of here—if there was a way to get out. If he wasn't back by the next day, Trenton would know something had gone wrong and he'd come looking for him. He had to stop him before he came or Trenton would never leave the fort alive.

Joe remembered something that his master, Linden Rothford Kingsley III, had taught him: almost every man has a price; you just have to find out what it is. With Zeb McKinney, it was the price of hidden gold stolen from a train years before. Joe used the same story Trenton had used a couple of years earlier in the same jail.

"How do you know there's gold hidden in those hills?" McKinney was still skeptical.

"My friend Hawkins told me."

"You mean the half-breed that Wainwright is trying to find?"

"That's the one. Who would know better than the man

whose mother hid the gold?''

McKinney's eyes lit up for the first time. ''If that's so, why didn't he get it before now? He doesn't need you.''

''He wants his son. His kid is more important to him than that gold. You get me out of here and help me get that kid, I can promise you that Hawkins will be real grateful.''

''How do I know that I can trust him? If I get his kid out, he doesn't have to give me anything.'' McKinney thought for a minute. ''No, I'll help get you out, but you tell your friend I want to see some of that gold before I help him get his kid.''

''How do we know if we can trust you? If he gave you some gold, you might just take off and never help us.''

''Not if you just give me a little, so that I know you mean to keep your part of the bargain. I'm not one who's likely to walk away from a fortune in gold.''

Joe believed him. ''All right, Zeb, you have yourself a bargain. You help get me out of here tonight, and I'll see to it that you have some gold. And if you help us get this kid out of here, you'll be a rich man. You can leave this army and travel to some far-off place where no one will ever find you. Just think of it, Zeb, you'll be rich enough to do anything you want.''

''Yes,'' Zeb agreed, his eyes containing a far-off look when he left the jail cell.

Trenton paced around the campsite, nervously throwing bits of twigs on the rocks. Where the hell was Joe? He should have been back hours before, by sunset at the latest. Something had gone wrong; Wainwright had figured out who he was and was holding him until he knew Trenton would come in to save his friend. He felt like riding into the fort now, but he knew it was best to wait until tomorrow. Joe had told him not to worry if he wasn't back that night, but Trenton knew something was wrong. Nonetheless he would wait for Joe. Joe had made him promise not to come into the fort unless it was absolutely necessary. Well, he'd wait until tomorrow and if Joe wasn't back by then he'd go in after him, no matter what the consequences.

Joe shouted for the guard, falling against the bars as he did so. It took a few minutes before the guard came in. Joe moaned, holding on to his chest, begging the man to help him.

"I can't open the bars, mister. Not for nothing."

"Help me," Joe muttered in agony, grasping onto the bars. His eyes were barely open, but he saw Zeb McKinney sneak up behind the guard and hit on the head. Joe jumped to his feet and dragged the guard inside as Zeb unlocked the cell. They tied and gagged the man, then locked the cell. Joe followed Zeb out of the guardhouse and onto the wooden sidewalk.

"I know a way to get you out. A friend of mine is on guard duty tonight. I'm gonna take him some whiskey and talk to him a bit. While I do that, you take the rope I've brought you. Climb the ladder to the parapet, tie the rope on top of one of the posts, and climb over. There's a horse waiting for you about a half-mile down the road."

Joe pulled on Zeb's arm. "Which house is Wainwright's?"

"That one." Zeb pointed across the empty yard to a neat two-story house. "Now come on. I don't fancy being hung for helping you escape." Zeb walked Joe over to a part of the wall that was guarded by only one sentry. "When I get talking to him, you go on up and over. Do it quickly. Someone could be walking across the yard and see you. They'll shoot first and ask questions later.''

''Thanks, Zeb.''

''Don't thank me yet. Thank me when you've got the boy and I've got my gold.''

''Yeah,'' Joe muttered to himself, not wanting to think of the consequences when Zeb found out there was no gold.

Joe hugged the wood, blending into it as if he were an animal of the night. He waited and watched until Zeb had the sentry engaged in an animated conversation with his back turned. Joe hastily mounted the stairs to the parapet, tied the rope which Zeb had given him around one of the poles, and shinnied down. He dropped lightly, checking to make sure he wasn't being watched before he ran away from the fort. He didn't stop running until he found the horse that Zeb had left for him and he was on his way back to camp. The hell with the stagecoach, Joe thought frantically as he rode, we'll get Nate tonight. Wainwright will never expect it and it's our best chance. Probably our only chance.

They left their horses in the same place Zeb had left the horse for Joe. Joe approached the fort first and discovered the rope still hanging from the parapet, hidden by the darkness. Zeb hadn't yet had a chance to take it down. Joe shinnied up the rope after waiting for the sentry to turn back toward the gate; then Trenton followed. They waited silently in the dark as the sentry walked toward them on the parapet and when he turned back toward the gate, Joe stepped up and hit him over the head, taking his rifle and instantly assuming the man's position on the parapet.

Trenton waited until Joe started walking; then he

climbed down the stairs and looked out across the empty parade ground. He moved along the inside wall of the fort to the east side until he came to Wainwright's house. Crouching down, he ran on all fours to the back. He considered the house for a moment, walking slowly around it. There were two stories and it had a balcony facing the parade ground. In the back was a door that led to a pantry which in turn led into the kitchen. Both doors seemed to be well locked. Trenton decided his best chance of getting into the house was through a window. After finding all the ones on the ground floor locked, he climbed up a trellis to the second floor. The first window he tried was locked and holding on to the window frame, he stepped to the next window. He tried it and was able to lift it enough to squeeze his body through the opening. He balanced himself on his hands, walking forward until his entire body was through he window. He remained on all fours, unmoving, until his eyes became accustomed to the darkness. He glanced around him and discovered an empty room. He walked to the door and opened it, peering out into the hall. There were two doors to the left of this room and double doors to the right. The double doors probably belonged to the Wainwrights' room, he surmised, the room facing the yard with the balcony. He walked to the left, his moccasined feet unused to the hardwood floors. He quietly opened the door and looked inside. It was empty. He shut the door and walked to the next one, opening it and stepping inside. He shut the door behind him, knowing this had to be Nathan's room. He waited for a moment, feeling the pain of excitement, then he walked to the small lump in the bed. He bent down, seeing the golden curls peek out from the covers. He touched Nathan's hair and for a moment was tempted to grab him in his arms and flee the house. He did not. Instead, he glanced around the room, wondering if this would be better for his son, if his grandparents would give him a better life than he could, raising him out in the open. But as he asked the question of himself he knew the answer—no, his grandparents could not give him a better life. They could not give him the love of a father or the freedom of living unencumbered by possessions. They could not teach him to respect nature or to live by her rules; they could not teach him that one of the most beautiful sights in a lifetime was an eagle soaring high in the air, its wings held steady by the wind. They could not teach him all of the things he wanted his son to know about; they could not be his father.

He gently nudged Nathan's shoulder, but the boy did not move. He whispered his name and shook him, hoping that he wouldn't be frightened, praying that he would remember him.

"Nathan, it's your pa."

Nathan was silent and still, rubbing his eyes. He looked up at Trenton, then he sat up. "Pa?" he asked in his childish voice. "Pa," he said without question, putting his small arms around Trenton's neck. Trenton held him tightly, feeling the tears that threatened to fill his eyes.

"Nate, I've come to take you home. We're going home, Son."

"Yes, Daddy. I want to go home. I don't like it here."

"All right, Son. We're going to play a little game. We're going to sneak out of here. I'm going to carry you and I want you to be real quiet. Can you do that?"

"I can do that, Pa. Can we say good-by to Grandma and Grandpa?"

"We'll say good-by another time, Nate. Right now we have to hurry. Joe's waiting for us."

"Joe. I want to see Joe."

"I know you do." He stood up, walked to the dresser, and pulled out a bunch of Nathan's clothes which he stuffed into a pillowcase. He wrapped a blanket around the boy and lifted him up. "You've grown; you're heavier."

"I'm a big boy now." He put his arms around Trenton. "I love you, Pa."

"I love you, too, Nate. Be quiet now. Don't make a sound."

Trenton walked out of the room, shutting the door behind him. He went down the hall to the staircase and holding Nathan in his arms, carefully walked down the wooden steps. He was halfway down the staircase when he heard a door open upstairs. He stopped for a second, clapping his hand over Nathan's mouth as he turned his head. He couldn't tell who it was and he didn't want to find out. He hurried down the stairs to the front door, undoing the latch and noiselessly running out onto the porch. He checked the parade ground and the sentry tower to see if it was clear. He ran to the spot which Joe was guarding. He climbed the stairs, placing Nathan on the parapet, and signaled his partner.

Joe grabbed his rifle and ran to Trenton. "Let's go, boy; I think we're pushing our luck."

"Put your arms around my neck and don't let go, Nate. We're going to climb down this rope. Hold on to me now; don't let go." Trenton followed Joe down the rope. He dropped to the ground and shifting Nathan to his arms, he and Joe ran to their horses. They mounted up, riding west for a few miles, then doubling back and riding east. Trenton wanted to confuse Wainwright. He was going to lead him away from Aeneva and her people because he would go back to Aeneva and start his life with

339

her and his son. Perhaps now their life could be more peaceful; perhaps now he could teach his son all the things he had so longed to teach him. Now life would begin for them all.

Although Trenton was an experienced tracker, Long Nose was even more experienced. He knew from the beginning what Trenton was trying to do and he knew that eventually he would head back to the small Cheyenne band.

"You're sure he's going back there? What if he really is going west? We'll lose him for sure."

"He would not do that. He has no people there. The only people he has are these Cheyennes. He will go there."

"Well, if that's what you think, we'll be there first."

"You must take many men this time. They will be angry for what you did to their chief the last time."

"I don't care if I have to kill every one of those damned Indians; I'm going to get my grandson back and I'm going to make sure Trenton Hawkins hangs."

"I will find them for you again, soldier man, but I will not stay to help you this time. Stalking Horse has two grandsons and a granddaughter; they will not forget what you did to their grandfather."

"What have I to fear from two boys and a girl?"

"You have much to fear. The grandsons are proven warriors, as is the granddaughter. But that is not all."

"What do you mean?"

"Sun Dancer, the wife of the chief you killed, is a medicine woman. She has much power, it is said."

"So? I'm not afraid of an old woman and three children."

Long Nose shrugged. "You will see. There is some-

340

thing else."

"What?"

"The granddaughter is also Hawkins' woman. Do you understand?"

"I understand. It means if I can get her, I will be assured of getting my grandson back. It will be his life for hers."

"You do what you want, but I will not be there."

"You fear the Cheyennes; I didn't think the Crows feared anyone."

"A man would be stupid not to fear the Cheyennes, white man, especially when he has hurt or taken one they loved. I do not envy you when they find you."

"They'll never find me, I'm protected by the United States Army."

Long Nose contemplated Wainwright for a long time, his narrow eyes penetrating. "They will find you, white man; have no doubt of that. They will find you." Long Nose walked away; he almost wished he could be there when the Cheyennes found Wainwright. It would be worth it just to hear the man's screams.

It was easy enough for Wainwright and his men to take the Cheyenne camp full of women, children, and old men. The men were out hunting and could do nothing by the time Wainwright's men rode into the camp from the side by the river. When the Cheyennes came back to camp, they found their women and children held hostage.

"What do you want?" Brave Wolf rode forward, not waiting for a council chief to ask questions.

"Who are you?" Wainwright demanded.

"I am Brave Wolf, grandson of Stalking Horse." Brave Wolf spoke clearly in English. "Are you the one who killed my grandfather?"

"I am the one." Wainwright nodded, a slight smile on his face. "It was not meant for anyone to be killed. I just wanted my grandson."

"He does not belong to you. Do you always take things that do not belong to you? Is this the way of the white man?"

"He does belong to me!" Wainwright growled. "I won't allow my grandson to be raised here with you people."

"And do you think you could teach him better than we?" Brave Wolf's voice was low and controlled.

"Of course I can. He will have the finest clothes, live in the finest homes; he will go to the finest schools."

"And what if he learns to hate you because of all the fine things you have given him?"

"He will not hate me," Wainwright shouted loudly, looking around as if suddenly remembering where he was. "It does not concern me what you think, young man. I have come here for a reason."

"What is your reason, white man?"

"I want a girl—your sister, I believe. She is Trenton Hawkins' woman?"

Now it was Brave Wolf's turn to feel uncomfortable, but his eyes never wavered from Wainwright's. "She is not here. She is with another band of our tribe."

"You are lying. She is here, waiting for Hawkins and the boy."

"She is not here."

"You are lying."

"She is my sister. Do you really think I would just give her to you?" Brave Wolf laughed derisively.

"You would if I told you I would kill all of your women and children." Wainwright's eyes sparkled with hatred.

342

Brave Wolf looked down at the group of frightened women and children. How could he sacrifice them? How could he sacrifice his own sister?

"You are taking too long to decide, Brave Wolf. Either you give me your sister or I start shooting these women and children. I think it's simple enough even for you to understand."

There was a movement from the back of the warriors and Brave Wolf heard a horse stop next to his. "It is I you want. I am the wife of Trenton Hawkins." Aeneva sat with straight back and head held high; she showed no signs of fear.

Wainwright began to smile. "So, you are the one. You are Hawkins' squaw."

"Let the women and children go. I will go with you peacefully."

"I will decide what to do, girl. I am in charge here."

"Perhaps you think you are in charge," Brave Wolf intervened, "but you are still on our land. You might kill some of us, but others of us would live to kill some of you. You would be the first to die, white man. We will not die without a fight."

Wainwright looked at the warriors and saw a determination that was not in the eyes of his men. They might be able to kill some of them, but not all of them. Even the women and children looked determined. "All right. You come with me now, girl, and I will let the women and children go."

"Aeneva . . . ." Brave Wolf spoke to his sister, but she ignored him and rode forward. She was immediately encircled by horses and her reins were taken from her.

Wainwright looked at the Indians in front of him and considered fighting them, but he decided not to do that. He wanted to live to enjoy his grandson, not lie here rotting away on the prairie by some Cheyenne bullet.

"Tell Hawkins that he can come for his woman, but he must bring my grandson and he must be willing to remain in the woman's place. That is the only way she will be set free."

"Do not hurt her, white man." Sun Dancer's voice came suddenly from the camp and everyone turned.

"Who are you?" Wainwright asked as he watched the old woman walk toward him. There was no fear in her eyes.

"I am Sun Dancer, wife to Stalking Horse, grandmother of Aeneva."

"Sun Dancer," Wainwright repeated lightly, remembering what Long Nose had said about her. Long Nose was frightened of her and of her powers.

"Did you hear what I said, white man?" Sun Dancer repeated.

"I heard what you said, old woman. I am not frightened by threats."

"You are indeed foolish then," Sun Dancer replied confidently. She walked past Wainwright, through the circle of his soldiers, to Aeneva. She reached up and took her hand. "Do not be frightened, child; you will be all right. I know this."

"I am not frightened, Grandmother." Aeneva smiled, squeezing Sun Dancer's hand.

Sun Dancer nodded and walked back to Wainwright. "We will tell Trenton your words when he returns. It is up to him to decide about his son's future, not you. And as for my granddaughter, if she is hurt in any way, you and your family will pay dearly. Do you understand, white man?" Her voice sounded ominous; it was more than a threat.

Wainwright didn't answer Sun Dancer. He held up his

344

and, leading his men out of the camp in an orderly fash-
ion. Aeneva was surrounded on all sides; there was no
way she could escape.

Brave Wolf dismounted and stood with his arm around
his grandmother. "He will pay for this," he said bitterly.

"Yes, he will," Sun Dancer agreed, knowing that
Wainwright would die. She did not know how, but she
knew he would soon be dead. And for once in her life,
she didn't feel haunted by the prospect of someone's
death.

Aeneva looked out between the bars of the small prison
cell. Her heart pounded in her chest as she tried to feel the
evening breeze that was blowing through the fort. She
could feel none. It had been over a week now and there
had been no sign of Trenton. She knew that he would find
a way to save her; but with each day that passed, her
hopes diminished and her fear increased. There were
times when she felt as if the walls themselves were closing in on her; she begged for a breath of fresh air. There
had been a soldier next to her for three days who had done
nothing but taunt and tease her, but she had tried not to
pay attention; she didn't let him know that she understood
every disgusting word.

And there were the times that Wainwright came to
speak with her alone. Sometimes he would just stare, at
other times he would shout and yell, lashing out at her
with words and fists. He was a man obsessed, there was
no doubt, and Aeneva was a central figure of his obses-
sion. He told her numerous times that if he didn't hear
from Trenton soon, he would hang her, right here in her
cell.

Aeneva was not afraid to die, but she was afraid to die
here, in this small, dirty place. She would not let Wain-

wright take her life from her. She would kill herself before she would let him have the satisfaction.

She sat down on the bunk, pressing her hands to her abdomen. There was also the child to think of and she was not doing that now. She was being selfish. She had to think of a way to save herself so that she might save her child. But how? How was she to find a way out of here when there was no possible way. Then she remembered Trenton's words: "If something should happen and we get separated, believe that I will always come back to you." That is what she had to do now—believe in Trenton. She had to trust and believe in him enough to convince herself that he would find a way to get her out of here. It was her only chance; he was her only chance.

"He is not coming? Do you know what that means? That means you will die."

Aeneva stared back at Wainwright with eyes as hard as his. "Did you think he would be so stupid as to fall for your silly trap, white man?"

Wainwright struck her, knocking her back across the bunk. "You talk too much. I thought Indian women were taught to keep their tongues."

"You do not know very much about Indians." She rubbed the sore place on her cheek and sat back up on the bunk. He would probably strike her a few more times before he left; it was always this way. He never really hurt her, but she sensed it was his way of letting out his frustration. "He will not come. I know him."

"Then you will die," Wainwright yelled again angrily.

"I am prepared to accept that, but you do not seem to be. Why is that?"

"I would kill you in a second if I had to."

346

"I do not think so. I do not think you are a cruel man. If that were true, you would not have such love for your grandson."

Wainwright looked at Aeneva and sat down, wiping his arm across his face. "I don't like to do these things. It's his fault. If he hadn't taken my Lydia away—"

"You daughter died in childbirth. There was nothing that could be done."

"That's his story."

"He cared for your daughter. He did not want to see her die."

"Another lie."

'No, he does not lie. If your daughter were still alive, he would not be with me. He would still be with her. Whatever you may think of him, he is not disloyal. He would have stayed with her. She is the one who wanted to leave him."

"That's enough! I don't want to hear any more, not from you, of all people. He left her for you. It's your fault as much as it is his." He stood up and pushed the chair away. "I said before that I don't like to do these things, but I will do anything I have to to get my grandson back, including hanging you from the front of this fort." He stared at Aeneva a moment longer as if wanting to say something, but yelled for the guard and left.

Aeneva lay back on the hard bunk, rubbing her face. So, she had misjudged him after all. He would kill her. He would hang her where everyone could see her death, see her humiliation. She looked around the small cell for a sharp object. She had to be prepared in case Trenton did not come. She and her child would not be humiliated like animals in front of these white people; she would not die without honor. She would not.

CHAPTER XVII

Trenton was thinking just how good it would be to hold Aeneva in his arms again. It had been a hard two weeks, but he was sure he had succeeded in leading Wainwright away from the Cheyenne camp. He looked up at the bright moon that lit the way in front of them and he felt a contentment he had desired for a very long time. Holding his young son in his arms and knowing that he would soon be with Aeneva gave him a fulfillment he never had thought possible.

"What're you thinking about, boy?" Joe's voice came to him out of the darkness.

"What do you think?"

"Your woman."

"It seems as if I've wanted her forever, Joe. I can't believe we're finally together."

"Well, you'd better believe it. She is some woman. A lot like her grandmother."

"More than she realizes." Nathan moved in the saddle in front of him and Trenton held him tightly. "Do you think I'm doing the right thing, Joe? I mean by raising Nate clear out here away from civilization?"

Joe laughed contemptuously. "We both know about civilization, don't we, boy? I was a slave for most of my life and we were both locked up in prison for no good reason. I don't know that I'd call that all that civilized."

"You know what I mean."

"I know what you mean and I think you're doing the right thing. You can teach him how to read and write and all those things, but you can't teach him about the things you've always lived if he's stuck in a city somewhere. Your pa was able to do it with you and you still chose to live out here. You can give him the choice when he's old enough, but I think he'll want to stay right here. Any sane man would."

"What about you, Joe? I thought you were going to travel all around the world. You don't owe me anything. You've done enough for me already."

"I know I don't owe you anything, but I kind of like it out here. Makes a man feel peaceful inside. You know?"

"Yes, I know."

A coyote yelped nearby only to be answered by another. The sound was not a lonely sound, but rather, a joyous sound, like one friend calling out to another.

"Thanks, Joe," Trenton said finally. "You've been a good friend. The best friend I've ever had."

"Don't start going soft on me, boy. Let's just get ourselves home."

"Home, that sounds good." It was a word he hadn't been able to say with true meaning since his childhood when his parents were still alive. Now he again knew the meaning of the word and all that it implied. Home was not a word to be taken lightly.

They rode into camp before dawn. A few campfires smoldered, and the camp dogs barked excitedly at the horses. When guards waved them through, they rode straight to Sun Dancer's lodge. Trenton and Joe walked quietly into the lodge, not wanting to wake Sun Dancer or Aeneva, but Sun Dancer was already up, sitting with her back to the door. "*Haahe,* Sun Dancer," Trenton said softly, walking over to her. "I have brought your great-grandson." Sun Dancer looked up at Trenton with great sad eyes. Taking Nathan in her arms, she kissed the boy on the head and cradled him in her arms as Trenton and Joe sat down next to her. "Where is Aeneva?" Trenton asked eagerly. "Has she gone out hunting before the sun even comes up?" He laughed gently. "Marriage has not changed her. She is still a warrior at heart."

"She is not out hunting, Trenton," Sun Dancer said gravely.

"Something has happened to her." Trenton knew by the sound of Sun Dancer's voice. "Where is she?"

"The white soldiers came into our camp when the hunters were out. They captured the women and children. Their leader said he would kill them all if Aeneva did not come with him. She, of course, went with him willingly."

"The bastard." Trenton thought for a moment. "What else? Did he leave a message?"

Sun Dancer nodded. "You are to bring Nathan into the fort yourself. He will take Nathan and then he wants you in exchange for Aeneva."

"The man certainly doesn't give up easily," Joe said. "Did he set a time limit, Sun Dancer? Did he say when Trenton was to go to the fort."

"No, only that if he came in with Nathan, Aeneva would be set free."

"Well, I don't have any other choice. The bastard will kill her if I don't take Nate back."

"And he'll kill you when you go in there, boy. You can't do it."

"What in the hell am I supposed to do, Joe? I can't let Aeneva stay there much longer. You remember what it

351

was like in the dirty little cell. I could barely stand it; it will drive Aeneva crazy in no time. Indians aren't used to being locked up."

"I agree with Joe." Sun Dancer's calm voice interceded.

"I can't leave her there, Sun Dancer. She'll die."

"She will not die. I promise you that."

"How do you know? One of your visions?" Trenton asked bitterly, then shook his head. "I'm sorry, Sun Dancer, forgive me."

"I understand. I myself did not trust my visions for many, many winters. They frightened me; I always saw death in them. Then as I grew older, I also saw life. I know that Aeneva will live to be very old, with you. She will not die in that prison."

"Even if you're right, I still can't leave her there. Believe me, it will be worse torture for her to be locked up like that than if she were beaten."

"She is strong, Trenton; she will survive."

"I can't believe you're asking me to leave her there. Why, Sun Dancer?"

"Because you must make him come to you."

"He'll never do that."

"He will if you send him a message."

"What kind of a message?"

"Tell him that he must bring Aeneva to you or he will never see his grandson again."

Trenton looked first at Sun Dancer, then at Joe. "Are you crazy? He'll kill her first."

"You must trust me, Trenton; he will not kill her. He wants Nathan back more than anything. He knows that if he kills Aeneva, he will never see Nathan again."

"She's right, boy. If you go in there, he'll kill you for sure. Then what good's that going to do Nate and Aeneva?''

''I don't trust him. He'll kill her anyway. He's not going to come out here and trade for Nate.'' He shook his head uncertainly. ''He'll never go for it.''

''Send him the message, Trenton. You must not go in there.''

''I thought you said in your vision that I would live a long life with Aeneva.''

''That does not mean you will not suffer unduly.''

''Then it may also mean that Aeneva might suffer unduly; is that right?''

''It is possible.''

''Then that's it. I'm going in there. Neither of you can stop me or talk me out of it.'' He stood up.

''Sit down, Trenton.'' There was a note of authority in Sun Dancer's voice that Trenton had never heard before. He complied immediately. ''There is something else you must know. Aeneva is with child.''

''Jesus.'' Trenton rested his head on his hand, eyes closed. He envisioned Aeneva being tortured; and the sight of her hemorrhaging to death just as Lydia had, was clear in his mind. ''Why did you tell me this? Surely you know that I have to go now.''

''I told you so that you would not go. Do you not see, Trenton? Once he has you he will not let her go. Why should he? Has he proven to be a man of his word?''

''Once he murders you, boy, he'll do the same to Aeneva. There'll be no stopping him.''

Sun Dancer glanced sharply at Joe. ''He will not kill her, but he could harm her and the child. Do you understand why you must not go in there, Trenton? You must make him come out here.''

''I told you before, he won't do it.''

''He'll do it if you make him believe that you don't

care what happens to Aeneva. Make it seem as if it would be nice to have her back, but you're not risking your neck for her."

"Joe is right. He will do anything to get Nathan back, including bringing Aeneva to you. It must be done this way."

"I could just go in there by myself at night—"

"Sneaking into a fort and breaking into a house is one thing, boy, but breaking into a prison is another. You and I were both in there and we both know it's not easy to get out of."

"I still don't like it."

"You don't have to like it; just do it. It's the only way."

"Who will take the message?"

"I will."

"Hell, he'll kill you, too, Joe. No, I want Brave Wolf or Coyote Boy to do it."

"No, they cannot go in either. He knows they are related to Aeneva; he already saw how much they care for her."

"You two won't let me have a say in any of this, will you?"

"Don't get so steamed up, boy; we're just trying to think of the best way to save Aeneva and you, that's all."

"All right, Joe, you take the message in to Wainwright. But if you don't come back by tonight, I'm coming in there after the both of you."

"All right, all right. Don't worry, he's not going to do anything to me, especially when I tell him you expect an answer by evening."

"All right. I guess I don't have much choice." Trenton reached over and ruffled Nathan's hair, watching him as he slept peacefully in Sun Dancer's arms. "If anything

354

happens to her—''

''She will be all right, Trenton. You must believe that.''

''I'll believe it when I see her, Sun Dancer,'' he said abruptly and walked out of the lodge.

''I feel for that boy. He's been through a hell of a lot in his short lifetime. All he wants is to be with Aeneva and Nathan. It must be eating at him that he can't help her.''

''I am sure that it is, but I do not trust that white man. If he gets Trenton alone in that fort, I am sure he will kill him.''

''But you said—''

''I lied. What else could I do?''

''You lied about Aeneva also?''

''No, I told the truth about her. It is Trenton I am most concerned about now. You must make sure he doesn't go off on his own.''

''Well, it'll be almost dawn soon. I'll get ready to take off.''

''You must rest first, Joe.''

''I can rest later. I want to get that message to Wainwright as soon as I can.'' He stood up and stretched, looking at Sun Dancer strangely. ''What's it like to be able to see into the future? It must be scary.''

Sun Dancer thought for a moment, reflecting back on her childhood. ''The first vision I ever had was of my brother being killed. It haunted me for many years.''

''Did he get killed?''

''Yes, just as I had seen. But I did not know when. He lived a fairly long life, an honorable one.''

''Honor, that's real important to you people, isn't it?''

''I would say it is the most important thing. But you would know about honor, would you not, Joe?''

''What would I know about honor?''

"Honor and pride are much the same thing. You say you were a slave for most of your life; yet you do not strike me as a man who could be mastered."

"You are too wise for your own good, Sun Dancer." Joe smiled. "I owe you a knife for scraping."

"And I owe you a robe for the winter."

"We were both wrong."

"Or we were both right. There is always that possibility."

Joe laughed loudly, slapping his thigh. "You are something, Sun Dancer. You are very special. Anyone ever tell you that?"

"Yes." Sun Dancer recalled her father and brother telling her that long ago—what seemed like hundreds of winters ago.

"Well, they were right." Joe bent down and kissed Sun Dancer on the cheek. "You and my ma would have gotten along fine. She was full of wisdom, too."

"She is no longer living?"

"No, she died when I was real young, before they moved me up to the big house. She was the one who helped me have pride in myself. She was the one who made me believe in freedom. She died believing I'd be free someday."

"And she was right."

"Yes, she was right. I just wish she could've been here. I wish I could've taken her with me to this place, to this land. She would've loved it here. She would have loved you."

"Perhaps I will see her when I go to the other side. I will tell her that you are well."

"I thought just Indians went to that place."

"To Seyan? I do not believe that. I believe all who deserve to will go there. I know I will see my brother, Jean, for he was as much Cheyenne as I or Stalking Horse. And perhaps your mother will be there also.''

"Well, I hope you're not planning to go there real soon. We can't do without you just yet.''

Sun Dancer smiled, realizing that Joe knew she was speaking seriously of her future death. She liked him even more for that. "No, I will remain here until I am sure that Aeneva is safe and that you all are proceeding down a safe road in life.''

"How can you be sure that any of us has chosen a safe road?''

"I cannot; I can only hope. I can die thinking that you are all happy and safe, just as your mother died thinking that you would be free. It is very simple, Joe. Your mother was a smart woman.''

"You're right, she probably is in that Seyan place. When you get there, tell her I'm as free as any man can be. Tell her that, will you?''

"I will tell her.''

Joe nodded and ambled out of the lodge. Sun Dancer watched him as he left, thinking that in spite of the difference in the color of their skins, Joe and Jean were very much alike. She knew that Joe would watch out for Trenton, just as Jean had watched out for Stalking Horse. It would be a lifelong bond that could not be broken by anyone or anything, just as Jean's and Stalking Horse's bond had not been broken. Wistfully she thought of them both and she smiled a secret smile. "I will be there soon, you two. Do not be impatient. Soon my work here will be done and I can finally rest. Soon.'' She closed her eyes, the smile still on her face long after she was asleep.

"This is outrageous! He can't really expect me to go into hostile Indian territory.''

"You've done it before," Joe replied sarcastically.

"But he wants me to come alone. I can't trust him."

"You want him to come alone. Why should he trust you?"

"That's different. He is a deserter and he murdered my daughter."

"He's no deserter and he didn't murder your daughter. I was with them both when it happened."

"You were there?"

"She died in childbirth. It couldn't be helped."

"It could have been helped if she had been with a decent doctor."

"She was with a decent doctor."

"I don't believe you."

"You don't want to believe much of anything, do you? Well, I'll tell you something else you don't want to believe. Your daughter railroaded Trenton into that marriage with your help, and then when she realized what she had done, she wanted to do the decent thing and leave him. That's what she was planning to do after she had the baby."

"I don't—"

"You don't believe me. I know, but it's the truth. She wrote you letters. She told me. I suppose you didn't believe her either."

"He made her write them under duress."

"There is no getting through to you, is there, man? You just won't see the truth for what it is. Nathan is Trenton's son and he'll never give him up. Never."

"Then why did he send you here?"

"To tell you that you can do whatever you want with his wife, but he won't give Nathan up. Do you understand, Wainwright? He feels he owes it to her family to get her back, but he feels no obligation toward her. You

358

know how it is with white men and their squaws.'' Joe watched as Wainwright's cheek twitched nervously.

"I don't believe you."

"I don't really care what you believe, but you'd better know something else. If you kill that girl, her brothers and the rest of the band and probably a few more Cheyennes are coming after you, and they won't stop until they find you. I'm surprised your Crow friend didn't tell you that.'' Joe reached into a box on Wainwright's desk and took out a cigar. He rubbed it between his fingers, smelled it, then bit off the end and stuck it in his mouth. "Look, Wainwright, I don't really care what you do, but you'd better give me an answer soon. If I'm not back by tonight, then Hawkins is taking his son and they'll be long gone where no one will ever see them again."

"All right, all right," Wainwright replied uneasily. "Tell him I'll bring the girl. But I must have some guarantee from him. I won't go out there alone."

Joe thought for a moment, then nodded. "All right, say you bring some men with you, not more than ten. I'll ask Hawkins if you can talk to the boy alone."

"I want more than that. I want to be able to see him grow up. He is all that I have left of Lydia."

Joe studied the man for a time, almost feeling sorry for him until he remembered Stalking Horse. "I'll do what I can. I'll talk to Hawkins and be back here again tomorrow. If he agrees to your terms, then we'll arrange a time and place to meet."

"Yes, I will wait for you until tomorrow."

"What about the girl? Is she all right?"

"She is fine."

"I'd like to see her. It would reassure her brothers somewhat. They're getting a little impatient, if you know what I mean. I don't know if you could handle a full-scale

Cheyenne and Sioux uprising.''

"Don't push me. I could just as easily keep you here.''

"You could, but you won't. You want to see your grandson, remember?''

"All right. You can see her for five minutes. No longer.''

"Five minutes is long enough.''

Joe remembered the dank smell of the cells where he had been imprisoned not long before. It had been easy for him; he had been used to being enclosed for as long as he could remember. But for someone like Aeneva, who had never known anything but the freedom of the outdoors, it would be almost unbearable.

"Hello, Zeb.'' Joe walked up to the guard.

Zeb looked up, mildly interested. "Wondered what became of you. Figured I'd never see that gold.''

"Sorry, Zeb, but I had to get my godson out of here. Hope you understand. Nothing personal.''

Zeb looked around before answering. "I understand. I know how crazy Wainwright can be.''

"Thanks, Zeb. Can I see the girl now?''

"Come on.''

It was still fairly dark in the cells, the sun not coming through until the afternoon. He saw her lying on the floor, a blanket wrapped around her. He squatted down, reaching through the bars with his two hands. "Aeneva.'' He spoke softly, not wanting to startle her. She was awake instantly and sitting up. Hearing her name but not recognizing the voice, she looked at the bars.

"Who is it?''

"It's Joe.''

"Joe?'' There was a joyful sound in her voice that tore at Joe's heart.

"Come closer; I want to talk to you.''

360

She moved to the bars, sitting down and taking Joe's hands in hers. "You have come for me? Trenton has sent you?" There were dark circles under her eyes and bruises on her face where she had been struck.

Joe reached up and touched her lightly. "Has he hurt you much?"

"Not much. I would never let him know even if it was too much."

"You are well?"

"I am well." Her voice had already lost some of its joy; she had already guessed he was not there to take her out.

"You look thin, too thin."

"I am well." She squeezed his hands. "You are not here to take me out, are you?"

"No."

"Why are you here then?"

"I've just had a talk with Wainwright. He will be taking you to Trenton in the next day or two."

"I do not understand."

"Your grandmother and I did not think it safe for Trenton to come in here after you. We were sure Wainwright would have murdered him on the spot, and then you. Do you understand?"

"Yes. And Trenton?"

"He wanted to come in here after you, of course. But we talked him out of it. Instead, I came with a message for Wainwright telling him that if he wanted to see Nathan again he was to bring you back to your people."

"Yes, it is a better plan."

"There is something else. I told Wainwright that Trenton did not really care for you, that the only reason he wants you back is for your family. He must believe that you are worthless to Trenton or he will kill you."

"I have already told him that Trenton would not come in after me. Now he will believe me."

"Good."

"How is Trenton? He is well?"

"He is crazy knowing you're in here. He'd do anything to get you out."

"Tell him I will be fine. I am strong."

"That's what your grandmother said."

"She is right as usual."

"All right, Joe, it's time." Zeb opened the door behind Joe.

"Be right there." He looked back at Aeneva. "You'll be all right? It won't be long now."

"I will be fine. Please tell Trenton . . . No, I will tell him myself. Thank you for coming, Joe."

"I'll see you soon, girl. Real soon."

Aeneva watched Joe as he left the cell and she stood up on the bunk and peered through the bars to watch him as he walked across the yard. Soon, he had said, real soon. She breathed in a lungful of fresh air and sat down on the bunk. She pressed her hands to her stomach and rocked slowly back and forth. She was glad she would not have to kill herself and her child. If she had done that, she would not have been allowed to go to Seyan and she would not have seen her grandfather, *Naxane* Jean, or her parents. She got down on the floor, reached back underneath the bunk, and pulled out the stone. It was flat and thin and sharp on one side, where she had rubbed it continually against another rock. It was to be the weapon with which she killed herself, but now she would not need it. She felt its sharp edge and threw it back underneath the bunk. Soon she would be back with Trenton; soon she would be home. Suddenly that was the most important thing in the world to her.

Wainwright waited as his men readied themselves. He smiled as he thought of the black man; he hadn't believed a word he'd said, and he certainly wasn't stupid enough to ride into a trap that Hawkins had set. No, they would be off their guard until the next day when the black man came back with a message from Hawkins. He had until then to get into the Cheyenne camp and do what he had planned from the beginning. None of them deserved to live and if he had to kill them all in order to get Hawkins, that is just what he would do. And he would take the squaw with him and let her see just how cruel he could be. He would let her watch and he would kill her, too. If he could not have his grandson, no one would.

Sun Dancer woke up suddenly, opening her eyes to the darkness inside the lodge. They were coming tonight; the soldiers were coming tonight. She sat for a minute, recalling her vision: Wainwright and his soldiers, many of them, were riding in the darkness to ambush the Cheyennes. They had Aeneva with them. It was this night. She did not know why. Nothing in the dream told her that it was this night; she just knew. "Trenton . . ." She spoke softly, knowing that he would not be sleeping, just as he had not slept the night before.

"What is it, Sun Dancer?"

"The soldiers, they are coming tonight."

There was movement across the lodge and Trenton was beside her. "You have just had a dream?"

"I saw the white soldier with many of his soldiers riding here in the darkness. They had Aeneva with them."

"How many did you see?"

"More than the other times. Two long lines."

"So, he's not taking any chances." Trenton did not

doubt Sun Dancer this time. "Joe, wake up."

"What is it, boy?" Joe was instantly awake and next to Trenton. "Is it time for me to go?"

"No. I want you to wake the people in the lodges on the far side of the camp; I will wake the ones around here. Sun Dancer says that Wainwright and his soldiers are coming tonight."

"And to think I almost felt sorry for the bastard."

"Tell the men to get their arms and meet me here. Are Brave Wolf and Coyote Boy on guard?"

"Yes."

"Go to them and tell them what I've told you. Brave Wolf will know what to do."

In less than twenty minutes, all of the people of the camp were in a large group next to Sun Dancer's lodge. She told them of her dream. All of them, including the women and some of the older children, carried weapons.

"The women and children will go across the river and into the woods. White soldiers cannot sneak up on you there," Brave Wolf said with authority. "Coyote Boy, you lead a group of men to the east side of the camp, but remain outside of it so you are not seen. Black Bear, you take a group to the west side of the camp along the river. We don't want them coming across the women and children. The rest of you will come with me to the north side of the camp. We will await them in darkness, as they wanted to surprise us in darkness. Trenton, you will come with me. Joe, you will go with Coyote Boy."

There was quiet, efficient movement as all did as they were told. The women, children, and old men moved across the river into the woods, while the men separated into three different groups. They unstaked their war horses from in front of their lodges and hurriedly rounded up the older horses that were grazing and staked them in

364

front of the lodges. They wanted the camp to look as normal as possible. They settled down to wait.

It was early in the night when Sun Dancer had had her dream and by midnight, when the moon was high in the sky, there was still no sign of the soldiers. Some of the women and children slept and many of the men grew impatient, but Brave Wolf, Coyote Boy, and Black Bear reminded them all that there were many hours yet left in the night.

As the hours wore on, Sun Dancer grew more impatient than anyone. She was beginning to doubt her dream vision. Perhaps she had grown old and feeble and was unable to distinguish a dream from a vision. Perhaps she had only dreamed that the soldiers were going to come; perhaps they were not really going to come at all. She held Nathan in her arms and covered him more tightly with a blanket. She would miss not seeing this one grow up; he would be like his father but much different. Already he showed signs of having great patience and acceptance of things that happened. Unlike his father, he did not fight everything that happened to him. She closed her eyes and rested her chin on Nathan's head. She was tired; she always seemed to be tired these days. She was much too impatient to be on her way down the Hanging Road to meet Stalking Horse and Jean. She hated the fact that they were having so much fun without her. She would miss her grandchildren, but all of her family and friends were now in Seyan: her parents, her brother, her good friends Laughing Bird, Spring, Calf Woman, and Broken Leaf; they were all there waiting for her.

"Sun Dancer, "—a hand touched her gently on the shoulder—"I think they are coming."

Sun Dancer opened her eyes and listened, her body tense. She heard the horses in the distance and she knew she had been right. She had read the vision correctly; she had been able to do a good thing for her people before she died. Nathan wiggled in her arms, trying to find a more comfortable spot, and he laid his head against her chest. "Sleep, little one, for when you awake it will be all over. Your life will then begin." She kissed him lightly on the head and looked out across the river to their empty camp.

"This will be easier than I thought," Wainwright whispered to his sergeant in the darkness. "They don't even have any guards keeping watch."

"They don't usually have need of guards, sir."

"Well, they should have been more careful. They should always be ready; it's their own fault they're going to die. It's their own fault." Wainwright stared at the empty camp. "I suppose there's no time like the present, Sergeant. Remember, no one is to touch my grandson. I'll kill any man who even fires in his direction. Is that understood?"

"Understood, sir. But isn't this a little dangerous, sir? Your grandson could get caught in the crossfire."

"Well, it's up to you to make sure he doesn't get caught in the cross fire. Find him, do you understand? Kill anyone who stands in your way."

"Yes, sir."

"Is everyone ready, Sergeant?"

The sergeant passed word down the two columns of men. "Everyone is ready, sir."

"Good." Wainwright held up his hand, then brought it down sharply. "Now!" he yelled and led his men into the Cheyenne camp. They rode furiously, charging in and firing their rifles and yelling. They knocked their rifles against the lodges, waiting for the people to come out. When no people appeared, Wainwright went crazy. "Get

them out of their lodges. Search the damned things!''
Wainwright ordered his men to dismount and go into the
lodges. While most of the men were searching the lodges
and riding around the camp, the three separate groups of
Cheyennes slowly closed in on the camp, spreading out to
make a wide circle. They waited silently until one of the
soldiers looked up and saw them. ''Look!'' he cried with
a strained, frightened voice, and pointed to the unbroken
circle of Cheyennes. Many of the men stopped to look,
but they didn't fire their rifles; the Cheyennes all had
their rifles and weapons aimed on the soldiers in the
camp.

Ready to reprimand his men, Wainwright came out of
one of the lodges. When he looked up, he saw the Cheyennes and Trenton. ''You,'' he said bitterly, raising his
rifle and firing. Trenton fired first, shooting Wainwright
in the arm. Wainwright looked up at Trenton. ''How did
you know we were coming?''

''Do you remember the grandmother the Crow told
you about? She had a dream you were coming.''

''No, that's not possible.''

''It's not only possible, it's what happened. She
warned us that you were coming, Wainwright.'' Trenton
shook his head in disgust. ''Why did you do it? I was considering letting you see Nathan once in a while. I thought
it was only fair that he know his grandparents.''

''I didn't trust you.''

''Have you ever trusted anyone in your life?''

''I could never trust a half-breed who murdered my
daughter. You're scum, Hawkins.''

''I didn't murder your daughter; I told you that before.''

''And I told you I didn't believe you.''

''Well, it doesn't matter now anyway. I'm going to

make sure the army knows all about your personal vendetta against these people.''

''They won't care. They're starting to move many of the tribes westward anyway. They'll applaud me and they'll hang you.''

''I don't think so, not when I tell them the truth.''

''The truth as you see it.''

''The truth, Wainwright.''

Wainwright looked around the camp. ''Where's Nathan?''

''He's safe.'' Trenton looked around at Wainwright's men. It suddenly occurred to him that Aeneva was not with them. ''Where is she?''

''Did you think I'd be so stupid as to bring her here? I thought about it. In fact, I was going to make her watch while I killed you and her family. But then I decided to leave her there, just in case something like this happened.''

Trenton stepped forward, smashing his fist into Wainwright's face. ''You're a pig; you know that, Colonel?''

Wainwright wiped the blood away from his injured nose and smiled at Trenton. ''You do care for her, don't you. I knew it.''

''If you've hurt her—'' Trenton grabbed Wainwright by the collar.

''I haven't hurt her too badly; just slapped her around a bit. I told my men that if I'm not back by tomorrow at sunset, they can do whatever they want with her; then they're to hang her. You got that, Hawkins?''

''You son of a bitch!'' Trenton slugged Wainwright again, this time knocking him to the ground. He jumped on him, pressing him to the ground with his knees while he pummeled his face with his fists.

''That's enough, Trenton. You're going to kill him,

boy." Joe pulled Trenton away from Wainwright.

"I want to kill him."

"No, we may need him to get back into the fort."

"If I had my way, I'd shoot him right now."

"So would I, but that won't help you get Aeneva out of there, will it?"

Trenton looked at Wainwright's bloody face and he backed away, rubbing the knuckles of his fists. "All right. Let's get all these men tied up first; then we'll talk about what to do."

"Now you're talking, boy."

They tied all of the soldiers together; first their hands behind their backs, then one long rope through the wrist ropes so they were all connected. Next their ankles were tied together, one soldier to the next, so one man couldn't escape without taking everyone else with him. A special place was reserved for Wainwright in the middle of the camp. His feet and hands were tied together by a rope that also went around his neck. If he moved too quickly or tried to stretch the rope, he could easily strangle himself.

"You can't get into that fort without me," Wainwright said coldly.

"We got into it before, and there won't be as many men guarding it. You didn't plan very well, Wainwright."

"I left enough men to guard the place. More than enough."

"How about your wife? Is she guarded, too?"

"What? Wainwright was suddenly alert. "What are you talking about?"

"I'm talking about your wife. It was fairly easy for me to get into your house once before. I think I'll do it again and I'll take your wife along for insurance. Just in case any of your men don't want to help me."

"Leave her out of it. She hasn't done anything to hurt you."

"Neither had Aeneva, but you took her away from me, didn't you?"

"It's because of her that you left Lydia. You never loved my daughter. You made her life a constant torment."

Trenton squatted down in front of Wainwright, seeing now what Joe had spoken of before. His voice was almost gentle when he spoke. "You're right about one thing. I didn't love Lydia, but she knew that when I married her. I never deceived her. I did everything I could to make her happy."

"No, it's not true." Wainwright shook his head miserably.

"Listen to me, Colonel. She was going to leave me and go back to live with you and your wife after the baby was born. The only reason she married me was to give the child a name. She was afraid you were going to make her give the child away if she stayed with you."

"How could she think that? I wouldn't have done that."

"She did what she thought was right."

"I suppose she did." Wainwright looked up at Trenton, his eyes no longer filled with hatred. "What are you going to do with me?"

"As soon as I get Aeneva, I'm going to return you and your men to the fort."

"What about me? You said you were going to tell the army about me."

"I don't think I'll have to do that, not if you plan on retiring soon."

"You're forcing me to retire?"

"No. I'm giving you a choice: you can leave the army

honorably or dishonorably. It's up to you.''

"You don't give me much choice.''

"At least you have a choice, Colonel. Oh, there's one other thing. I'd like to have my record cleared of desertion charges.''

"Never.''

"I didn't desert. All I did was help Lydia.''

"So you say.''

"All right, believe what you want.'' Trenton stood up. "I feel sorry for you, Wainwright. You're a man who has nothing.''

"Don't you feel sorry for me, you bastard. I don't want your pity.''

Trenton ignored him as he walked away, Wainwright's words falling on deaf ears. The only thing on Trenton's mind now was getting Aeneva out of prison before it was too late.

CHAPTER XVIII

It was very simple. Instead of having to rescue Aeneva from the fort, Trenton and the Cheyennes merely walked the soldiers within view of the sentry. They waited until the large doors opened and Trenton rode forward.

"What do you want, Hawkins?"

Trenton recognized one of the men he had ridden with before. "Take a look out there, Jacob. We've got your colonel and most of your men tied up."

"Just what do you plan to do with them?"

"Nothing if you'll cooperate."

"The girl?"

"Yes, the girl. I want her. If she's set free, all of these men will be released unharmed. It's a hell of a lot more than he would have done for us."

"I don't know. I have my orders. . . ."

Trenton turned on his horse, pointing back to the Indians. "You see those Cheyennes out there? Well, they're growing kind of restless. You see, you have one of theirs and they're real tired of having you ride into their camp unannounced. You also killed one of their great chiefs."

"I had nothing to do with that. Wainwright's the one."

"Well, you're the one now. Bring the girl out here."

"Wainwright will probably hang me after all this is over."

"Wainwright will probably be booted out of the army

373

if word of his personal vendetta gets around. You don't have to worry, Jacob.''

"All right. You wait inside the fort. I'll get her.''

"I'll come with you.''

"No, you wait here. Make sure your friends can see you. I don't want them thinking we've done something to you, too.''

"All right.''

Trenton dismounted and leaned against one of the tall gates, waiting impatiently while Jacob went for Aeneva. He looked out at his friends who completely encircled the white soldiers. They looked proud and unafraid; the paint on their bodies stood out even at this distance. He remembered having talked to Stalking Horse when he was just a boy. Stalking Horse had spoken to him of his fears concerning the white man. He had believed Sweet Medicine's prophecy and he felt that someday the Cheyennes would be destroyed by the white man.

Trenton thought about it for a moment until a shot broke his reverie. He looked across the yard and saw Mrs. Wainwright pointing a rifle at Aeneva. She fired again and this time Aeneva fell to her knees. Trenton started to run across the yard yelling, "No, don't shoot," but Mrs. Wainwright kept shooting at Aeneva until there were no more bullets; then she let the rifle fall from her hands.

"I'm sorry, Trenton. I tried to shield her," Jacob was saying as Trenton knelt next to Aeneva.

"It's all right, Jacob. Just get that crazy woman out of here." Aeneva had been shot in three places: twice in the leg, once in the back. "Jesus," Trenton muttered, as he tried to get a look at the wounds.

"Leave them." Aeneva spoke suddenly. "Take me out of here, Trenton. I want to go home."

"You can't be moved like this. You'll bleed to death."

"I would rather die where I can feel the sun on my face than die in a place like this. Please."

Trenton nodded and lifted her up in his arms, carrying her as carefully as he could to his horse. He propped her in front of him so that her back wound was not irritated by his body. He turned his horse and rode out to the rest of his people, watching Aeneva as she looked up at the sun. He couldn't tell if she was just enjoying seeing the sun again after so long a time or if she was preparing to say good-by to it. "You must be in great pain. I'm sorry."

"I do not feel any pain. I am happy to be with you and to feel the wind on my face and the warmth of the sun on my skin. There is no better day to die."

"Don't say that. You're not going to die."

"Do not worry, my Husband; it is just that my grandfather always said that it would be good to die on a sunny day."

"Don't speak any more of dying, do you hear me?"

"I hear you." She closed her eyes and Trenton noticed that she was paler than before.

Before he reached the group, Brave Wolf, Coyote Boy, and Joe rode out to meet him. He answered their questions before they asked them. "She's been shot."

"Who did it?"

"Wainwright's wife. She was crazy."

"Then she will pay," Coyote Boy said bitterly, drawing his rifle from its holder.

"No," Aeneva said softly. "Do not kill anyone."

"Look what the woman has done to you, little Sister. She and the white soldier must pay for everything they have done to our family."

"It will serve no purpose, Brother. The woman has suffered enough. She blames me for the loss of her daughter; she is not unjustified in thinking that.''

''You talk in riddles. The man must pay,'' Coyote Boy said finally.

''Coyote Boy . . .'' Aeneva tried to sit up and look at him. Her voice was strained but clear. ''What good will it do? It will not bring grandfather back. If you are doing it for him, he would not want you to do it.''

''I am doing it for myself because of what the man has done to you.''

''Then do not do it for me. Let him go; let them all go. I just want to go home. Please, my Brother, do this for me.'' She shut her eyes and leaned back against Trenton.

''He will do it, little Sister,'' Brave Wolf asserted and looked over at his brother.

Coyote Boy looked back at Wainwright and then at his sister and he finally acceded to her wish. He reached out and stroked her arm. ''I will do as you say, little Sister. But only because you ask it of me.''

''Thank you, Brother,'' Aeneva responded in a low whisper. She did not open her eyes.

''I'm going to take her back to camp as soon as I bandage her.''

''Go ahead, Brother,'' Brave Wolf said firmly. ''We will wait until you are well on your way before we let these men go.''

''Do not bother,'' Aeneva said softly, but Trenton proceeded to bandage the wounds as best he could.

''I'll ride ahead and tell Sun Dancer to be waiting for you.''

''Thanks, Joe.''

Joe reached out and squeezed Trenton's arm. ''Don't worry, boy, she'll be all right. She's one of the strongest women I ever met. She's a perfect match for you.''

Trenton smiled weakly and nodded his head; he was

not even aware that Joe had already ridden off. He finished with Aeneva, then started home. He rode as carefully as he could, but every time the horse took a step it seemed to jostle Aeneva around. When he noticed that she was unconscious he decided it didn't matter how fast he went; it was just important that he get her to Sun Dancer as quickly as possible. He looked down again at her pale face and noticed the beads of perspiration that had formed. He couldn't believe this had happened. To have gone through so much only to lose her. He couldn't imagine life without her; most of his life had been spent thinking about her.

He rode for what seemed like an eternity until he saw the camp in the distance. It was a welcome and painful sight. This could be the place where Aeneva would live to be with him; or this could be the place where she would die, never to be with him again. He kissed the top of her head and urged his horse into a full gallop. He felt as if he were racing against all odds, against time itself, against death. He had never been so frightened in his life.

Sun Dancer worked over Aeneva for many hours, never stopping to rest. Trenton watched her as she tried to remove the bullet from Aeneva's back, but was unable to; so she removed the bullets from Aeneva's leg. When she was through, she covered her with a blanket. Sun Dancer purified herself and Aeneva by burning the leaves of the sweet grass, and she held her hands over the smoke and pressed them to the wounds on Aeneva's body. Then she did something which Trenton had never seen her do before—she prayed. She sang a song about life and strength while shaking a rattle to drive away the evil spirits that lurked in Aeneva's body. Sun Dancer continued to pass her hands through the smoke and lay them on Aeneva's wounds. She even prayed to the Maiyun and to Heammawihio himself, stating that she would gladly exchange her life for that of her granddaughter's. Continuing to chant and pray for many hours, she never stopped or seemed the least bit tired. After a long time, Sun Dancer reached for the old medicine pipe that Horn, her teacher, had given her. She filled it and offered it to the earth, the sky, and the four directions, and she passed it through the smoke of the burning sweet grass. She smoked it until it was empty and she laid it by the fire. Mixing a special tea, she held Aeneva's head up, forcing her to drink the tea. She refilled the pipe, passed it through the smoke, offered it to the earth, the sky, the four directions, and she smoked it again. During the entire healing process, Sun Dancer had drunk no water. It was as if she possessed some unnatural power while she healed so that she didn't feel tired, thristy, or hungry. Finally, she rested for a time, sitting quietly next to Aeneva, not sleeping but keeping watch over her.

Trenton heard a sound and woke with a start; he had been sleeping. He looked over and found Sun Dancer shaking the rattle and chanting in a loud, angry voice. She was threatening the evil spirits with her power, the power that had been sent to her by the Maiyun. Trenton wanted to talk to Sun Dancer, but he knew he could not disturb her from her concentration. She was working harder than she had ever worked before in her life. He looked over at the still form of his wife and he got up and left the lodge.

He walked through the camp and to the river. He sat down on the bank, staring at the water. He hadn't even seen Nathan since he'd been back; he'd thought of nothing but Aeneva.

"How is she, my Brother?" Brave Wolf sat down next to Trenton.

"I don't know, Brave Wolf. She hasn't moved since I brought her to your grandmother."

"And my grandmother, does she work hard over my sister?"

"She hasn't stopped. I fell asleep for a while and when I woke up Sun Dancer was still chanting."

"She is chanting then? Umm." Brave Wolf sighed deeply. "I believe my grandmother when she says Aeneva will not die. You must believe her also."

"I want to believe her, but when I see Aeneva lying here it's hard to believe anything."

"She will live; I am sure of it."

"How can you be so sure, Brave Wolf? Just because Sun Dancer told you she had a dream that Aeneva would live till old age?"

"My grandmother has had many dreams and I do not remember a time when she was wrong. She knew you would come back here to us someday; she knew of my grandfather's and Jean's deaths; she knew of the white soldiers' coming. Yes, I do believe her because she has seen it in a dream."

"You seem almost happy. Your sister is dying and you're happy."

"I told you, my Brother, she will not die. It is not just that my grandmother had the dream, but I do not feel she will die."

"What do you mean you don't feel it?"

"You must know by now that we Cheyennes believe much in our feelings, our intuition. I feel, no, I *know* she will be all right. Why should I not be happy?"

"I'm half-Indian and I don't feel good about her."

"That is because the white part of you will not let your true feelings come through. You are willing to believe the worst. It was not always so with you, Swiftly Running

379

Deer.''

Trenton looked up; he hadn't been called by his Arapaho name in years. "No, it was not always so. There was a time when I was more Indian than you.''

"Yes, and it troubled me greatly. How, I asked myself, can a boy who has white blood in him be such a good hunter and tracker? It made no sense to me. But then my grandfather explained that blood makes no difference. *Naxane* Jean was more Cheyenne than many of our own people.''

"Perhaps I have to relearn many things, Brave Wolf. It seems as though the last few years of my life have been spent running and being chased. I am tired. I want only to live with Aeneva and our children in peace.''

"You have no desire to go back to the white world?''

"I have no good memories of the white world. My father taught me all about the whites and what they were like so that I would be able to choose in which world I wished to live.''

"And you have chosen?''

"I chose a long time ago when I first saw Aeneva, you and Coyote Boy. I saw things in you three that I envied and admired. You all had such a free spirit; your lives were filled with laughter; you knew in what direction your lives would go.''

"It has not been easy for you, has it, my Brother?''

Trenton shook his head. "And it will not be easy for Nathan. He is three-quarters white, one-quarter Arapaho. I would not expect him to deny that part of him which is white, just as my father did not expect me to deny it.'' He threw a rock out over the river where it skimmed lightly across, making delicate swirls on the water. "I will raise him here, but one day he must choose.''

Brave Wolf pressed Trenton's shoulder firmly and

stood up. "You are more Indian than you realize, my Brother. Perhaps it is I who should envy you."

Trenton turned to ask Brave Wolf what he meant, but he had already gone into camp. He picked up another stone to throw it, but he stopped. Through the low overhanging branches a shaft of sunlight had penetrated. It was so bright on the water that Trenton had to squint his eyes. He stared at it for a long while and then he smiled and nodded. "If you are testing me, Great Father, I do believe that Aeneva will live. She will live." He stood up, skimming the rock across the water, spreading the sunlight in all directions.

When Trenton walked back to Sun Dancer's medicine lodge, Aeneva was awake, but she didn't seem happy to see him.

"Are you in pain?" he asked as he knelt down next to her. He kissed her on the cheek, but she turned her face away.

"Go away, please."

Trenton pulled her face back. "What is it? What's the matter?"

"I do not wish to see you. Please. I am tired."

Trenton looked up at Sun Dancer, his face wearing an anxious expression. "What's the matter with her?"

Sun Dancer motioned him to follow her and they walked outside. "Come, let us go for a walk. We have much to talk about." Neither of them spoke until they were well out of the camp. Sun Dancer stopped. "Do you mind if I sit? I am slightly weary." With Trenton's help she sat down on the ground.

"What is it, Sun Dancer? What's the matter with her?" A thought suddenly struck him. "Did she lose the child?"

"No, the child is fine as far as I can tell. There is something else."

"What?"

"The bullet in her back, I was not able to get it out. It is too near the spine."

"What are you saying? You are going to leave it in? Will she die?"

"She is unable to move her legs."

"Paralyzed?" Trenton was incredulous. "I don't believe it. Not Aeneva."

"I am afraid, Trenton. If I leave the bullet in, it could cause great damage. If I try to take it out, she could be paralyzed forever. I wanted to talk with you first."

"What does Aeneva want?"

Sun Dancer's eyes were grave. "She wants to die."

Trenton nodded wearily, knowing how this news would affect Aeneva, how it would affect any vibrant human being. "Then you must take it out. If she can't move her legs now and you leave the bullet in, isn't there a possibility that the bullet could move?"

"I know very little about this, Trenton. Jean told me once that if a bullet was left in the body it could travel or a person could live many years with it in his body."

"But not right next to the spine."

"I do not think so."

"Take it out."

"I am frightened, Trenton. I do not have the kind of tools that are necessary for this. Jean told me that your people have good doctors, men who learn just to cut people open and take things out."

"Surgeons."

"Yes, that is the word. I think we should take her to one of your surgeons."

"No," Trenton replied adamantly.

"But Trenton . . ."

"No! I trust you, Sun Dancer. I know you can make her well again."

"Ah, Trenton, this is something I had not foreseen. I did not think that I would have to make such a decision for Aeneva."

"You aren't making it, I am."

"I do not know if I can do it, Trenton. You do not understand; my powers only go so far. Perhaps the Maiyun have only instilled me with so much power—"

"The hell with the Maiyun, Sun Dancer. You don't need them."

"Why do you say that? If they hear you they may get angry at us and make Aeneva suffer."

"Now you are talking nonsense. I have known you for a long time and I've never known you to take them so seriously before. You have always relied on your own abilities, Sun Dancer, not those of the Maiyun."

"But the Great Father has given me these powers through the Maiyun."

"I don't believe that and I don't think you do either. You have worked hard all of your life to learn what you've learned. You studied with Horn and you worked with him. The Maiyun did not teach you any of those things. You learned them all on your own."

"But she is my granddaughter; if something should go wrong—"

"Then you will have done your best; no one will blame you. But you cannot leave her the way she is; she would rather be dead now anyway." Trenton saw the uncertainty on Sun Dancer's face and he put his arms around her. "I know this must be difficult for you, but you have done it before. You have worked on Stalking Horse and Jean and many of your friends. You can do it, Sun

Dancer. You are good enough." Then suddenly, incongruously, he smiled. "Besides, I know she will be all right."

"How do you know that? My vision?"

"I've had a sign of my own. I took some advice from Brave Wolf to believe a little more and now I do. She will be all right, with your help."

"How can one so old and feeble as I refuse one so handsome and quick with the tongue as you, Trenton Hawkins?"

"I am hoping that you cannot."

"All right, but it will not be today. Today I will rest. Tomorrow I will take the bullet out."

"I'll watch her. You go to your lodge and sleep."

"You will call me if she needs me?"

"I'll call you. Go now." He gave Sun Dancer a little push. "Thank you, Sun Dancer."

"Do not thank me yet, Trenton. Let us wait to see what happens."

"I know what will happen," Trenton yelled after her and she turned and smiled at him. Trenton watched her as she walked slowly away and he realized just how much he loved and respected her. She was unlike anyone he had ever known and she had filled a void made by the death of his own mother. When Sun Dancer was gone, and he felt now as he had never felt before that she would soon be gone, there would be an emptiness that could not be filled by anyone. Sun Dancer was a special human being and her memory would go on long after she was gone.

Trenton waited with Aeneva until she opened her eyes. When she looked away from him, he pulled her back to face him. "You cannot hide from this thing. You must face it."

"I want only to be dead if I cannot walk. I will be useless."

"Do you want to give up without a fight? You have changed, Aeneva."

She looked at him. "What do you mean?"

"I mean that there is a chance you will walk if your grandmother takes the bullet out."

"How can she do it? She told me it is too dangerous and she will not do it."

"She changed her mind."

"You mean you changed her mind for her."

"Aeneva, she can do it and she will do it. You must also believe that she can do it."

Aeneva shut her eyes and turned her head away. "I am tired, Trenton, but I do not want to die and I do not want our child to die."

"Then you must fight."

"I am fighting now."

"Good. I know you will be fine."

"How are you so sure? Another of grandmother's visions?"

"No, I had a sign."

"You had a sign?" Aeneva smiled broadly.

"Can't I have signs, too? I am half-Indian also."

"I know. I am just surprised that you would believe in anything like that."

"A man must believe sometimes." He bent down and kissed Aeneva on the cheek, taking the cloth from the bowl and washing her face. "I am staying with you tonight. Sun Dancer will be here tomorrow. She wanted to rest."

"Poor Grandmother, this must be very difficult for her."

"It is difficult for her, but she can do it. It is from her

that you get all your strength, you know.''

"Yes, I think you are right." She looked at him and took his hand. "How is your son? I have not even met him yet."

"Would you like to?"

"No, I will wait until I am well. It will be better when we have time to get to know each other."

"All right. You rest now. You'll need your strength. I'll be here if you need anything."

"Will you be here tomorrow?"

"Yes, I'll be here. Don't worry, when you wake up you'll be able to move your legs again."

Aeneva nodded her head and closed her eyes. She was asleep within a few minutes and Trenton watched her for a long time before he lay down next to her. He would need to be rested, too; tomorrow would not be an easy day.

Sun Dancer waited until she was sure Aeneva was sleeping deeply, from the special tea she had given her, before she made the incision. She used the knife that Joe had given her. It was long, it had a very thin blade and it was extremely sharp. She cut next to the wound, away from the spine, using cloths to absorb some of the blood. She washed her hands in a bowl of water and then began probing in the open wound for the bullet. She had done this many times before, but this time counted more than the others. Even when she had worked on Jean and Stalking Horse, they already had led fairly long lives, but not so with Aeneva. She was still so young and she still had so much to live for, including the baby that was growing inside of her.

Sun Dancer's stomach lurched as her fingers felt something hard. When it moved around in the flesh, she knew she had the bullet. "I have it, Trenton," she said calmly, maneuvering the bullet away from the spine and out of the wound. She withdrew her bloody fingers from the wound and dropped the bullet into the bowl. "There it is."

Trenton continued to swab at the blood in the wound, trying to contain his excitement. "I am not surprised."

Sun Dancer smiled at him and shook her head, rinsing her hands and picking up the bowl that contained the poultice she would apply to the wound. When she was through, she covered the wound with a warm, moist cloth; then she sat back.

"Well, it is over. Now we will have to wait and see."

"Whatever happens, Sun Dancer, I am proud of you and I admire your courage. I want you to know that."

"Thank you, Trenton."

They waited together, one resting while the other watched Aeneva. It was sometime in the night when Aeneva caught them both sleeping. She opened her eyes and looked over at Trenton lying on his side on a robe, at her grandmother sitting back against a backrest, her head up but her eyes closed. She tried to reach out to her, but pain shot down her back and she remembered. She tried to move her legs, but the slightest movement caused excruciating pain. Her face was covered with sweat and she shut her eyes. Tomorrow would be soon enough to find out; let them sleep peacefully for now. Tomorrow would tell.

There was a noise and they all looked up. "Daddy?" Nathan came walking into the medicine lodge, blinking his eyes against the darkness. "Daddy?"

Trenton sat up. "I'm here, Nate."

"Nathan Hawkins!" Joe's voice came from outside,

then in a quieter voice by the lodge door. "Boy, is Nate in there? That little rascal's run off again."

"Come on in, Joe."

Sun Dancer reached for Nathan and he went to her immediately. "Have you run away from Joe again? You know you are not to do that, *Mohe*."

"Yes, Grandmother." Nathan's eyes focused on the still form of Aeneva. "Is she sick, Grandmother?"

"Yes, very sick and we must be quiet."

Joe sat down next to Trenton, shaking his head. "I tell you, if that boy is half as fast in a few years as he is now, won't be nobody who can run him down."

"He is swift like his father." Aeneva's voice was soft but clear. She smiled as everyone looked at her in surprise. "Why do you all look at me so?"

"I thought you would sleep for much longer," Sun Dancer said with concern. She knelt down and felt her head. "You do not feel overly warm."

"I am fine, Grandmother."

"How is the pain?"

"The pain is great, but you told me it would be so."

Trenton knelt down next to her, kissing her lightly. "Would you like to meet my son now? Our son."

"Yes. I have waited a long time for this." She held out her hand and Nathan took it boldly.

"Pa told me you were shot. Does it hurt?"

"Yes, it hurts, but it will be over soon."

"Are you going to be my mother now?"

"If you will let me, I would like that very much. Did you know that you look very much like your father when he was young."

"You knew him then?"

"Yes. We played together and hunted together. We even hunted a buffalo together."

Nathan sat down, suddenly intrigued. "What else did you do?"

"Well, we swam and rode and had foot races and sometimes we argued. But we were always friends."

"Pa told me he saved you from quicksand once."

"Yes, he saved my brother and I. If your father had not come, we would have been swallowed alive." Aeneva smiled as Nathan's eyes got larger and rounder.

"Gosh."

"All right, Nate, that's enough for now. Aeneva is tired and she needs to rest. You go back with Joe and if I hear you ran away from him again, I'll make sure you can't sit down for a long time."

"Yes, Pa." He looked over at Aeneva and smiled. "I hope you feel better real soon."

"Thank you, Nathan, I will."

"Good-by, Aeneva. Glad to see you're doing better."

"Thanks, Joe."

"And how do you feel, child?" Sun Dancer asked again.

"I am glad that it is over with."

"Have you any feeling in your legs?"

"Not yet, but do not worry, Grandmother. I am sure I will walk again. So is Trenton. He had a sign."

"So he told me, but he has not told me what kind of sign he had."

"You know that I cannot tell you that, Sun Dancer. That is very personal."

"Bah, if I did not know better I would think you were Stalking Horse's grandson." She picked up her medicine basket with false disgust. "Do not stay long, Trenton, she must rest. It is important that she get strong now. *Na-ase.*"

"*Mohe.*" Trenton turned to Aeneva. "How are you

feeling?''

Aeneva looked up through the smoke hole to the sky. *"E-toneto.* It is cold.''

Trenton reached to cover her, but she pushed the blanket away, smiling. ''Why are you smiling like that?''

''I am not cold. It feels cold; winter will come soon.''

''Yes, you're right. Soon your people will break down their lodges and find shelter for the winter.''

''Was it a good hunt?''

Trenton shrugged. ''Some of the older ones say it is the worst hunt they have ever seen. The herds are getting smaller and more skittish. They never used to be afraid of the Cheyennes, they say.''

''What is wrong? Where have they all gone?''

''I think they've been killed by soldiers and people coming west. Mostly by soldiers though.''

''Soldiers. They do not like the Indians, do they? They seem to hate everything about our life.''

''It's because they know so little about it. I think there are many of them who have great respect for you.''

''Do you remember when we were children, you and I and my brothers found the carcasses of the dead buffalos? You said soldiers had killed them and they would kill even more every year. It seems you have been proven right.''

''I would rather have been proven wrong.''

''What will my people do, Trenton? What will we do?''

''We will keep moving west until it is safe.''

''And what if there are no buffalo there? What will we do for food and clothes?''

''Don't worry, it'll be all right. There are always deer.''

''But deer do not graze in large herds as the buffalo do,

and they are harder to hunt."

"What's the matter, Aeneva? Why are you worrying about this now?"

"Because it frightens me. We know nothing about the West. *Naxane* Jean told me there are great mountains that you must climb and that beyond those mountains, few people have ventured."

"The unknown never frightened you before."

"I was never with child before."

"Yes." Trenton looked at her as if for the first time. "I think I understand now."

"You do not think me foolish?"

"How could I think you are foolish? I don't even know what it's like to carry a child."

"But you know the fears of being a parent."

"Yes, and I understand what you are fearful of. But I think we have enough time to talk about the future. I want you to get well first."

"I am already well."

"You can move your legs?"

"No, but I am certain that I will be able to."

"So am I." He kissed her softly and stood up. "I'll be back later. I want you to rest now. We will talk when you are well."

"Trenton?"

"Yes?"

"*Ne-mehotatse.*"

"I love you, too."

She smiled and closed her eyes, her body giving in to the physical exhaustion she now felt. She remembered her grandmother once telling her that she could not remember a time when she did not love her grandfather. That is how she felt about Trenton. It seemed as if she had always loved him. It seemed as though her path in life had been carefully chosen for her. She tried to think, but her mind grew too confused and everything faded into darkness. A slight smile appeared on her face as she thought of their child growing inside of her and then it quickly vanished as her face relaxed and she fell into a deep sleep. Her breathing came steadily now and Sun Dancer watched her, her eyes filling with tears. She reached out and stroked Aeneva's silky hair.

"I will miss you most of all, my Granddaughter. You have brought me much joy. So much joy." She laid her head against Aeneva's for a time and sat up, wiping the tears from her face. This was not a time to feel sorry for herself, this was a time for rejoicing. Soon Aeneva would be well and would go with Trenton and their people to the mountains for the winter, while she, Sun Dancer, would return to Stalking Horse's burial place and start on the Hanging Road. Soon she would be with Stalking Horse and Jean and everyone she missed so. But something was wrong. She did not feel as she had thought she would when it was time to go; Stalking Horse had told her it would be a good time, that she would feel no sadness. She remembered the look on his face when he died; it was a look of contentment. She remembered her parents' faces as they rode away from the band to die alone; their faces were joyous and content. Why, then, did she not feel the same? She shook her head and picked up her healing basket again. It was probably just seeing Aeneva so sick. As soon as she was well, the contentment she sought through death would come easily. She knew it would.

Sun Dancer walked out of the medicine lodge and started through the camp to the lodge of Dancing Bear and his wife, Yellow Fish. Both were suffering from stomach cramps and nausea; probably they had eaten something that did not agree with them, she thought to herself.

"*Haahe,* Grandmother."

Sun Dancer turned, smiling broadly at Brave Wolf. "How are you, Grandson? It seems that I do not see enough of you and your brother now that you have your own lodge."

"We are well, Grandmother. Did you see the meat we left for you?"

"No. I have been at the medicine lodge all night."

"Trenton tells me Aeneva is doing well."

"You do not seem surprised."

"I am not. I knew she would get well."

"You knew more than I then."

"You knew that she would get well also. You were only surprised that she was wounded so badly. You were not prepared for it."

"Perhaps. What is it you want? I am expected at the lodge of Dancing Bear and Yellow Fish."

"We will be breaking camp soon. Look." He pointed at the mountains in the distance. "See the dark clouds that are there. Winter will come early; already the air is cold. Coyote Boy and I want to pack your things for you. You will not have time."

"No. You do not have to pack my things for me, Brave Wolf."

"But we want to, Grandmother. We promise we will not get into any of your medicines."

"Yes, I remember well catching you two mixing up all of my medicines. Do you remember what I did?"

"How can I forget? You painted our noses red and made us walk around camp like that for a day."

Sun Dancer laughed. "It was a cruel thing to do, but you two would not learn."

"Well, we are older now and we promise not to get into any of your medicines."

"I trust you, Brave Wolf, but I do not need your help."

"You will not have the time. You spend all of your extra time with Aeneva."

"I will not be going to the mountains this winter."

"Where will you go then? You will not stay here?"

Sun Dancer looked at her grandson, seeing so much of his father in him. She reached out and touched his cheek with her hand. "I am going to be with your grandfather."

"No."

"I am tired, Brave Wolf, and I have grown old. I do not want to live so long that I become a burden to you and your brother. I do not want to grow so feeble that you must pull me on a travois when we travel."

"But you have always told me how important it is to respect the old people of the band. They are living history, you said."

"It is true. We are important, but my time here is over. I have done many things in my lifetime, Brave Wolf, many good, exciting things. Now I am ready to rest. When I am in Seyan with Stalking Horse, I will be at complete rest."

Brave Wolf turned away from Sun Dancer, staring out at the mountains that his grandfather so dearly loved. "It will not be the same without you."

Sun Dancer touched his shoulder, forcing herself to keep control. "Do not think this will be an easy thing for me to do, for it will not be. I love you, Coyote Boy, and Aeneva much more than I could ever express. You three have given me so much joy in my life and many times you have made me feel young although I was very old. It will be very difficult leaving you three, but I know that you vill do well. You are our grandchildren, are you not?"

Brave Wolf turned around, his eyes glistening slightly. 'Yes, we are your grandchildren and we will do well. We will make you proud of us."

"I am already so proud of all of you, Brave Wolf. Do you not know that?"

"But when you look down on us with Grandfather, you vill be even more proud. I promise you."

Sun Dancer dropped her basket and embraced Brave Wolf, for once not caring if anyone saw this outward display of affection. She would not have many more opportunities to hug her grandchildren. She backed away, er expression changing from one of sadness to one of oy. "I want Aeneva to have all of my things; you will ack them for her?"

"You will want some things to take to Seyan with ou."

"I will choose those, but the rest will go to Aeneva. he horses you will divide among you."

"All right." Brave Wolf nodded and looked up at the ky. "We are going to a different camp this winter."

"Where is it?"

"Northwest. We have heard from other bands that here is plentiful game and many places for shelter."

"No," Sun Dancer replied softly, rubbing her temles. "You must not go there."

"What do you mean, Grandmother? Are you all ight?"

"You must not go there."

"Why?"

"I do not know why."

"But you cannot tell me that—"

"Danger. Danger awaits you if you go there."

"What kind of danger?"

"I do not know." She rubbed her temples vigorously; she felt dizzy. "Something is wrong, Brave Wolf."

"Come." Brave Wolf picked up her basket and put his arm around her. "You must rest. You are tired."

"No, that is not it. I feel well enough. Something else is wrong. I do not yet understand what kind of danger you face in this new place."

"Grandmother, I think you worry overmuch. You do not even know where we intend to go. We do not even know ourselves."

"Please, Brave Wolf, you must trust me in this. I know that you are all in some kind of danger."

"All right, Grandmother; we will talk about it later. Now you must rest. Perhaps when you have slept you will see that we do not face any danger; perhaps you will see that it has only been a vision brought on by your lack of sleep."

"I hope you are right." Sun Dancer leaned against Brave Wolf, feeling suddenly quite exhausted. By the time she reached her lodge and lay down on her robe she was almost asleep. Brave Wolf covered her and stood up, watching to make sure that she was all right before he left. When he was satisfied that she was well, he left silently, wondering as he did so, just what had upset his grandmother so much that she had almost fainted. He had seen her before when she had had visions, but she had never acted this way. Something was wrong. He intended to find out more about this place in the northwest before they all went there. He trusted his grandmother and he trusted her visions, and something told him that she was very right about this one. He had seldom doubted her before; he did not intend to start now.

CHAPTER XIX

Sun Dancer felt strangely uncomfortable traveling to this new place. She still could not say why she had bad feelings about the place; she only knew that something would happen there. She turned and looked down at Aeneva, who was sleeping on the travois behind her. She was healing well and growing stronger every day. Her legs were also growing stronger and along with them, her spirit. She seemed very happy to go to this new place that Brave Wolf and Coyote Boy had heard of, although Sun Dancer could sense a well-hidden feeling of apprehension. Aeneva felt something, too.

They followed the Big River for many days until it led into country with which they were unfamiliar. The landscape started to change: there were more pine trees, more mountainous areas, and the air seemed even colder. When they had traveled for almost two weeks in a northerly direction, they cut westward and rode until they found the Powder River. The area here was quite beautiful and as Brave Wolf had been told, there were many places where a band could find shelter for the winter. The trees probably held an abundance of animals and there were beavers and fish in the river. Everyone was pleased to make this their winter home.

While the men secured an area for the band and cut down saplings for lodgepoles, the women began to set up camp. They helped each other erect their lodges and they began to unpack their things from their travois. Sun Dancer was hard put to make Aeneva rest while she worked.

"I am well enough to help for a while, Grandmother." She stubbornly refused to be treated as an invalid.

"You should not tire yourself, child. You are only now healing. You still must rest."

"I have been resting all day on that thing,"—she pointed to the travois—"and I will go crazy if I rest anymore today."

"If Trenton sees you he will be angry."

"He will not be angry. He will be glad to see that I am up." She took some things from Sun Dancer's hands. "Now, let me have those and you see about your medicines. I will carry in the other things."

Sun Dancer saw that there was no point in arguing and she unpacked her things from her horse. She was reaching up to pull down some of the bags when she had a sudden blinding pain in her head. She stopped and leaned against the horse, overcome with dizziness. Faces flashed before her, like bizarre scenes out of a nightmare. She saw the children of the camp and she heard voices, but she could not understand what it all meant.

"Grandmother, are you all right?" Aeneva put her hand on Sun Dancer's shoulder. "Come, you must come inside and rest."

"I do not want to rest, Aeneva. I want to know what it means. I keep having these pains in my head and I see things, faces and scenes, but I do not understand any of it. I think it is bad, but I do not know for sure."

Aeneva looked around her. "You think it is this place? You think this place holds some kind of danger for us?"

"Yes. You feel it, too."

"Yes, I have felt it for quite some time, but I did not understand it either. When Brave Wolf told me you were frightened for all of us I could understand why."

"But what does it mean, Aeneva? For the first time I am unable to 'see.' This has never happened to me before."

"Perhaps you will make some sense of it soon. Do not worry yourself so."

"I cannot help but worry. What if something happens and I am not able to warn all of you?"

Aeneva took Sun Dancer by both shoulders. "Grandmother, not everyone has someone like you to protect them. It has been wonderful for us and you have helped many people and saved many lives because of your special gift. But we cannot count on you. When you are gone we will have to face life on our own. You cannot always protect us, Grandmother."

Sun Dancer nodded slowly, finally understanding what it all meant. Perhaps she was not meant to understand this final vision because she was not meant to be here any longer. Perhaps it was time for her to go. "You are right, of course. I will make sure you are all set up; then I will leave. I do not wish to endure another cold winter. I want to be with Stalking Horse where it is always warm."

"But you said you would stay until after my child is born."

"You will be fine, Aeneva, you do not need me any longer."

"I am sorry, Grandmother. I have offended you with my words."

"No, you did not offend me, Aeneva. You spoke the truth. It is time for me to go. Do not feel sad; I do not. I am eager to go."

"But you would have stayed through the winter if I had

not spoken so.''

"Perhaps I would have, but I might have been out of my mind trying to understand those visions. I do not think I am meant to understand them. The Maiyun are telling me that I have no more powers to 'see.' ''

"I am sorry."

"Do not be sorry. I am glad that I do not have to 'see' things anymore. It has been very tiring, Aeneva. Horn told me it would make me very tired and that when my time came, I would welcome the opportunity to go. He was right."

"You will not go today?" Aeneva's eyes were wide and anxious, much like those of a small child.

"No, I will not go today, but I will go soon. Very soon."

The first storm came the next week. It lasted for four days and people were only able to come out of their lodges for minutes at a time. Strong winds whipped at the surrounding trees, knocking them into some of the lodges. Snow fell heavily and some were unable to get out of their lodge doors. Sun Dancer lay on her robe, sullen and withdrawn. She had wanted to leave days ago, but her grandchildren had not let her.

"Are you still angry with me, Grandmother?" Aeneva offered Sun Dancer a bowl of soup which she refused.

"Yes, I am still angry."

"Why? We did not want you to go in this storm."

"You are all silly children. What does it matter if I am killed in this storm? I am going off to die anyway." She turned on her side away from Aeneva.

"Aeneva took the soup and poured it back into the pot. She sat down next to Trenton who was holding a sleeping Nathan in his lap.

400

"You cannot blame her," Trenton said softly.

"I do not blame her. I just do not want her to go."

"You and your brothers are being selfish. Can't you see how unhappy she is?"

"We are not keeping her from going. We only want her to wait until it is safe."

"You want her to wait indefinitely until she finally says she will die here."

"That is not true."

"Yes it is, Aeneva, and you know it." He reached out for her hand. "I understand how much you love her; I love her, too. But you must allow her to decide for herself when she is ready to die. You cannot deny her that."

"It is a matter of honor," Aeneva repeated to herself. How often had she heard her grandfather say that. "You are right, of course."

"I want to take her, Aeneva. I want to make sure she gets to Stalking Horse. That is the only place she wants to die."

"Yes, she would like that. You tell her." She reached out and took Nathan.

Trenton walked across the lodge and sat down next to Sun Dancer's robe. "Are you awake, Sun Dancer?"

"Yes, I am awake." She turned over and looked at him. Her eyes were amazingly clear for those of an old woman and when she smiled, Trenton could remember the first time he had seen her and how beautiful she had been. "What is it, boy?"

"When you are ready, I will take you to Stalking Horse."

Sun Dancer looked at him a moment as if not quite comprehending what he was saying and her eyes clouded with tears. "You would do that for me?"

"I would be honored."

She looked over in Aeneva's direction. "What does my granddaughter think of this?"

"She agrees that it is a good idea. She wants me to take you."

Sun Dancer sat up. "You do understand, don't you, Trenton?"

"Yes, I think I do."

"You have always amazed me. The Arapaho in you has made you very sensitive to Indians, while the white in you makes you wary. It is a good combination. You have turned out well."

"Thank you."

"When will we leave?"

"After this storm is over." When Trenton saw the angry expression on her face he shook his head. "I am not lying to you, Sun Dancer. It would be best to wait until this is over. I would not like for us to get caught in this and die somewhere out in the snow. Stalking Horse would be angry with us both."

"Yes, you are right. Better wait and get there safely."

"Good." Trenton stood up, then squatted back down. "What about Brave Wolf and Coyote Boy? They will want to come with us."

"No, I will say good-by to my grandsons here. It will be easier for us all that way. Aeneva understands that already." She looked over at her granddaughter. "You will take care of her and your children?"

"You know I will. Children? How many children?"

Sun Dancer laughed. "That is my secret. Now go back to your wife." She lay back down and pulled the robe up over her shoulders, suddenly feeling sleepy and content. Soon she would be with her love. Soon they would be together and nothing would ever separate them again. This time would be for eternity.

Sun Dancer was ready. She had turned everything over to Aeneva. She had taught her as much as she could about healing, medicines, and calling on the Maiyun and the Great Father for help. She had tried to remember everything she could about the art so that Aeneva could pass it on to someone else, hopefully one of her own children. Aeneva took to it naturally, easily understanding all that Sun Dancer taught her and making it easier for her grandmother to leave. When the actual time came for Sun Dancer and Trenton to leave, Sun Dancer packed a few things and went through the camp to say good-by to everyone. They all wished her a safe and good journey on the Hanging Road to Seyan, and many asked that she take good wishes to members of their families.

When she returned to her lodge, Trenton, Joe, Nathan, and her three grandchildren were waiting for her. She embraced Joe and smiled, returning his knife to him. "You will need it much more than I."

Joe put up his hand and gave the knife back to Sun Dancer. "I hear there are many buffalo in Seyan. You will need a good knife for scraping hides."

"Thank you, Joe. You are a good friend. I will send your greetings to your mother."

"Have a good journey, Sun Dancer."

Sun Dancer turned to Nathan, picking him up in her arms. "You are so tall already; I can barely hold you."

"Where are you going, Grandmother?"

"I am going on a journey to be with my husband."

"Will you come back?"

"No, I will not come back, Nathan, but I will always be watching over you."

Nathan hugged Sun Dancer tightly. "I will miss you, Grandmother. *Ne-mehotatse.*"

"I love you, too, Nathan. Take good care of you father and my granddaughter. You will do that for me?'

"Yes."

"Good. You are a good boy." She kissed him onc more and put him down. Next she turned to Coyote Boy

"Do not look so sad, Grandson. This is a good day.'

"For you perhaps."

"Be happy for me, my Grandson. It will make my journey so much easier."

"I am happy for you, Grandmother. But I am also self ish; I will miss you."

"As I will miss you." Sun Dancer hugged him tightly remembering how he had always been so willing and eager to fight as a boy, so unwilling to show his true feel ings. *"Ne-pevo-mohta-he?"*

"Haahe. Na-pevo-mohta. I am well. Journey safely Grandmother."

Sun Dancer smiled at Coyote Boy once more and moved to Brave Wolf. He was her first grandchild, strong yet gentle, named for her brother. "I will miss you Grandson. You have been a good boy. You have alway lived honorably."

"I will not let you down, Grandmother."

"You could never do that, Brave Wolf." She hugged him, touching his cheek softly. "Take care of you brother and sister."

"I will do that. Have a safe journey, Grandmother Tell Grandfather and *Naxane* Jean that I hope they have good hunting."

Sun Dancer nodded and moved to Aeneva. Her grand daughter stood tall and straight beside her brothers and husband, her stomach slightly rounded from the child within. She smiled broadly as if truly understanding how joyous this was for Sun Dancer. They hugged each other and Sun Dancer kissed Aeneva on both cheeks, staring into the beloved face for a moment longer. "I will miss you so much, Aeneva."

"As I will miss you, Grandmother."

"If you need help at any time, call on me. I will try to help you."

"That is comforting. It will be good to know that you are smiling down on me, there to help me if I need you."

"I must go now. I have waited long enough." She patted Aeneva's stomach. "What will you name the child? Have you thought on it yet?"

"If it is a boy, he will be called Stalking Horse. If it is a girl, she will be called Sun Dancer."

Sun Dancer nodded, lowering her eyes to keep from crying. "You do not have to do that."

"We do not want your names to be forgotten." She hugged Sun Dancer once more. "I love you, Grandmother. Journey safely. Make sure that Grandfather and *naxane* do not play all of the time."

"I will make sure of it." Sun Dancer stood back, taking one last look at her family; then she walked out of the lodge door, followed by Trenton. She mounted her horse, pulled her robe around her shoulders, and rode away from the camp, her back straight, her head held high. She started to turn around once and look back, but she did not permit herself to do so; already it was proving too difficult to leave. She would remember them all as they were, smiling and happy; she would not want to remember them standing outside in the cold, waving good-by with sad expressions on their faces. She looked over at Trenton and found him staring at her.

"Are you all right?"

"I am well, Trenton. I am better than I have been in many winters."

Trenton seemed satisfied and turned his attention to the path in front of them. Sun Dancer followed, her body free at last but her mind still troubled by some unknown thing. She breathed deeply and looked up at the sky above her. It was dark and the clouds were swirling, but there was no snow. It would take them many weeks to get to where Stalking Horse lay, but that was the only place where she could rest peacefully. Beside him, her body as well as her mind would be free.

Aeneva and the other women walked through the trees, trying to find as much wood as they could. They dug in the snow to find branches that had been covered and they dragged them back to camp. Aeneva had a full bundle and she draped it over her back and started back to camp. Snow was beginning to fall and she stopped to look up at the sky. She laughed with delight as the small, soft flakes fell on her face and she tried to catch some on her tongue. She brushed the snow from her face and started forward when she heard a noise in the trees behind her. She looked around, thinking it was an animal, but she could see nothing. Standing still, she listened again. Animals were not so noisy; only man could make so much noise. "Who is it?" she asked. There was no reply. Trudging through the snow with her bundle of wood, she hurried back to camp. At the edge of the camp, she saw Nathan and some of the other boys playing, and she yelled at them to get back into their lodges. She assessed the situation quickly. Most of the men were out hunting; only the old ones were left. Dropping the bundle of wood, she ran to her lodge to get her rifle, telling the women of the camp that they were in danger and to go inside their lodges. She found Red Fox, one of the young men who was left to guard the village.

"Red Fox, you must find the others. We are being watched by someone in the woods."

Red Fox was instantly alert. "Who are they?"

"I do not know. Crows, perhaps Shoshonis. Whoever they are, they do not wish us well. They saw the men leave the village."

"I will send one of the other boys to find the hunters. I was ordered by Brave Wolf to stay here until he returned."

"All right. Do it quickly. We must have help." Aeneva stood guard while Red Fox sent one of the younger boys out to find the hunters. He returned in a short time and took her place.

"You should return to your lodge, Aeneva. It is dangerous here."

"I do not fear danger, Red Fox. I am an able warrior."

"I know that you are able, but you are also with child. You must be careful."

"I will be careful. You will need me. I will find all the women in the camp who are the best shots; the others I will arm. They will shoot if an enemy comes into their lodges." Aeneva went quickly about the camp, seeking out the women who could handle rifles, arming a few of the others who stayed inside their lodges. They were also armed with knives, lances, war clubs, bows and arrows.

"We are ready, Red Fox."

"Go to your place at the other side of the camp, Aeneva. I have heard them. They are coming."

"They have spoken to you?"

"No, but I heard them. They are noisier than a herd of buffalo."

"They are being noisy on purpose. They want to make us uneasy." Aeneva started for her spot when she heard a voice.

"Cheyenne woman, why do you run away? Are you frightened of us?"

Aeneva stopped, walking back to Red Fox. Red Fox motioned her back into the camp, but she ignored him. "Who are you that I am supposed to be frightened of?"

"I am Spotted Shield of the Shoshoni tribe."

"What do you want, Spotted Shield?"

"Do you speak for your people, woman? Do the Cheyennes always let their women speak for them?"

"When the women speak well enough they do."

A loud laugh resounded in the woods around them. "I like you, Cheyenne woman. What is your name?"

"Aeneva."

"What does it mean?"

"You speak our tongue; do you not know?"

"I do not know."

"It means 'winter.' "

"It is a good name. Perhaps I will take you for myself."

"Perhaps I will not let you."

"So, you can fight, too?"

"Well enough."

"Are you the Cheyenne woman I have heard talk of? The one who fought as well as any warrior?"

"Perhaps there are others, I do not know. I have fought in many battles."

"And done well or you would not be here."

"I ask again, what do you want, Spotted Shield?"

"We want your women and children. We have lost many of our own through sickness."

"Is that the only reason you want the women and children?"

"As you well know, winter woman, we Shoshoni have no great love for the Cheyennes."

"As we have no great love for you."

"You have a sharp tongue, woman. Too sharp."

"Perhaps you would like to come in here alone and try to make it less so?"

Spotted Shield laughed again. "You are cunning also. I can see that you would be a worthy catch."

"I will be no man's catch, Spotted Shield. And you cannot have our women and children."

"There is nothing you can do about it. All of your men are hunting."

"But we have sent someone to find them. They will be here soon."

"You mean the boy on the brown mare? You disappoint me, winter woman. Did you think we were so stupid?"

"You have him?"

"We have him"

"He is all right?"

"For now."

Aeneva looked over at Red Fox, nodding at him to be alert. "Do you always fight innocent boys, Spotted Shield?"

"When I have to."

"No wonder you are afraid to come into this camp and face me alone."

There was no laughter this time. "You have spoken too sharply this time, woman. We will come for your women and children. There is nothing you can do to prevent it."

Aeneva turned, raising her rifle to the women in the camp. They went to different spots around the camp, waiting until the Shoshonis appeared. They were not to fire until the Shoshonis were close enough so they couldn't miss. Although Spotted Shield had indicated that they would attack directly, the Shoshonis did not come. Aeneva understood what they were doing—they were playing a waiting game. It was a game of nerves. They were hoping to wear down the Cheyennes and then attack them unexpectedly.

Aeneva looked over at Red Fox. He seemed unusually calm for a young man who had never yet fought. "Are you well, Red Fox?"

"Well enough, Aeneva. It is not always easy to have a woman speak for you."

"I am sorry."

"I understand. You have more experience than I. You spoke well."

"I made him angry."

"No less than I would have."

"Thank you, Red Fox."

"Aeneva, I know it is not my place to speak to you this way, but I want to ask something of you."

"What is it?"

"When the Shoshonis attack, I want you to run. I want you to find some place to hide. You must save yourself."

"I cannot do that, Red Fox."

"But you must. You must think of your child."

Aeneva felt the child kick inside of her. "I am always thinking of the child, Red Fox, but I cannot run away."

"But your brothers will blame me if something happens to you. And I would not forgive myself if something happened to you."

"Thank you, Red Fox. Do not worry; I will be fine. My brothers and the others will come back soon and the Shoshonis will wish they had not chosen this band to attack."

"I hope you are right, Aeneva. I hope you are right."

* * *

Sun Dancer sat up; it had all come clear. The vision was much clearer this time. The women and children were being attacked by Indians and she could see Aeneva alone, firing her rifle. "Trenton, you must go back."

Trenton stirred under the tree and rolled toward Sun Dancer. "What did you say, Sun Dancer?"

"I said you must go back."

"Go back where?"

"You must go back to the camp. There is danger; I have seen it. I have also seen Aeneva alone in the middle of it."

Trenton sat up. "What kind of danger?"

"Indians—I do not know what tribe."

"Crows or Shoshonis," Trenton muttered to himself, pulling his robe around his shoulders. "Tell me what you see."

"I see the men out hunting and I see these Indians attacking the camp, taking the women and children."

"Aeneva?"

"She is firing a rifle; that is all I can tell you."

Trenton stook up, pulling his robe off the ground. "We'll go back then."

"No, you go back. I cannot ride as quickly as you."

"But I might not be back here for many days. Will you be all right?"

Sun Dancer nodded her head, smiling. "Is that not a silly question to ask a woman who is ready to die? Of course I will be all right. I will wait for you."

"I'll be back as soon as I can." Trenton swung up on his horse and rode as rapidly as he could through the darkness. Sun Dancer watched him until he was gone and she lay back down on her robe. What had eluded her for so long had finally come clear—she had finally been able to see the vision plainly. She just hoped she had seen it early

411

enough to help everyone.

Aeneva fired off a shot. The Shoshoni dropped, emitting a loud scream. They seemed to come from all directions. She fired at one, then another. When one rifle ran out of ammunition, she picked up another loaded one. Some of the women who weren't good enough shots had come out of their lodges to help the others reload their rifles. It had worked out well and saved time. A few more volleys were fired back and forth and without any sign, the Shoshonis stopped.

"Have they gone away?" asked Little Woman.

"They will be back. They want us to wait a little longer so they can take us by surprise again. Was anyone wounded?"

"I do not think so, Aeneva. Everyone seems to be well."

"Good. You are all doing well—especially you, Red Fox. Your father would be proud." Red Fox's father had died the spring before along with Stalking Horse, when Wainwright's men had attacked them.

"Thank you, Aeneva. But I am still worried. It is dark now. We will have trouble seeing them."

"As they will have more trouble seeing us. We are going to change positions. I want all fires put out and the children kept quiet. When next they attack, we will not be where they expect us to be."

They waited for almost two hours before the next attack came. Aeneva was right; the Shoshonis came at them, thinking they would be positioned in the same places, but found out too late that the Cheyennes had moved. Shots were fired and the attack was soon over. It was a black night and it was impossible to see anything. Apparently, the Shoshonis decided to wait until the next morning before they attacked again.

Aeneva rested fitfully that night, relieved by one of the other women. She slept with a rifle at one side of her in case the Shoshonis decided to come back, and Nathan at the other side. She tossed and turned and finally sat up, rocking back and forth. She kept thinking about her grandmother and Trenton and she hoped that they were having a safe journey; and she wondered especially if her brothers and the other men of the camp would get back in time. A camp full of women, old men, and boys could only hold off a Shoshoni raiding party for so long.

Soon it was morning and the war cries of the Shoshonis rang throughout the camp. Aeneva jumped up, pushing Nathan back down as she did so. "You stay in here as you did yesterday. Do not come out." She stuck her head out of the lodge door and quickly pulled it back inside. She ran to Nathan, jerked him to his feet, wrapped his robe around his shoulders, and put his hat on. "Come with me."

"But you just said—"

"The Shoshonis are in our camp, Nathan. I am going to try to get you out." They went to the back of the lodge and Aeneva knelt down, sticking her knife through the thick hides. It was difficult to cut a hole in the hides, but she finally made one large enough for Nathan to squeeze through. "All right, Nathan, I want you to go out through here and hide in the woods. Do not say anything. Stay there until I or your father come for you."

Nathan looked up at Aeneva, his blue eyes reflecting his fear. "What do I do when it gets dark?"

"You stay there, you understand?" She pulled him to her. "Do not worry, Nathan, it will be all right. Just find a good place to hide and one where you can keep warm. Do not come out until someone calls for you. Go now."

413

She pushed him through the hole and peeked out to make sure he didn't hesitate. He did not. He scurried off into the woods as quietly as if he had been born to them. Aeneva smiled to herself and nodded her head. She picked up one of her backrests and placed it in front of the hole. In case the Shoshonis came inside, she did not want them curious about the hole in the lodge. Aeneva breathed deeply and walked out the lodge door, just as one of the Shoshonis came to her lodge. He grabbed her arm and pulled her to the center of the camp. When all of the women, children, and old men had been captured, the Shoshoni chief, Spotted Shield, stepped forward.

"Where is the Cheyenne woman who calls herself Winter?"

Aeneva did not hesitate. She stepped from the group of people. "I am Aeneva."

Spotted Shield walked up to Aeneva, appraising her greedily with his eyes. "Yes, it fits you. It is a good name."

"Do you plan to make war on all of us, Spotted Shield?"

"No, I plan to take you back to my tribe. If any of you prove worthy, I and my men will take you as wives. The children we will adopt." He looked around with a cold eye. "The old men and women we will kill."

"No! You cannot do that."

"Why can I not do that?"

"It is a cowardly thing to do."

"That is the second time you have accused me of being a coward, woman. I do not like it."

"Prove me wrong."

"What, by taking them with us? Ah, they are useless baggage."

"They are human beings. Let them go. They will do

414

you no harm.''

"And if I do?''

"I will go with you.''

"And why is that such a bargain?''

"I am strong; I am a proven warrior; I am also a healer with much knowledge of medicines.'' She stepped forward, pulling back her robe, revealing her round stomach. "I am also carrying a child. This child could be raised as a Shoshoni.''

"You think highly of yourself, woman.''

"I know my own worth.''

Spotted Shield laughed, cupping Aeneva's chin in his hand. "You are also very pleasing to the eye.''

"I do not know about that.''

"Humility does not become you, Aeneva. Come''—he took her arm—"and we will talk. If what you say pleases me, then I will let the old ones live.'' He ordered his men to tie up the prisoners and he made Aeneva lead him to her lodge. "I am hungry. Get me food.'' Aeneva brought him a bowl of rabbit stew and some tea. Spotted Shield looked at the liquid. "What is this?''

"It is tea. It is very relaxing.''

"Relaxing enough to put me to sleep. Ah!'' Spotted Shield threw the tea onto the ground and pulled Aeneva down next to him. "What of your husband? He is with the hunting party?''

"Yes.''

"You do not seem too eager to talk about him.''

"I am not.''

"Why?''

"It is my business.''

"Your answer does not please me.''

"I do not like my husband. He is cruel and loathesome.''

415

"So you long for a real man, eh?"

"I do not long for any man."

"That is because you have never had a real man. Cheyennes are pigs, Shoshonis are men." He hit his fist against his chest. "I have never known a Cheyenne woman who was so willing to raise her child as a Shoshoni. You are not telling me something."

"I have never been accepted by my people; I have always been strange to them. Did you see the way the women looked at me out there? They have shunned me for a long time now because I fought with the men, and the men think I am a witch because I can heal. It is not so strange."

"Yet you stayed."

"I had family. My grandfather was a great chief. I could not leave him or my grandmother."

Spotted Shield looked at her, handing her the bowl. "More food." Aeneva complied immediately, bringing him more stew. Spotted Shield watched Aeneva as he ate. "Why is it you are not afraid of me?"

"Perhaps I am, but do not show it."

"I like you, woman. You will make a good Shoshoni."

"You will let the old ones live?"

"I must think on it some more."

"Our hunters will be back soon. You will have to decide quickly."

"I will decide when I am ready. Now, lie down here beside me." He placed the bowl on the ground and opened Aeneva's robe. "You are strong and slim, even with the child inside of you."

Aeneva tried to control her fears. "Have you any children, Spotted Shield?"

"Three. I also have two wives."

"You would not mind another?"

"Not if she proved worthy." He practically pounced on Aeneva before she could push him away.

"Wait. I will undress for you." She stood up, dropping the robe on the ground. She untied the front of her dress, exposing the tops of her swelling breasts. She dropped the knife that she wore at her waist and bent down to pull her dress over her head. As she did so, she withdrew the small knife that she wore strapped to her thigh. She dropped her dress and stood facing Spotted Shield. "Do not move. I can assure you that I know how to use this." She bent down and picked up her larger knife. "Put your hands in back of your head and do not move." Spotted Shield did as he was told and Aeneva backed over to her robes, retrieving one of the extra rifles. She walked forward again. "I do not want to kill you, Spotted Shield."

"What do you plan to do with me then? My men will not let you live when they discover that you have killed me."

"I will not have to kill you."

"You should kill me, woman, for if I can get hold of you, I will do you the same favor."

Aeneva walked around behind him and with the butt of the rifle, smacked him in the back of the head. Spotted Shield slumped forward. Aeneva listened for a breath to make sure he was still alive; she really did not want to kill him. She tied his hands behind his back, then his ankles, and she connected the two with a rope around his neck. She stuck pieces of cloth inside of his mouth so he could not shout. She went to the pot of tea, *miskahets*, and added more of the tops and stems of the plants. She boiled them for a few minutes, then took the pot and some bowls outside. She walked to the Shoshoni who had been with

Spotted Shield.

"*Ne-tsehese-hestse-he?*"

"I speak some Cheyenne."

"Your chief wanted me to bring this tea to all of you. It will warm you quickly." Aeneva poured some into the bowls and waited until the men had drunk; then she refilled the bowls.

"This is bitter. I want no more."

"Your chief says you are to drink it. He does not want you to freeze to death. It is a good tea. Our warriors drink it often before they go hunting in the snow."

The Shoshoni looked at her skeptically, but drank, nodding to the others to do the same. When they were finished, Aeneva collected the bowls.

"I must get back to your chief now. He will wonder where I am. I will bring you more tea later."

"And food."

"Yes, and food." Aeneva walked calmly back to her lodge. Once inside, she sat down and waited. She made sure her rifles were loaded and she began to pray to all the gods in the heavens that the Shoshonis would soon get sleepy.

Trenton could see the Shoshonis in the middle of the camp, but there was something strange. They seemed lethargic, not alert as they should have been. He crept out of the woods on his belly to the camp and their lodge. He saw the small footprints leading from their lodge into the woods and when he saw the rip in the lodge skin he knew that Aeneva had sent Nathan into the woods. He stuck his hand into the hole and felt something in front of it. He moved his hand around until he was able to move the obstacle and peer into the lodge. He faced a rifle barrel.

"Jesus, Aeneva," he groaned, trying to squeeze himself through the small hole. He ripped it some more with his hands until he was able to fit through. "Would you mind putting that rifle down?"

"Trenton!" Aeneva threw her arms around him, kissing him square on the mouth. "I am so glad to see you."

"Yeah, we'll talk about that later. Tell me what's happened."

Aeneva led him over to Spotted Shield and related the story as quickly as possible. "I thought those Shoshonis looked kind of strange. They're hardly moving."

"It is working then."

"Maybe you should go out and offer them some more. No, on second thought, why don't I just walk on out there and see just how alert they are?"

"No, you cannot do that. It may not work on all of them."

"How many are there? I counted ten that I could see."

Aeneva nodded. "Eleven, counting Spotted Shield."

"Well, we're not going to have to worry about him for a while." He picked up the rifles that Aeneva had loaded and placed them under his arms.

"Let me go with you, Trenton."

"You have been in enough danger the last day. Now it's my turn."

"If you had not come back, I would have had to go out there. I can still fight."

"I know that, Aeneva. Thanks to you everyone will probably make it out of this mess. I just worry about you."

"Because of this child?"

"Because of you. I love you. I've come close to losing you too many times."

"You will not lose me, Trenton." She took one of the

rifles from him. "I will let you lead."

"Thanks." Trenton peered out of the lodge door in the direction of the Shoshonis. Some were sitting on the ground, two were leaning against trees, and the rest were asleep. "Be quick. Some of them are still awake." Aeneva followed Trenton out of the lodge and into the center of camp. The Shoshonis looked at them sleepily, but did nothing. By the time any of them reacted, Trenton and Aeneva had taken their rifles and other weapons away from them. Aeneva untied the people of the village and they in turn tied up their Shoshoni captors. Just as they were walking back to the lodge to check on Spotted Shield, they heard horses. The hunting party had returned.

"They are a little too late. Just as I was."

"But at least they are back. This will teach them never to go off and leave the camp so poorly guarded."

"I'm sure you will tell them."

The villagers greeted the returning riders with a mixture of anger and gladness. "You have been busy while we were gone, little Sister."

"Busier than you, I see, Brother." Aeneva referred to the empty packhorse Coyote Boy led.

"We had much difficulty. We have brought back some fresh meat. We will have to go back out again."

"Only a few of you will go out. You will not leave this village so poorly guarded again."

"You are right, Aeneva. It was a foolish thing to do." Brave Wolf gazed at Aeneva holding her stomach. "You are well?"

"I am well, Brother. Except for the excitement of the past two days. I have not been a warrior for some time now."

"But I see you have not lost any of your ability." He

420

glanced back at the Shoshonis. "What do you want us to do with them?"

"Let them go. They did us no harm."

"If that is what you want—"

"But they came into our camp and tried to take our women and children," Coyote Boy protested. "They should be killed."

"They killed no one, Coyote Boy. I do not want them killed. As soon as they wake up, we will warn them that we will never be surprised like that again. We will tell them that they should heed our warning or the next time we will not be so generous."

"Do not argue with her, Brother. She is the one who captured them. She should be the one who decides their fate."

"I will not argue with you, Aeneva. I admire your courage, Sister. I am proud of you."

"Do not look so shocked, Aeneva. Coyote Boy has always admired your ability."

"I know that and it pleases me that he feels so." She put her arm around Trenton and looked at Brave Wolf. "I will not be fighting anymore, Brother. That is, unless I have to."

"Better for us then. You make us look bad, Aeneva."

"I have other things to do now. I have Grandmother's work to carry on; I will soon have a child, and there is Nathan . . . Nathan!"

"Where is he? In the woods?"

"Yes, I sent him there when I heard the Shoshonis in the camp."

"I'll get him. He'll be fine."

"Hurry, Trenton. He will be so cold."

"I'll stay with Aeneva. Come on, girl. Let's see if that Indian is awake yet."

While Aeneva and Joe waited anxiously for Trenton to return, Spotted Shield woke up and lay motionless. Trenton returned not long afterward with a cold but happy Nathan. He ran to Aeneva when he saw her.

"I did just what you told me, Aeneva. Did I do good?"

"You did very well, Nathan. I am so proud of you. You were quieter than any hunter."

Nathan smiled up at his father and then over at Joe and Spotted Shield. "Hiya, Joe. Did you catch that Indian?"

"No. Aeneva caught him."

"You did? All by yourself?"

"Yes, but I was very lucky."

"Did you hear that, Pa? She caught him all by herself."

"Yes, I heard, son. Listen, why don't you go over and get yourself some of that stew? It'll help warm you up."

"O.K."

Trenton waited until Nathan was farther away. "What do you want to do with Spotted Shield?"

"I told you before; I want him set free."

"But you told me he tried to hurt you."

"He did not hurt me and I do not think he would have." She took the knife from her waist and bent down, cutting the ropes that bound Spotted Shield. He sat up, rubbing his wrists and ankles.

He inclined his head in Trenton's direction. "You told me you hated your husband."

"I lied."

Spotted Shield laughed as he had done so many times previous. "You are a better warrior than I, winter woman. You have courage and you lie well."

Aeneva smiled, nodding her head in thanks. "You and your men are free to go, Spotted Shield. But please do not come here again. Our men will not make the same mistake again.''

Spotted Shield gave the men surrounding him a disdainful glance as he stood up. ''I do not think you need these men. You seem to be warrior enough for the entire village.''

''Go on. My people will soon grow impatient. Some of your men are sleeping; you will have to carry them.''

''The tea. It was a drug?''

''Yes.''

''Ah, you are very good, winter woman. Very good. It is too bad you are not Shoshoni. You could be great.''

''I would rather be a good Cheyenne.''

Spotted Shield glanced at her once more and left the lodge.

Aeneva followed him out. ''Spotted Shield, we will have to keep your horses and weapons. You understand?''

''I understand. It is good. May the Great Father look kindly upon you, winter woman. I will not forget what you have done here today.''

Aeneva watched him walk away and she smiled, glancing up at the sky. ''You would have been proud of me today, Grandfather. I think I understand now what you always said about killing. It does not make one feel whole to kill. It is a much better victory to win without taking another life. You were right.'' She walked back to the lodge, suddenly feeling better than she had felt in a long time. She felt the child move within her and she knew that soon her grandmother would be with the man she loved. All was well. It was a good day.

Aeneva looked down at Trenton's face in the firelight and she lowered her mouth to his. They kissed deeply and he held her gently, loving her as he had never done before. His love-making was gentle but urgent and Aeneva responded in kind. Their bodies moved over the soft robes, their skin moist and hot. They made love until they were both exhausted and they lay in each other's arms.

"Did I hurt you?" Trenton smoothed the damp hair away from her face.

"You did not hurt me. It was wonderful. I have missed you."

"I don't ever want to be away from you again. It gets harder every time I go."

"This will be the last time. When you have taken Grandmother to her resting place, we will always be together."

"Aeneva. I want to talk to you about something."

"What is it?"

"How would you feel about leaving the band someday and going out on our own? It wouldn't have to be soon. I've just been thinking about getting some land somewhere and raising some cattle and horses and planting a garden. . . ."

"You want to live among the white people?"

"No. I want to live alone, with you and our children. I don't want them to forget their Indian heritage, but I want to give them a chance for a future."

"You do not feel there is a future here?"

"I don't know. Things are happening too fast. Sun Dancer says that there will be few Cheyennes left by the time our children grow up."

"Did she ask you to take us away from here?"

"Yes, but I've been thinking about it myself. It's not something we have to decide on right away. I just want you to think about it."

"I will think on it. I only know that I always want to be with you, Trenton, no matter where that is."

"I feel the same way. If you decide you want to stay with your people, we will stay."

"We will talk later. Let us love now. The morning will come too quickly."

"I love you, Aeneva. I will always love you."

As Trenton took her in his arms, Aeneva prayed that their love would be as strong as her grandparents', that it would withstand all things and last for all eternity. It was a lot to ask, but she could settle for nothing less. "I love you, too, Trenton." And she meant it more at the moment than she ever had before.

Sun Dancer glanced over at Trenton, unable to keep the look of anticipation from her face. Ever since Trenton had come back for her, Sun Dancer was barely able to conceal her pleasure. She was happy that her grandchildren and her people were all well so she could join Stalking Horse. She hadn't eaten in four days and she was growing steadily weaker. By the time they reached Stalking Horse's resting place, she would be ready to go to sleep and never wake up.

The trip seemed interminably long to Sun Dancer. Trenton had forced her to eat; he had told her there was no possible way she could make the trip without food. She had relented and eaten small bites, but only enough to keep her strength up. She felt as if they would never reach their destination, but finally she recognized their mountains. She seemed to gain immeasurable strength just from that sight. She smiled over at Trenton. They rode for three more days and finally they reached the spot where Stalking Horse lay. Sun Dancer took her things from her horse and walked to the scaffold. She laid her head against it and nodded wearily. "I am here, my Husband. At last I am here." Trenton left her alone while she

425

changed into her best dress and covered herself with her best quilled robe. She took down her hair, combed it out, and rebraided it with beads and feathers. She sat down below the scaffold. She smiled up at Trenton when he came back. "How do I look?"

"You look more beautiful than the first time I saw you, Sun Dancer. Stalking Horse will be pleased."

"I hope so." She grew serious for a moment and reached up and unhooked the necklace. "I want you to have this. I want you to give it to Nathan."

"No, I can't take it. I wanted you to have it forever."

"You are a good boy, Trenton, but please take it. It has quite a history, does it not? I think Nathan will be quite interested in it someday." She held it up.

Trenton walked over and sat down, taking the necklace from Sun Dancer. "I will miss you, Sun Dancer. You have been special to me."

Sun Dancer took his hand and brought it to her lips, kissing it gently. "You have been special to me also. Thank you for making Aeneva so happy."

"It is an easy thing to do."

"I must ask one thing of you, Trenton."

"Anything."

"Will you place me on the scaffold next to Stalking Horse when I am gone?"

"Of course I will. I will hang your things next to his and I will make sure everything is as it should be. Do not worry."

"Thank you, Trenton." She leaned her head against a leg of the scaffold. "I am tired now, Trenton. Just keep watch to make sure the wolves do not drag off this old body."

"I will be near. Have a good journey, Sun Dancer. *Nesta-va-hose-voomatse*. I will see you again."

426

"Ne-aoh-ohese." Sun Dancer watched Trenton as he walked his horse away and out of sight. She knew he was somewhere close, but he was giving her her privacy until she was gone. "I am so tired," she muttered softly. She rocked slightly, feeling the welcome sleep overcome her. She laid her head against the pole and she felt her body relax. It was so simple; so very simple. "I am coming, Stalking Horse. I am coming, my Husband." She lay against the pole until her body gave way and fell to the ground. That is how Trenton found her, with a smile on her face and an expression of such extreme peace that he was warmed by it. He held her slight body against his, feeling the tears as they rolled down his cheeks.

"We will miss you, Sun Dancer. We will all miss you." He climbed up the scaffolding, holding Sun Dancer tightly in his arms. He laid her gently down next to Stalking Horse, wrapping her in her good robe, and covering her with another heavier robe which he secured with rope. He tied her body to the scaffold so it would not fall down. He hung her medicine bags next to her, as well as the other things she had chosen to take with her. When he was finished, he looked at the covered body once more and descended from the scaffold. He looked up at the two bodies lying there and he spoke in a solemn voice. "Oh, Great Father, guide Sun Dancer safely to your world. Grant her and Stalking Horse peace in their next life for they knew very little in this one. Look favorably upon them for you will find few better people. Let them find each other for they are incomplete without each other. Grant that they may love through all eternity for no one deserves it more than they." Trenton looked up at the scaffold one more time; then he mounted his horse and rode off in the direction of his family and his life. His life was yet to be lived, yet he hoped he could face death with

427

as much grace as Sun Dancer had faced it. He kneed hi
horse and rode into the cold winter wind. He looked up a
the sky and saw a patch of blue peek through the clouds
"She picked a good day to die," he thought and rode
harder, eager to get home to his family.

It was strange that she did not feel tired. She felt ligh
and weightless and young again. She walked the starry
road, unafraid of what was ahead. Her father had ofter
told her that the Hanging Road was the road where the
footprints all pointed the same way, and that eventually
they led to the camp in the stars. She looked around her a
the glistening stars and she felt strange, almost as if she
could laugh. She was dressed in her best dress and he
best robe, and she had all of her medicine bags. She
walked for a long time; yet she never felt tired. She fol
lowed the footprints until she came to a camp filled with
white lodges. People were walking about, women were
tanning robes, meat was hanging on racks to dry, mer
were laughing and gambling. It was just like . . . it wa
just like the other place.

She walked into the camp and wandered around. She
knew there were many camps here and she did not knov
where he would be. She walked on and on, passing
through many different camps, smiling back at all of the
people who waved to her. She came to a river and looking
out over the clear water, she walked to it. She bent dow
and picked up a stone, skimming it across the water. I
skipped seven times before it dropped to the bottom.

"You have not lost your touch, little Sister."

She turned and saw her brother, Brave Wolf. How lon;
had it been since she'd seen him? Thirty, forty winters'
"Is it really you, Brave Wolf?" She reached out and
touched him. He felt real, just as she did.

He smiled and took her hand. "Yes, it is I, Sun Dancer. Come, I will lead you to him. He has been waiting a long time for you."

They walked along the river until they came to a grassy spot. "I will leave you now."

"No, do not go."

"I will see you later. There are many who wish to see you."

"Mother and Father?"

"And your children and friends."

"Little Flower and Young Eagle. Laughing Bird, Broken Leaf, Spring, they are all here, too?"

"Yes. I must go now."

She watched him walk away, but she did not feel sad. She turned back to look at the spot where he had taken her and Stalking Horse was standing there, tall and straight, more handsome than she remembered. She walked to him, holding out her hands. "It is you, Stalking Horse? I am not dreaming?"

"You are not dreaming, Wife. We are in Seyan." He put his arms around her and held her tightly. "It has been much too long a time without you."

"I had many things left to do there, just as you said I would."

"You are here now; that is all that matters." He took her face in his large hands, kissing her lightly. "You are so beautiful. So very beautiful." They kissed deeply and embraced for a long time.

"*Mon dieux!* She does not even tell me she is here. She runs to this savage first."

She turned around abruptly, pulling away from Stalking Horse. "Jean, oh, Jean!" She ran to him and he enclosed her in his thick arms. "*Oui,* it is I. Can you believe I made it here? I thought I would wind up in some other place."

"Why must you always interrupt? I have not seen my wife in an eternity and you must interrupt."

Jean shrugged his big shoulders. "That is the way, *mon ami*. You would not have it any other way."

Sun Dancer reached for Stalking Horse's hand and together they walked with Jean along the river. She bent down and picked up a rock, skipping it across the top of the water. She challenged Stalking Horse and Jean with her eyes and they attempted it, but neither could get his stone to skip more than five times.

"She was always too good at this, *mon ami*. It is good we did not wager with her."

"She was good at many things, *Veho*." Stalking Horse put his arm possessively around Sun Dancer and glared at Jean. "You must have some woman you can go visit."

"*Oui*, one or two. But I will be back later. You are still the most beautiful, Sun Dancer."

She smiled and turned in Stalking Horse's arm. "Will we be together for always?"

"Always."

"I cannot believe it. I feel as though someone will pinch me and—"

"Do not say it. Just know that you are here with me and we will be together for all time. Nothing can change that now."

She looked around her at the shimmering water and the blue sky and she felt as if she had been reborn. "It is a good day to begin our lives anew."

"Then let us begin."

They walked along the river, the sun shining down on them, the water reflecting their happiness. It was a good day to love. It was a good day to be alive.

BESTSELLING ROMANCES BY JANELLE TAYLOR

SAVAGE ECSTASY   (824, $3.50)
It was like lightning striking, the first time the Indian brave
Gray Eagle looked into the eyes of the beautiful young settler
Alisha. And from the moment he saw her, he knew that he
must possess her—and make her his slave!

DEFIANT ECSTASY   (931, $3.50)
When Gray Eagle returned to Fort Pierre's gates with his
hundred warriors behind him, Alisha's heart skipped a beat;
would Gray Eagle destroy her—or make his destiny her own?

FORBIDDEN ECSTASY   (1014, $3.50)
Gray Eagle had promised Alisha his heart forever—nothing
could keep him from her. But when Alisha woke to find her
red-skinned lover gone, she felt abandoned and alone. Lost
between two worlds, desperate and fearful of betrayal, Alisha
hungered for the return of her FORBIDDEN ECSTASY.

BRAZEN ECSTASY   (1133, $3.50)
When Alisha is swept down a raging river and out of her savage
brave's life, Gray Eagle must rescue his love again. But Alisha
has no memory of him at all. And as she fights to recall a past
love, another white slave woman in their camp is fighting for
Gray Eagle!

*Available wherever paperbacks are sold, or order direct from the
Publisher. Send cover price plus 50¢ per copy for mailing and
handling to Zebra Books, 475 Park Avenue South, New York,
N.Y. 10016. DO NOT SEND CASH.*

THE BEST IN HISTORICAL ROMANCE